The Road
to Kandahar

John Wilcox

headline

First published in 2005
by HEADLINE BOOK PUBLISHING

First published in paperback in 2005
by HEADLINE BOOK PUBLISHING

13

ISBN 978-0-7553-0985-6

Typeset in Times by Avon DataSet Ltd,
Bidford-on-Avon, Warwickshire

Printed and bound in Great Britain by
Clays Ltd, Elcograf S.p.A.

Headline's policy is to use papers that are natural, renewable and
recyclable products and made from wood grown in sustainable
forests. The logging and manufacturing processes are expected to
conform to the environmental regulations of the country of origin.

HEADLINE BOOK PUBLISHING
A division of Hodder Headline
338 Euston Road
London NW1 3BH

www.headline.co.uk
www.hodderheadline.com

For my daughter Alison

Acknowledgements

THE ROAD TO KANDAHAR was the first of the Fonthill novels to be read by my agent Jane Conway-Gordon, and her cheerful encouragement led to the publication of it and the others in the series. At Headline my editor, Marion Donaldson, displayed patient courtesy in coping with my idiosyncratic twists of syntax and story development. The staff of The London Library were, as ever, most helpful in allowing me to plunder their books and newspapers to ensure that, as far as possible, I was able to recreate the Britain and Afghanistan of 1879–1880 with reasonable accuracy. I am also grateful to Dr Patrick Craig-McFeely for ensuring that my account of Simon's recovery from his injuries is medically credible. I must thank my wife Betty, who read several drafts of the novel with determination and only the occasional whimper. Finally, like every other author who looks back at the Victorian sub-continent, I owe gratitude to those magnificent old Indian hands, Field Marshal Lord Roberts and Rudyard Kipling, who recorded it with verve and accuracy.

J.W.
Chilmark,
May 2004

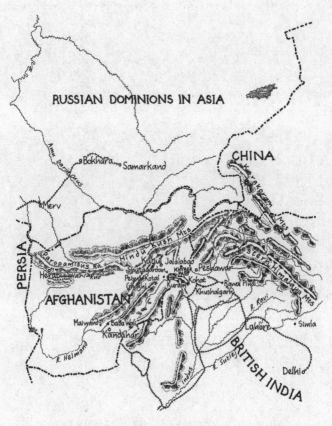

Afghanistan and Surrounding States in 1879

RUSSIAN DOMINIONS IN ASIA

CHINA

AFGHANISTAN

BRITISH INDIA

Afghanistan and Surrounding States in 1879

Chapter 1

Natal, South Africa, July 1879

Simon Fonthill guided his horse carefully through the detritus of an army in the field. For half a mile back from the banks of the Tugela River, the tents sprawled in a dishevelled array. Originally they had been pitched in impeccable rows; now their orderliness was eroded by limbers strewn across the lines, camp fires which smoked between the tents and a forest of damp bedding that hung from clotheslines and steamed in the early-morning sunlight.

The smells which met Simon's nostrils melded together in a pot-pourri of nostalgia and disgust and he wrinkled his nose. The damp washing – moist, warm and domestic – brought back the safety of Martha's wash-house, at the back of his parents' home on the Welsh borders: a place of refuge and welcome, away from his mother's strictures and his father's gentle but reproving eye. The other odours were army: feet, sweat and cheap tobacco. All around him sat, stood and sprawled soldiers in varying states of undress: some wearing only long-john combinations, others with braces dangling from regulation blue trousers, bare-chested in the morning heat yet still retaining the cool night's woollen comforters on their heads. This was an army relaxing; an army pleased with itself, having done a job well. A victorious army.

Instinctively, Simon's eyes searched in the middle distance for the pickets on the far edge of the lines. There were none, and then he remembered that the Zulus had gone, defeated. There was no danger now.

He trotted on and glimpsed a band boy, no more than twelve years old, buffing his bugle as he smoked an incongruously long clay pipe. The lad knelt, as if in supplication to his glistening instrument, and Simon's mind switched back to the last bugler boy he had seen, held aloft by a Zulu, skewered like a piece of pork on the warrior's assegai. Isandlwana was only six months ago. The difference was all around him but still he shivered.

As usual when this black dog came to sit on his shoulder, Simon looked round for the reassurance of Private Jenkins 352, late of His Majesty's 24th Regiment of Foot. Jenkins rode behind his officer, his feet balancing on the very edge of his stirrups, his knees bent so that he sat high, like a jockey – and with a jockey's confidence. Jenkins's head swivelled constantly as he, too, took in the scene. He mouthed to Simon: 'Bloody army!'

Nodding, Simon repeated to himself: 'Bloody army. Bloody army indeed!' Although he had resigned his commission – and bought Jenkins out of the army – shortly after Rorke's Drift, their subsequent work as civilian scouts for the re-invading column in the south still linked them, however intangibly, to the military. It was not a position which suited either of them.

He hailed a private of the Buffs, one of the few soldiers in scarlet uniform. 'Where's the Commander-in-Chief's headquarters?'

The soldier gave both horsemen a keen glance. There was a tone of command to the question that sat ill with the appearance of the questioner. No air of military smartness distinguished Fonthill. He slumped in the saddle, his shoulders slightly hunched, his legs thrusting the stirrups forwards and upwards. He wore the loose flannel shirt, cotton corduroy breeches, dirty, scuffed riding boots and slouch hat of a Boer hunter but, unlike most Afrikaners, he was clean-shaven and his face was open, with wide-set brown eyes. He was also carrying at his belt the new .38 calibre Webley-Pryse officer's revolver, and an army-issue Martini-Henry cavalry carbine protruded from the saddle holster by his knee. Fonthill was only in his middle twenties, but he sat his horse gingerly, almost with the air of a man expecting to be tossed at any minute, in great contrast to the ease of his companion. This was not the only contrast between them. Jenkins was bare-headed, obviously much shorter, and his very broad shoulders, dark eyes, spiky black hair and wide moustache gave him the air of a mounted stevedore. They were a strange couple to be seeking the Commander-in-Chief.

The soldier delayed his reply long enough to weigh the odds, then decided that it would be wise to give them the benefit of the doubt. Lord Chelmsford's Zululand army was full of traps for the unwary.

'Straight ahead for about a quarter of a mile along this track. Then you'll see the General's standard on your left.'

Simon raised a finger to his hat brim and urged his horse forward. Jenkins drew alongside.

'I don't much like being back in the army,' he said. 'Do I have to start calling you sir again?'

'We're not back in the army, so don't talk rot.'

Jenkins sucked in his moustache. 'It's all right for you. You're supposed to be a gentleman. But ridin' back 'ere, along the lines, like, I feel as though they could put me back on fatigues as soon as look at me. I feel . . .' he searched in his

3

narrow vocabulary, 'vulnerable is the word, see.' In the manner of the valley Welsh, Jenkins's voice rose mellifluously at the end of each sentence, as though he was asking a question.

Simon smiled to himself. 'You've never been vulnerable in your whole life, 352.' He looked down. 'For God's sake, loosen those stirrups. You look as though you're riding in the four fifteen at Chepstow. And fall back behind. There's not room for two of us.'

Jenkins lapsed into a half-heard grumble, now familiar to Simon. 'You're a fine one to talk,' he muttered, 'with your toes stickin' up like candles in church. Uh.' But he reached down to lengthen his stirrups and dropped back behind Simon.

It was as well that he did so, for the nearer they rode to the centre of the camp, the more congested the track became. The Tugela was low at midsummer, but even so, the humidity hung heavily around them and made their shirts stick to their backs like plaster. Yet the moisture that seemed so prevalent did not break into rain, and the dust from the stream of carts, riders and slouching soldiers added to the discomfort, making teeth gritty and giving a harsh edge to their tongues.

'Why d'you want me with you anyway?' called Jenkins. 'I could 'ave been doin' something really useful back at the camp, like the washin', see.'

Simon turned in his saddle. 'Because, as I told you before . . .' he began, but paused as Jenkins's hard gaze over his shoulder made him turn back.

Coming towards them, at a gentle canter, rode a major of Hussars. He was a gorgeous sight amongst the dust and dishevelment all around. The sunlight danced off the buttons and epaulettes which decorated the ridiculous half-jacket, half-cape which he wore on his left shoulder, and he rode with a back as straight as a colour standard, his buttocks – so tightly rounded that it looked as though his breeches had been painted on – rising and falling to the rhythm of the horse's gait. One white-gloved hand lightly held the reins while the other pointed directly to the ground, in the approved parade-ground fashion.

As he saw Simon he did not slacken his pace but lifted his disengaged hand and waved him aside. Instinctively, Simon tugged momentarily at the reins to pull his horse aside, off the track. As he did so, he looked into the pale blue eyes of the Hussars officer. In an instant a series of images flew across his mind: the sardonic features of Lieutenant Colonel Covington at his trial, his lip curled, his eyebrows raised in mock astonishment; the jowls of Colonel Pulleine as he looked up from his campaign table at Isandlwana and said, 'Johnny Zulu doesn't frighten me . . . I've got twelve hundred men of the regiment here; and the Zulus breaking the line, rushing in, hacking and stabbing. He pulled his horse's head round again, stopped and waited, leaving only a small space for the Hussar to pass, between him and a parked wagon.

The major stared with his china-blue eyes, chin strap cutting a furrow into his jaw. 'Out of the way.'

Slowly, Simon edged his horse forward. As he did so, he felt the head of Jenkins's mount nuzzle the back of his left thigh. His man, as ever, was right behind him. The weight of the two horses forced the Hussar to edge off the track, tangling his low-slung sabre scabbard between the spokes of the wagon wheel. 'What the hell . . .' he began.

Simon waited until he was level with the major. Then, leaning forward so that his face was only inches from that of the other man, he said quietly, 'Fuck off.'

'What? What!' The Hussar's face had turned vermilion, a combination, perhaps, of heat, too much mess port and extreme anger. 'How dare you,' he shouted, attempting to wrest the head of his horse round. But the solidity of the other two mounts forced him to give way. Simon edged by and gave a perfunctory flip of his hat brim. Jenkins followed, and bestowed on the cavalryman one of his most beatific smiles, the kind of grin that made his huge moustache bend upwards so that it almost touched his ears. 'Mornin', Major,' he said. 'Nice day.'

The Major steadied his mount, looked after them and made to follow, then thought better of it. 'Bloody Boers,' he shouted, and then, head up even more belligerently than before, if that was possible, rode on.

When the track widened, Jenkins drew abreast of Simon and for a while they rode in companionable silence before the Welshman spoke, in a light, conversational style. 'Yes, well then. We're in deep trouble again, isn't it? That'll be two court martials for you now in six months an' one for me, though I didn't even say a bleedin' word, look you.'

'Rubbish. I keep telling you, we're no longer in the army.'

'Just as well, if you ask me. I'm not much good at this bein' shot at dawn business. Bit too early, see.'

'Shut up.'

'Very good, sir.'

A few minutes later they dismounted at a tent before which stood a crudely painted wooden sign announcing 'Colonel George Lamb, CB, Chief of Staff'. The sentry enquired their business and disappeared into the tent, but not before he had looked the pair up and down with clear disapproval. Simon turned to Jenkins. 'Look, I've no idea what Colonel Lamb wants of me, but whatever it is, it could include you. So I think it best for you to wait here. Just in case we need you.'

'Very good, bach sir.'

The sentry's manner had changed when he returned. 'Mr Fonthill, sir, the Colonel will see you right away.'

The interior of the small bell tent was dominated by a long trestle table, its top seriously bowed in the middle from the weight of the papers piled on it. Behind this barrier sat a small, tanned man smoking a cheroot. He was in shirt-sleeves, a foulard silk scarf loosely knotted at his throat, and his scarlet jacket hung on the chair back. As Simon entered he threw down his pen and advanced to meet him, hand outstretched.

'Damned glad to see you, Fonthill. Damned glad. Take a pew.' At five foot nine, Simon was no giant. But he seemed to tower over the Colonel, who pumped his hand as though trying to draw water. 'Sit down, do.'

Simon removed a ribbon-tied cardboard file from a camp stool and sat facing the Colonel, whose nut-brown face beamed at him from above the piled papers.

'Sorry about all this,' he said, waving his cheroot deprecatingly at the mound. 'Boney – or whoever it was – was wrong. An army doesn't march on its stomach. These days it staggers about on arse paper like this.' He regarded Simon through the blue smoke, a half-smile on his face. 'Look like a bloody Boer. Gone a bit native, eh?'

Simon shifted uneasily. 'Well, sir . . .'

Lamb held up his hand. 'No. No. Necessary for the job, I know.' He gestured to the scarf at his neck. 'Envy you. Glad to get out of a tunic whenever I can. General's away so I can today.'

Simon smiled at the familiar staccato sentences. Yet it was not like Lamb to beat about the bush. The summons to see the Chief of Staff had been urgent, and there was an air of unease about the little man's jocularity. Simon wondered what was afoot. But, hell, he had had enough of the army! It was not his place to make it easy for the Colonel. So he sat on the camp stool and waited.

'Cheroot?'

'No thank you, sir.'

7

'Right. Yes. Well. Good. Good.' Lamb picked up a piece of paper from the right side of his desk and put it to the left, without looking at it. 'Must be wonderin' what this is all about. Right? Right?'

Simon gently inclined his head. 'Sir.'

'Jolly good. Yes, well then. Right.' Colonel Lamb shifted in his chair and blew a smoke ring. 'Right. Three things. First, a word of congratulations. You and your man . . . what's his name?'

'Jenkins, sir, 352.'

'Three five two?'

'That's his last three numbers, sir. The 24th is a Welsh regiment, as you know, and there were six Jenkinses in his holding company at Brecon, four of them with the same initials. The only way to distinguish between 'em was to use their last three numbers.'

'Ah, I see. Well, anyway. You and he have done a first-class job over the last four months. Absolutely first class. Stopped us gettin' caught with our breeches down again, like at Isandlwana.' The Colonel pulled on his cheroot and waved it in the air. 'Good scoutin', too. Yes. First class. First class.'

'Thank you, sir.' Simon waited. He had not been summoned to the Chief of Staff to be patted on the head. There must be something else. But he was damned if he was going to help Lamb to get to it.

'Yes,' the Colonel repeated. 'The General was most pleased. Particularly after . . .' his voice faltered for a moment, 'after that court martial nonsense.'

Simon's gaze remained expressionless. 'It wasn't nonsense, sir. I could have gone to a firing squad.'

'What, eh? Well, yes, I suppose so. Miserable business. But you were acquitted, so everything turned out right in the end. Eh? What? Good.'

The Colonel smiled, almost in supplication, and Simon was forced to smile back. 'Quite, sir. What do you want of me now, then?'

'Right.' Lamb delved among the papers on his desk. 'Second thing. Got something for you. And for 376 or whatever his damned number is.' He handed two envelopes across the table and Simon opened the one addressed to him. Inside was a money draft for thirty-five guineas.

'I don't understand, sir.'

Lamb cleared his throat gruffly. 'It's your pay. And the other's for, whasisname, 762.'

'Three five two. But we have been paid for our scouting work.'

The little man shifted uneasily in his seat. 'Yes, but that's the difference between scouting pay and what's due to you as a soldier. Same for your man.'

Simon shook his head. 'But we are not soldiers any more. I resigned my commission four months ago and I bought Jenkins out of the army at the same time.'

'Ah yes. Well.' Now the Colonel looked openly embarrassed at last. 'Truth is, Fonthill . . .' he dug back into the confusion on his table and produced another two envelopes, 'I've been sitting on these: your resignation and your request to get your man out.' He shrugged his shoulders disarmingly. 'I just didn't forward them on to the Horse Guards so, you see, you're still in the army. Thought I'd better tell you now and give you your back pay, so to speak.' He smiled. 'Chance to buy a decent shirt, at least, don't you think?'

Simon stared into the blue eyes facing him. 'Do you mean to tell me, sir,' he said slowly, 'that I've been a second lieutenant in the 24th these last four months – all the time I've been scouting for John Dunn?'

The older man held his gaze and slowly nodded.

'But you had no right to delay my resignation. No right at all.'

'No, Fonthill. I didn't delay it. I stopped it.' This time Lamb spoke slowly and firmly.

Simon stood up. 'Colonel Lamb. You cannot stop me from resigning from the army. The terms of my commission allow me to do so after the first three years of service. And as for Jenkins, I checked. He had served five years and I can buy him out. In fact, I have paid to do so.'

'Your cheque is in your man's envelope. It has not been cashed.'

Simon swung on his heel. 'Then I'll have no more of this.' He spoke over his shoulder. 'I shall see Lord Chelmsford.'

'Come back.' The words came like a whiplash. Despite his anger, Simon paused at the tent flap and looked back at the Colonel. The little man remained seated but pointed at the vacant chair. 'Sit down, Fonthill. We have not finished yet.'

Slowly, Simon returned to the chair.

'Good. Now listen to me.' Lamb stood up and perched one buttock on the crowded table in front of Simon. All embarrassment was now gone. 'I want you to withdraw that resignation and, if you wish, your request to buy out three nine seven, or whatever his number is!'

The Colonel lifted his hand as Simon began to interrupt. 'No. Hear me out.' His voice took on a warmer tone as he leaned forward. 'I can well understand your disenchantment with the army, my boy. It must have been, well, frightening to say the least to have been court-martialled for cowardice. All that bloody fool Covington's doing. But you *were* cleared and you must remember, Fonthill, that that bloody fool is also a most gallant soldier and a splendid CO of his battalion. He thought he was doing his duty.

'Now.' He walked round the table and selected and lit

another cheroot. 'You have also shown that you have become a first-class soldier over this last strange year, in rather unusual circumstances. Not only in the work you have done as – forgive me – a so-called civilian scout during our advance into Zululand, but also in the intelligence-gathering which you carried out for me in the months leading up to that dreadful business at Isandlwana.' He blew a spiral of blue smoke into the air. 'Same goes for your man Jones, too.'

'Jenkins, sir. Jenkins.'

'Ah yes. Quite so. Jenkins, yes. Three five two, isn't he?'

'Oh well done, sir.'

'That will do, Fonthill. Don't be impertinent.'

'Sir.'

'Look here. I believe you have a future in the army. I know very well that your father was a distinguished soldier – got a Victoria Cross in the Mutiny, didn't he?'

Simon nodded.

'Quite so. The line is there. The tradition is there. This court martial business will soon be forgotten. You owe it to your family and to yourself to continue. Besides which,' the Colonel's face relaxed once more into a smile, 'and this is the third thing. I have a job for you. It is very important work and there are few I would entrust it to. But I am sure, in view of your experience here, that you would do it well.'

Simon stood up once more. 'I rather thought that there might be something like that behind this, sir. I am very grateful to you, I really am. I appreciate all you say and all that you have done for me. But I do not wish to continue serving in the British Army. I insist on resigning.'

The Colonel was silent for a moment. Thoughtfully, he removed a fragment of tobacco from his tongue. 'What, then, will you do?' he asked quietly.

'Don't really know, sir. Jenkins wishes to stay with me as

11

my servant, and I am lucky enough to have a few pennies of private income. I thought perhaps we might try our luck in India. Tea, perhaps, something up in the hills.'

'Capital. Absolutely capital!' The Colonel, too, was now on his feet, once again displaying the enthusiasm of a small boy. 'This work I have for you – and at this stage it is absolutely confidential – is in India and, dammit, beyond. You must do it.'

Simon smiled, as much at the enthusiasm as the offer. 'Can I do this as a civilian?'

'Good lord, man. Of course not. This is vital work. Can't trust it to a feller...' he sought for words of sufficient condemnation, 'in a tweed jacket and flannels.'

'Then I am sorry, sir, but the answer must be no. I do not wish to remain in the army.'

The Colonel blew out his cheeks in resignation, sat down again and gestured for Simon to do the same. 'Very well then, young man. I must play my last card.' He leaned back in his chair and blew smoke towards the top of the tent pole. 'You will remember – yes, of course you will remember – what I understand was the turning point of your court martial?'

'I am not sure that I know what you're driving at, sir.'

'Well,' the Colonel's eyes were now half closed in contemplation of the conical top of the tent, 'I was not there, of course, but I am told that what swung the court round in your favour was the last-minute intervention of a witness who confirmed your story about your capture by King Cetswayo and your escape from his camp. Eh? What?'

Simon felt his heart lurch. 'Yes, sir,' he said slowly. 'John Dunn's daughter, Nandi, was able to prove that I had not been telling a pack of lies, as Lieutenant Colonel Covington had implied.'

'Quite so.' Lamb's eyes were now distinctly twinkling.

'Quite so. But the court had already reached its verdict, I understand, and almost certainly would not have allowed a girl – and a half-caste Zulu at that – to give evidence at such a late stage if it had not been presented with a letter from me asking them to hear her.'

The Colonel's chair came crashing back and he leaned across the paperwork in mock puzzlement. 'And do you know, Fonthill, I'm damned if I remember ever writing such a letter!'

The crack of a whip outside and the rumble of wagon wheels broke the silence. Simon could think of nothing to say. 'Really, sir,' he croaked.

'Must have been a damned forgery. Eh? What?' The blue eyes now positively danced in that seamed brown face. 'And done, of course, by that remarkable young lady who telegraphed to me in the Cape from Durban: Miss Alice Griffith, of the *Morning Post*. Damned good friend of yours, Fonthill, I'd say. And smart too, don't you think?'

Simon cleared his throat. 'I am sorry, sir,' he said woodenly. 'I knew nothing of that. What is important is that I was not guilty of the charge brought against me. You must believe that.'

The Colonel's face hardened and he rose to his feet again and walked round the table. He put his hand on Simon's shoulder and looked sternly into his face. 'I do believe it. I know that you are not a coward. The letter said only what I would have written had there been time for me to do so before the court rose – which there was not, of course, hence the forgery. But you have one thing to learn about me, Fonthill.' He lowered his face towards Simon's in emphasis. 'I am absolutely ruthless where the interests of my Queen and country are concerned. I want you for this job. If you continue to refuse, then I shall have no hesitation in making public the fact that the letter was forged and demanding that the court martial be reopened.'

He walked back to his chair and pulled out a gold timepiece from the debris on the table. 'Take your time to consider. I will give you exactly thirty seconds.'

In the ensuing silence, Simon felt he could hear the watch ticking. He stared at the nut-brown countenance before him. Little bastard. Just like the rest of them in this army of Queen Victoria. Single-minded to the point of blackmail. Should he call the little man's bluff? Would Lamb dare to reopen the trial and risk renewing the storm of criticism back home which had followed the slaughter of Isandlwana? If he did, then Simon would stand no chance of an acquittal this time. The Colonel's gaze was centred on his watch; one eyebrow raised as if disbelieving the time. No hint of indecision there; just an impersonal air of sang-froid. Ruthless bastard. Simon felt trapped. He sighed. 'Very well. What do you want me to do?'

Immediately, Lamb's face broke into a beam. 'Good man. Knew you'd see sense eventually. Sorry about the hard stuff. Don't mind playing dirty if I have to, y'know. Now.' He leaned forward. 'What do you know about the North West Frontier?'

Despite his anger, Simon felt his heart leap. The part of him which, despite his disillusion, remained a British soldier could not but be interested. The Frontier, India's border with Afghanistan, presented the greatest opportunity for action and advancement for any officer in the army. It offered danger and hard employment and it did so because it was a vulnerable, half-open door to the richest possession of the Empire: India. The tribes of the independent state of Afghanistan were a militant hotchpotch of feuding warriors in constant conflict with the British garrisons of the Frontier. But they were comparatively unimportant compared to the threat posed by the other great imperial power, Russia, whose own territorial ambitions had taken the double-headed eagle banners of the Tsar right to the northern frontier of Afghanistan, leaving that cussedly independent nation as a kind of buffer between the two great imperial locomotives of the nineteenth century. The North West Frontier of India was Russia's obvious point of entry to India. Afghanistan, then, was a playground for power politics – and a forcing ground for military careers.

'Not much, sir,' said Simon. 'Only what I learned at Sandhurst and what I've read in the papers. And there's been little chance to do that lately. I'm afraid I'm right out of touch.'

'Well, you'll need to be brought up to date damned quickly.' The Colonel turned in his seat and pushed with his toe at a pile of maps on the ground. Selecting one, he turned back. 'While we've been farting around with Cetswayo down here, the Russkies have been stirring up quite a bit of trouble in Afghanistan. Here, look.' He unrolled a map of the region, put an inkstand at the top to prevent it re-furling and walked round the table to join Simon.

The map was depressingly empty. The corner of India fronting the border with Afghanistan bristled with hatched lines depicting railways and was studded with townships – Lahore, Rawal Pindi, Kohat, Banu – but the territory that was Afghanistan seemed to consist mainly of shaded mountain ranges and little else. The western Himalayas to the east linked with the Hindu Kush mountains running from east to west to form a seemingly uncrossable spine across the country. No railways, few towns and fewer roads. Across the country's northern border lay white expanses marked 'Russian Dominions in Asia'. Here, large blank areas were broken up by names romantically evocative from Simon's childhood classroom: Samarkand, Tashkent, Bokhara, Khiva, Merv. But again no roads and few railways, although one, advancing menacingly due south from Merv to the Afghan border, caught Simon's eye. It was marked 'Under Construction'.

Lamb noticed Simon's frown. 'Yes. Not much in the way of cartography. One of our problems. Damned nuisance. But look.' He jabbed a thumb on Afghanistan's southern border with India and swivelled his forefinger on to the northern border with the Russian territories. 'Whole bloody country's only three inches wide. The Russians could be across those mountain passes in three weeks and be down on to the plains of the Punjab before we'd hitched up our knickers.'

'What's to stop them, then?'

The Colonel wrinkled his nose. 'Apart from world opinion – and that can't be relied on – it's the Afghans. Awkward buggers. They don't like us. You will remember that we invaded in 1840-something and got a bloody nose, but they're not too fond of the Russkies either. So they play one off against the other. But you'll know all this.'

Simon did, more or less. The Russian threat to India, via Afghanistan, had been a perennial topic of dinner and mess table conversation throughout Britain before he left for South Africa more than a year ago. In Zululand he had heard of a British invasion of Afghanistan and, vaguely, of a British victory somewhere in the hills. But he knew little of what had ensued. He told Lamb as much.

'Right,' said the Colonel, lighting another cheroot. 'Won't take long to paint you the picture.' His briskness and obvious delight in this pedagogic role made Simon smile inwardly and took him back to a humid room in Cape Town, where Lamb had lectured him on Zulu history. But he listened intently. The Colonel was good at this.

'Now,' said the little man, his eyes sparkling, 'about ten months or so ago, St Petersburg put great pressure on Sher Ali – he's the Amir, the guv'nor, of Afghanistan – to accept a Russian mission at his capital, Kabul. The Afghans didn't fancy this, so they did their old trick of turning to us, asking if we would come to their aid if the Russians attacked. Delhi got the wind up and vacillated. So old Ali was forced to accept a pretty strong contingent of Russkies at Kabul. This meant that the latch was off the Afghan gate to India and our government got the wind up again, from a different direction, so to speak.' The blue eyes smiled through the cigar smoke. 'Follow?'

Simon nodded.

'Good. Now we demanded the same facilities, and when the Afghans hummed and hawed, we sent a mission that was firmly but politely turned back at the frontier. Naturally we couldn't have that, so we invaded.'

Simon nodded again. 'Naturally,' he said, but his irony was lost on the Colonel. 'We sent in three columns.' Lamb jabbed at the map. 'Lieutenant General Sir Donald Stewart took his Kandahar Field Force in from Quetta, here, to Kandahar and occupied that.' He pointed to the south-east corner of Afghanistan. 'At the same time, Major General Roberts's Kurram Field Force marched from Kohat over the Peiwar Kotal mountain range here in the centre, and Lieutenant General Sir Sam Browne's Peshawar Valley Field Force invaded through the Khyber Pass here towards Jalalabad in the east.' He shrugged. 'Not much choice really. These are the only routes in. Anyway, Stewart and Browne didn't have much trouble, though Browne got a bit bogged down in the Khyber. It was Roberts who was opposed and got the fighting. He took on most of the Amir's men up in the mountains here, at Peiwa Kotal, outflanked 'em in a brilliant move and cleared the way to Kabul. Conveniently, old Sher Ali fled and died quickly and his successor, Yakub Khan, decided to negotiate. Don't blame him, with three British columns encamped in his damned country.'

Lamb flicked the ash off his cheroot. 'There was a treaty concluded here, at Gandamak, on the border, under which the Kurram valley and Khyber Pass were assigned to us and we also gained our mission at Kabul *and* control of Afghan foreign policy, in return for which Yakub was recognised as amir and an annual British subsidy was agreed.' The Colonel sighed. 'It's always bloody rupees in the end, you know, in that country.'

Simon nodded slowly. 'And the Russians?' he asked.

'Still there, of course, but a bit squeezed out. They relied on us getting beaten and we weren't.'

Simon raised his eyebrows. 'So everything's all right, then?'

'Ah, not quite. Roberts is still there – left in charge, so to speak, right in the south of the country – but the other two columns have withdrawn. Our mission has gone to Kabul, but Roberts is uneasy. He thinks there could be an uprising at any time. Trouble is, he's got no reliable intelligence. So . . .' Lamb smiled. 'He wants me to go out there and organise this for him. He's my old boss, you see.'

'Yes, but where do I fit in?'

'I want you to be my main intelligence officer out there. Do what you've done so well here. Sniff out the feeling amongst the tribes. Give us warning of an uprising. Tell us where and when it might come.'

Simon's eyebrows rose again. 'But I don't know Afghanistan, neither the country nor the language.'

'Lack of lingo and local knowledge didn't stop you doing a good job here.' Lamb stood. 'Look, you will need a bit of training out there, but there isn't much time.' He riffled through the papers on his desk again, drawing out a letter written in green ink in strong, sloping handwriting. 'Here. This is from Roberts to me. Confidential, of course. Highly.

Take it and read it overnight and then bring it back. It will fill you in. Right? Right?'

Simon sighed. The whole project sounded crazy: delegating highly sensitive intelligence work to a man who had never visited the country and knew nothing of its customs or its language. Crazy? No, homicidal. Was it the army's way of getting rid of him? Unlikely. It would be far too contrived and expensive for the Horse Guards. It must be their inherent stupidity. He made one last try.

'Surely General Roberts will have established sources of intelligence far more experienced and skilled than me?'

Lamb snorted. 'Oh yes. But he doesn't rate 'em. Wants a soldier.' The blue eyes twinkled. 'Looks as though he's going to have a reluctant one.'

Simon stood. 'Very well, sir. I'll go. But I must take Jenkins with me. He's discreet, and anyway, he's a far better shot and horseman than I am. And I fancy you will need both on the Frontier.'

'Agreed.' The Colonel waved in a motion of dismissal, then paused. 'Before you go, tell me one more thing.'

'Sir?'

'Why are you so unhappy at the prospect of staying in the army?'

Simon frowned. What to say? 'It's, well, rather personal, sir.'

'Anything to do with Covington?'

How far to go? Attack his former CO, who had suspected him of cowardice, hounded him for two years and then falsely accused him of desertion in the face of the enemy? Simon fixed his gaze on the tent wall behind Lamb's head and took a deep breath. Go the whole way . . . . 'Yes, it has. With no disrespect, sir, I have not been impressed by the standard of serving British officers, either at home in peacetime soldiering or out here, on active service. Colonel Covington was allowed to conduct a campaign of persecution of me, a junior officer in his command, for eighteen months back home and then bring a charge of cowardice against me here in Natal. In addition to that, at Isandlwana, mistakes were made in conducting the defence of the camp that I find hard to forgive. We lost so many men needlessly that day, some of them my friends.' In for a penny, in for a pound. He took a breath to continue, but the Colonel interrupted impatiently.

'But Covington wasn't there. It wasn't his fault.'

'No, sir. I know that. But the General's enquiry seems to have put the fault for the defeat on the fact that the native levies broke and fled. That wasn't the real reason. I was there and I saw it.' Simon's pace hurried now, as the indignation took over. 'Firstly, the camp was left open and unlaagered. It was easy for the Zulus to rush us once the ammunition ran out. And that's the second point: the ammunition *did* run out – not because we didn't have enough but because the damned screws and the steel bands had rusted into the boxes. We just couldn't get them open. The Zulus were upon us before we could get cartridges to the line. The men had virtually nothing left and our volley firing just died away. The Zulus saw that. They were not fools.'

Simon was now looking indignantly at Lamb. 'Sir, this column had been in enemy country for several weeks and no one bothered to check the ammunition reserves. It was poor soldiering and the officers were to blame, not the black levies.'

The Colonel snorted. 'Dammit, Fonthill, mistakes occur on a campaign, you know that. Anyway, we've now won the war and finished off the Zulus once and for all. Ulundi was a perfectly executed battle.'

'With respect, sir, we fought the battle from a defensive square just as though we were at Waterloo, sixty-four years

20

ago. If the Zulus had not attacked so bravely we would probably still be looking for them now. I saw no evidence of generalship there. Anyway, it was terribly one-sided. They had spears and incredible guts. We had Martini-Henrys, Gatling guns and cannon. It was like shooting fish in a barrel.'

The two men faced each other across the table, the tension almost visible between them. Eventually, a rueful smile crept across the face of the Chief of Staff. 'Hmmmn.' He rubbed his jaw. 'I see what you mean about your determination not to serve again. Your . . . opinions are not quite what we would expect from a young officer.'

'Exactly, sir.'

'And Covington?'

'The last time I saw him I promised to stick an assegai in him the next time we met.'

'How charming of you, Fonthill.' For the first time both men laughed together. Then Lamb's face became thoughtful and he walked slowly round the table to join Simon. 'After hearing all that, I really ought to put you under arrest. But look,' he said, 'I have an idea. I want you for intelligence work – out in the field, working on your own, or with this bright Welshman, if you like. You've shown you can do that, adapting to a strange environment and all that. But it's not a task that can be carried out while staying within the confines of normal army discipline. And you certainly won't have to work closely with the type of regimental officer,' the Colonel's voice took on a dry note, 'whom you don't exactly seem to admire.'

He leaned against the tent pole. 'You know I'm an Indian Army man, out here on secondment?'

'Yes, sir.'

'Ever hear of the Guides?'

'I don't think so.'

'Part of the Indian Army. Raised in the Punjab and patrol the North West Frontier. Wonderful bunch of men – cavalry and infantry. Indian troops, of course.' He smiled. 'Not exactly regular, y'know. In fact, damned irregular. Work as much in native dress as they do in uniform. I could get you a captaincy in the Guides, with sergeant's rank for your man. Easy enough to do a transfer that way, from the home force to the Indian, though more difficult t'other way round. Chaps who are finding things a bit expensive in the line regiments do it all the time, though this doesn't apply to you, o'course. Pay's not bad – and, of course, you would be away from the men you admire so much in Her Majesty's regular army. What do you think?'

'Well, if I have to stay in the army, that sounds pretty good to me.'

'Good. There is one very final point, Fonthill, and in view of what you have said, it is not unimportant.' Colonel Lamb drew himself to his full height and the word 'bantam' came into Simon's mind. 'As I said, I am going to India too, to be Roberts's chief of staff and to take charge – among other things – of this intelligence work. This means you would report to me. Now, how do you feel about that? I don't want you threatening me with an assegai or – even worse – mopin' around all bitter and twisted like a rusty corkscrew.'

The two men regarded each other from either side of the tent pole. 'I could live with that, sir,' said Simon, half smiling at the challenging, combative face before him. 'But no more playing dirty, please.'

The blue eyes twinkled again. 'Only if I have to.'

They shook hands and, clutching his envelopes, Simon re-emerged into the morning sunlight. He looked around and the sentry nodded to his left. There lay Jenkins, fast asleep, curled innocently around a tent peg, one arm hanging from the guy rope. 'I tried to get 'im to move, sir,' said the sentry, 'but he . . .

er . . . was a bit rude, like. I was goin' to call the guard.'

'No need,' said Simon. 'We're off now anyway.'

With his toe he gently stirred the sleeping Welshman, who disentangled himself from the guy rope and scratched himself. 'Gawd, you've bin ages,' he yawned. 'I almost dozed off. What's happenin', then? We goin' to be shot, is it?'

'No.' Simon gathered up the reins of the horses. 'Worse than that. We're back in the army.'

'What? What?' Jenkins's consternation was real, and in his haste to catch Simon, his foot slipped from the stirrup as he tried to mount. 'Not me, boyo,' he called plaintively after Simon. 'Oh no. Not me.' The sentry watched in disbelief as the strange couple rode away, the shorter one behind calling after the slim young man, who rode on, down to the Tugela ferry crossing, a half-smile on his face.

As they crossed, Simon began telling Jenkins of what had ensued with the Colonel. The Welshman listened quietly, occasionally pulling at his moustache. Across on the Zululand side of the river, John Dunn, formerly one of King Cetswayo's *indunas* and now chief of intelligence for the southern column of Lord Chelmsford's army, had erected his own tents away from the mud of the main campsite. Simon was glad to find that Dunn was away so that he was able to complete the briefing of Jenkins without interruption. Jenkins gave no response but walked slowly to a large bowl, where he had left the washing. He lifted a shirt from the tub.

'Ah, bach, what on earth did you do to this shirt? I can't get rid of this stain no how, see.'

Simon inspected the wet lump thrust under his nose. 'Hmmn. Red wine, I think. Sorry, 352.'

'Well, I can't do much with it.' Jenkins slapped the shirt between hands as wide as paddles. Then his face lit up. 'Tell you what,' he beamed. 'Tell the girls it's blood. Marks of a wound received in a terrible fight against the savage Zulu.'

Simon smiled. Jenkins was getting round to it, he knew. The Welshman looked down at the shirt and spoke without glancing up. 'So we're goin' to swap the savage Zulu for the savage Afghan, is it?'

'Sort of. Though I hope we won't be exactly fighting him. More a question of getting to know him and of reporting on his movements, that sort of thing.' Simon waited. Jenkins's reaction was vital. Despite the Colonel's threat, Simon would refuse to go to India if Jenkins did not accompany him. Life in the field without the Welshman would be unthinkable.

A sniff came from beneath the big moustache. 'I don't think I'd be much good at spyin', wearin' turbans and all that.'

'Well, I'm not sure that I'll be much good at that either. But the Colonel seems to think that we would make a better job of it than the people doing it now.'

The sniff came again. 'So I'll have to start calling you sir again, salutin' and so on?'

'No, not really. Not to me, anyhow, and I don't think we will be seeing much of the regular army.'

Jenkins smoothed out the shirt. 'Well, if you go, I'll go. You'll need me to look after you.'

'Rubbish. I don't need a bloody nursemaid.'

'You do when you're tryin' to sit on a horse.'

'Oh, come on. I'm much better than I used to be.'

Jenkins suddenly smiled, his teeth all the whiter beneath the black moustache. 'Sergeant, eh? Well, well, well. What will they think about that back home, eh, bach?'

'They'll be as astounded as me. Come on. You've got to pack. We leave for Durban in the morning.'

* * *

Simon crept into his tiny bell tent, sat on his trestle bed and opened the letter from General Roberts to Lamb. It had been written from Gandamak, the border town in eastern Afghanistan where the treaty had been signed, and dated 26 May, six weeks before. It was in two parts. The first was couched in formal language, penned in a clerkly hand, and had obviously been dictated. It updated Lamb on the situation and told Simon nothing that the Colonel had not already related. The second, much shorter, slanted across the pages in a scrawl that exuded urgency. It had been written by Roberts himself, a few hours after the treaty had been signed, and concentrated on his intelligence needs. It was clear that the General had little confidence in the agreement made with the Afghans.

> The Afghans are an essentially arrogant and conceited people. No great battle has yet been fought and the Afghans have nowhere suffered serious loss. It is not to be wondered at if the fighting men in distant villages and in and around Kabul, Ghazni, Herat, Balkh and other places still consider themselves undefeated and capable of defying us.
>
> Both Stewart and Browne are withdrawing their columns. I am to stay and a mission is to go to Kabul, with just a small contingent of Guides to join them. I have fears for their safety but my intelligence is most ineffective.
>
> Look here, Baa-Baa, I need you quickly to organise this. Neither the nature of the country nor the attitude of its people permit me to make effective reconnaissance. Afghan sources are not to be trusted and the political officers, whose job this is, have proved to be useless in conditions of war.

I have heard about Isandlwana and I am sorry about it. But you should have no trouble in quelling the Zulus now with the resources I understand you are receiving. So please get out here as soon as you can. I have cleared this with Delhi and London and I know that Chelmsford will let you go. You will need help. Bring with you whoever you trust. This affair will undoubtedly get worse. Our treaty has only brought us a little respite. The Russians are still behind it all . . .

Simon put down the closely written pages, lay back on the bed and closed his eyes in concentration. He knew little of Roberts except that he had fought that fine action on the ridges of Peiwa Kotal, and that Lamb clearly idolised him. The Pathans of the Afghan hills had fought the British for years. They were renowned as fine, if ill-disciplined warriors, but fierce and cruel. To be captured by them could mean being killed by slow torture. Simon frowned as he forced himself to contemplate this. The women of the tribes were supposed to do the business, he recalled. They used knives and hot coals . . .

He lay quietly for a moment. No. He remained physically unaffected by the prospect. No perspiration. No slump of the heart and dryness of the mouth. Had he cured himself at last of his fear – fear of the actuality and, even worse, of the unknown? Well, there was only one way to find out: go there and see.

His thoughts turned to the nature of the work. Roberts wanted intelligence: information about tribal movements and notice of confederation against him; news of massing in the hills, the size of the gatherings and likely direction of strike; that sort of thing. But if the experts on the spot – what were they called, political officers? – couldn't provide this, with all their knowledge of the country and the people, how on earth could he? Simon sat up quickly. To hell with it! If Lamb felt he could do it, then he could. If he could fight the Zulu, he could fight the Afghan. And of course – he smiled – Jenkins could fight anyone.

That evening, Simon put on as clean a shirt as Jenkins could find for him, struggled into his only other pair of breeches – he had long ago given away his army uniform – and re-crossed the Tugela. He turned right along the riverbank, skirting the periphery of the camp, until he found a small stream. He followed it away from the camp until it reached a quiet clearing where half a dozen tents were pitched, each at a distance from the other. A notice nailed to a tree announced that this was the 'Newspaper Compound'. He saw a familiar black figure laying a fire before one of the tents.

'George. Where is Miss Griffith?'

'In the tent, baas. Shall I call her?'

'Yes please.'

Simon dismounted, tied the reins loosely to a bush and waited. Eventually, a slim young woman in her mid twenties emerged from one of the tents and hurried over to him, tying back long fair hair into a bun at the nape of her neck. She was dressed purposefully in a simple cotton blouse, riding breeches and long boots, and her bronzed face broke into a smile of greeting.

Without hesitation she kissed him on the cheek, put her arm through his and walked with him back towards her tent.

'I haven't seen you since Ulundi,' she said. 'What did you think of the battle? It was my first, and I have to say, I took no joy in it. Tell me, what did you think?'

As she referred to the battle, she frowned and her grey eyes looked with concern into Simon's. She was not conventionally pretty, the set of her jaw and the line of her mouth giving her perhaps too masculine an air, but her figure was tall and slim, her skin clear, her cheekbones high and her hair the colour of soft honey. Alice Griffith was attractive enough to have turned many a head since she first arrived in South Africa nine months ago. Now, her earnest enquiry and the concern of her gaze made it difficult for Simon to resist a smile. He must not smile, though. She hated condescension.

'I suppose, Alice,' he said, 'no battles are very edifying. We had to shoot down the Zulus before they could get to the square and then . . . then . . .' he hesitated for a moment, because the memory was unpleasant, 'then we had to send out the cavalry to hunt them down to make sure the defeat was complete.'

'I know. I saw it. I rode out after the Lancers and saw them do it. Do you know, Simon,' she swung him round so that she could look into his eyes, 'most of those natives had thrown away their weapons and were trying to run away. Some just lay down and put their shields over their heads. It was pathetic. But the cavalry still killed them with their lances, as though they were spearing pigs.' The grey eyes filled with tears. 'It was just sport to them. Brutal. Brutal.'

Simon blinked at her vehemence and marvelled anew at the change in the girl he had first met three years ago. Then, to confound their parents' scheming, she had made him confess that there was no love between them and agree that they would become good friends. But that was long ago, and it was a woman of the world who confronted him now. Then, as he held her gaze, the fire slowly died from her eyes and she smiled.

'Sorry. I know it's not your fault.' She shouted to her servant. 'George. Tea. Quickly now.' She ducked into the tent and emerged with two small camp chairs, and they sat together

28

in front of the fire which George had succeeded in lighting. 'Now,' said Alice comfortably, 'what are you up to?'

'Well, I do have something to tell you.' He related his meeting with Lamb. To his surprise, she was not at all disconcerted by the revelation that the Colonel knew of her forgery. She simply shrugged her shoulders and buried her nose in the tea mug.

'Well, he was too smart not to find out sometime. But it was good of him to keep it quiet – even if he has used it to blackmail you.' She laughed. 'Shrewd old devil.' She gave Simon a cool glance. 'But he obviously thinks a great deal of you to use his dirty trick to get you to go to Afghanistan.' She nodded thoughtfully. 'Simon, I must say that you have grown, well, much older, my dear, in the last eighteen months.'

Simon laughed ruefully. 'You mean that I have grown up. Well, I suppose I have, and perhaps not before time.'

The sun had long since gone and the flames from the camp fire threw shadows across Alice's face. They gave golden highlights to her hair and silhouetted the gentle thrust of the breasts beneath her shirt. Simon felt again the stirrings of desire he had first experienced long ago.

'Alice,' he began tentatively.

'No, Simon.' Her eyes were now laughing at him again. 'I shan't miss you, for the simple reason that I am leaving here.'

'What! You are going to India too?'

'No, I wish I was. I can't say that I like wars, but they do give one the best possible material for writing – and I agree with Roberts that I think the Afghan business will flare up again. No, I'm going home.' She looked around her. 'I'm not sorry to leave here and I don't think that my reports have particularly endeared me to the army.' She laughed again. 'So no one here will grieve at my departure. But the

Morning Post has been very kind to me. The editor has instructed me to take the first ship to England now that the campaign is over. I understand that dear old Gladstone is preparing a great attack on the Government for its handling of foreign policy and these colonial wars, and my editor wants me to come home to cover it.' Alice's voice took on an air of excitement. 'I do so admire Mr Gladstone, and reporting on his campaign will be capital experience for me and should further my career.' For a moment, the woman of the world had become a girl again.

Simon did not dislike the regression. He took her hand. 'I am so pleased for you, Alice. I am impressed that you have made your own way so successfully. It cannot have been easy for a woman – and such a young one at that.'

Alice came as near to blushing as was possible for a newly hardened war correspondent, and she gave a half-embarrassed smile of thanks. Simon retained her hand and they sat silently for a moment, gazing into the fire. Then Simon stood. 'I must go now, for I have much to do before the morning.' Despite slight resistance from her, he kept her hand in his and drew her towards him. 'Alice, I shall forever be grateful for the way you helped me. Goodbye, and God bless you.'

He kissed her briefly on the lips and then walked away. As he mounted his horse, he looked back to see her framed against the firelight, one hand raised in silent farewell.

Eighteen hours later, he and Jenkins were riding the dusty road towards Pietermaritzburg, Durban, and a ship for Bombay.

John Wilcox

Chapter 2

By craning his head to look forward through the dirty glass of the carriage window, Simon could see the foothills of the mountains of Swat to the right, and to the left, those of Waziristan, which looked down from Afghanistan on to the border with India. Although the train had not climbed very far from the hot plains of India, he could already detect a certain freshness in the air, a crisp harbinger of the snows of the Hindu Kush.

Opposite him, Jenkins stirred and opened one eye. 'Where are we, then?'

'Just coming into Khushalgarh, I think,' said Simon, flattening his cheek against the glass in an attempt to look ahead. As they had already learned, opening the window let in not only the heat but also the soot-laden fumes from the twenty-year-old engine, straining two carriages ahead. 'In fact, I think I can see the Indus now.'

'Is this where we get off, then, bach sir?' Jenkins yawned and stretched his arms luxuriantly. 'I've just about had enough of this old puffer, look you.'

Although it was little more than three weeks since they had left the army of Lord Chelmsford in South Africa, the two men carried no trace of their military background. Both were dressed in nondescript mufti: simple khaki shirts tucked into lightweight cotton trousers, with loose-weave white

31

jackets slung above their canvas bags on the rack above their heads. They could have belonged to almost any stratum of the heterogeneous working population of British India: engineers, railway officials, or civil servants from the growing class of bureaucrats that kept the sub-continent functioning. The casual observer, however, might have puzzled about their ethnic origins. While both – and particularly Simon – carried with them something of the nonchalant air of confidence that went with their undoubtedly European clothing, their skins were quite dark and gave them the appearance of Indians or Eurasians. Simon's brown eyes and, especially, the black coals of Jenkins added to this impression.

'No, not yet.' Simon had to raise his voice to be heard above the hiss of escaping steam as the train slowed itself to a halt at Khushalgarh station. 'The one after this is for us. Kohat. About another twenty-five miles. Then it's back on to horseback and up into the hills.'

As he finished speaking, the door crashed open and a round-faced English officer, with captain's stars on his shoulders, a tropical topi with a pugree wound round it on his head, and dressed in lightweight khaki and brightly gleaming Sam Browne belt and riding boots, started to climb into the carriage. On the second step, however, seeing Jenkins and Simon, he paused, stepped down again, swung the door back to look at its exterior, and then, with a frown, put his head into the compartment.

'Look here, this is a first-class coach, isn't it?' It was more a statement than a question and he gestured vaguely with a swagger stick as he spoke.

'Yes, do come in,' said Simon. 'There's plenty of room.'

'What . . .?' The officer blinked at Simon's smooth tones, took a quick look at Jenkins and climbed into the compartment. Gingerly, he took a corner seat as far away from Jenkins as possible and put a small valise on the rack, stealing a glance at the two men's luggage as he did so. What he saw obviously decided him.

'Now look here,' he said again, pointing with his cane to Simon, 'you know perfectly well that only Europeans are allowed in first cl—'

'Fonthill,' Simon interrupted him, stretching out a languid hand of introduction. 'Guides. Captain.'

'Queen's *Own* Corps of Guides,' added Jenkins, helpfully.

The captain's jaw dropped. 'Barlow,' he said automatically. 'Eighth Foot.' He looked again from Simon to Jenkins and back again. Outside a whistle blew.

'Oh, sorry,' said Simon. 'This is Jenkins, 352.'

'Sergeant,' added Jenkins proudly, his white teeth cutting a swathe through his black countenance as he gave Barlow a huge grin. Then he jumped to his feet, grabbed the bewildered captain's hand, shook it vigorously and sat down again.

'Sergeant!' spluttered Barlow. 'Sergeant!' He swung round to Simon, who was still sprawled in his corner. 'You know very well that non-commissioned officers do not travel first class.'

'This one does,' said Simon imperturbably.

'What?' Barlow turned from one to the other uncertainly, before addressing Simon again. 'I am *not* travelling in the same compartment as an NCO. Dammit, I wouldn't do it even . . . even . . . even if the man was English.'

Jenkins retained his smile but his eyes had hardened. 'Ah well, look you, sir,' he said. 'I'm Welsh, so perhaps that's all right, is it?'

'Damn your impertinence. Get out of this carriage.'

Jenkins looked quickly across at Simon, who shook his head.

'I said get out.' With a swift movement, Barlow grabbed

Jenkins by his shirt front and hauled him to his feet. But Simon was even quicker. He sprang from his seat, slipped one hand under Barlow's belt and clamped the other on the back of his uniform collar and swung him away from Jenkins towards the open door. Then, his foot against the man's buttocks, he ejected him through the doorway like a bullet from a gun. At that point, with a hiss, the train began to move forward.

Unhurriedly, Simon pulled down Barlow's valise and threw it out after him, as the train gathered speed. Then he leaned out, closed the door with a thud and resumed his seat in the corner.

Jenkins stroked his moustache for a moment and then broke the silence. 'Now we shall both be blown from the mouth of a cannon,' he said. 'Or *you* will. It was nothing to do with me, look you. I thought you were supposed to be gentle and quiet, like?'

'Pompous bounder,' murmured Simon. And closed his eyes.

An hour later, the old engine wheezed into Kohat. It was not the end of the line, for the tracks now turned south to complete a loop at Dera Ismail Khan, but it was the nearest point to the Frontier south of Peshawar. Kohat certainly looked like a border town. There was no platform, and the two men stood with their bags in a rough square bounded by wooden shacks. Through a gap they could glimpse the tents of an army cantonment.

'Where to now, then, bach sir?'

'Now,' said Simon looking around him, 'we find the stables of one Sheram Khan, Pathan and dealer in fine horses. I'm told it's near a market. It can't be far.'

The two men picked up their bags and began walking

down a rough cart track between shacks, which soon opened out into a busy bazaar. The street became lined with stalls selling a colourful selection of northern Indian foods and artefacts: almond curd balushai sweetmeats; delicious-smelling boluses of spiced mutton, fried in fat with cabbage and onions; tobacco; trinkets of silver, turquoise and, perhaps, gold; dung cakes and firewood; long swathes of cotton and gauze in colours which sang the skills of the dyer. For Simon and Jenkins, who had had little time to explore Indian village life during their brief time in the sub-continent, it was all breathtakingly colourful. Nor did they feel out of place. Kohat had been the departure point of Major-General Roberts's column, and the little town hummed with the business this had brought. The bazaar thronged with an eclectic mixture of castes and nationalities – wild-haired Akalis from the Sikh states; short, fat Gujarat traders from the south; tall Pathans with kohl-rimmed eyes and noses like eagle beaks; a sprinkling of dowdy, cotton-suited Eurasian clerks; and, everywhere, off-duty sepoys of the Indian Army, in their khaki drill, turbans and puttees, mixed with the occasional British Tommy, turning over the wares of the stallholders with dismissive fingers.

'Just like Rhyl, bach,' murmured Jenkins, as they picked their way through the crowd.

A stall selling saddlewear and other leather pieces showed them to be near their goal. Behind the stall, a low archway opened on to a surprisingly spacious stable containing about a dozen horses in rough stalls. A small boy sat cross-legged, splicing a hempen halter.

'Sheram Khan?' enquired Simon. The boy, wide-eyed, gestured towards an open doorway to their left. A tall Pathan, his distinctive hill man's robe hitched at the middle by a deep embroidered Bokhariot belt, rose as they entered.

Simon gave him a respectful Musselman's salaam and said, '*Starrai Mashe! Khwar Mashe, janab ali.* Sheram Khan?'

The hill man bowed in silent acknowledgement and observed Simon with sharp eyes.

In English, Simon said: 'The cholera is bad in the south. I trust it has not come here?'

'The cholera has not reached us.' Sheram Khan spoke in excellent English and smiled slightly behind his long, grey-flecked beard. 'Good. I have been expecting you. The General and Lamb Sahib are most anxious that you travel up to their camp as soon as possible. I am to tell you that you must travel on as soon as . . .' he paused for a moment, 'I can turn you into respectable Persians.'

He stepped forward and examined the two men's faces in turn. 'The walnut dye is good,' he said, rubbing Jenkins's cheek gently with his thumb.

'It's not walnut, I understand,' said Simon. 'Our people in Gharghara have found something better now. This is supposed to last for about nine months before it starts to wear slightly.'

The Pathan nodded in approval. 'Your Pushtu sounded well. Can you speak it fluently?'

Simon grinned sheepishly. 'I'm afraid not. You see, we have only had three weeks' training at Gharghara.'

Sheram Khan regarded him impassively. 'Then, my friend,' he said, 'you will last for two weeks in the hills, perhaps three if you are lucky and can shoot well.'

'No. We will be supplied with an interpreter to travel with us when we reach the General's camp. And, of course, we are to be Persian traders from Mashad in the north, who do not speak the Pushtu of the Afghan.'

The Pathan nodded slowly. 'You are of the Guides?'

'Yes.'

'Then I respect you. The Guides fight well. Come, we have little time.'

An hour later, two Persians left the stable. They were dressed in the flowing robes of their race; one rather more finely than the other, with the edges of his turban cloth edged in gold and a Delhi-embroidered waistcoat showing beneath the loose top-garment. He rode a fine Balkh stallion ahead of his companion, who was mounted less richly on a serviceable horse from Herat.

'You've no right to be ridin' 'im,' hissed Jenkins from the rear. 'I should have had that one. You'll fall off if you 'ave to gallop. This one would 'ave suited you better. It might just pull a milk cart on a fine day.'

'Shut up, 352,' murmured Simon. 'Just try and be a little more Persian-like, there's a good chap.'

Jenkins snorted in disgust and pulled hard on the long rein that linked him to the laden donkey reluctantly trotting behind. Then, silently, they picked their way through the streets of Kohat to the plain beyond. There they set their horses' heads almost due west, towards the dark hills which rose before them and merged imperceptibly into the silver-capped escarpment dominating the far skyline.

Major General Roberts's main camp lay roughly fifty miles ahead of them, at the Afghan fort of Kuram, at the head of the Kuram valley, although the General had established a forward post higher in the hills at Alikhal. Simon's orders were to press on with all speed along the route taken by Roberts's little army of five thousand men and to meet the General at Kuram, where he would receive instructions for his mission. The orders, as paraphrased orally by Sheram Khan, were cryptic: don't delay; the route is only partly patrolled and the local Afridis are not to be trusted, so be on your guard.

The pair camped the first night at Thal, a little township

which Roberts had used as the last springboard for his invasion. There they met the stony tributary of the Indus which flowed from north-north-west and which was to be their guide into Afghanistan proper. Although they were climbing gradually and the air was undoubtedly crisper, the sun beat down relentlessly, and Simon and Jenkins slipped off their top garments and rode only in shirts and breeches, retaining their turbans as much for solar protection as for disguise.

Their track followed the river, which, although shallow in this high summer, and rock-strewn, varied from fifty to a hundred yards in width. They were now entering the Kuram valley, a barren, rocky plateau bordered by tall, magnificently wooded mountains. These were highest to the north and east. But Simon and Jenkins's route led to the north-west and the Sufed Koh range, where, directly ahead of them at the nine-thousand-foot high pass of Peiwa Kotal, Roberts had fought his battle to clear the way to Kabul.

Steadily they climbed until the mountains closed in and the stream, hissing and gurgling joyfully on its downward passage to the Indus, narrowed perceptibly. Their way now lay through craggy defiles, and Simon marvelled that Roberts had been able to take his army this way, with its camels and elephants carrying the heavier guns. It must have been continually susceptible to ambush.

He screwed up his eyes and peered up at the heights on either side. Was Roberts able to post scouts up there to protect his flanks as he advanced? Just about possible, perhaps. But the two men had no such luxury now, and they rounded each bend in the track with care, hoping to meet an army patrol, for the General had said that he was taking pains to keep the route open.

Rocks and crags, however, were all that met their gaze. The valley had now narrowed further to become a gorge and the distant vista of snow-capped peaks had long since disappeared. To the front and above them was a succession of spurs, covered with dense forests of deodar. Simon realised that, as the junior of the three invading generals, Roberts had drawn the shortest straw. This was by far the toughest approach to Kabul.

'Do you know, bach sir,' said Jenkins from the rear, 'I think I'd rather have Zululand. At least we could see where we were goin'.'

Simon looked up at the rapidly darkening sky. The sun had slipped away over a peak an hour ago and it was noticeably colder. 'We'd better camp here,' he said, pulling his horse's head away from the track towards a mossy bank, which stretched invitingly under a rock overhang. 'It should be safe to light a fire.'

The two men dismounted and Jenkins began relieving the donkey of part of its load. The horses were hobbled – an unnecessary precaution in truth, because they could not have wandered far – and Simon gathered wood and began lighting a fire as Jenkins broke out their sleeping rolls and took water from the stream.

It was quite dark by the time they had eaten. 'Snug enough, though, isn't it?' said Jenkins comfortably.

'Hmmn. Perhaps just a bit too snug.'

Simon got to his feet and walked softly to the edge of the trees that came down to the rock overhang. He peered into the darkness and stood still, listening. Then he sniffed. Equally quietly, he walked back to Jenkins and crouched down beside him.

'I don't like it, 352,' he said. 'This big overhang stops the fire being seen to some extent, but the smell of wood smoke is strong and will carry up the gorge. If there is anyone about it won't take long for them to know we are here.' He looked around. 'I think we shall have to forsake the fire. Come on.'

Together the two men unlashed some of the carpet samples that gave them credibility as traders, and laid them out like bed rolls, spoked away from the guttering fire. Then, taking their blankets and rifles, they stole quietly into the steep forest, finding a spot nearby which afforded them a view of the camp and where they could find cover, to some extent, by burrowing into the leaves and pine needles which covered the rocks.

'I'll take first watch,' whispered Simon.

'Kick me if I snore, then,' said Jenkins, wrapping his blanket round him so that his moustache protruded over the edge like a little black rodent at rest. Within seconds he was asleep.

Simon, after a cold and uneventful first watch, was fast asleep when a gentle dig in the ribs from Jenkins's rifle woke him. The half-light of dawn revealed the gorge as Simon inched himself alongside the Welshman to look down on their campsite.

At first he could see nothing, then, as his eyes grew accustomed to the light, he spotted them. At either side of the rock overhang, two men – four in all – stood motionless. So still were they that it was difficult to pick them out, in their dun-coloured clothing, from the grey of the rock. Then, moving like cats, one man from each side approached the camp fire.

Simon focused his eyes carefully in the gloom and saw that the two remaining men carried long-barrelled Afghan *jezails*, or muskets. The men tiptoeing towards the campsite seemed to be unarmed, until a charred ember of firewood slipped and caused the dying fire to blaze momentarily. The two men froze for a second, but not before the flame had caused the knife blades in their hands to flash. Jenkins lifted his rifle.

'No,' Simon whispered into his ear. 'I want to see what they're going to do first. Don't fire till I do. Then I'll take the two in the middle. You shoot the men waiting – they're the hardest targets.'

'Oh, thank you very much, I must say,' mouthed Jenkins. But he carefully took a bead on the most distant Afghan.

As the two men converged on the fire, the watchers saw that they were Pathans: tall, slim men, wearing turbans wrapped precariously like bundles of washing on their heads. They stole in noiselessly on soft sandals, slightly upturned at the toes.

'Do you think there are more in the trees?' whispered Jenkins, without taking his eyes off his target.

'Don't know. We'll have to take that chance.'

The Pathans each moved towards what appeared to be a sleeping man. Then they exchanged glances. One nodded, and both men swung their arms up and down in terrifying arcs and plunged their daggers into the sleeping forms.

'Right,' hissed Simon, and fired.

Almost simultaneously Jenkins too pulled his trigger. One of the two attackers immediately fell, as did 352's target on the edge of the trees. Simon and Jenkins quickly grabbed second cartridges from the rock by the side of their rifles and, using their thumbs, pressed them into the depression behind their back-sights and fired again. Despite the fact that he had to swing his rifle round, Jenkins got his shot away before Simon and dropped his second man as the Pathan fired his cumbersome musket. The second attacker, however, had run into the blackness of the trees before Simon could sight on to him.

'Damn,' he said. 'And damn again. Come on. There's nothing to be gained by hiding now.'

The two men got to their feet and crashed down in a shower of rocks to the campsite, running to where the Pathan had disappeared into the forest. He was, of course, nowhere to be seen. Rifles at their hips, Simon and Jenkins stood back to back for a moment, facing the trees, expecting an attack, or, at the least, a volley of firing from the darkness. But there was nothing. Only silence.

Jenkins looked quickly over his shoulder at Simon. 'You all right, bach sir?'

'For God's sake, yes. Look about you, into the trees. He must be there somewhere.'

His words were interrupted by two reports from the forest, some hundred and twenty yards above them, one from the right, the other from the left. The first ball hit the rock immediately above Simon's head, causing splinters to fly, before ricocheting down the gorge with a mournful whine. A rock splinter caught Simon above the eye and he felt blood trickle down his face. The other slug whistled through the loose folds of Jenkins's shirt and thudded into a tree behind him.

'Quick!' shouted Simon. 'Get them before they can reload. You take the left . . .'

But Jenkins had already gone. Moving with remarkable agility for such a thickset man, he bounded up the rock face and had disappeared before Simon could finish the sentence. Simon peered into the gloom. Dawn was flooding the gorge with light but the forest remained almost impenetrable. Concentrating hard, however, he thought he saw the remnants of a wisp of smoke lingering by the branch of a fir tree, about a hundred yards above him to his right. He thought quickly: how long did it take to reload a musket? It was a fifty-fifty chance. Heaving himself up by a tree root, he scrambled into the dubious protection of the forest darkness, using his rifle as a lever to push himself upwards and sometimes scraping along on all fours. He could hear no sound save that of his own noisy progress as he crashed through the undergrowth, but concealment was of no importance. The Pathan – God, could there be more than one? – had seen him enter the forest and would either be scrambling away himself or, more likely, thrusting the ball down the long barrel of his *jezail* and filling his pan with powder.

In fact, when Simon finally saw his man, he was doing neither of those things. He was waiting: his musket perfectly balanced, his head still behind the crude rear sight and his thumb in the act of cocking the flintlock. Simon flung himself to one side as he heard the first, tiny explosion in the priming pan, and then the second, much louder, as the powder in the main charge at the base of the gun was fired. So close was he that he felt the blast of the ball as it missed his right shoulder.

Simon had no time to aim, so he fired from the hip. A dull click was the result. In his anxiety to chase the assassins, he had forgotten to reload – and the Martini-Henry was a single-shot rifle.

The Pathan reacted quicker than Simon. Throwing aside his musket, he pulled from the cummerbund at his waist a long curved dagger and threw himself at his assailant. Instinctively, Simon presented his rifle to the Pathan as though it carried a bayonet at the end. The result was almost as effective as if it had done. The muzzle caught the Pathan squarely in the midriff as he hurled himself forward. Just under four feet long, and weighing nine pounds, the Martini-Henry was a most effective longstaff and the blow completely winded the Afghan. Simon had a momentary impression of a face contorted with surprise, the cheeks blown out and black eyes popping above a strong, hooked nose, before he himself was knocked to the ground by the force of the collision.

43

Together the two men rolled down the hill, crashing from tree to tree as each clawed at the ground for purchase. Simon was brought up sharply at the base of a large deodar, hitting his head on the trunk. Dazed, he was half aware that the Pathan was scrambling back up the slope towards him, knife in hand, when a solitary shot rang through the forest and the Afghan fell, a black bullet hole neatly drilled above his left ear.

Unsteadily, Simon rose to his feet and saw Jenkins twenty yards away, slipping another cartridge into the chamber and lowering the lever behind the trigger guard to cock the rifle.

'Thanks, 352. I think he would have had me that time.'

'You're very welcome, sir bach. I couldn't shoot earlier because you two was lovin' yourselves all over the ground, see. But I did see you present the bayonet to 'im, just like you was on the parade ground.'

Simon smiled and looked quickly around. 'I didn't hear you shoot before. Did yours get away?'

Jenkins looked offended. 'Oh no. Like you, in the fuss, like, I didn't have time to reload. So I used this, see.' From his belt he drew a knife and scabbard and, slipping off the sheath, showed Simon the blood-stained blade. He nodded to the dead Afghan. 'Two can play at that game, look you.'

Simon wrinkled his nose. 'Jenkins, you never fail to amaze me.'

'Well, I dunno why. I'm good at killin', you know that.'

Simon looked around. The sun was now penetrating the foliage in bright shards of light, bringing little coils of steam from the wet pine needles and making the rock outbreaks glisten. The tree trunks marched relentlessly above them, climbing vertically from the forty-five-degree slope. But no sound came from them: no birdsong or scuffle of wildlife, and no sight or echo of human activity.

The two men stood quietly, each moving his head slowly to scan the forest and straining to hear a twig snap or a pebble slide. Nothing.

'Well, if there were more of them, they've gone now all right,' said Jenkins eventually.

'Hmmmn.' Simon frowned. 'I wonder. Damn! The horses. They might have doubled back. Quick.'

The two half ran, half slid down between the trees to the trail below and to the camp under the rock overhang. But the two horses and the donkey were undisturbed, grazing happily on the mossy bank. Simon and Jenkins loaded the donkey and mounted their horses, to resume their ascent along the rocky trail. They now rode with their rifles in their hands, eyes constantly scanning the rocks and trees that climbed above them either side of the fast-flowing water. Each bend in the trail was now approached with great caution, Simon, in the lead, edging round the rock face while Jenkins covered him, rifle at his shoulder.

This, and the fact that the going became steeper as they climbed, made for slow progress, and Simon estimated that they had covered only perhaps a mile and a half in the first hour when they met the army patrol.

The encounter showed how inadequate their precautions would have been if the ambush had been for real. Simon edged round one particularly awkward bend in the trail, where a jagged tooth of a rock made the corner completely blind, and called Jenkins to follow. Immediately, a dozen rifles poked at them from the top of a rocky ledge on the right and a young voice shouted at them in Urdu.

'Damn,' breathed Simon. Holding up his hand with the palm towards the cliff face, he cried: '*Allah kerim. Allah kerim.*' He could see no sign of the speaker; only the rifles pointing down at them, with what appeared to be a brown face behind each one. The voice again shouted either a command or a question in Urdu.

Standing in the stirrups, Simon replied in Pushtu: 'You must forgive this traveller, but I do not speak the language of the Indus.'

There was another pause, and then the speaker replied, this time with some exasperation, 'Well, dammit, do you speak English?' It was a voice from the playing fields of any English public school, high-pitched and querulous.

Simon smiled. 'Yes, dammit, I do. But it would be better if I could see who the hell I'm speaking to.'

At this, a slight figure emerged above the parapet and scrambled down to the road. He was dressed in a tight-fitting uniform of dark green, with a pistol in a black leather holster at his side and a black topi on his head. He might have cut a sinister figure in those hills but for his face, which was cherubically pink and sported a startlingly blond moustache. He could not have been more than twenty-one years of age.

'Sorry, old boy,' he said, as he approached Simon. 'Had to be sure you weren't a couple of *pahari choors*.' He held up his hand. 'Chambers. Second Lieutenant, 5th Gurkhas.'

'Glad to see you.' Simon shook his hand warmly. 'Fonthill. Captain, Corps of Guides. This is Sergeant Jenkins.'

'Oh, sorry, sir.' Chambers briefly stiffened into a formal salute and then nodded cordially to Jenkins. 'Don't see many white NCOs in the Guides – if you are white, that is.'

'This one's a bit special. How far are we from General Roberts's camp?'

'About half a day, if we get a move on.' The young man turned and shouted an order in Gurkhali. Immediately the rifles disappeared from the ledge and, within seconds, some twenty Gurkha infantrymen appeared on the trail and fell in loose order. Simon looked at them with interest. He had heard about these little mountain men from Nepal. They had a formidable reputation as fighters, yet now they appeared almost childlike in their green uniforms and pillbox hats, which they wore jauntily to one side. They seemed like page boys on a day's outing from a London gentleman's club. Yet they carried their rifles with easy grace and every man had a broad-bladed kukri hanging from his belt.

Chambers regarded Simon and Jenkins with an ingenuous smile. 'I must say, you Guide chaps do go native magnificently,' he said. 'You certainly look the proper article. My chaps nearly blew your heads off as you rounded the bend.'

'Ah, that's because we're Welsh, see,' interjected Jenkins helpfully, his smile cutting a great white gash under his moustache.

'What? Oh, I see. Yes. Well.' Chambers looked puzzled for a moment. Then his smile returned. 'Welsh, eh? So you're used to the mountains, of course.'

'Not really,' said Simon. 'Don't you think we'd better get on? We had a bit of trouble back there.'

'Eh? Oh. Yes, sir. Of course. We thought we heard firing down the pass about an hour ago, so we hurried on down. We were sent out to escort you in, because the Afridis here are a two-faced lot. They profess friendship but they'd as soon cut your throat as shake your hand. This route is supposed to be open back to the border but it needs constant patrolling.'

Simon looked down at the little men with their ageless brown faces. 'Aren't the cavalry used for patrolling?'

'What? Good lord, no. Not here. These chaps are the best in the world in this territory.' Chambers gazed at his platoon with pride. He seemed like a school prefect out with a party of fourth-formers. 'Horses are no good here. My chaps are the thing for these rocks. You'll see.'

He barked a further command, and immediately, two men splashed through the stream and disappeared on the far side, while another two climbed among the trees and went ahead on the right bank. Half of the remainder fell into double file ahead of Simon and the rest behind Jenkins. Then the little column set off, Chambers chatting continuously to Simon as he strode beside him.

Simon soon saw the young man's point about the Gurkhas. They moved silently and, seemingly, effortlessly along the rocky path, maintaining a far faster pace than the two horsemen had managed. The trail was now very steep, and Simon was happy in the knowledge that flank men were out ahead of the party.

As they neared Kuram, the trail widened and flattened, and they fell in with a company of Punjab Cavalry who had been out on patrol on the plain. They made a fine sight with their lances, coloured turbans and great beards, and Simon felt that Jenkins and he were being escorted into Kuram by the pick of the Indian Army.

The town itself was little more than a handful of huts clustered around the brown mud walls of an Afghan hill fort. The ramshackle fort could not house all Roberts's men, and the white bell tents of the troops surrounded the fort like a besieging army. Although the sun was still quite high in the sky, it was noticeably colder here, and Simon shivered as they were escorted through the guard lines.

A major on the General's staff received them in the fort, and here Simon said goodbye to Chambers, who trotted off with his soldiers as though they had all just got out of bed. Here, too, he parted company with Jenkins, who was dispatched to the sergeants' mess of a British line battalion, there being no unit of Guides in the camp.

'Now try and behave like a sergeant,' whispered Simon.

'Very well, bach sir. I'll try and find someone to shout at, then.'

Both the General and Colonel Lamb – the latter having only arrived at the camp himself two weeks before – were out on reconnaissance, and Simon was ordered to wait on the General at nine that evening, after dinner. General Roberts, he was told, was anxious to see him as soon as possible.

Simon was allocated a tent and advised that he could eat at the officers' mess of the Punjab Cavalry. But after washing himself thoroughly in a hand bowl, he chose instead to wander among the huts of the Afridis who lived at Kuram and farmed the surrounding inhospitable plateau. He bought a bowl of goat stew and some coarse Afghan bread, and sat cross-legged in the dust, his back to the wall, feeding himself fastidiously, using his fingers and the bread, impervious to the curious gazes he elicited.

Precisely at nine o'clock, he presented himself at the General's headquarters. The fort was a gloomy place, built for defence rather than comfort. The walls were about twelve feet thick and enclosed a cramped quadrangle. But they were flaking and crumbling here and there, and Simon estimated that they would be unlikely to withstand even a light artillery bombardment. He was led into a small, stuffy anteroom, lit by rush flares flickering on the walls. It was medieval and primitive; not at all how he imagined the palaces of the Raj to be. In fact, he reflected, Afghanistan was completely unlike India. If the predominant colours of the sub-continent were bright – the yellow of saffron, the silver of silk, the bright blue of the sky – then the land of the Pathans was painted in browns and greys.

The call came quickly, and Simon was ushered into a much bigger room, lit by candles and a large fire, with unglazed windows through which he could glimpse stars and hear the murmur of the camp. Two figures, silhouetted against the fire, rose to greet him. As they did so, Simon almost gasped in disbelief. The two men could have been twins, so similar were they in stature and bearing.

The first figure was that of Colonel Lamb. The second, however, seemed almost a replica of the Colonel: also five foot two, slightly built, flag-staff straight and with Lamb's direct gaze. Frederick Sleigh Roberts, VC, had been Quartermaster General of the Indian Army when the call had come to lead the Kuram Field Force. He had won his Victoria Cross in the Mutiny as a subaltern twenty-five years earlier, but he had seen comparatively little active service and had never commanded in the field until now. His success in the fierce skirmish at Peiwa Kotal had been his first victory as a commander, and it had won him instant fame.

Roberts did not advance to meet Simon, but stood by the fire, his hand extended. As he approached, Simon realised that height and posture were all that the General shared with Lamb. While the Colonel was sunburned and cleanshaven, Roberts's cheeks were pink and he wore side whiskers which ended in a short, grey-flecked beard. Both men wore comfortable smoking jackets, with loose scarves at their throats. They could have been two English country gentlemen – the squire and the doctor – finishing their port after dining well.

'You had trouble on the way up, I hear,' said Roberts. He spoke softly, with nothing of Lamb's staccato delivery.

'Yes, a little, I'm afraid. We had to kill four Afridis.'

Roberts gestured to a chair. 'Tell me about it.'

Simon told the story as briefly as he could. He would have been briefer, in fact, but the General continually interrupted him to ascertain details – 'At what range did you fire?' 'Why do you feel there were no more attackers?' 'Describe Jenkins to me; is he as well disguised as you?'

His account finished, Simon was silent. The General looked at him without speaking. Colonel Lamb shifted in his chair, but he too said nothing. Simon began to feel embarrassed.

Eventually, Roberts spoke. 'I don't like it,' he murmured. 'Sir?'

'You are supposed to be agents. I didn't expect that you would thunder into the hills, virtually shooting on sight.'

Simon bristled. 'With respect, sir, if we had not done so we would both now be dead.'

The General scratched at his beard. 'What rifles did you have?'

'Martini-Henrys, sir.'

'Ah. There you are then!' Roberts rose to his feet and began to pace around the room. 'Where did you get them?'

'We . . . er . . . brought them with us from Zululand, sir.' Simon stirred uneasily.

The General stopped pacing and stood before him. 'Did it not occur to you, young man, that a Persian carpet trader from the north and his servant would be highly unlikely to go about their business carrying the latest British Army rifles?' He still spoke quietly, but every word was uttered with precision. It occurred to Simon that Roberts's career as Quartermaster General of the Indian Army meant that his life had been one of careful planning and attention to detail.

He too stood up. 'Yes, sir. That's why we kept them carefully concealed until we were attacked.'

'Hmmmn.' The General's blue eyes were completely expressionless. 'Nevertheless, it's not like the Afridis to attack a couple of merchants in the middle of the night. They would be curious about you . . . want to talk to you and offer you mint tea before slitting your throats. No. It's my bet that they saw your rifles and took you for what you are – a couple of *gora-logs*, playing the game.'

'The game, sir?'

Roberts looked at him sharply. 'How long have you been in India?'

'Just under a month, sir.'

'What training have you had here?'

'A little over two weeks in the school at Gharghara, in the hills. We learned some Parsi and a little Pushtu, native manners, how to measure distances by keeping our foot paces consistent . . . that sort of thing.' Simon suddenly felt inadequate. 'There was time for little else. I was told to hurry on to you by this date. I am sorry if . . .'

For the first time Roberts smiled. 'Do sit down, Fonthill. Here, have some . . . dammit, Baa-Baa, you've virtually finished the brandy!'

An unusually quiet Lamb stood up. 'I'll fetch some more,' he murmured and walked to the door.

Roberts leaned forward. 'Yes, I was aware that you had little time for training here. Frankly, Fonthill, I've been forced to take a gamble with you. Lamb tells me that you and your man were the best intelligence people he had in South Africa. I asked him to bring you out because we are damned short of that sort of material here. Not that we don't have some fine men operating. Cigar?'

Simon shook his head and the General leaned back and blew blue smoke to the ceiling.

'Both we and the Russians have had agents working in and around Afghanistan for the last forty or fifty years; white men but living like natives, surveying the passes and roads, watching each other's movements, gauging which tribe is friendly and which isn't. That sort of thing.'

He smiled. 'The newspapers back home have called it "The Great Game", and in a way it is. Except that there aren't any rules.' Roberts's eyes narrowed. 'It's a very dangerous game, Fonthill. But then . . .' the smile came back, 'you'll know about this sort of thing because you've played it in Zululand.'

Simon's heart sank. The last thing he wanted was to be regarded as some sort of master spy, skilled at subterfuge and disguise.

'Not really, sir,' he began. But Lamb had returned, and the next few moments were taken up with the brandy bottle. Despite the fire, the open windows made the room cold, and Simon was glad of the warm liquor. It helped to stop his heart from thumping. The Great Game sounded frightful.

The General settled back in his chair and sipped at his glass. 'My irritation of a moment ago was caused by the fact that your disguise may well have been penetrated by the Afridis who attacked you. If it was, you have two chances. Firstly, you may have killed all the members of that attacking party. Secondly, even if a couple of the Pathans did get away, their particular tribe could well keep the news to themselves in the hope that they can pick you off themselves later to settle the score.'

For the first time, Colonel Lamb now intervened. 'You may well wonder, Fonthill, why we would even think of sending a blacked-up chap into hostile territory which he doesn't know and where he can't speak the lingo, eh? What? What?'

Simon smiled. 'I must confess, it had occurred to me, sir.' He tried not to sound ironic.

'Quite. Quite.' Lamb bounced in his chair, pleased that he had so successfully put himself in the other's place. 'Well, we're not such duffers as we seem. You see, this godforsaken country is really a loose collection of little kingdoms, which, although they formally owe allegiance to the Amir in Kabul, act very autonomously. There's not much cross-fertilisation between 'em, so to speak. That's one reason why those Afridis might not pass on to their neighbours the news of your presence.

'The other – more important – point is that Afghanistan is a sort of crossroads. It's the link between India and central Asia. All kinds of queer Johnnies are always travelling through it. Traders from Persia. Horse dealers from Samarkand. Fakirs from India. Teachers and their *chelas*. They speak their own tongues and often no other. So if you play your parts properly, you won't seem at all unusual to the *paharis* – that means hill men – whose territories you pass through.'

The Colonel sank back, satisfied that he had made his point well. Simon nodded thoughtfully. 'But I must be able to communicate, mustn't I?'

A great grin seamed Lamb's face and his teeth gleamed in the firelight. Even the General smiled faintly. 'We've taken care of that,' said Lamb. 'We're giving you a Sikh interpreter. He's a Guide and he knows the hills, the tribes and the dialects well.'

'He is, I understand, a trifle . . . ah . . . eccentric,' interposed Roberts. 'But the best man for the job, without a doubt. You will meet him in the morning.'

Simon nodded. 'Thank you. Now, sir. What exactly is it you want me to do?'

Roberts took a reflective puff at his cigar. 'You've read the briefing notes which I sent to Colonel Lamb?'

'Yes, sir.'

'You will know, then, that we have agreed peace terms with the Amir, Yakub Khan. Under the terms, mine is the only column that has been allowed to remain in Afghanistan.' He smiled wryly. 'And, as you can see, we're not camped very far into the country. The other two columns, under General Stewart at Kandahar, and Sir Sam Browne's force in the Khyber, have both been withdrawn.'

The General stubbed out his cigar in an earthenware dish. 'However, we do have a military mission in Kabul itself, the capital. Sir Louis Cavagnari has gone there with a small force to set up the Residency.'

Roberts looked at the floor momentarily before continuing, and Simon intuitively felt that this straight-talking man was about to dissemble. 'Cavagnari's a good man, of course. Knows the country well. First-class diplomat – in fact, it was he who negotiated the treaty. His dispatches sent here for onwards transmission to the Viceroy in Simla are all full of optimism.' Now the General held Simon's gaze again. 'But I don't like it.'

'Why not, sir?'

'The Afghans may not be the world's most united nation, but they're quite cohesive in the sense that, not unreasonably, they don't like their country being invaded by foreigners – particularly unbelievers. They're mainly Musselmen, you see. They are fine fighters – although not as good as they think they are – and the trouble is that we've not defeated them properly in battle yet. Our southern army just went straight through to Kandahar without any fighting at all. In the Khyber, we had a few skirmishes but little else. Here, we gave 'em a bloody nose on the high pass, but you can't say that the nation has been defeated.'

The General looked across at Lamb and smiled. 'So I believe the pot is simmering. I want to know where, when and how it might boil over, and that's why I sent for Colonel Lamb.

'You see, Fonthill, I have found our intelligence to be poor here. Yes, we have a much-vaunted system of political officers. But although these people have military rank, they are really civil servants and lack what I consider to be a proper strategic sense of our situation here. They're all damned optimists and placators, it seems to me. The other point is that each officer is limited to his own territory and has no perception of what is happening, or likely to happen, in the valley next door.

'As a result of this, I have asked Colonel Lamb to create an *army* intelligence operation to serve the Field Force here. Lamb rates you highly, so he has brought you with him to be in the van, so to speak.'

'The van, sir?'

Roberts nodded. 'I want you to go to Kabul. Cavagnari has only been there a month, but he will have settled in by now. Of course you will inform him of any development which you believe will have relevance to his work. But you will not report to him. You will deal with Colonel Lamb, who will remain here.'

Simon's brow creased into a frown. 'But I can't stay at the Residency, sir.'

'Of course not,' Lamb interjected. 'You and 457 – whatsis-name – and your interpreter must live in Kabul as carpet traders. Sir Louis will need to refurbish the Residency, so there is every reason why a Persian merchant should visit him. But you must find lodgings in the city.'

The General now rose to his feet and Simon did the same, sensing the dismissal. 'What we need from you, Fonthill,' said Roberts, 'is news of that pot. I want to know if there is an amalgamation of the mullahs in the hills; where the tribes will gather for it; and, of course, when they are likely to strike.'

Roberts seized Simon's arm in emphasis. 'The possibility of the tribes massing is what interests me most. If they stay disunited, I can pick them off separately. If they unify, it will be a very different matter. We would be outnumbered by a hundred to one.' He smiled and held out his hand. 'Good luck, my boy.'

'Thank you, sir.' Simon shook hands with both men and turned for the door.

'Fonthill.' It was Colonel Lamb who called. 'I will walk with you to your tent.'

Once outside the General's quarters, Lamb bustled into a quick walk, along the corridor, across the enclosed ground and through the massive gates of the fort towards the British lines, all the while gripping Simon's arm.

'Sorry about the early rubbishing,' he said. 'But Bobs was worried that you had blown everything when you killed those hill men. And you may well have done. Can't be helped. You had no alternative. I understand that. But you're at greater risk than ever, my boy.'

Simon gulped. 'I'm not sure I'm the best man to be a spy, Colonel. For one thing—'

'Rubbish.' Lamb stopped at the lines of the Punjab Cavalry. The distinctive smell of horses and manure filled the air. 'You did well in Zululand. No different here. Two things, though.'

'Sir?'

'Exchange those Martini-Henrys for a couple of old Sniders. They don't shoot as well, but they fit better. A Persian trader would never be able to get his hands on Martini-Henrys, but Afghanistan is full of old Sniders.'

'Very good, sir. And the second thing?'

Colonel Lamb looked up at Simon quizzically. 'Did you throw a certain Captain Barlow of the 8th Foot out of a railway carriage at Khushalgarh?'

Simon examined the stars above, set like diamonds in blue velvet. 'I certainly did, sir. Man's a bounder.'

The Colonel sighed. 'I suppose I was aware that you were not enamoured of what we might call conventional army officers. Very well. But get out of here as soon as you can in the morning. Barlow has filed a formal complaint and I can deal with it much better if you are lost somewhere in the hills.'

'Thank you, sir. Good night.'

'See me first thing in the morning. Sleep well, Fonthill.'

Chapter 3

Simon rose before dawn. While Jenkins collected their supplies for the journey to Kabul and their replacement rifles – snorting at their obsolescence – Simon reported to Colonel Lamb's tent to receive his final briefing. He was given a rough map for the road ahead and a code to memorise and destroy, for use in written reporting. His interpreter, a sepoy from the Guides, was then brought in.

He was undoubtedly a Sikh, taller than Simon, blue-turbaned and heavily bearded, but dressed in the manner of a hill man. Incongruously, he crashed to attention before the Colonel and gave both men an impeccable salute.

Simon spoke quickly. 'That will be the last time you will salute me,' he said. 'From now on I am a Persian merchant from Mashad, with my servant, and you are our guide and interpreter. You will show me conventional respect as an employee would. But that is all.'

The Sikh's eyes glowed. 'Very good, sahib.' His voice was remarkably high-pitched for such a big man.

Simon sighed. 'And that is the last time you will call me sahib. Do you understand? What is your name?'

The Colonel, sitting behind his desk, coughed slightly. 'Ah, his name appears to be . . .' and he consulted a note before him, '. . . er . . . W. G. Grace.'

'What? But he's a cricketer, isn't he?'

59

'Ah no, sir.' The Sikh spoke firmly. 'I believe that you are mistaken in degree, sir. W. G. Grace is not a cricketer, sir. He is the King, sir.'

'King? King? King of where?'

'King of cricket, sir. He is the Emperor and King of all cricket, sir. The best, sir. The very best, sir. He is King.'

'What the dickens . . .?' Simon looked at the Colonel in supplication. Lamb shrugged his shoulders, a half-smile playing on his lips. 'Look here.' Simon tried again. 'You can't call yourself after this man. I mean, well, he's a Gloucestershire doctor or something. An English cricketer. You're a Sikh and a Guide. It won't do.'

The Sikh's finely arched eyebrows rose. 'With greatest of diffidence and respect, sir, and to repeat myself just this once more without giving offence, W. G. Grace is not simply a cricketer. He is greatest cricketer world has known.' Simon took a breath to intervene, but he was too late. 'Eight years ago, sahib, the honourable doctor scored ten centuries in one season. Imagine, sir, ten whole centuries. He was first man to do that. And then, in '76, sir, he hit highest ever score of three hundred forty-four. But more than that, sir . . .'

He turned to Lamb. 'If the Colonel will allow?' The little man, one hand across his mouth, waved acquiescence with the other. The Sikh took up the ruler from Lamb's desk. 'Now, sir.' He held the ruler as a cricket bat, his left hand above the right, bending his knees so that his bottom stuck out and the base of the ruler tapped the ground behind his right sandal, as though he was taking guard. It was an incongruous sight, and Simon noticed that the Colonel now had his hand across his eyes.

'Now, sir,' the Sikh repeated. 'Before Dr Grace, batsmen would play ball so.' And he took a half-pace forward and brought the ruler diagonally down from his right shoulder, so that he ended up with his body twisted, his head looking to the left. 'What happens? Bally ball goes under bat, because bat has swung across line, and hits wicket. Out, sir!'

He smiled, confident that he had made his point. 'Dr Grace changed all that, sir. Look.' The big man settled into his crease once more, then took half a pace forward again with his left foot. This time, however, he brought the ruler down vertically and completely straight, his left elbow high – and seemingly awkwardly – in the air. He stayed in the pose for a moment to demonstrate. 'You see, sir, ball has nowhere to go but plonk on to bat. Result? Straight back behind bowler for four of the best. This Mr Grace devised.' He straightened up. 'He is almost, though not quite, as great as revered Queen Empress.'

A silence fell on the tent, relieved only by Lamb blowing his nose. Simon did not know quite what to say. 'How, ah, how do you know all this?' he enquired.

The big Sikh smiled. Digging beneath the folds of his quilted coat, he produced a yellowed cutting. '*Illustrated London News*, sir. I have been great admirer of Dr Grace since reading this.' A look of modest pride came over his countenance. 'I also play, sir, and scored century last year in Rawal Pindi. Not out, sir. Not out. With many covering drives, so . . .' and, bending his right knee, he executed a graceful cover drive, finishing with the ruler in the air.

Holding the pose, he directed a stern eye at Simon. 'So, sir,' he said, 'last year I change name as indication of great respect for great man. I am no longer Inderjit Singh, sir. I am W. G. Grace. Though,' he smiled winningly, 'everyone calls me W. G.'

The big man stiffly stood upright and shared his smile with Colonel Lamb. Simon looked at the cutting in his hand.

It showed a sepia drawing of a large, thickset man, with a full beard and a round face topped by a rather ridiculous peaked schoolboy's cap. He looked sharply at the Sikh. But for the headgear, they could be the same person. He folded the cutting. 'Would you wait outside for a moment, please?'

The Sikh sprang to attention and was about to salute, then he stopped, gave his big smile and turned towards the tent flap. There he paused for a second, before whirling round and approaching Simon. 'I would like to have Dr Grace's story back, sir, if it is allowed.'

'Oh, of course.' Abstractedly Simon returned the cutting and watched as the big man left the tent. He turned to the Colonel, who was now unashamedly wiping his eyes.

'Really, sir,' said Simon, 'I can't have him. The man's a buffoon. W. G. Grace indeed . . .'

'Well,' said Lamb, blowing his nose again. 'I've been to Lord's many times, but that was just about the best "covering" drive I've ever seen executed with a ruler. Haven't laughed so much for years.'

'It won't be any laughing matter if he starts talking this cricket nonsense to the mullahs in the hills if they nab us.'

'Oh, don't be so stuffy, Fonthill.' The Colonel replaced his handkerchief and walked round the table, his eyes twinkling. 'Goodness me, you'll be throwing NCOs out of first-class compartments soon.'

Simon smiled. 'But we need somebody really good for this trip. Jenkins and I will have to depend on him.'

'I know.' The Colonel raised his eyebrows. 'Do you know who recommended dear old W. G. as your interpreter?'

Simon shook his head.

'The General himself. I haven't been here long enough to know, but it seems that, whatever else he is, W. G. is not a buffoon. Last year he spent nine months in the north of

Afghanistan going through Merv, Bokhara and Samarkand
with Lieutenant Cavendish of the Guides, looking at Russian
dispositions on the border there. Just the two of them.'

There was no laughter now in the Colonel's eyes. 'Three
months ago he returned carrying Cavendish's body slung
across his camel. He'd been shot on the last lap back near Ali
Masjid in the Khyber. W. G. himself had a bullet wound in the
upper arm.' Lamb allowed himself a smile. 'Though it doesn't
seem to have affected his cover drive. More importantly, he
had preserved all of Cavendish's coded notes, written on rice
paper. Know how?'

Simon shook his head again.

'By rolling them in a piece of goatskin and keeping them
concealed up his arse in case he was captured.' He smiled
again. 'Damned uncomfortable riding on a camel, I imagine.'
He took Simon's arm. 'I shouldn't worry about this cricketing
Sikh, if I were you. The General tells me that, in addition to
Urdu and English, he speaks both dialects of Pushtu – the
soft, Pashtu, and the hard, Paktu – as well as Persian Parsi,
which you are supposed to speak. He's as good a shot as your
sergeant, by the sound of it, and he once broke a man's neck
in a wrestling match in Balkh. Oh, and he knows the passes
and mountain trails around Kabul like the back of his hand –
or his cricket bat. Convinced?'

Simon nodded. 'Sold, sir. Though you wouldn't be pulling
another dirty trick on me, would you?'

'Get out, Fonthill. Before I confront you with Barlow's
very reasonable complaint.'

The two men shook hands. Outside the tent, Simon called
to the Sikh. 'W. G., it is good to have you with us. I am sorry,
though, that we only have two horses and a loaded donkey.
You must walk, I fear.'

A smile broke the Sikh's beard. 'I am glad that you do not

63

have camels, sir. At the moment, I am peculiarly glad not to have to sit on camel, sir, or anything for that matter. I am glad to walk.'

'I think I know what you mean,' said Simon. 'Come on and meet Sergeant Jenkins.'

The party set out shortly afterwards, Simon in the lead on the stallion, looking every inch a dealer in fine Persian carpets; Jenkins behind on his serviceable mount; and W. G. at the rear, walking with long, loping strides, leading the donkey.

Almost immediately the route led upwards towards the pass of Peiwa Kotal, the only way across the Safed Koh range, which marked the end of the Kuram valley and the entrance to Afghanistan proper. It was here that Roberts had been faced by an Afghan army vastly superior in numbers and shrewdly positioned to deny him passage. The pass itself was merely a depression in the range, some 9,400 feet above sea level and commanded on each side by high pine-clad mountains rising to 14,000 feet. As the track – it was little more than a zigzag goat path, littered with rocks and boulders – approached the summit, it grew precipitously steep, and each short, straight stretch was flanked by breastworks of pinelogs and stones, emplacements for rifles and cannon.

For the first time, Simon began to appreciate why the General was so well regarded in the Indian Army. While the two senior officers had taken their columns along settled trading routes through the wide, comparatively low passes of Khyber and Kohjak, the little Quartermaster (his substantive rank was only Major) had been allocated this most difficult of paths to Kabul. Meeting these substantial fortifications, he had feinted to attack frontally. Then, leaving his camp fires burning and his tents erect, he had led his main force on a mad night scramble up through the forested mountains to attack the pass from the rear just as dawn was breaking. It had been touch and go through the day but he had eventually sent the Afghans reeling back towards Kabul, leaving their baggage and cannon behind. The detritus of the retreating army was still evident as the three men mounted the crest.

'Glad we missed this one,' said Jenkins as they picked their way through splintered rock and pines gashed by shot and shell.

That night they camped just outside the army outpost at Alikhal and then pushed onwards and upwards again towards the Shutargardan, the last mountain range before the descent to the Logar and Kabul valleys. They had passed the high-water mark of the English invasion and were beyond the reach of army patrols. This was now completely Afghan territory, for the tiny English mission at Kabul would not stray from the capital.

The Shutargardan itself formed a distinct crest and the little party paused to rest and regain breath. Although the Sikh was quite impervious to the altitude, despite the fact that he walked while the others rode, Simon and Jenkins found the pass's eleven-thousand-foot elevation made breathing difficult. Reassuringly, however, the view from the crest to the north-west showed a fertile valley. The road fell away somewhat into the valley, but not as steeply as the climb to the pass, for they had now reached the central high plateau of the Amir's kingdom. Nevertheless, it revealed a promising prospect towards the little township of Kushi, which they glimpsed after an hour's march from the summit.

Simon chose not to linger in the town, and they picked

their way with dignity through the dirty, sleepy streets, attracting only perfunctory glances.

'Looks as though we're gettin' away with it,' hissed Jenkins as they left the last dry-stone wall behind them and headed once again into open country.

'Don't count chickens,' said Simon, wrapping his cloak around him. Although it was only September and the sun's rays cut cheerfully in daylight hours through the thin, high air, a steady wind blew down the valley from the snowy peaks of the Hindu Kush directly ahead of them. It whispered of a cruel winter to come.

They now followed the Logar river, and camped that night above the settlement of Zahidabad, some fifteen miles from Kushi, taking it in turns to stand watch. But the night, like the days before it, was uneventful. They passed through a pretty little village called Charasia, which nestled in orchards and gardens, and then approached the gorge of Sang-i-nawishta, through which the Logar river gurgled and jumped. As they neared it, the Sikh gently lengthened his stride so that he caught up with Simon in the lead. Diffidently, he tightened a strap on the big horse, and without raising his head, addressed Simon in Parsi, speaking slowly so that the Englishman could understand.

'May I suggest that my lord slowly turns his head towards . . .' here he paused, and then lapsed into English, 'cover point . . .' before continuing in dialect, 'and looks at the two big rocks that stand proud, like virgin's breasts.'

Unaffectedly, Simon did so, taking in the large boulders to his right, some two hundred yards away, and then innocently looking up at the sky, back down the trail and to the front again. 'I see nothing.'

'Two men have been following us on foot since we left Charasia. I saw them regard our carpets as we passed through

the square. I believe them to be covetous of them, master.'
The Sikh hardly moved his lips as he spoke. 'They are moving
ahead of us and I expect them to strike as we pass through the
gorge.'

'Thank you, W. G. I would not have seen them. You have
the eyes of a hawk.' Simon thought hard for a moment. 'I do
not want to kill unless we must. So let them make the first
move. Warn Sergeant Jenkins.'

The Indian inclined his head slightly and fell back,
whispering to Jenkins as he did so.

Within ten minutes the trail narrowed and became more
stony as they approached the gorge. Here the river had carved
its own passage through the low range of hills which overlooked Charasia and blocked the passage to Kabul, creating a
narrow defile only a hundred yards or so in length, before
opening out again to the valley beyond. The road had become
little more than a rough path, which followed the course of
the Logar, tumbling turbulently fifty feet below.

'This is no place for shaking 'ands and sayin' 'ow d'yer do
politely,' hissed Jenkins from the rear. 'Let's gallop through
with our guns a-blazin'.'

'W. G. can't gallop, remember. No. Sit it out. They could
have fired on us long ago. I have a feeling we are being tested.'

They had not long to wait. Hardly had the party picked
its way through the first ten feet of the narrow path before a
bend revealed their way blocked by two tall Afghans. They
stood, expressionless, each holding a *jezail*, stock on hip,
long barrel pointing to the sky. Bandoliers were slung around
their chests, and swords and daggers protruded from their
wide cummerbunds. Their turbans were loosely wound and
seemed to be sitting only precariously above their bearded
faces. They looked wild but were undoubtedly creatures of
the terrain.

Eventually the taller of the two spoke. With relief, Simon recognised the language as Pushtu, and not the Parsi which a Persian trader would undoubtedly speak. He gestured W. G. to come forward and, in Parsi, loudly delivered the phrase he had rehearsed so well that he could utter it fluently: 'Give the blessings of Allah to this man and explain that, alas, I cannot speak the language of the Amir, but would ask his wish and how I can satisfy it.'

W. G. inclined his head and spoke quickly to the Pathan. The two Afghans exchanged glances and remained silent for a moment, their black eyes taking in every detail of the three men, the horses, the donkey and its load. Their muskets remained pointing skywards, however, and Simon mentally calculated the chances of being able to ride the two men down before they could bring their guns to bear. Fifty-fifty, perhaps. Not good odds. Behind him he heard Jenkins cock his rifle, and Simon hoped that the Welshman had the Snider hidden. He didn't want to precipitate shooting. Then the Afghan spoke again, a little more eloquently this time, gesturing towards the pack animal.

W. G. turned to Simon and, again speaking slowly and clearly, translated. 'Master, this man sees that we bring carpets. He says his mullah in the hills here would like to buy. What is your price?'

Simon raised a hand dismissively. 'Say we go to Kabul to keep a promise,' he said, speaking equally slowly and grasping for the Parsi phrases. 'We cannot trade here, in this place.'

The Sikh now spoke quite animatedly, swinging his arm around to take in the barren nature of their surroundings and then indicating Simon, clearly describing the high standing of his employer and the worth of his products. Simon maintained a fixed expression of languid disinterest. Inwardly he began to bless Roberts for providing an interpreter with so rich a tongue and so keen an eye. He also prayed that, for once, Jenkins would remain silent.

The conversation continued for some minutes, with the Sikh now disdaining to translate for Simon and growing increasingly indignant at the delay. Eventually, the Afghan shrugged his shoulders and, gesturing to his companion, climbed a few feet up the slope and allowed the little caravan to resume its progress. Gently digging his heels into his horse's flanks, Simon nodded and moved away, letting the horse find its own speed among the rocks and keeping his gaze to the front. No musket shot sounded and no ball thudded into his unprotected back as the party wound its way through the gorge and down on to the plain below.

'Phew,' said Jenkins, edging alongside. 'You took a risk there, bach sir. Why didn't you just show 'em our guns and ride straight through 'em?'

'Because, 352, I don't think that is the way a Persian carpet seller would behave. He would not want to make enemies because he would wish to return this way – it is, after all, his sales territory. He would not wish to upset the locals. And nor did I.'

Simon let his horse fall back. 'W. G., well done. What did you say?'

The big Sikh swatted a fly off his donkey's rump and his face broke into its wide grin. 'I explain, sir, that you are very important Persian lord indeed and that we had big contract to fulfil in Kabul. Anyway, I told that we would never do trade in that place. The place, sir, called Sang-i-nawishta, which means "place of inscribed stone". I say that Persian gods don't like trade in holy places and please get out of our way plenty quick.'

Simon allowed himself a smile. 'Do you think they really wanted to trade?'

69

'Ah no, lord.' W. G.'s grin disappeared. 'They come from Mullah Mushk-i-Alam. He is holy man who lives in mountains above Kabul and hates the British. He wants *jihad*, or holy war, against you, sir, begging your pardon, sir. The men I think are sent to see if you are really Persian carpet men or *gora-log* spies.'

'Mullah Mushk-i-Alam. Do you know him?'

The Sikh shook his head. 'No, lord. But I know about him. Oh yes. It was his people who killed Lieutenant Cavendish and put bullet through my arm.' His face clouded over. 'Very worrying at first, sir. Thought I would not be able to hold cricket bat again, you know. Of very great concern. Oh yes.'

'I am sorry.'

'No need to be sorry now, lord. Wound is of no consequence, in eventuality. But mullah is very powerful man.' He gestured to the mountains away to their right. 'He is a Ghilzai from back near the border, but he lives in those hills now. He very old and a very cruel man. They say even the Amir is afraid of him, sah . . . lord.'

Jenkins had been listening. He wrinkled his nose with impatience. 'That's all very well, Gracey, but do you think we passed the test back there? Will they come back when we're not lookin' and cut off our cricket balls? Eh?'

The Sikh's grin returned. 'Not exactly easy to say, sir. Difficult to tell with Afghan. We have a saying: trust a Brahmin before a snake, and a snake before a harlot, and a harlot before a Pathan. But we are very much alive, indeed. So far so good, eh?'

Simon looked behind and around them. The valley had opened out and seemed deserted. 'So far so good, indeed. Well played, W.G.'

They rode through pleasant countryside for another hour, skirting a series of villages that told them they were nearing

70

Kabul. Despite the wind, it was a fertile area, and behind stone walls they could see a profusion of fruit growing: mulberries, peaches, plums, apricots, apples, quinces, cherries, pomegranates and even vines. Soon they met the Kabul river, wide and shallow, running over and between hundreds of rocks that caused the water to swirl and foam.

Then the walls of Kabul itself came into view, looking forbiddingly down on to the river. Jenkins edged his horse alongside Simon. 'Where to now?'

'We will go straight to the Residency.' Simon rose in his stirrups. 'It is near a kind of fortress place, called the Bala Hissar, on the south-east side of the city, so we should see it soon. W.G. knows where it is.' He smiled at Jenkins.

Jenkins 352, now sergeant in Her Imperial Majesty's Corps of Guides, was a fine horseman, a magnificent shot and a soldier with the heart of a lion. But he was notorious for not having the slightest sense of direction. To him a compass was a watch that told no time and the sun a most unreliable point of reference, since it wandered about in the sky.

'Stay close,' said Simon.

Jenkins looked sheepish. 'I shall 'ang on to your 'orse's tail, bach,' he muttered.

W. G. led them through a narrow, high gate in the wall and they followed him and the donkey along a maze of streets lined with houses made of mud, interspersed, here and there, with stone-walled gardens in which grew a rainbow variety of flowers and fruits. Kabul was a city of colour and fragrance, despite its grim exterior.

It was clear that their disguises were effective. Indeed, it was the Sikh, with his distinctive turban and formidable build, who attracted most glances as they picked their way through the teeming lanes to the Bala Hissar. This massive citadel, not unlike a Crusader's castle, was set high on a saddle just beneath

71

the Shahr-i-Darwaza heights. The Residency, situated some two hundred yards away from it, was a large, mud-plastered building arranged around a hollow courtyard, with a further open space before it. As Simon painfully dismounted, he noted that the building was overlooked on three sides by the upper storeys of the surrounding houses, some of which overhung the street.

In heavily accented English, Simon announced that he had business concerning carpets with the Resident, and while the others waited, he was ushered without delay into the presence of Major Sir Louis Napoleon Cavagnari, the man who had negotiated the end of the war with the Amir, and who now had the responsibility of building the peace.

Slim and elegant in a dark blue military uniform whose provenance was unknown to Simon, Cavagnari rose and extended his hand. 'You are most welcome, Fonthill. I have been expecting you, of course.'

Simon shook hands and bowed. The face that looked into his bore an expression of faint amusement. The brow was high, like that of a scholar – an impression heightened by the receding hairline – but the mouth, beneath the full beard, was firm and, like the eyes, carried a faint smile. Simon had made it his business, on arriving in India, to discover as much as he could about this man, who had already become something of a legend on the Frontier. Son of an Italian aristocrat and an Irish mother, Cavagnari had been brought up in England and had entered the old East India Company as a military cadet, later being commissioned into the 1st Bengal Fusiliers and fighting throughout the Mutiny. He had switched to the political service in the early 1860s and had spent the last sixteen years on the Frontier, earning a reputation for energy and courage. He had also, however, revealed a ruthless sense of ambition, concealed beneath a smooth air of imperturbability. Now he had become a firm favourite of the Viceroy, Lord Lytton.

'It's good to be here, sir,' said Simon, taking the seat offered. He was aware that he was under close scrutiny.

'Well, I must say,' said Cavagnari eventually, 'you've blacked up well. Look a damned fine Persian to me. Almost inclined to buy a carpet from you.'

Both men laughed. 'They've got a new dye in Gharghara which seems to last wonderfully,' said Simon. 'And Sheram Khan did the rest at Kohat.'

Cavagnari's smile was replaced by a slight frown. 'Sheram Khan. Yes. Good man. I trained him.' He raised an elegant finger to his cheek. 'May I suggest you do not mention his name again. He can stay alive and do good work for us as long as it is not known that he is one of our agents.'

'Of course, sir. I am well aware of the rules of the game.'

The Resident raised an eyebrow. 'Well, yes. I should hope so. You will have to live by them here, of course.' He sighed faintly. 'You have been a regrettably short time in India, have you not?'

A feeling of annoyance began to steal over Simon. He hated condescension. 'Regrettably short, I'm afraid. But I understand that General Roberts was anxious to improve the standard of intelligence-gathering here, and I . . . well . . . had some experience of this in Zululand.'

'Ah, yes. That bit of nonsense with the Kaffirs.' Cavagnari's mouth twitched. 'I think you will find the wily Afghan a rather different kettle of fish from your naked aboriginal. Had time to acquire the language at all?'

'Very little, sir.'

'Know what a *choor* is?'

'Er . . . a thief, isn't it?'

'Well done. What's a *kala admmi*?'

'It's a black man – and I believe it is a great insult to call a Pathan that.'

'It is indeed. Who or what is Bhodisat?'

'The Buddha, or one of his incarnations.'

'And the Kaisar-i-Hind?'

'The Queen Empress of India.' Simon took a deep breath. 'But surely, sir, these are Hindee expressions?'

'Quite so. But they are common terms across the tribes that straddle the Frontier here. Do you have an interpreter?'

'Yes, and a good one.'

'*Shabash*.' Cavagnari crossed his legs and leaned back in his chair. 'Look here, Fonthill, I have no objection to you being here and . . .' he waved his hand languidly, 'learning on the job, so to speak. The point is that I don't believe there is much of a job to do. You see, I feel that matters are well in hand here. We are not an army of occupation. I deliberately kept my escort here down to fifty men to avoid causing provocation. I have the full support of the Amir, whose palace is only a stone's throw away. I negotiated an acceptable peace with him and there is every indication that that peace is going to be kept to the full satisfaction of both our countries.'

Cavagnari's head was now back and he seemed to be addressing the ceiling, as though rehearsing arguments to himself. 'We did not need to crush these people to bring them into the British Empire – even under mandate. No, they realise that we are the most powerful nation on earth and can bring untold benefits to them. We have much to teach them and they know it.'

Simon frowned. Not another lecture on the benefits of empire! He had heard so many since landing in India. But the Resident was now addressing him directly again.

'Of course, in an uncivilised country such as this, there are always risks. For instance, we have contingents of the Afghan army back here from Herat, where they saw no fighting in the war at all, and they are damned cocky. They sneer at the fellows who got a bloody nose from Roberts at the Peiwa Kotal and say that *they* could see off the British quite easily.' He looked rueful for a moment. 'It doesn't help that they haven't been paid for months and they think we have lakhs of rupees to distribute. They're camped out at Sherput, two or three miles north of here.'

For a moment the mask of insouciance had slipped. Aware of it, Cavagnari smiled again. 'But dogs that bark do not bite.' He raised his hands in mock indignation. 'Bobs does *worry* so! He seems to feel that I have no sources of intelligence of my own. I in no way wish to deprecate what you can do, but my ear is very firmly to the ground, I assure you. And I am not exactly alone here. My escort is small but it is made up of Guides, and – as I am sure you will agree – one wouldn't wish to have a better body of men to protect one. But the main point is that I am sure that the Amir, Yakub Khan, will turn out to be a very good ally and that we can keep him to his engagements.'

He stood up. 'Now, I really fear you must excuse me, for there is a dispatch to be written.' He called to a bearer. 'I have arranged lodgings for you not far away. They are expecting a Persian merchant, so maintain your position.' They shook hands. 'Ahmed will take you there. Come back and see me tomorrow afternoon at four. Then we shall discuss how you can be of service.'

The tone was dismissive and conclusive. The audience was over. Simon gave a half-bow and followed the servant, collecting Jenkins and W.G. from the anteroom on his way out.

As Ahmed led them through the steep streets, Simon looked carefully about him. There was no air of sullen resentment on the faces that passed him; no sign of a people on the edge of revolt. Yet it seemed that every third man carried a *jezail* or a more-or-less modern rifle, and the gazes that met his were direct and unswerving. The very walk of the Afghan – an undulating, unhurried, hip-swinging stride – seemed to reflect independence and even arrogance.

Come back and see me tomorrow . . . then we shall discuss how you can be of service . . . Simon fumed at the lofty tone and the memory of the crude test of his Hindee. It was the assumed air of superiority that annoyed him. There was nothing wrong with the Empire; it was the people who administered it from middle to top who were at fault. It was the same with the army: long years of insularity had bred a contempt for natives and all outsiders. It was as though incest had been allowed to creep into a distinguished family. A type of sanguine sickness had resulted, which left the victim brave and bold enough in action, but lacking in perception and openness of mind.

Simon sighed. It was clear, anyway, that Cavagnari expected little 'service' from this newly arrived parvenu. To what extent, though, did that languid air conceal a shrewd player of the game? After all, Cavagnari had been making his way on the Frontier with skill and subtlety for nearly two decades now. He knew the ways of the Pathans better than Simon, and even, probably, Lamb and Roberts. He must surely know if he was sitting on a powder keg.

The house to which they were led was unpretentious and small, yet comfortable enough after their days on the road. They were received with a polite indifference and given mutton rice and delicious mint tea. Simon, with much on his mind, went to his bed roll early, leaving Jenkins and W.G. playing dice in monosyllabic whispers.

Chapter 4

Simon awoke the next morning aware of a background noise. It was a distant, high-pitched rumble but not consistent in level; there were peaks and troughs. Intrigued, he walked to the open window and looked down on to a completely empty street. He squinted up at the sun. It was quite high. He had slept late. Forgetting his nakedness, he leaned out, the better to hear. Frowning, he concentrated and the rumble took a form: it was the noise of a mob shouting. And it came from the direction of the Bala Hissar.

Pulling on his shirt, Simon ran to the room shared by Jenkins and W.G. The Welshman was sitting on his mattress, carefully cleaning his rifle.

'Damn,' said Simon. 'Why didn't you wake me?'

Jenkins was unfazed. 'Thought we could all do with a bit of a lie-in after that journey, bach sir.' He squinted down the barrel of his Snider. 'This hubbub started about half an hour ago, so I've sent old Gracey off to see what's up, like. Didn't want to wake you if they was just lettin' off steam for nothing, see.'

Simon frowned impatiently. 'It sounds as though it's coming from the Residency. We'd better get down there.'

Jenkins rose to his feet and sucked in his moustache. 'Don't you think we ought to wait till W.G. gets back? We might not find 'im in the crowd, and if we do lose 'im, we'd be about as

79

useful in this place as a three-legged Welsh pony.'

Simon shook his head. 'Can't help that. If there's trouble at the Residency we can't stay here. We must help.'

They were interrupted by the sound of sandalled feet climbing the stairs and the Sikh entered the room. He bowed to Simon. 'Sahib...' he began in his strong, deliberate tones.

'Parsi,' hissed Simon.

'No, lord. There is no one in the house. I have checked. We can speak English. Everyone seems to have gone to great fort, the Bala Hissar. There is big crowd there.' He spread his arms wide. 'All very angry about the Amir and begging your pardon, lord, the English.'

'Wait. Tell me as I dress.'

The two followed Simon into his room. The house was eerily quiet. 'Now,' said Simon, pulling on his soft, baggy trousers, 'tell me what you know.'

The Sikh spoke quickly and quietly. 'The crowd is about three hundred, perhaps four hundred, lord, and they all seem to be soldiers of the Amir who have recently returned from Herat. They did not fight His Excellency General Roberts in war, sahib,' W.G. shrugged his shoulders. 'In fact they fought no one. They are like hounds who smelled the wild pig, lord, but were not allowed to chase.'

'What are they demonstrating about?'

'They want wages, lord. They have not been paid for half a year, they say. They think that the Lord Cavagnari has money and they shout that he should pay them.'

'Are they armed?'

'Ah,' the Sikh nodded his head, 'that exactly is point, lord. Many of them went off to their camp at Sherpur to get rifles, sir, so I came back here, pretty damn quick. I think they will attack the building where lives the Lord Cavagnari.'

'Right.' Simon was now fully dressed. 'Get the rifles, 352. If this mob is armed, no one will notice three more men with guns. Leave the horses, though.'

Jenkins opened his eyes in mock alarm. 'What about the carpets? Look you, we could make a sovereign or two sellin' to them fellers dressed in the dirty washin' with the bundles on their 'eads.'

'Don't be flippant. Come on.'

The three men hurried through the deserted streets towards the Balar Hissar. As they approached, the noise grew louder but, thankfully, they heard no shots. It was clear that the mob had now congregated in the small square that faced the Residency. It had also spilled out into the narrow streets surrounding the high-walled building, so that it was difficult for Simon and his companions to push their way through. As they attempted to do so, they attracted some attention, but the crowd's main interest centred on the gates of the Residency, which had now been firmly closed.

Simon realised that it would be impossible to approach the building, let alone enter it, and he looked around him keenly. The mob was clearly militant, in origin as well as attitude. Most of the gesticulating men wore the dun-coloured garments – seemingly half uniform, half mufti – of the Afghan army, with brightly swathed turbans or wide fur *poshteens* on their heads and broad belts at their waists. Through these were tucked daggers, sometimes two or three. Many had bandoliers worn across their shoulders and breasts, but so far there seemed to be no rifles. Simon noticed that the crowd was now being swollen by citizens of Kabul, street vendors and traders who shouted and gesticulated as strongly as the soldiers. Here and there, marked by their comparative inanimation, stood shorter but impressive-looking cavalrymen from the north, wearing leather jerkins and long kid riding boots. They watched impassively from under black sheepskin Turkoman caps, the fringes of which hung over their eyes and framed their cheeks. Simon wrinkled his nose. The mob had its own distinctive smell – not just of sweat, dust and a hundred cooking pots, but of something else: excitement, anger and, yes, a kind of passion.

Behind the bars of the Residency gate Simon could see a unit of Indian Guides watching the mob expressionlessly, their Martini-Henrys at the port, their young English subaltern standing to one side, as still as his troops. For a moment Simon caught his eye, but there was no flicker of recognition. Nor should there have been. To him, Simon's was just another dark, turbaned face in the crowd.

The mob quietened for a moment then let out an angry roar as the slim, erect figure of Cavagnari appeared on the flat roof and moved to the edge of the parapet. For a few seconds the Resident looked down on to the crowded square, taking in quite coolly the distorted faces and raised fists. He wore the elegant blue uniform which Simon remembered from the previous day, but this time it was ablaze with orders and medals and a white topi hid the receding hair.

Then Cavagnari raised his hand for silence. It did not come at once, but as he began speaking in high-pitched, fluent Pushtu, the crowd quietened. Simon strained to gain the sense but failed.

He turned to W.G. 'What is the English lord saying to the people?' he asked in his slow, stilted Parsi.

The Sikh shook his head in concentration. Then, as a howl broke out from the Afghans – a shout of derision and renewed anger – he cupped his hand and whispered loudly in English into Simon's ear, 'The Sahib is promising them two months' rupees, which I think is only one little third of their wages. I think they do not like it much.' He smiled.

Cavagnari turned and spoke to an aide by his side, who hurried away out of view. Then he took off his topi and held it above his head in another plea for silence. Once more he addressed the multitude, this time, it seemed to Simon, raising his voice perhaps a little petulantly. His words evoked an even louder reaction and stones began to fall around him.

'What? What?' hissed Simon.

'His Excellency says he has no more money,' the Sikh whispered into Simon's ear. 'He says that he will send messengers to the Amir to ask for payment for the soldiers. But they do not like this either.'

As they watched, Cavagnari slowly – almost contemptuously – turned his back on the square, replaced his topi and walked out of sight. Bricks and stones followed him. Simon felt a nudge in his ribs and Jenkins nodded silently to the right. There the front wall of the Residency turned at right angles and formed one side of a narrow street which ran away from them. Through a small post-gate halfway along, a trio of cavalrymen Guides emerged and began to move cautiously, carbines at the ready, away from the square, pushing their way through clusters of Afghans. Suddenly, a stone hit one of the Guides. Without hesitation, he raised his weapon and fired, bringing one of the Afghans nearest to him to the ground. The rest hung back under the threat of the carbines and the three Guides backed away up the street and then disappeared into a side turning.

'Gone, I respectfully suggest, lord, to gain help from Amir,' said W.G.

But the incident seemed to be the signal for which the crowd were waiting. From the fringes of the square shots began to ring out and spurts of dust and patches of dried mud sprang from the walls of the Residency. Within seconds, the square was echoing to the sound of gunfire as the soldiers behind the gate levelled their pieces and fired through the wooden bars into the crowd. The Residency was now besieged.

Simon raised his own rifle and fired vaguely in the direction of the building. Taking their cue, the others did likewise. Then, firing as he went, Simon led the trio quickly through the rapidly dispersing crowd to the comparative safety of a doorway at the edge of the square. Here, the noise of the shouts and gunfire was so loud that he could speak freely in English.

'Listen,' he said. 'There is no chance now of us getting into the Residency. But the men there are in real trouble, I fear. Our best hope of helping them is to find a place from where we can safely direct our fire at the mob without being seen – at least for a while.'

Jenkins looked reflective. 'Well, bach sir, we shall be lucky to get away with that, look you. Any fool can see where the firing's coming from.' He gestured around. Distinctive puffs of smoke were now issuing from windows overlooking the Residency.

'No. If we can find a building or room to ourselves and direct our fire from well inside, away from the windows, we shall stand a chance. Anyway, there is no alternative. Come on.'

The three flitted from doorway to doorway until they found entry to a house situated at the side of the square and partly flanking the street up which the Guides had departed. There was no sign of occupancy at street level nor on the first storey. But above that, the first room they entered sheltered a large Afghan soldier who was carefully aiming his *jezail* through the window at the rooftop of the Residency. Without a word, Jenkins drew his dagger, sprang across the room and, in one movement, pulled back the man's head with one hand and slit his throat with the other. The Sikh's eyes widened for a moment.

'Don't 'ang about, Gracey bach,' said Jenkins. ' 'Elp me pull the bugger out the way.'

As they did so, Simon looked into the room next door. It was empty. Not so the only other room on the floor. There, two Afghans crouched at the window, one aiming through it, the other inserting a long ramrod down the barrel of his *jezail* in the act of reloading. This man slowly rose to his feet, and for a brief moment he and Simon regarded each other in silence, the Afghan's black eyes travelling the length of Simon's figure, taking in the gold-edged turban, the fine brocaded waistcoat and the Snider rifle. Puzzled, the Pathan frowned and took a half-step forward, his hand falling to the curved dagger in his waistband.

This was an incongruous place, Simon reflected, for a Persian carpet seller to be. He raised his rifle and, firing from the hip, sent the bullet into the breast of the man before him. At this his companion swung round, threw his empty musket at Simon and leapt upon him. Like most Afghans, he was tall and lithe and the force of his spring sent Simon crashing to the floor, the Pathan on top of him. The fall temporarily winded Simon, but his adversary was not so disadvantaged. In a second his hands were upon Simon's throat. Desperately, Simon drove his knee into the Afghan's groin, but the man's long garment muffled the thrust and his grip tightened, wrists like steel rods resisting all efforts to tear them apart.

A roaring started to sound in Simon's ears, and the Afghan's dark face, inches from his own, was slowly beginning to become indistinct when, suddenly, the grip was relaxed and the weight pressing him down was removed. As his vision swam back, Simon saw the Pathan's heels dangling above him and the man's head forced back unnaturally by W.G.'s forearm under his chin. Almost lovingly, the giant Sikh relaxed his grip for a second and then tightened it again with a jerk. Simon heard a crack and a cry and saw W.G. throw the man to the ground.

'I am sorry to be late, lord,' said the Sikh, bending over Simon and carefully raising his head. 'It does not do to fight these men so. They do not play cricket. They do not fight fair. Is the sahib recovered?'

Simon grabbed the big man's arm and shakily regained his feet. 'My God, W.G.,' he whispered, feeling his throat gingerly, 'I am glad you arrived. Thank you. You saved my life.'

The Sikh's teeth flashed. 'It is absolutely nothing, lord. I am thinking it was a sticky wicket you were playing on there.'

'Quite so. Where's Sergeant Jenkins?'

'He is in the next room, lord.'

'Can we fire into the square from here?'

'Absolutely, sir.'

Next door, Jenkins had installed himself well back from the window, his rifle resting upon an upended table. He was firing coolly and carefully, inserting his single cartridges slowly to avoid overheating the Snider.

He glanced up. 'Got the place to ourselves, 'ave we?'

'We have now. Let me take a look.'

The window commanded the roof of the Residency, part of the interior courtyard and some of the houses facing the square. The attack on the building had only been in progress for ten minutes or so, but already three Guides were sprawled dead on the roof and a further ten lay crumpled behind the gate. The fire from surrounding buildings might not have been accurate, but it was so heavy and close that the defenders stood little chance if they showed themselves. It was also clear that the dried mud of which the Residency was constructed could not withstand a bombardment at such short range. Already the walls were pitted like a colander and the masonry round the windows was breaking, revealing the interior.

'Have we been seen yet, do you think?' Simon asked Jenkins.

The Welshman sniffed so that his moustache rose in an arch under his nose. 'Don't think so, but it's only a matter of time.'

'Right.' Simon gestured. 'Aim your fire at the snipers in the buildings across there, but switch to the square as soon as there is a frontal attack.' He turned to the Sikh. 'You too, W.G. We will take a room each. Back from the windows like Sergeant Jenkins.'

'Very good, lord.'

Simon returned to the room where the two dead Afghans lay. He stood for a moment and looked at them, massaging the place on his neck where the Pathan had gripped him. Both men lay on their backs, their sightless eyes seemingly studying the ceiling. A year ago, he reflected, such a sight would have horrified and disgusted him. In fact, a year ago he could not have killed. But Zululand and Afghanistan had brought home the reality of soldiering. At the end of the day, it was about this – not sitting a horse correctly, nor wheeling a column of fours quickly into line, nor passing the port the right way in the mess – it was about killing men.

He knelt down and gently closed the eyes of both men and crossed their hands upon their breasts. He then took up his position back from the window and began firing, taking aim with care.

For more than an hour the three men kept up their sniping, staying well back in the shadows and taking steady toll of the

Afghans firing from the houses opposite and those at the back of the square. It seemed that they were undetected, for no answering fire came their way. Nor was any attempt made to enter their stronghold. It also appeared that the Residency was holding out. Somehow, the defenders were returning fire from their windows and from loopholes cut in the mud walls. Twice, as the attackers rushed to the gates, Cavagnari led forays of Guides, bayonets levelled, to dispel them. The second time, the young English subaltern was among the bodies left behind in the square as the sallying party, its job completed, withdrew into the Residency.

Then the door leading on to the roof opened and men appeared carrying furniture and timber which, under fire, they somehow erected as a form of shelter at the leading edge of the roof, opposite the square. It was an obvious attempt to command the square and so repulse the attacks across it. Simon recognised Cavagnari leading the operation. He appeared almost languid as he directed the positioning of the protection, occasionally raising his revolver and firing at the snipers, as though at target practice on Salisbury Plain. For the first time, Simon's heart went out to the man. His courage was superb. But his cause was hopeless.

The protection was quite inadequate, given that much of the fire was coming from above the roof. As Simon watched, one bullet took Cavagnari in the shoulder, spinning him round. Then another hit him in the breast and he collapsed. As he lay, further shots thudded into the blue-clad figure and other near-misses sent up spurts of hard mud at his side, as though the marksmen were trying to trace his body outline in the dust. It took only a few more minutes before the little party on the roof were all killed.

Then a boom rose above the crackle of musketry.

'Artillery,' called Jenkins from the next room. 'Where's this Amir bloke then?'

Looking across the square, Simon saw that a cannon had been hauled up the narrow street immediately facing the Residency gates and that its first shot had crumpled the wall at the side of the gate. As he watched, a second crashed through the main building and immediately a tongue of flame came from the interior, taking hold on a wooden window frame and licking quickly along the Residency's façade. Whoever was directing the fire knew his business, for a third shot brought the wooden gates crashing to the ground.

Simon's thoughts raced. Until Cavagnari's death there had somehow seemed hope for everyone in the Residency – and, indeed, for Simon and his companions. The defenders were well armed and, despite recent happenings in Zululand, the British and Indian armies *always* won in the end. The prestige of these soldiers resounded throughout the Empire. At least the Zulus at Isandlwana were disciplined, well-trained warriors. Here, however, the attackers were a rabble, perhaps as many as three or four hundred of them, but a rabble for all that. The Guides could not, *must not*, be overrun by these people. And yet . . . His heart in his mouth, Simon ran into the little corridor behind him. He caught Jenkins's eye. The Welshman did not look frightened – fear seemed to be alien to him – but Simon could see that he was concerned now, all right. There was perspiration on his forehead and his black eyes seemed to be gleaming un-naturally. The thought did not help Simon. 'They will try and storm the building now,' he cried. 'Aim at the leaders as they run across the square.'

He regained his position, and as he did so, the first wave of Afghans ran towards the gap where the gates had been. Simon fired at the same time as Jenkins and W.G. so that their shots sounded as one. Immediately three men in the front rank of attackers fell. But Simon and his colleagues were not the only marksmen. The first two rows of assailants seemed to crumple away as the front of the Residency lit up with rifle fire, and the remainder of the attackers ran for the shelter of the buildings surrounding the square. Then the cannon boomed again and a spurt of flame broke through the roof of the besieged building. The fire was gaining hold rapidly.

'Try and pick off the men servicing the gun,' shouted Simon to Jenkins above the tumult.

'Can't get a line on the devils, look you.'

It was true. From where the three were firing, only the barrel of the cannon could be seen. It fired again into what was now becoming a blazing mass. The structure of the Residency still held, but the roof was crackling with flames and tongues of fire licked upwards from every window. The heat was so strong that Simon and his companions were forced back from their windows for a moment.

Jenkins and W.G. joined Simon. In horror they watched as sparks flew high from the roof and timbers fell inwards with a crash.

'Poor devils,' murmured Jenkins. 'No one can have survived in there.'

But he was wrong. What was left of the door at the front of the building crashed open and a little band of Guides ran out – perhaps twenty in number. They were dishevelled, with scorch marks and dust staining their tunics, and several displayed wounds. They all, however, carried rifles or carbines and their discipline and bearing seemed quite unaffected. Led by a *jemadar* of the Guides, they trotted to the centre of the square and formed a loose crescent in two ranks, the front rank kneeling, the second standing, facing the cannon and the surrounding buildings. At a command, the kneeling

Guides fired a volley and coolly began to reload as the second rank fired.

For a moment there was a lull between the volleys and Simon saw a tall Afghan run into the centre of the square with arm upheld. He shouted something to the *jemadar* and then held both hands low, as though in supplication.

'What's he saying, W.G.?' yelled Simon.

'The Pathan is saying that Afghan people have no quarrel with fellow Musselmen, lord. He says that if they will surrender, no harm will come to them.'

'And?'

'And the honourable *jemadar*, sir, has told him that his mother was a camel and the Guides do not do business with camel shit.'

As the three watched, the Pathan made a derisive gesture with his hand and walked back with dignity to the edge of the square. The Guides punctiliously withheld their fire until he had reached the protection of the buildings. Then they recommenced their volleys.

Simon put his hand to his mouth and found that tears were coursing down his cheeks. 'Magnificent,' he murmured. 'Bloody stupid, but magnificent.' He cleared his throat. 'Back them up. Quick. Rapid fire.'

The others ran back to their windows and they all fired as quickly as their single-shot Sniders would allow. How effective they were they would never know, but it was clear that the little band in the square, enfiladed from the flanks, could not last long, despite the obvious inaccuracy of the Afghan fire. Eventually – it seemed an age but was probably only about three minutes – the *jemadar* looked round at his men, of whom some two thirds were now lying in the dust. He gave an order and the remainder fixed their bayonets. Another shout and the Guides charged across the square, bayonets levelled, straight at the crowd of Afghans who bunched in front of the cannon.

To Simon it seemed as though the mob opened up and then simply swallowed them. He was reminded of fish food being tossed into a crowded pool: there was a swirl of bodies, a flash of swords and then – nothing.

Simon pulled a rag from his pocket and wiped both perspiration and tears from his eyes. 'So much for the Amir keeping to his engagements,' he said softly. Then the first bullets began to thud into the wall near his window.

'We've been spotted,' shouted Jenkins. 'An' there's a bunch of them comin' across the square to get us.'

Simon ran into the corridor. 'Jenkins. Drag out chairs and beds and whatever and block the staircase. It might give us a minute or two. W.G.'

'Lord?'

'See if you can find a way up on to the roof.'

Thrusting a cartridge into his rifle, Simon ran down the narrow stairway, doubling round on the first landing and then straight down to the half-open door. It was rickety but the key remained in the lock on the inside. As he reached it, so too did the first of the Afghans who had run across the square. To Simon, the man seemed huge, filling the frame of the doorway, all black eyes, white teeth and curved sword. But the narrow entrance prevented him from swinging the blade and Simon fired again from the hip. The explosion sounded like a cannon shot in the narrow corridor, but somehow, thanks to Simon's unsteadiness after running down two flights of stairs, the bullet missed. The flash, however, was enough to make the Afghan flinch and pull back momentarily. Simon thrust the Snider like a spear into the man's face and he fell backwards, into the path of his followers. This gave Simon just enough time to slam the flimsy door shut, turn the key and run back up the stairs.

On the top floor, Jenkins had already wedged beds, mattresses and chairs across the head of the stairs, leaving a small space for Simon to climb through before the barricade was completed.

'Where's W.G.?' demanded Simon.

'Disappeared to long bloody leg or somewhere,' said the Welshman. 'Honestly, he's a lovely boyo but I think he's a bit mad. Rushed down the corridor saying it was time to change the bowlin' or somethin'.' He shook his head sadly.

From below came the splintering of wood. Simon's eyes widened. Oh God! Was this the end? How could they possibly get out of this? He gulped and shook his head to overcome the shaft of fear that ran through him. He *must* concentrate and give leadership. 'It won't take them long to get up here,' he shouted. 'Quick. Help me drag these natives out.'

With Jenkins's help, he pulled the dead Pathans into the corridor, and clumsily propped them behind an upturned chest, their *jezails* at their shoulders, seemingly ready to fire down the corridor.

Jenkins nodded approvingly. 'There's a lovely idea, bach sir. That might give us another 'alf a minute, just time to get on the roof. Or somewhere,' he added plaintively, looking along the little corridor.

Indeed, there seemed nowhere to go. There was no skylight, no other stairway or ladder and no aperture in the whitewashed ceiling. The three rooms all faced on to the narrow street running into the square and a crowd could be heard milling below. Of W.G. Grace, there was no sign.

With a crash the door below was pushed in and Simon and Jenkins heard the sound of many feet rushing up the stairs. The two men rushed to the barricade and levelled their rifles.

Jenkins's bullet took the first Afghan to round the bend immaculately between the eyes as the man squinted up the stairs. He fell back on those behind and Simon's shot shattered the shoulder of the second man on the narrow stairway. It was enough to gain respite as the attackers retreated for a moment behind the turn of the stairs.

'Now what?' asked Jenkins. 'Can't stay 'ere all day, look you.'

The answer came from behind them. In a shower of plaster, whitewash and mud, the ceiling at the end of the landing crashed in, bringing with it the dishevelled figure of W.G. Grace, dust coating his face, beard and turban. He picked himself up quickly. 'Back to pavilion now, lord,' he said, gesturing to the roof above him. 'Bowling a little too hot down here, I am thinking.'

'W.G., you're brilliant,' shouted Simon. 'How did you get up there?'

'Through window, lord, and out on roof. We can get away across rooftops but I have been seen climbing up. They will come after us.'

At that moment, they heard the scrape of a ladder against the window frame in the middle room. Jenkins ran into the room, fired quickly at the Afghan about to climb over the windowsill and, as he disappeared with a cry, grasped the ladder ends. Bending his short legs, he expanded his chest and twisted the ladder round, despite the weight of the three men already on it. Then, with a flick of his shoulders, he hurled the ladder and the men into the crowd below. A shout arose from the street and bullets smashed into the wall near his head.

Simon ran to the barricade and extricated a chair. He fired off a shot at a turban peering round the stair bend and threw the chair at Jenkins. 'You and W.G. get up on the roof. I'll hold them off here and at the windows until you're away. Then pull me up.'

'No, bach,' shouted Jenkins. 'Let Gracey pull you up. I'll stay. I'm stronger and a better shot. I can get up quicker.'

Simon let off another round down the stairwell and ran to one of the windows. 'No. Do as you're told. Go now. That's an order.'

His appearance at the window evoked a howl of rage and a ragged fusillade from the crowded street below, but no attempt was being made to reposition the ladder. Simon sprang back to the barricade and, from the corner of his eye, saw Jenkins being pulled up from the chair through the hole in the ceiling. The attackers on the stairway were not showing themselves around the bend, but he could hear their hoarse whispers. He looked behind him. Jenkins had disappeared, and from the head of the stairs Simon could not, of course, command the windows in the three rooms. It was impossible to defend all four positions at once. A trickle of perspiration ran into the corner of his mouth. He was quite alone. He felt again that once-familiar lurch of the stomach and drying of the mouth that attended the onset of fear. But why hadn't he felt it before? He closed his eyes and considered for a moment. Too busy. That was why.

'For God's sake, bach sir. Come on.' The voice seemed to come from far away – and from the heavens. Simon blinked and saw the arm and head of Jenkins hanging down from the hole in the ceiling. 'They'll be through the winders in a minnit, look you. Come on.'

Simon turned from the barricade and, as he ran, sensed rather than saw the rush up the stairs. He hopped over the dead Pathans, who were still maintaining their silent vigil, and climbed on to the chair. As he did so, the first of the Afghans crashed through the barricade and turned into the corridor. Immediately, seeing the raised muskets seemingly poised to shoot at him from behind a second line of defence, he threw up his arm to warn his followers and fell back. In doing so, he gave Simon twenty precious seconds to throw up his rifle and grab Jenkins's beseeching hands. The first bullets cracked down the corridor as his legs wriggled through the hole and on to the roof.

'Gawdstrewth, bach sir. What were yer doin'? Day-dreamin'?'

Simon scrambled to his feet and picked up his rifle. 'Something like that. Sorry. Where's W.G.?'

Jenkins gestured. The roof was quite flat, though dotted here and there with crudely plastered chimney pots. At the far end the Sikh stood, calmly holding a plank of wood. Beyond him, the roofs stretched away, providing a bizarre second level of city, uninhabited and crossed with narrow canyons, like fissures in a rock face. Simon and Jenkins ran towards him and he laid the plank across the parapet. It was just long enough to span the gap.

'Oh no! Not me. I can't stand heights.' Jenkins had blanched under his dyed skin. He turned despairingly to Simon. 'I'll just 'ang about 'ere and stop them fellers from following us and meet up with you later.'

'Rubbish. Get over. Just hold my hand and don't look down.'

W.G. had already crossed the chasm, which because of the overhanging nature of the top storeys was only about eight feet wide. He stood on the far edge of the plank and held out his hand to Jenkins. Wide-eyed, the little Welshman began to edge along the plank, his rifle extended towards the Sikh, his other hand clenching that of Simon. Eventually, although the plank bent under their joint weight, they were over.

Jenkins collapsed on to the roof. 'Oh bloody 'ell.' His

round face was drenched in perspiration and his moustache resembled a drowned rodent. He looked up at Simon. 'Sorry, sir. It's all right for you. Nothing frightens you now. But I just can't stand heights, see.'

Simon smiled, a little sadly. 'Jenkins, you'd be surprised how much I do see.' He extended a hand and pulled him up. 'Sorry. But you will have to do it again. We've got a bit more roof-hopping to do yet.'

Jenkins's groan was interrupted by a crack from W.G.'s rifle. 'They are trying to follow us, lord.' He gestured towards the hole in the roof.

'Right. You cover us from here until we are over the next gap. Then we will cover for you. We must kill anyone who shows his head through the hole to stop them from seeing which way we go. But keep away from the edge. We don't want to be followed from the streets below.'

So began the trio's escape across the rooftops of Kabul. It soon became clear that concentrating their fire on to the hole in the roof discouraged pursuit from that route, and the crowd seemed to have stayed in the square, probably now looting what remained of the Residency, for the streets below were empty. Even so, their escape was far from easy. Apart from Jenkins's vertigo, which reduced each crossing to three minutes of cajoling, prodding and blaspheming, the escapers had to take care not to attract attention from below – and also to concentrate on their route back to the stable yard of their lodging. Luckily, the Sikh seemed to know this elevated Kabul as well as the streets below, and although the sun was now setting, its warm westerly light helped their navigation. Simon thanked the emerging stars also for the fact that Kabul's architects had espoused conformity. Most of the buildings in this quarter, at least, seemed to have been built to the same height, and their plank served them well.

After about half an hour, the Sikh gestured cautiously and they slid down the sloping roofs of two outhouses to land in the courtyard of the stables next to their lodging house. It was deserted at this late hour, except for a small boy who stared in amazement and some fear at the three dusty, begrimed figures, their faces blackened by cordite, who climbed down a drainpipe into the stable yard.

The two horses and the donkey were in their stalls, saddles hanging nearby.

'Mount up and go right away, eh?' enquired Jenkins.

'No,' said Simon. 'We must settle our account and take the rest of our belongings. But be quick.'

Within ten minutes they were riding through strangely quiet streets, with W.G. lugubriously astride the donkey. Their host was clearly puzzled at their rapid departure, but happy with the coins he had earned. And, a little later, happier still when he found the fine carpet samples left behind in the strangers' rooms. This time, Simon reasoned, they had to travel light. They must reach Roberts quickly to tell him of the sacking of the Residency and the butchering of the mission – and in time to warn him before the Amir and his forces fell upon the English outpost at Alikhal. The fact that the Amir had not gone to the aid of Cavagnari did not necessarily mean that he was behind the attack. But it was not unlikely, and in any case, he had clearly done nothing to help the defenders. The whole country would now arm itself for war. It was no time to be wandering through it, pretending to sell carpets.

Quietly, then, they picked their way towards the city gate. As they rode, the sky ahead was already a dark blue, pinpricked by the first evening stars. Behind them, however, it was a lurid golden, as the last embers of the Residency hissed and crackled. Simon hoped that there would be enough of the building left standing to offer loot to the mob. This, he reasoned, might prevent any organised pursuit.

Nevertheless, his heart was in his mouth as they reached the huge gateway. As when they had arrived the previous day, there were no guards mounted – there was no army threatening the city, nor levies to be collected at the entrance – and there was sufficient traffic on the thoroughfare to offer some cover to the two Persians and their Sikh attendant. The trio were not challenged, although a hundred pairs of eyes followed them as they rode through the gate.

Once beyond the city limits, the three urged their mounts into a steady canter and headed for the dark mountains ahead of them.

Chapter 5

Alice Griffith nodded at the two policemen on duty outside the Corn Exchange and was thankful to find a cab rank. It was only 4.35 but already nearly dark, and the harsh wind that blew from the Firth of Forth made her grateful for her bonnet and muff.

'Waverley Market, please, as quickly as you can. I must reach there before Mr Gladstone.'

If the cabbie, perched high at the back of the hansom, was impressed, he showed no sign. He raised a chilblained finger to his tam-o'-shanter, flicked his whip at the horse and they were off.

Inside, Alice laid aside her muff and fumbled in her bag for her compact. She did her best to inspect the face that peered back at her from the small mirror. She still retained a little of her South African tan and frowned at the thought. It was not seemly to resemble a milkmaid, and she dabbed a little face powder on to her cheekbones. Damn this wind! It made her face glow like a golden apple.

The cabbie had turned off the main thoroughfare and was picking his way through the drably lit side streets which gave him a short cut to Waverley Market. The alleys were narrow and the soot-blackened walls glistened with recent rain. The ride was jerky, for the cobblestones were strewn with litter: sodden rags, broken red bricks bleeding their fragments into rusty puddles, a shattered cartwheel, old newspapers. Away from Princes Street and its Georgian squares, Edinburgh had no right to call itself the Paris of the North.

Alice held a lace handkerchief to her nose and then pulled out her silver watch and squinted at its face. Good. She was about ten minutes ahead of Gladstone, who, after his marathon ninety-minute address at the Corn Exchange, would still be listening to a vote of thanks before he too set off for the Market. Her mind raced through what she could remember of the economic *tour d'horizon* just presented by the Great Man.*

Once again Alice marvelled at the remarkable performance she had witnessed that afternoon. In front of an audience of five thousand people, Gladstone had spoken for an hour and a half, seemingly without notes, and had hardly hesitated in his destruction of the Tory government's fiscal policy.

The cab entered a wider street, better lit, and Alice scrabbled for her notebook. Gladstone had reeled off a sequence of statistics with a precision that had made Alice once turn round to see if some giant prompt sheet had been hidden at the end of the hall. She held her notes to the window. She had only been able to get down the main figures to mark the thrust of the old man's argument: Disraeli had increased expenditure on the armed forces from . . . she waited until they clopped past a street light . . . £25,903,000 in his first year to £27,286,000 in his third. Another lamp: a deficit on India of £2,183,000 increased to six million. Yes,

---

* Gladstone was not yet the 'Grand Old Man'. Although he was seventy, an ex-prime minister and had been a member of Parliament since he was twenty-two, his great rival Disraeli, the Prime Minister, was his senior by five years.

but what was this sum of £493,000? Why had she recorded that?

Alice sighed and leaned back. She was simply not good enough at straight reportage and she *must* improve her note-taking. Part of the problem was that she was enthralled as much by the man as by what he said. She had found her mind wandering as he spoke, and although she had noted – or tried to note – his key statistics, she had also looked at his boots and wondered why they turned up at the toes, and speculated on why this defender of the poor so loved dukes, and how a politician who had presented more national budgets than any man alive could deliver these bewilderingly new figures without reference to notes.

She was by now well used to the power and eloquence of William Ewart Gladstone – his ability to construct balanced, orotund sentences worthy of Gibbon and deliver them with the passion of Browning. The address that afternoon had been the eighth of his Midlothian campaign and she had listened to and reported on them all. This marathon series of speeches – a similar number were scheduled for the following week – had been undertaken to launch his Liberal candidacy for the Midlothian seat in the general election, which the voters of Britain expected to be called in the spring of 1880. More importantly, the campaign was also marking his move from the parliamentary back benches, to which his resignation of the Liberal leadership in 1874 had consigned him, back on to the world's political stage.

The force, the sweep and the content of this review of world affairs had now begun to attract the attention of the international press. About twenty reporters had gathered to hear Gladstone's first speech, earlier in the week. Today, in the Corn Exchange, sixty correspondents had clustered awkwardly round the press table, seeking room to rest their elbows as they scribbled away. This was why Alice had scurried away before the meeting had closed. She was anxious to ensure her place in the Waverley Market.

The cab sashayed to a halt and Alice put away her notebook and descended in the gloom. If the Corn Exchange, with its air of late-Victorian hard-nosed mercantilism, had exuded middle-class prosperity, the Waverley Market was undoubted working class. Huge and forbidding, it reeked of vegetables. Fragments of sprouts, cabbages and leeks had been ground into the pavement to form a dirty mosaic.

'Sorry, miss.' The large constable, glistening in his cape, held up his arm. 'The place is full.' Teeth flashed under his moustache. 'And no place for a lady, I can tell yer.'

'Full!' Alice hauled out her watch. 'But it's only ten to five. How many are inside?'

'We reckon about twenty thousand. They've come from all over Scotland.' He laughed again. 'There can't be that many voters in Midlothian, that's for sure. Och, the mon's a great attraction.'

Alice showed her press pass, and after the customary show of first disbelief and then amazement that a woman was representing one of the great newspapers, she was ushered inside.

It was a booming barn of a place, its iron arches and vaulted roof reminding her of the great railway stations that newly marked each British provincial city. It was true: the Market was packed, with men standing shoulder to shoulder, separated only by barriers erected – as at football matches – to prevent crowd surges which could lead to some being trampled underfoot. As Alice was led down a narrow aisle she looked above and behind her. The gallery, which swept round three sides of the Market to form a second storey, was packed with women. Something about them made Alice look again. There was hardly a bonnet to be seen, only rows and rows of head shawls, with an occasional bare head, hair swept behind into a tight knot. The men who turned to look at her as she made her way down the aisle were also dressed roughly: dirty scarves tucked into collarless shirts, jackets of the cheapest broadcloth, hard, seamed faces under old caps. At the Corn Exchange, the platform had been graced by one marquess, two earls, at least five peers and one duchess. The audience had glistened with top hats and elaborate bonnets. Here, however, it was very different. Somehow the working class of south-eastern Scotland had left their factories, fields and fishing boats to make a pilgrimage to this vegetable market to hear their champion, 'the people's William', share with them his philosophy of government. It was enough to stir Alice's radical heart, and she lowered her head to hide an unexpected tear as she was shown to the roped-off enclosure, in front of the platform, which housed the press's long table, stretching almost the width of the hall.

Most of the seats at the table were already taken, but Alice determinedly thrust her way to a chair that remained free. She took out her notebook and looked about her again. Unlike the Corn Exchange, Waverley Market was sparsely decorated: merely a few banners and mottoes at the rear and sides of the hall. Above the speaker's table, however, hung a rather bizarre replica of an earl's coronet, from the points of which flared brilliant jets of gas. Alice was contemplating the reason for such aristocratic bravura in so plebeian a setting when she felt a sharp nudge on her shoulder.

'Excuse me, miss, just make way and let 'im lie doon a wee while an' he wull be a' right. There's nae room else, yer ken.'

The policeman who had spoken was carrying, with a

colleague, the limp form of someone from the audience, who hung, white-faced and perspiring, from their arms.

'Of course. Of course.' Alice stood up and moved aside. 'Can I help?'

'Nae. We'll just lay 'im doon here, wi' the rest.'

Then Alice saw, at the side of the press table, a row of men propped against the wall; some half conscious, others mopping their foreheads and blowing out their cheeks in seeming exhaustion.

'They've been handing them down over the heads of the crowd for the last hour.' The voice came from behind her, from the man sitting next to her on her right.

'Oh, how awful! I suppose it's because it's so hot in here.'

'That and the fact that they're so tightly packed. And half of them look as though they haven't had a square meal for days.'

The speaker was a young man, not much older than Alice, although he possessed the faintly cynical world-weariness of the experienced journalist. His hair was fair and worn long, so that it merged with the full moustache and trimmed beard – grown, thought Alice, almost certainly to make him look older. His frock coat was severe and correct, but his waistcoat was of a lush cream and his tie red and full-knotted. He looked at Alice now with a half-smile, his blue eyes showing a frank interest.

He stood and made a little bow. 'Campbell. John Campbell. Central News.'

'Oh, the news agency.' She extended her hand. 'Alice Griffith. *Morning Post*.'

'Yes, I know.' He shook her hand in a manly, collegiate fashion. Alice liked that.

'How did you know? I don't think we've met before.'

Campbell laughed and showed crooked white teeth behind

the beard. 'Oh, come now, Miss Griffith. There can't be more than three or four ladies working on news coverage in Fleet Street. And few of them have covered a foreign war. I heard you were here and I am pleased to meet you. I read your reports from Zululand with pleasure and admiration.'

To her annoyance, Alice felt herself blushing. Compliments about her appearance and femininity she could always take without embarrassment. Her sexuality was strong and she was not averse to flirting – with the right man. But tributes to her work from fellow professionals were rare. As a woman in a male-dominated profession, she was more used to being met with distrust and disapproval from colleagues she encountered on assignment.

'You are very kind,' she said, a little coldly. 'Were you at the Corn Exchange?'

'No. I am here to do a full verbatim report. As you know, the Great Man doesn't give out texts – he doesn't even seem to use notes – so papers such as yours use people like me to do their bread-and-butter stuff. The old varmint speaks for so long that one man can't cover two speeches in one day and get it on the telegraph in time.' He suddenly frowned. 'You're not doing full verbatim, are you?'

Alice laughed. 'Good gracious, no. I can't do a word of shorthand – although,' she added hurriedly, 'I do admire people who do. No. I am here to do what I think is called "a colour piece".'

'Really?' Campbell regarded her again with that air of direct interest which Alice found faintly disturbing. The blue gaze seemed to take in every feature of her face and body without leaving her eyes. 'What does that mean?'

Alice laughed a little too loudly. 'Oh, it's the latest idea of our editor. He wants me to report, analyse the main thrust of the speeches and give background colour too. Rather as a correspondent would from abroad – particularly from a campaign, say.'

'Hmmn.' Campbell tilted his head to one side slightly, while holding her eyes. 'I don't seem to remember reading any of those in the *Morning Post*.'

Alice felt herself flushing again. 'No. As a matter of fact, my stuff seems to be appearing in the leaders, if it appears at all. The colour and the analysis is kept, but the newspaper's editorial policy is overlaid, so that opinions are inserted which, frankly, I don't completely share.' She felt she had gone too far. Why was she revealing to this young stranger feelings of which she was only just becoming aware?

He nodded his head. 'Ah, I see. So you are not exactly sympathetic with the strong Tory views of the *Post*?' His half-smile had returned.

Alice paused for a moment. 'Mr Campbell, I have always felt that one's political views should remain one's personal property, until, that is, one is prepared to share them.' She smiled sweetly, rather pleased that she had regained her composure. 'Don't you agree?'

'No, not entirely. But it is of no consequence. For my own part . . .'

But his words were drowned by a great cheer which rose from the hall as side curtains on the platform were pulled apart and the speaker's party filed on to the stage. The cheering reached a climax as Mr Gladstone appeared, nodding gravely in thanks to the audience as he strode to his chair. Alice's eye took in again the familiar figure: the wisps of hair and the side whiskers, contrasting strangely in their whiteness with the black eyebrows; the long stern face, with deep seams running from the nostrils to the jaw; the upstanding white collar cutting into the flesh of the neck; the severe black tie, inelegantly knotted; the rough tweedy jacket, waistcoat and trousers; and those dreadful boots. The figure of Liberal Britain; the awkward, long-winded, cussedly moral and very rich opponent of expansionist empire.

Appropriately before such an audience, it was a local blacksmith, William Fairbairn, who proposed that the Earl of Rosebery should take the chair, and this was met with acclaim. His Lordship wasted no time in introducing the star speaker, and then the old man was on his feet and on his way again.

There was no doubt, Alice felt, that even Gladstone, accustomed as he was in this campaign to addressing large audiences of the faithful, was impressed by the size of the gathering in the Market. His great beaked nose turned as, in silence, he surveyed the ranks before and above him. 'This great ocean of human life', he called it. And Alice hastened to scribble down the phrase, determined now to capture the orator's bons mots as well as those endless damned statistics.

This time, however, Gladstone eschewed economics, matching both the content and the language of his address to the sentimental, rough-hewn nature of the audience before him. His theme was the rights of overseas people to govern themselves and his form was an attack on Disraeli's policies of intervention in the affairs of the 'struggling provinces and principalities of the East'.

As Alice scribbled to keep up, her cheeks flushed as the opinions that had been taking shape in her mind for the last eighteen months were put into words by the old man. She looked sideways at Campbell, who was effortlessly capturing the address in his strange cryptography, having time even to sideline the most newsworthy points. Alice sighed and gave up her attempt to record, sitting back to listen. Looking into

Gladstone's black eyes only a few feet away, it seemed that he was addressing her alone.

'I think of the events which have deluged many a hill and many a plain with blood,' he said to her, 'and think with shame of the part which your country has had in those grievous operations. In South Africa – that a nation whom we term savages have, in the defence of their own land, offered their naked bodies to the terribly improved artillery and armies of modern European science and been mown down by hundreds and thousands and who have committed no offence but that of having the duties of patriotism.'

Alice closed her eyes to prevent tears. She heard again the boom of the guns at Ulundi and saw the corner of the British square open to release the cavalry. She recalled the heat of Zululand and the whoops of the Lancers as they lowered their lances and charged after the defeated Zulus.

'Turning to Afghanistan, I fear that there has been a sadder night than there has been in the land of the Zulus.' Gladstone was unrelenting. 'Many of the facts belonging to that war have not been brought under the general notice of the British public. I think that is a great calamity.

'You have seen that, from time to time, attacks have been made upon British forces and that in consequences of these, villages have been burned. Have you ever thought of the meaning of those words?' For the first time for weeks, Alice thought of Simon. Was he in those hills? Was he burning villages?

'These hill tribes have committed no real offence against us. If they have resisted, would you never have done the same? Their villages were burned. The meaning of these words is that women and children were driven forth to perish in the snows of winter. Does that not appeal to your hearts and make a special claim on your instincts? To think that the name of England for no political necessity except for a war, as frivolous as ever was waged in the history of man, should be associated with consequences such as these!'

Alice realised that tears were streaming down her cheeks, but she forbore to draw attention to herself by fumbling for her handkerchief. Gladstone thundered on, declaiming – to roars of approval – that the sanctity of life in the hill villages of Afghanistan, among the winter snows, was as inviolable in the eyes of Almighty God as that of the audience themselves.

Alice became suddenly conscious of a pressure on her thigh. Under the table, a large white handkerchief was being offered to her. Campbell, however, did not look at her. His head down in concentration, he continued with his right hand to record the Liberal leader's every word.

'Thank you,' Alice mouthed, and took the handkerchief surreptitiously, blowing her nose gently to cover the wiping of her tears. She picked up her pencil again and returned, chastened, to her note-taking.

At last Gladstone finished, to the inevitable standing ovation. Campbell threw down his pen and drew out his watch. 'Not too bad,' he said. 'Only forty-five minutes – probably no more than two columns. Mind you, I'm told he reeled off twenty columns in all last week.'

Alice smiled, glad that no reference was being made to her weakness. 'Yes. He went on for an hour and a quarter this afternoon.' Shyly, she handed back the handkerchief. 'Thank you. I am most grateful.'

For the first time Campbell looked a little embarrassed. 'No. Keep it. You must have a cold. It's the weather up here . . . this wretched wind.'

'Yes.'

A vote of thanks was being proposed by a worthy at the

end of the line on the platform. The pressmen were all scurrying away. Campbell closed his notebook.

'Did you, did you . . . er . . . get it all down?' whispered Alice.

'Yes. But now I must transcribe and get it on the telegraph before the Press Association and Reuters.'

'I do think you are clever to be able to do that.' Alice regretted the words as soon as they were spoken. Although meant sincerely, they sounded gushingly schoolgirlish.

Campbell looked embarrassed again. 'No, no. It's not difficult once you've mastered the business of it.' He regarded her with his half-smile 'It's not really reporting, you know. It's not *writing*. A clerk could do it.'

'Oh no.' Alice was glad to sound professional again. 'It *is* reporting. It certainly wasn't beneath Dickens.'

'True. Perhaps I shall progress to making my fortune by writing novels.' He gathered up his papers. 'You must excuse me, Miss Griffith. I must file my copy.' The vote of thanks was drawing to an end. Campbell leaned towards Alice. 'Where are you staying?'

'Very close. The Waverley.'

'Ah.' A grin split his whiskers. 'So am I. Would you . . . would you care to have supper with me when I have filed my copy? We both must eat.'

Alice felt uncomfortable again for a moment. 'That is very kind. But I must decline. I, too, have to put my story on the telegraph.' She smiled. 'And I have to cover both speeches, you see, and, alas, I don't write quickly. A snatched sandwich is all I can expect.'

He regarded her expressionlessly. 'Quite so. Well, if you need any help . . .' he adjusted quickly, 'I mean with your notes, not your story, of course, I am in room seventeen. Don't hesitate to call on me.' He smiled again to remove any misunderstanding. 'I know how difficult it is to decipher notes. And even if you're not doing a verbatim, you will need references. *Au revoir*.'

He rose and, head bowed in deference to the formalities still being observed on the speaker's platform, shuffled out of the hall. Alice gathered her things more leisurely and followed him. She gave a half-apologetic look behind her to the platform and found Gladstone watching her with – was she imagining it? – a small smile playing on his hard mouth.

Back in her room in the solid Waverley, Alice summoned a maid to light the fire, arranged her copy paper on the table and gazed out of the window, which gave her a much-prized view of Edinburgh Castle. She had just two hours to compose a thousand words – and she hated writing to a tight deadline. Luckily the post office, with its telegraph service (what a boon to newspapers!) was almost next door. Pen in mouth, she mused.

Campbell was much luckier. It was true that once you had mastered shorthand, reporting politicians verbatim was comparatively easy. The main news pages of all of the London dailies tomorrow – *Times, Telegraph, Morning Post, Daily News, Standard, Morning Advertiser* – would lead with: 'Mr Gladstone said . . .' and run without cross-headings or interruption for four or five columns, giving every word the great man had uttered – *and* marking every pause for applause and cries of 'yes, yes' and 'hear, hear'.

Alice sighed. Her problem lay not only in meeting her deadline. She was slow to get her first words on paper, but once she had her introduction and basic theme, she found her copy flowed. No, Campbell had been shrewd enough to outline her main difficulty: how, in writing an analytical piece, could she express her approval of Gladstone's opinions without obviously clashing with the pro-Tory policy of the *Morning Post*? In comparison, reporting from Zululand had been easy. There, she had gathered facts and they were sacred. Although some of her more direct criticism of Lord Chelmsford and his staff had been softened back in London, the fact that Isandlwana had been a tragic disaster was self-evident, and she had been allowed to show why. But it was one thing to criticise the direction of an obviously unsuccessful British army in the field and quite another to attack government policies which her employers espoused. She sucked hard on the pen and began to write.

After ten minutes she had covered three pages, writing uncharacteristically clearly so that the telegraph clerk would have no trouble transmitting the copy. She sat back and read her introduction with approval: 'Twenty-five thousand people – perhaps ten times the number eligible to vote in the Midlothian constituency – heard Mr Gladstone in Edinburgh yesterday continue his wide-ranging and devastating' (she frowned and then, reluctantly, deleted those last two words) 'attack on the record of Lord Beaconsfield's government. His targets, in two major speeches in the Corn Exchange and Waverley Market, were, respectively, the Government's fiscal and foreign policies, and there was no doubt that Mr Gladstone's audiences in both places felt that his shafts had hit their targets with unerring' (she crossed that out and substituted 'devastating') 'accuracy.'

Alice nodded slowly. Good. Facts, not opinion. No one could argue with that. She read on and then threw down her pen in disgust. Damn! Once again she had forgotten to write in cablese. The telegraph service had been nationalised and brought under the Post Office only nine years before, and the resultant lower charges had virtually revolutionised news-gathering costs and enabled daily newspapers to carry large reports the day after the news had broken. But thousand-word dispatches were still expensive to transmit and all reporters were trained to condense their copy into simple, money-saving codes. This was a discipline which Alice had learned the hard way but still often overlooked when deadline pressure was heavy. It would never do to look unprofessional, and she pulled fresh copy paper to her and began writing again, as quickly as clarity allowed:

25,000 people – prps ten times t number eligible to vote in t Midlothian constitcy – heard M Gladstone in Ednbrgh ysty continue hs wide-ranging attack on t rcrd o Ld Becnsfld's govt. His targets, in two major spchs in t Corn Exchange and Waverley Market, wre, respectively, t Govt's fiscal and foreign policies, and th ws no doubt tt Mr Gldstne's audiences in bth places felt tt his shafts hd hit thr targets wi devastatg accuracy.

Good. That must have saved at least tuppence. Brow furrowed, she continued to write, her pen now fairly racing over the paper. After an hour, she had covered about fifteen pages, and she allowed herself time quickly to read through what she had written. It wasn't perfect, but she felt that she had captured the passion of the man without letting her approval of the arguments intrude.

Alice looked out of her window at the yellow gaslights in the streets below. Why did Gladstone wear rough tweed trousers and waistcoat with a worsted tailcoat? Was he dressing down for his audience? Better the smooth cream of Campbell's double-breasted vest. Such white teeth, too, and so charming a smile . . . Alice shook her head in annoyance, rang for tea and settled down again.

She was finished well within the hour. The teapot was still warm as she gathered the pages together, put on her coat and hat and half walked, half ran through the door, down the corridor and stairs into the cold air outside. The telegraph office was only three minutes' walk away and she was fifteen minutes within her deadline as she handed her copy to the clerk, paid for the transmission and pocketed her receipt.

'Well done.' Campbell rose from the bench beside the door. 'I thought you said you didn't write quickly. I have only just filed my own copy.'

'Oh, I er . . .' Alice felt uncharacteristically flustered. She tucked a strand of hair back beneath her hat. 'Thank you. You have been very quick yourself. Goodness,' her brows rose as she made the calculation, 'you must have written at least twice as much as me.'

The white smile came again, reminding Alice disconcertingly of Simon Fonthill. 'Nothing to it. As I told you, it's formulaic, really.' He gestured to the door with his curly-brimmed bowler. 'Look, we have both finished work now. Do let's have supper together. I am hungry and I am sure you are too.'

Alice regarded him quizzically. He had been sitting with his back to the wall of the telegraph office as she had entered and spoken to the clerk. If he had only just filed his own story he would still have been at the desk. Obviously, he had been waiting for her. She felt a slight anticipatory tingle. 'Oh, very well,' she said. 'But I insist on paying my share.'

'We can argue about that later.' He ushered her through the door. The wind hit them sharply, forcing them to turn up coat collars and bow their heads. He gripped her arm and turned his body to shelter her. 'Would you mind if we did not eat at the hotel? There are so many of the agency fellows there and, anyway, the food's not very good. I know of a splendid restaurant literally round the corner where we can get oysters. What do you say?'

His face was now frowning in supplication and the wind had turned his cheeks a bright red. Alice thought how young he looked. She decided to succumb to the tingle. 'Why not?'

The restaurant was quite full, but a table was found for them and, without consulting her, Campbell ordered a bottle of '75 Chablis while they studied the menu. For all his youthfulness, Alice noted, he carried an easy air of authority and worldliness. This was no louche boy from the provinces.

They gave their orders and Alice found herself chatting to the young man with no awkwardness. He had a habit, she noted, of asking questions directly. There was no gentle skirmishing, no deployment of small talk. He wanted to know how she had got her job, so he asked her. It was not what she was accustomed to, this directness. But she made no objection. After all, it was what they both did for a living, asking questions.

She related how she had begun by writing to the letters page of the *Morning Post*, and then contributing articles on matters of the day, usually foreign policy. Gradually she had become a regular contributor, signing her covering letters to the editor 'A. Griffith', although, of course, she had received no by-line in the newspaper. Occasionally she was allowed to sign her articles 'From a Special Correspondent'.

Campbell's eyebrows rose. 'So they never knew you were a woman?'

'No.' Alice grinned.

'When did they find out?'

'When I applied for a job as a foreign correspondent to cover the North West Frontier of India and the Afghan War.'

'Good lord.' Campbell slowly put down his glass. 'I must

117

say, you have got nerve . . . but that's always been obvious.'

Alice decided to take this as a compliment. 'Thank you.'

'But you didn't get sent to the Frontier. You ended up in Zululand.'

'Quite. Cornford, the editor, liked my articles and had agreed to see me, not knowing, of course, that I was a woman.' Alice pushed away a stray lock of hair, and a gleam of satisfaction came into her eye at the memory. 'I had him at a disadvantage, of course, because he had written praising my pieces and he was curious to meet me – although there was never any offer of a position on the paper.'

'So?'

'So, eventually, after a lot of arguing, I did a deal with him.'

Campbell's eyebrows rose again. 'A deal? A deal? One doesn't do a deal with editors.'

'Oh yes one does – if one is determined. He would not hear of me going to an "active" area like the Frontier, but I managed to persuade him that, through my links with the 24th Regiment – my father was a brigadier and both battalions had been posted to South Africa – I could be useful to him there.'

Alice smiled at the memory. 'There seemed little threat of war there so Mr Cornford eventually agreed to my offer to pay my own way if he would refund the expenditure if I made the grade.'

'And then came the war?'

Alice nodded. 'Yes, rather out of the blue. More to the point, then came Isandlwana. I reported on that . . .' she paused, and then smiled, half apologetically, 'adequately. The cost of my fare was refunded and I was taken on the staff and stayed to cover the rest of the war.'

Campbell nodded. 'Yes, and you did well. I remember. Very descriptive stuff. I admired it.'

'Thank you.'

For a moment, their knuckles touched as they gripped the stems of their wine glasses. Campbell's fingers relaxed, extended, and lay along the back of Alice's hand. She let her hand remain there for a second or two before raising the glass to her lips. The young man held her gaze and smiled, as if in recognition of the gesture. Alice felt again that inward surge of excitement. She sat back and cleared her throat.

'So there you are. My life story; or, at least, my professional life story.'

Campbell still held her gaze, his head now slightly on one side, quizzically. Then, slowly, he raised his glass. 'I toast you. Beautiful but talented. Compassionate but determined.'

Alice snorted. 'Nonsense. Anyway, I'm not the first woman to do this sort of thing. Frances Whitfield covered the siege of Paris for *The Times* – you know that she floated her dispatches out by balloon? How marvellous!'

Campbell leaned back in his chair. 'That may be so, but it's still rough trade, this. Do you remember what John Stuart Mill said about it?'

'No.'

The young man frowned in recall. 'Now, let me get this right. Mill wrote: "More affectation and hypocrisy are necessary for the trade of literature and especially the newspapers than for brothel keepers." '

'Hmnn.' Alice drained her glass and then accepted the remainder of the Chablis. Campbell, again without conferring, ordered another bottle. 'Well,' she said, 'he may have been right fifty years ago, or whenever he said it, but things have improved considerably since then. Do you know,' she leaned across the table in emphasis, 'I do believe that we journalists are right in the middle of a sort of revolution in literacy. I read somewhere last week that, in Birmingham alone, about ten thousand people a day are visiting these new reading rooms to take in the dailies.'

The blue eyes crinkled. 'I'm sorry,' said Campbell, 'but I can't somehow see myself as a warrior in an educational crusade.'

Alice bridled. 'Very well. Laugh at me if you must, but I am sure I will be proved right.' She paused for a moment, frowning at the young, half-smiling face before her. It was a damned attractive face, for all its self-possessed, gentle air of superiority. She knew well enough now that all men when close exuded some distinctive odour, faint or strong; often tobacco, tooth powder, perhaps, or – most provocatively of all – an intangible, earthy smell that came from she knew not where. What would John Campbell smell and taste of?

Her reverie was interrupted by Campbell throwing up his hands in mock surrender. 'All right, all right. I give in. We are in a noble profession and I personally will welcome all women to it. Why,' he reached across to the new bottle and filled their glasses, 'if Miss George Eliot, or whatever her real name is, wishes to report on Mr Gladstone's campaign up here, I shall go so far as to sharpen her pencil with my own penknife.'

And so they went on, talking animatedly in great good humour, jousting happily, with a growing sexual attraction adding piquancy to the encounter. Campbell seemed reluctant to talk about himself, although Alice was able to elicit that he was a Highland Scot, his lack of accent explained by an education in the south of England. He said little at all, in fact, continuing instead to ply Alice with questions, as if he was determined to strip her of her mystery. Nevertheless, when at last the bill arrived, Alice realised that she had not enjoyed an evening so much since she had left South Africa, months before.

'Please tell me the total, so that I may share it,' she said, extracting her purse from her bag. 'I insist. We are colleagues.'

Campbell took a breath as though to argue, then smiled. 'We are indeed. Very well.' He examined the bill. 'With the tip, I believe that a sovereign and a half will cover it all.'

Alice fumbled in her purse and became aware for the first time that they were attracting the attention of other diners. But Campbell seemed unfazed, and meticulously counted out change for the coins she gave him. Outside the restaurant he took her arm again and she willingly allowed herself to be steered back to the hotel.

'Are you covering the whole campaign?' he asked, as they climbed the hotel steps.

'Yes. And you also?'

He stopped her at the doors. 'No, I'm afraid not.'

'Oh.' Surprised, she allowed her disappointment momentarily to show in her face. 'Do you go back to London? I am sorry.'

'Yes, tomorrow.' He drew her a little into the shelter of the impressive doorway, without, however, pushing through the large doors that led into the hotel – as though he wanted to share an intimacy with her which was not for others. 'This was my last assignment for Central News. I am joining the *Standard*, and I am to leave as soon as possible for India to report the Afghan business. You see,' and the attractive smile came back, 'I am becoming a true reporter at last.'

A mixture of emotions surged into Alice's mind. The first was of acute disappointment – a disappointment coloured by a kind of sexual frustration that momentarily embarrassed her. Then came a strong feeling of jealousy. She swallowed. 'I am so glad for you. My warmest congratulations. You are lucky. It is what I would most heartily wish to do myself.'

'I know,' he said. He did not smile, but held her arm for a moment before pushing open the doors.

They climbed the stairs in silence to the door to Alice's room. She inserted the key in the lock and turned to him. 'Goodbye. I shall think of you in Afghanistan.'

He put a hand on each of her shoulders, pulled her to him and kissed her hard on the mouth. 'Goodbye, Alice Griffith. I shall think of you too.' Then he spun on his heel and was gone. Alice stood looking after him for a moment with an overwhelming feeling of sadness and disappointment. Then she shrugged, turned and entered her room.

Early the next morning she was woken by a maid, who brought with her a telegram in its small brown envelope. 'It arrived about two a.m., miss. But the hall porter thought it could wait until morning.'

'Thank you.' Alice propped herself on her elbow and opened the envelope. It was from Cornford, her editor, and it ran:

CONGRATS ON BEST CVERAGE YET OF GLDSTNE STOP BELIEVE YOU WASTED ON POLITCAL REPORTG STOP AFGHAN WAR BROKEN OUT AGN STOP TAKE FIRST TRN LONDON AND PREPARE LEAVE FOR BOMBAY SOONEST END

Chapter 6

'Tell me, W.G., about the tribes who live in these hills.'

Simon's question was pitched in a low voice, for although the three men were huddled together around a small fire, they had taken care to find a narrow defile, protected on three sides by walls of rock, in which to kindle it and so reduce the chance of its glare being seen in the darkness. They felt vulnerable and apprehensive.

Since their flight from Kabul, twenty-four hours before, they had ridden hard. Even so, their progress had been slow, for they had forsaken the well-travelled track across the plain towards the border in the south, and headed due east, into the mountains, before turning south again. They had climbed steadily, if erratically, leaving behind them deodar, birch and pine until they were now among scree and rocks, making their way towards the Shutargardan with the aid of Simon's compass and the Sikh's knowledge of the country. They were wary and breathless, for even W.G. was unaccustomed to the altitude, and they had rested hardly at all during their night's flight from Kabul. Although it was hot during the day, with the sun burning through the thin air from a completely cloudless sky, dusk lowered the temperature alarmingly and reminded them that winter was near. Now they huddled in their cloaks around the low flames.

123

With a long black finger, the Sikh drew a wavy line in the dust at their feet.

'Here, lord, is the frontier with India.' Then he traced a line moving upwards and slightly to the left. 'This is Kuram valley, through which you and bach sergeant rode to meet lord general at Kuram.'

'That's where we was nearly jumped by them black fellers,' said Jenkins, his moustache resting on the knuckles of his right hand reflectively.

'Ah.' The Sikh nodded. 'They would be Afridis, probably Jowaki Afridis. They live in hills either side of pass. In valley itself live the Turis, who are Shiah Muslims and are respectful to her Grace, Queen Empress, upon whom sun shines and rose petals fall. But in the hills are the Afridis, who are fellows not to be trusted. Not to be trusted at all, I am telling you.'

'Go on,' said Simon.

The Sikh gestured to the west of his Kuram valley line. 'Here, lord, are the Mangals and Wazirs, tribes of the Khost district, who are very warlike and aggressive. Not friendly at all, sir. But here,' he drew a smudge in the dust across his valley line, 'here is where real trouble starts.'

He looked knowingly at both his companions in turn. 'Real trouble, sir. Real trouble. Am I making myself one hundred per cent absolutely jolly clear, sir?'

'Oh yes, W.G.' Simon nodded solemnly. 'Absolutely. And don't call me sir.'

'Sorry, lord.' He pushed his finger along the smudge. 'This is Shutargardan Pass – very high, lord, very high – and here,' he gestured to the north, 'everywhere in the hills are Ghilzais, one of great tribal groups in Afghanistan. Very fierce people, lord, who do not like *gora-logs*, begging your pardon, lord.'

'Ah, yes.' Simon nodded slowly. 'The two tribesmen we

met at Sang-i-nawishta who fancied our carpets, they were Ghilzais, weren't they?'

'Correct, lord.'

'And they are led by this mullah, yes?'

The Sikh inclined his head. 'Indeed, lord. The Mullah Mushk-i-Alam. He is an old man now. No longer does he lead his team on to field, lord, but directs operations now from pavilion, so to speak. But he is still great captain and is always trying to stir *jihad* or holy war against British. There is no doubt, lord, that he will now be trying to unite all Afghans to attack Lord General Roberts if he invades now.'

Jenkins lifted his head. 'But isn't this Amir bloke in charge around here?'

'Not really, Sergeant bach. Of course, Amir in Kabul is nominally captain of team but he is powerful only really on plain. The outfielders in the hills are very independent, and anyway, they do not follow Amir closely now because he lost to Roberts Sahib at Peiwa Kotal. Mullah Mushk-i-Alam is religious leader and will gather faithful around him.'

The three men fell silent. The fire spluttered a little and sent their shadows high for a moment on the rock walls surrounding them.

'Do you know where the mullah's village is?' asked Simon.

'No, lord, but he is thought to live in the hills to the south-east of Kabul.'

''Alf a minute, Gracey.' Jenkins raised an anxious head and turned to Simon. 'You know that I don't know my arse from my 'elmet, speakin' geographically, but, look you, isn't that where we are now?'

Simon nodded. 'More or less.' He looked at the Sikh. 'Do you think we could find the mullah's camp in these hills?'

' 'Ang on a bit.' Jenkins looked quite indignant. 'Why do we want to find his camp, anyhow? Isn't the idea to get to the

General and tell 'im about the massacre at Kabooli as soon as possible, like?'

'Yes, but I think we would be welcomed all the more warmly by the General if we could tell him where the main forces against him are massing and how many Afghans he's likely to have to fight.'

'Well, if you say so.' Jenkins looked around him gloomily. 'But if you ask me, this moolah is more like to find us than we are to sneak up on him, see. Every bloody rock looks the same around 'ere and that's a fact.'

The Sikh turned an impassive face towards Simon. 'The sergeant bach is right, lord. I am not very familiar with the field placings here and I do not know where the mullah is. He is, indeed, more likely to find us than we to find him. His men will know these hills backwards and frontwards, lord.'

Simon pulled his cloak more closely around him and stared into the fire. Eventually he rose to his feet, walked a few paces deep in thought and then turned back to his companions.

'Right,' he said. 'We will make a virtue of necessity. If we can't find the mullah, we will let him find us – or me, at least.'

'Lord?'

'I am tired of skulking about this place like . . . well, like a second-rate carpet salesman. I am sick of being an intelligence agent who has no intelligence to report. And I am getting fed up of running away. From now on, we shall be positive.'

Jenkins's mouth turned down under his moustache. 'I don't like the sound of this at all, bach sir,' he said. 'With just three of us against thousands of them, it sounds like a good time to be a bit negative. Look you, why can't we get down on to the plain again an' just ride 'ard towards this Shittygarden place?'

'For one thing, W.G. can't ride hard at all on his mule,

and for another, we could easily be picked off on the plain. No.' He returned to the fire, sat down and crossed his legs. 'Now, listen, this is the plan.

'We will keep careful watch tonight – and I think it's time to put out this fire now we've eaten. Then, in the morning, I will ride on ahead. I will ride quite openly, on the skyline, so that I can be seen. You will follow me, keeping careful cover, far enough away so as not to be taken with me, but near enough to keep me in your sight.' He thought for a moment. 'I will take the mule, so you will easily be able to keep up with me.'

'Then what?' asked Jenkins, whose eyes had never left Simon's face

Simon shrugged. 'If I am not taken, then nothing has been lost, because I shall keep heading towards the Shutargardan and General Roberts's camp. But if I am ambushed, I shall not resist and it is almost certain that I shall be taken to the mullah, if only,' he smiled, 'to be given a cup of tea.'

'Sorry, sir, but it's daft.' Jenkins shook his head in exasperation. 'They're more likely to shoot you first and then offer you tea later. Or cut your balls off, for a bit of fun, like. And anyway,' he held out a hand in supplication, 'what are we supposed to do while all this is goin' on?'

'I admit that that is the difficult part. But you must not interfere. Is that understood?' He looked at both men in turn. 'You must follow when I am captured and mark where the camp is.' He turned to the Sikh. 'You know how to use a compass?'

W.G. inclined his head.

'Good. Now, once in the encampment, I shall have to play it intuitively. I may be able to maintain my disguise as a Persian merchant—'

'On a mule?' interrupted Jenkins.

127

'I shall say we were attacked and I lost you two and the horses. But,' Simon's face clouded for a moment, 'if I have to confess to being a British officer I shall somehow have to bluff my way through long enough to gauge the mullah's intentions and the strength of his force.'

'And then what?' Jenkins remained unimpressed. The Sikh stayed silent.

'Somehow I must get a signal out to you two and, with your help, escape, and then we will all ride to Roberts to tell him what we know.'

'Just like that?' Jenkins sniffed and shook his head. 'Too many risks is what I think.'

'W.G.?'

The Sikh pulled on his beard for a moment. 'It may well work, lord. Pathans are fierce people. Good fighters. But not disciplined, you understand. Not trained soldiers. They are not often attacked in their homes because they live in remote mountains. So they keep poor guard on their camps. Am I making myself quite clear?'

Simon and Jenkins both nodded.

'Indeed. So if they hold you in camp, it could be possible to, ah, pull you out, so to speak. But lord, with greatest of respect, I do not think you should try to convince them that you are Persian. You do not speak much Pushtu at all and your Parsi is not good enough for a Persian. And there will be someone there who will speak Parsi. You will be revealed, master.'

'Very well.' Simon rose to his feet again. 'I shall be open about who I am and say I've been sent by Roberts in an attempt to persuade them to join him. Who knows, that might even work.'

'But, bach sir . . .'

Simon rounded on Jenkins. 'No more of that, 352. We

were sent here to gather intelligence The fact that the place has exploded round our ears is no excuse for not doing our job. Roberts needs to know what he's up against. Right?'

Jenkins nodded gloomily.

'Right. I will take first watch, W.G. the second and 352 will take over until dawn. Put out the fire. Watchman should be outside the circle. Now good night to you both.'

They were ready to move long before dawn, anxious to be on their way to welcome the first warming rays of sun. Simon mounted the scrawny, recalcitrant mule and rode out, not without difficulty. The others gave him five minutes and then followed, scrambling a little at first to catch up before they glimpsed his turban among the rocks ahead of them.

It was not easy for the two followers to keep Simon in sight intermittently and remain hidden themselves. Their way lay over loose shale and between large boulders, and the fact that they were well mounted helped them not at all. They were quickly reduced to leading their horses as they picked their way through stones and occasional scrub. Fortunately, they were helped by Simon's deliberate efforts to be seen. They could remain below the skyline as he rode up ahead, silhouetted against the blue.

For Simon, it was the most anxious morning of his life. Taking his direction by the sun, he let the mule pick its own way among the rocks, hauling its head over from time to time to keep them roughly on course. At any moment he expected to hear the crack of a rifle or the deeper cough of a *jezail*, and he wondered whether the ball would take him in the back or front. How pathetic to be shot in the back, here in these lonely wastes!

It was almost a relief, then, when he caught a glimpse of sunlight reflected from steel a little way ahead of him. Thank goodness they were not behind him. He kicked the mule and urged it onwards until he sensed rather than saw that he was in their midst, although there was still nothing tangible to be seen. Clearly, they were waiting to check that he was alone before declaring themselves – or killing him. Simon's mouth was as dry as a *wadi*, but he licked his lips and called out as firmly as he could: '*Allah kerim! Allah kerim*!' and lifted his hand, half in salute, half in greeting. He hoped that his cry would have carried to Jenkins and W.G. behind him.

Immediately, about twenty Afghans emerged from the rocks around him, their sudden appearance reminding him of the Zulus' capacity to merge into the terrain. These were big men, slim but tall, dressed in loose-fitting cotton over which had been slung a wild collection of belts and bandoliers holding curved daggers and short swords. Each man carried a *jezail*, and the eyes that stared at him from underneath the high turbans were black and impassive.

All this Simon had time to take in before, from behind him, a musket butt crashed into his head and several hands pulled him from the mule and on to the ground. Dazed, he crouched on hands and knees in the dust for a moment before he was kicked in the stomach and a *jezail* barrel hit him in the face, knocking him half unconscious. He was aware of being beaten again and then of being lifted.

He regained full consciousness, perhaps only a few minutes later, to find himself looking down at rocks and shale as they passed slowly and lurchingly a couple of feet beneath him. Blood from his head dripped on to the ground as he watched, and he was aware of a dull ache in his ribs and an excruciating throb in his head. He realised that he had been thrown over the back of the mule, and that underneath the belly of the animal, his wrists had been lashed to his ankles. Pain and nausea overcame him and he was sick, his vomit joining the blood on the ground to mark the mule's passage. He groaned involuntarily and was rewarded by a crack across the shoulders from a gun barrel.

He tried to lift his head to look around, but the pain was too intense. With his mouth closed he could not breathe, so, he reflected, that blow to the face had probably broken his nose. He shifted his position as best he could and the resultant pain, though bad, was not agonising; the ribs, then, were probably bruised but not broken. Good, that meant he could walk or even run if he had to. But what about Jenkins and W.G.? Had they heard his shout? Were they still following? His head swung to the rhythm of the mule's gait and he drifted into unconsciousness.

He came to as rough hands untied his bonds, lifted him from the mule and threw him on to the ground. Immediately, he was kicked again and jerked to his feet by an Afghan, taller than the rest, who put his face close to Simon's and then, slowly, hawked and spat on to his forehead. Simon steeled himself not to flinch and held the gaze of the Afghan a few inches away. They stood for a moment, face to face, each quite expressionless, until the Pathan drew away, shouted in Pushtu and then seized Simon's hands behind his back and tied them at the wrist. A halter was slipped over his head and jerked roughly, and he was led forward.

The camp that Simon entered had a look of permanence about it. Two hundred or more mud huts were scattered about a small valley that flattened out in the middle into a rough pasture on which scrawny goats grazed. Rock walls on three sides made the place a kind of amphitheatre, although at the far end a very high cleft could be seen. The dwellings were of no sophistication. Unrendered stone poked through the mud of the walls, windows were small and shielded from the wind by scraps of fabric, and smoke curled from a hole in each flat roof. Men, women and children, dressed in anonymous rags, walked between the buildings. Commanding the entrance to the valley was a crude fort, the only two-storey building in the settlement. It, too, was made of mud and stone, but the walls, judging by the entrance, were of considerable thickness and they were holed by rifle slits. Looking behind him, Simon saw that the track up which the mule had carried him was steep and narrow, with room for no more than three or four to walk abreast. Presumably, any attackers would have to approach the village by this route, under the guns of the fort. It was a formidable defensive position.

A jerk of the halter brought his head round again and he was led into the courtyard of the fort, where a gaggle of women and young children immediately circled him and began feeling the texture of his blood-stained coat and shirt, giggling and digging inquisitive fingers into his stomach and ribs, making him inhale and wince. One bedraggled crone drew laughter from the others by grabbing his genitals and squeezing hard.

The pain and the barbarity of it all sent terror surging into Simon's brain. Was he going to be summarily killed? The Zulus had a reputation for cruelty which was, in his experience, quite undeserved. They acted within a code of behaviour which, once understood, was practical and logical. Here, the savagery seemed gratuitous and uncontrolled. Were they going to torture him? Simon ran his tongue over dry lips. This was a childhood horror, and the old doubts about his courage began to invade his mind once again, bringing with them the edges of darkness that he remembered so well.

Damn and to hell with them! He raised a foot and kicked hard at the crone. Immediately, his halter was pulled hard by his guard, so that the rope burned his throat. But a *jezail* was thrust forward to gesture the ragged mob away from him. Simon realised with relief that he had won reprieve of a sort from the black horrors within him. Nevertheless, the relief was accompanied by despair and a growing feeling that his gamble had failed. No one seemed interested in holding even the beginnings of a civilised conversation with him, so giving him a chance of extracting the information he desired.

The pain and the heat from the sun grew worse, and once again he slumped to his knees. Immediately he was hauled to his feet and dragged to an old tree stump in the centre of the compound, with a rock at its foot. He was allowed to sit on the rock but was bound to the tree by body and throat. He lost consciousness again – or perhaps fell into a head-throbbing half-doze, his tongue protruding from between his lips as the rope cut into his throat.

When he awoke, the sun had almost set and long shadows were being thrown across the courtyard. The pain of his head and ribs was now overtaken by a thirst which clove his tongue to the roof of his mouth. Blood from the wound on his head had dried to form a crust across one eye, blurring his vision there. His broken nose forced him to draw air through a mouth that felt ulcerated and swollen. His distress drew a moan that came from a deep well of misery.

From behind him came a movement and an Afghan, shorter than the others, with a round, bearded face and eyes as black as a raven's, appeared and stood looking down at Simon for a moment. Simon tried to speak to plead for water but all that emerged was a faint croak. However, it was enough. Immediately, he felt blessed relief as the coruscating rope around his throat was removed and a pitcher of water brought to his lips. He drank greedily, the liquid coursing down his chin and soaking his shirt and breeches until he had had his fill. He nodded his thanks to his captor and the man disappeared behind him again.

The sun had vanished completely and Simon was beginning to shiver when a door leading from the compound into the fort opened and a retinue of Afghans appeared and approached him. They formed a semicircle around him and then respectfully made way for an old man, who, leaning on a stick, limped across the courtyard and stood looking down on Simon. A command was given and a chair was brought for the man, who lowered himself into it and then made a dismissive gesture, at which the others sat cross-legged in the dust.

With his one-eyed gaze, Simon did his best to observe the man carefully. There was no distinction about his dress, nothing to show seniority. He carried no weapons, only his staff, and the same type of robe worn by the others draped his shoulders, the same carelessly swathed turban sat on his head. But the air of command was very evident and the eyes that regarded Simon from within deep sockets were alive and, it seemed to Simon's aching senses, burning very brightly. A strikingly white long beard contrasted with the darkness of the lined face, and the hand that held the staff was dappled with age spots. Undoubtedly, Simon had found the Mullah Mushk-i-Alam.

For what seemed like minutes, the mullah remained motionless and silent, his eyes fixed on Simon. Simon returned the stare, resolutely holding his head back, although his neck muscles urged him to let it drop forward. Eventually the mullah turned and gestured to an Afghan sitting on his right. Simon felt that there was something familiar about the man's jaunty air.

Then the Pathan smiled and spoke, in perfect English. 'So you sold your carpets, then?'

Ah yes, of course, the confrontation with the two Ghilzais in the ravine before Kabul. Simon recalled the arrogant and nonchalant way the *jezail* had been held skywards, the stock on the hip, the head held to one side. The Afghan's smile was the same now, enquiring but sneering. Simon thought quickly of maintaining his cover but recalled W.G.'s advice.

'Ah,' he said. 'That was a pity. I had to leave them in Kabul.'

For a moment, the insouciance of Simon's reply appeared to disconcert the Afghan. His smile disappeared. 'You are not a Persian trader, then?'

'You know I am not. I am an English officer, Captain Simon Fonthill, of the Queen's Own Corps of Guides.'

The sneer reappeared. 'Then why do you dress as a Persian?'

'I carried important dispatches from General Roberts to the Residency in Kabul. The General did not wish to offend the Amir by sending troops to protect me, but, as you know, the Afridis of the Kuram are brigands who will kill all Englishmen, so I was forced to travel in disguise.'

'Humph!' The Afghan spat in the dust. 'Where are your two companions?'

'There was fighting in Kabul and the Residency was burned to the ground. We were separated in the fighting and I fear they were killed. I was forced to escape on the mule.'

'So you were running back to your general?'

'No. I had further work to do. I was looking for the Mullah Mushk-i-Alam. I seem to have found him.'

The mullah had been growing restive during the exchange, and now, hearing his name, he spoke tersely in Pushtu to the Afghan, who replied at length. The interrogator turned back to Simon.

'My lord, the Mullah wants to know what you want of him.'

Simon's throbbing head had cooled somewhat during the interrogation, while his brain raced to keep one pace ahead of his questioner. Perhaps now he had got through this first, dangerous phase. At least he had aroused the curiosity of his captors. He tried once more to ease himself within his bonds and sit erect. This time he directed his gaze at the mullah.

'I bring a message to the Holy One from the Lord General Roberts. The General is about to invade Afghanistan to avenge the death at Kabul of His Excellency the British Resident there, and to punish the treachery of the Amir, who has broken his word to the British Queen Empress.' Simon paused and ran his tongue over his cracked lips. He was taking a risk here that the mullah was no supporter of the Amir. The interpreter was listening intently, one eyebrow raised.

'The General has no argument with the people of Afghanistan, only with those leaders who broke their word and provoked the attack on the Residency, which had no soldiers to defend it. In particular, he has no quarrel with the Ghilzai or with the Holy One, whom he respects as a great leader.'

The interpreter said nothing, but Simon nodded to him and to the mullah, as a sign that his words should be translated. It was important to be in control here – and, anyway, he wanted time to think. The Ghilzai spoke quickly in Pushtu to his leader, who remained expressionless.

Simon cleared his throat and continued. 'The General values the friendship of the Mullah and, when he begins his advance, he pledges that he will make no attack upon the Ghilzai people. He does not expect the Mullah and his people to take up arms against their fellow Afghans. All he asks is that the Mullah will stay with his people in the hills when the British advance on Kabul and that they will trade, providing fodder for horses and food for which they will receive many rupees. The Mullah will know that the British do not break their word on these matters.'

Simon paused again while his words were translated. His mind galloped. God, he hoped that he was not overcommitting Roberts! As far as he knew, the Ghilzai had not been involved in the fight at Kabul – indeed, he believed they had not been at the battle at Peiwa Kotal either. Certainly, Roberts would not want them as a hostile force on his flank as he advanced through the hills and along the plain. But whether he had enough rupees in his war chest to bribe the mullah was another matter.

The mullah was speaking again, guttural and with obvious economy of words.

'How many soldiers does Roberts have?'

Simon blinked. Roberts's command was small for an invading army. Obviously there would be reinforcements and other columns coming through from India. He must be careful not to give information which could be helpful. On the other hand, this could be an opportunity to probe the size of the mullah's own force. 'Very many thousands,' he said, 'with many more in India, of course. More than would be needed to invade and occupy this country, if occupation was necessary.'

When this reply was conveyed to the mullah, he became agitated for the first time. He spoke quickly and at length, his words emphasised by the stamp of his stick into the dust, his voice rising until, at the end, he was shouting.

The Ghilzai interpreter bowed his head to his leader and turned triumphantly back to Simon. 'You talk camel dung,' he said. 'My lord knows exactly how many men your General has beyond the Shutargardan: he has seven and a half thousand men and twenty-two guns. He has only two brigades of infantry and one cavalry brigade. He has only eight mountain guns and just two Gatling guns. That is not many thousands. Why do you lie?'

Simon swallowed. That estimate of Roberts's strength sounded amazingly accurate. How did they know? 'I do not lie,' he said. 'There are men in close reserve beyond the Shutargardan. But the number of men is not important. These are great warriors with modern guns and great firepower. With much respect to the Mullah, I have seen nothing here or in Kabul which could stand against such troops.'

As Simon's words were translated, the mullah became increasingly agitated. Eventually he pushed his staff into the ground and, with its aid, rose to his feet and walked towards Simon. He was not a big man but he seemed to loom over his prisoner, who looked up into a face that appeared in the semi-darkness to be contorted with rage. Simon noticed for the first time that although the beard was white, the eyebrows were jet black. That, with the eyes blazing from their kohl-dark pits, gave the old man a demonic aspect as he began to rant at Simon, emphasising his words by thumping the butt of his staff into Simon's chest. Eventually, clearly exhausted by his tirade, he tottered back to his chair.

The interpreter spoke swiftly, as though anxious to end the charade now. 'My master says that you speak with the arrogance of all unbelievers. You and your people do not understand the force of the faithful. None of the men of the hills will trade with your general. They will fight him and kill him. The tribes are uniting under the banner of Allah – sixty thousand men will gather about Kabul soon. There are twenty thousand Russian troops on their way from the north to fight with us against the infidels, but they will not be needed. We shall crush your general and his pathetic force and leave their bones on the hills for the crows to pick them clean. But you will not live to see that.'

While the Ghilzai was speaking, the mullah struggled to his feet and, with a dismissive gesture to Simon, turned and walked slowly back to the fort, his retinue following him. At the end of the translation, the interpreter shouted an order and two Afghans untied the rope securing Simon to the tree and led him out of the compound.

The interpreter gave Simon a mock salute and shouted after him: 'Tonight, the women will amuse themselves with you, and in the morning we shall send your ears and testicles to your general.'

Simon looked around wildly. The women. The women. What did that mean? Oh God. Not torture. What would be the point of that? They had learned as much as they wanted from him. Why inflict pain needlessly? His eyes strained into the surrounding darkness. No sign of Jenkins or W.G.

He was hauled to his feet and taken to a hut at the side of the valley, close to the rock face. Here the earth was beaten flat and the ashes of a fire smouldered in front of the hut door. Suddenly a musket barrel struck him behind the knees so that he sprawled to the ground with a gasp. Immediately, his bonds were cut, he was rolled over on to his back and his arms and legs were pulled wide so that he was spread-eagled. Women suddenly appeared from the darkness and eager hands lashed his wrists and ankles to pegs that were driven, with some difficulty, into the packed earth. He lay flat, his legs forming a V either side of the ashes of the fire, the warmth of which he could already feel.

The two Afghans who had led him here looked down at him, quite expressionless. One of them spoke curtly to the crowd, which evoked a gale of laughter from the women, and then the men were gone.

Simon looked up at the faces that ringed his vision. There was no sign of compassion in any of the eyes that regarded him, only a kind of glee. Everyone was smiling. He clenched his teeth. He had heard of barbarities that had been inflicted on captured Englishmen. The advice he had been given during his brief training was explicit: just don't be captured. Well, he had gambled and lost. How long would it last? How could it be endured?

He became aware that fuel was being piled on to the embers between his legs to bring the fire to life again. 'Bitches,' he shouted. 'Hell-fired bitches. Damn you all to hell.' He pulled at his bonds but they held fast. He was no longer conscious of the pain in his chest and head. A helpless terror consumed him.

Suddenly the crowd parted and made way for a small, bundled figure. It was the old crone who had grabbed his testicles earlier. Slowly she lifted her skirts and put a foot either side of Simon's head, then lowered her skirts again, so that he was enveloped, tent-like, within their folds, and crouched down. The smell was disgusting. Simon realised what was coming and turned his head just in time to avoid the stream of urine which hit the side of his face and trickled on down to the ground. The crowd erupted into a shriek of approval and the trick was repeated six or seven times by other women.

The fire was now burning again and was beginning to make the insides of Simon's thighs and calves uncomfortably hot. The elderly crone, who clearly took precedence in this hell's kitchen, wiped the back of her hand across her mouth and gestured an order. Immediately, a knife was produced and was used to tear apart Simon's trousers and lower garments, so that his loins were exposed. Bound as he was, Simon shrank away as the woman crouched down beside him. He tossed his head frantically. 'Touch me and you will hang,' he cried, realising immediately how pathetic his voice sounded in this lost Afghan valley.

With the stick in her hand, the woman pointed at Simon's penis and, gums bared, addressed the crowd. The audience roared in approval and urged her on. Slowly she smiled and nodded, and, with the stick, lifted Simon's member in derision. Then she leaned beyond him to the fire and removed a burning brand, holding it for a while so that the flames died and the brand glowed red-hot. Then she slowly brushed it against Simon's penis, as a cook would seal a piece of meat.

Simon's scream rang through the night and immediately evoked an echoing roar of approval from the women gathered around the scene of torture. The hag nodded her head in approval as a smell of burning flesh rose. With precision she applied the brand to Simon's pubic hair so that it frizzled and curled.

The intensity of the pain caused Simon to faint. But a re-application of the brand and the ensuing agony ended that brief, merciful oblivion and he screamed again, his body arching and his head thrashing from side to side.

Then came the first rifle shot. It was high above the rock face but clear and distinct, coming seemingly from the cleft at the far end of the valley. It was followed by a second shot, and a third. The women turned their heads and one pointed in alarm. In the cleft, some two or three hundred feet above the valley, glowed a fire – perhaps a camp fire.

Immediately the camp came alive. Men came running from the fort and from the huts surrounding the grazing land. A rough command scattered the women, who then joined the men running towards the far end of the valley. All except the crone. She rose to her feet with difficulty, lifting her brand as though it would help her to see through the darkness to the flickering light high in the hills. Through the pain that consumed him, Simon realised that he was alone with her. He pulled desperately at the cords that bound him to the pegs, only succeeding in tightening them on his wrists and ankles, and drawing her attention back to him once more. She frowned and mumbled, and then turned and picked up a long-handled wooden shovel that stood propped against the hut wall. With a toothless grin she gestured to the fire and to his genitals, then began to load burning embers on to the shovel.

'No!' shrieked Simon.

An Afghan loomed up out of the dusk and shouted something to the woman. She lowered the shovel and turned to him.

'I said,' whispered the Afghan, as he reached her, ' 'alf a minnit, missus.' Then, with one expert movement, Jenkins whirled the woman round, put one hand on her mouth and slit her throat with the knife in his other. He gently lowered her to the ground by the side of the fire, thrust one end of the shovel which she had been holding into the ground and the other sharply into the folds of skin under her jaw, wrapped her hands around it and propped her up, as though she was sitting contemplating Simon.

The Welshman looked around quickly. All attention seemed to be directed towards the far end of the valley. His actions had gone unobserved. Quickly he kicked dust on to the fire to reduce the glare and then cut Simon free.

'Ah, bach. I'm sorry I've taken so long. Quick, can you walk?'

Simon tried to speak but could not. He lifted his head but a fresh wave of pain overtook him and it fell back again.

Jenkins looked down at the young man. Simon's genitals were red raw and the remnants of his pubic hair were black stubble, and from him came an acrid smell the like of which the Welshman had never experienced before. 'Ah,' he wrinkled his nose in disgust, 'you poor young bastard. What a mess.'

He looked around in desperation, seeking inspiration.

Then, from childhood, back over the years, came the memory of a very young boy running to his mother across the earthen floor of the kitchen, crying and holding his burned finger.

'Butter. That's it. Butter!'

He spun on his heel, ran into the hut and reappeared a moment later with a gourd. 'It ain't butter, bach, but it's some sort of fat, so it'll 'ave to do, see. Now excuse me, but I've got to get a bit familiar, like.'

With care, he lifted Simon's naked buttocks and began smearing the fat around his genitals. Simon had lapsed into unconsciousness again but Jenkins's rough ministrations renewed the pain and he whimpered, his eyes wide open.

'Good,' said Jenkins. 'No sleepin' on the job now, there's travellin' to do, see.' For the first time he noticed Simon's blood-encrusted face. 'Gawd. They've bashed your face in too, the bloody 'eathens. Now, we need something to wrap your bum in.'

Gingerly he lowered Simon to the ground again and looked up the valley. He could see the fire, high in the cleft, burning lower now, and small figures climbing up the rock face towards it. There had been no further firing but it could not be long before some of the tribesmen returned. He began to peel the shawl from the shoulders of the crone but heard a gasp from Simon.

'Not from her,' he said. 'I'd rather freeze to death.'

Jenkins nodded. 'Right you are. Probably crawlin', anyway. I'll use this.' He unravelled his turban and, pulling Simon to his feet, wound it round his midriff. 'Good. You look like one o' them fakeer blokes now. But can you walk?'

Simon attempted a step but his knees began to buckle and Jenkins caught him.

'No matter. I can carry you. Look you, lean forward over my shoulder. Now. Go.'

Simon had no difficulty in leaning forward – in fact he collapsed like wet washing across Jenkins and the broad little man lifted him easily and slipped quickly out of the fire's arc of light into the shadows by the rock face. He moved swiftly but deliberately along its edge until he found the fissure down which he had entered the camp.

Simon bit his lip to stop himself from moaning as the fabric of the turban rubbed against his burned skin.

'Now,' whispered Jenkins, 'we're goin' to do a bit of climbin'. You'll know I'm not very good at 'eights, so it's just as well it's dark. In fact, between you an' me, bach, I couldn't 'ave come down 'ere in the light. But it was no good me nippin' off to light that fire. I would 'ave lost me way in no time, so Gracey 'ad to do that bit. Now...' He sucked at his moustache and looked up into the darkness of the fissure above them. 'I shall need both 'ands, see, so you'll just 'ave to clasp yourself round me neck, 'ang down me back and 'old on for your life. All right?'

Simon nodded. As an afterthought, Jenkins secured the turban cloth round Simon's waist with the cord remnants he had taken from the pegs and tied a hitch around his own midriff. Then he bent his legs, heaved Simon on to his back and they were off.

The fissure, in fact, was not a difficult climb. It was a three-sided chimney up the rock face with plenty of foot- and hand-holds, but the night was pitch black, Jenkins, although strong, was no climber and they kept having to stop when unconsciousness threatened Simon as bursts of pain overtook him. Somehow, however, they reached a scrubby plateau about one hundred feet above the valley. Here, tethered behind a rock, were the two horses.

Jenkins lowered Simon carefully to the ground and brought him a water bottle. The Welshman's face was covered in perspiration. 'Gawd, I don't want to 'ave to do that again. I dursen't look down, otherwise we should 'ave been finished.' He glanced with horror towards Simon's groin. 'I could see what they were doin' to you, see,' he said apologetically, 'but I couldn't get down there till old Gracey 'ad fired his shots at the other end of the valley to create a diversion.'

Simon raised his head. 'Thanks, 352. You saved my life. Not for the first time. But how is W.G. going to get away? The whole tribe will be after him.'

Jenkins's teeth split the gloom. 'Ah, bach, don't you worry about 'im. 'E's like a mountain goat in these rocks. No.' The smile disappeared. 'We've got to worry about us. Look, I know you're badly injured, but you've got to keep aware now, see, because you'll 'ave to 'andle this compass thing. I can't make 'ead or tail of it, as you know. Gracey tells me that we've got to keep as near as we can to due south, though we shall 'ave to follow whatever trails we can find to make it easy for the 'orses. They're bound to come after us and we must ride to outdistance them.'

Simon sighed. 'I don't think I can manage to sit a horse. I've been . . . burned, you see.'

'Bless you, boyo, you've got to. We've got to make speed, see. Look, as a special treat I'll let you ride the Arab and I'll take the dobbin'. 'Ow's that, then?'

Simon forced a smile. The pain in his loins consumed him. It was as though he was on fire, and every touch of the turban was agony. But he saw the point. The horses were their only chance. 'All right. Get me up and help me mount. But stay close in case I fall.'

A strong moon had now risen: a blessing and a curse, for though it made it easier for the horses to pick their way among the rocks, it would also help their pursuers. Simon had no idea how long it would be before his escape was discovered, but he did not much care. The motion of the horse and the friction of the saddle sent surges of pain through him. He removed the turban and tucked it under his bottom, and the cool air brought – or seemed to bring – some relief to his burned flesh. The need to concentrate on the compass bearing to ensure that they did not ride in a circle helped somewhat to divert his mind from the pain, and they certainly made better time than they would have done on foot. Luckily, the ground was too stony and grassless for them to leave tracks to aid any pursuers.

Just before dawn they reached a high pass, and Simon realised that it was time to stop. It was clear that he had developed a fever and the burning now seemed to consume his body. Twice it was only Jenkins's arm that had prevented him from tumbling from the saddle.

'A cave, that's what we want,' muttered Jenkins, peering about him in the grey light. 'A bloody cave. Just like coppers. They're never about when you need 'em.'

But they did find a cave. Not much of one, admittedly, in that it was impossible to stand upright within it, but, more importantly, it was well hidden. They discovered it only when Simon's water bottle fell from his hand and Jenkins dismounted to scramble after it. A boulder half concealed the entrance and a stunted bush gave further cover. The entrance was only about four feet high, but the cave ran back double that distance and it was dry. Vitally, a mountain stream was gurgling nearby.

Simon half fell from the saddle into Jenkins's arms, and the Welshman carried him awkwardly through into the dark recess, squatting to lay him down, his head to the opening. Simon had now begun to shiver and Jenkins took off his cloak and wrapped it round the shaking man, laying Simon's rifle – left behind when he set off on the mule – by his side.

'Sorry, bach, we can't afford to light a fire. 'Ere, 'ave some water.' He held the canteen to Simon's lips and then, taking out his handkerchief, drenched it and tied it round Simon's forehead. 'Can't do much more now, see,' he said, half to himself. 'But what am I goin' to do with the bloody 'orses, eh?'

He crawled to the entrance and peered through the bush. The rising sun had thrown the mountain peaks to the east into black relief against a rosy sky. The air was crisp and clear. It was the beginning of a perfect day. He looked behind him into the cave. Simon was sleeping deeply now. As good a place as any to see the fever through, thought the Welshman. As long as I can keep him warm. No bloody flies, anyway.

Jenkins carefully poured a little water from the canteen into his cupped hand and then dipped his fingers into it before gently rubbing at the blood on Simon's battered face. The blood was congealed and crusted, however, and the ministrations had little effect. For a moment the Welshman stayed kneeling by the side of his charge, affected by an emotion that was, if not new to him, at least still somewhat alien. Then he patted the sleeping man's head, rose and began looking for the horses.

They had hardly moved from where he had left them, grazing tiredly on the sparse grass that poked between the rocks. The animals were a betrayal of their presence. They had to be hidden. But where? Then his eyes fell on the stream. It gurgled round a bend from a gentle slope in the mountainside some fifty feet from the cave mouth. It flowed fast but shallowly. Leading both horses, Jenkins took them upstream, splashing through the water for ten minutes before he stripped off the packs, leaving the saddles in case they needed to depart hurriedly. Then he hobbled the horses and returned warily to the cave.

The sun was now peeping above the jagged peaks but the morning remained quiet. In the distance, a bird cawed as it wheeled overhead, down the valley, but there was nothing else. With some difficulty, Jenkins dragged both packs into the cave, rearranged the bush to hide the opening and, rifle at the ready, lay down on his side with his head to the cave mouth.

He had no idea how long he had slept, but the sun was now well clear of the hilltops; he could tell by the absence of shadows on the track. But something had woken him. He listened intently. There it was again, a footstep, a soft rattle of stones.

W.G. or Afghans? If the latter, it was only a matter of time before they found the cave. Was it better to fight from the cave or outside it? Jenkins sniffed. Depended on the number of the enemy. He raised the Snider and sighted down the barrel. As he did so, an Afghan came into view. He seemed to be a Ghilzai – same nondescript dress, same bearing, same feline tread as the men he had watched in the camp. The Pathan carried a *jerzail* in one hand and led Simon's horse with the other. He walked slowly, quietly, his head turning from side to side. Jenkins followed him with the rifle foresight until man and horse disappeared behind the boulder.

Then another Ghilzai appeared, leading Jenkins's own horse with equal caution. Jenkins let him go and waited, watching as another three Afghans loped by. Five in all. But that did not mean there were no more. If it was a search party, they would be spread out, examining every nook and cranny, looking behind every boulder, now the horses had been found.

As the thought occurred to him, a shower of stones fell down from above the overhang to the cave's entrance, a few inches from Jenkins's nose. They were followed by a pair of sandals that dangled for a moment before the legs were lowered, landing in a half-jump in front of the Welshman's gun muzzle. Jenkins found himself looking at the rear view of an unusually tall Pathan, his back criss-crossed by bandoliers, his cotton pantaloons soiled by his descent.

The man did not look behind him but paused by the boulder, his head turning as he scanned the terrain. Suddenly his body stiffened and he half turned so that he was hidden behind the rock. Slowly he raised his *jezail* to his shoulder. He had obviously found an enemy. Jenkins's jaw dropped for an instant and, involuntarily, he took a quick glance at Simon in case, somehow, his comrade had crawled out of the cave. But the young man still slept, his breaths slow and even.

Slowly the Pathan pulled back the flintlock on his piece, carefully sighting it at a target Jenkins could not see. The man's finger tightened on the trigger, and as soon as the first small explosion occurred in the priming pan, Jenkins pulled his own trigger, so that the two main reports sounded as one. The Snider's bullet took the Ghilzai in the back of the head, shattering it and sending a mass of red and grey matter splattering along the wall of rock.

Jenkins quickly waved away the smoke from his gun barrel and slipped another round into the breech. He waited tensely and jumped as a hand closed on his ankle.

'Zulus, is it Zulus?' Luckily Simon was speaking in a whisper. Jenkins looked down at him. The sick man's eyes were red-rimmed and staring, and perspiration rolled down his face.

'No, bach. Nothing to worry about. Bit of firin', that's all, see, at pigeons. Somethin' to eat. Try and get some sleep now.'

As he spoke, he heard the distinctive crack of a Snider and in answer the characteristic coughs of two *jezails*, followed, after loading time, by another shot from the Snider.

Jenkins edged forward. 'Sounds as though there's a bloody war goin' on out there,' he murmured.

Rolling over on to his back, he inched himself awkwardly out of the opening, his rifle at his chest, looking above the overhang in case there was another Afghan following the first. But there were only the rocks and the brazen steely-blue sky. He turned back on to his front and crawled through the bush. Avoiding the dead Pathan, he put a cautious head around the boulder. He was in time to see both horses, some way down the track, break into a canter, the two Ghilzais who had been leading them lying seemingly dead in the middle of the path. A *jezail* sounded again, and Jenkins saw the turbans of the other three Pathans behind rocks on his side of the track. Who they were firing at remained unclear, but it was obvious that the target had been sighted by the man whom Jenkins had killed. The Welshman withdrew his head and glanced about him. It looked as though he and Simon had not been discovered. But were there more of the Ghilzais scattered in the rocks, and who the hell were they firing at? W.G.? Whoever it was, they were on the other side of the track. This meant that Jenkins should be able to get behind the Afghans.

He dropped on to his belly and began squirming around the boulder, using the high shoulder of the track as cover as he wriggled towards where the three Pathans were spread out behind rocks a little higher up the hill, where the track climbed and wound around a bend. Slowly he climbed, cradling his Snider in his arms, working his way upwards on elbows and knees, freezing from time to time to locate his position.

The firing had now ceased, and Jenkins wondered why. He lifted his head and saw that one of the three, the man furthest away from him, was himself crawling away to his left, obviously trying to outflank the enemy. And then the Welshman saw W.G. The big Sikh had taken cover on a ledge that overlooked the track on its opposite side. As Jenkins watched, the Afghan nearest began to crawl from rock to rock towards him, so that he could outflank the Sikh from the other direction.

But were there only three Afghans left? Jenkins sucked in his moustache and looked carefully around him. No sign of other life at all. Certainly, as he lay on his ledge, W.G. presented a good target to anyone following up from this side of the track, and if there were more of the Pathans lurking behind the rocks above Jenkins, they were showing remarkable forbearance. The Welshman risked another quick look at the nearest man. He, not realising his danger, had eyes only for the Sikh, and was edging along, on his belly, through the shale towards Jenkins.

Still Jenkins waited. He had to be sure of the number of the enemy. Two to two was easy – even three to two. More than that, however, and it could be difficult, given the cover for riflemen provided by the rocks, and the Pathans' obvious knowledge of the terrain. He wiped the sweat from his face and slowly counted to ten. Nothing. No sound, no movement from behind or above him. Then a slither of stones came from the other side of the boulder behind which he sheltered – disturbingly close. He couldn't wait any longer. Jenkins shortened his grip on the Snider and presented it around the boulder – almost into the ear of a Ghilzai who was nestling his cheek into the stock of his *jezail* as he sighted along the slim barrel towards W.G.

'Sorry, bach,' said Jenkins and pulled the trigger. So close was the muzzle of the Snider that the Pathan's head and turban half muffled the sound of the shot. Jenkins directed a quick glance towards W.G. The Sikh, clearly startled, was shuffling on his ledge to bring his Snider to bear on the new direction of danger when he recognised Jenkins and gave a quick wave of thanks. Jenkins jabbed his finger towards W.G.'s right, in the direction in which the furthest Pathan had crept. The Sikh nodded again and wriggled out of sight. As he did so, a bullet cracked into the rock sheltering Jenkins, forcing him to duck low behind its protection. Now, of course, he had been seen and it was to be hoped that the odds were only two to two.

He slipped another cartridge into the breech of his rifle and thought hard. He did not want to stray too far from the cave, leaving Simon unprotected, and his elbows and kneecaps were bleeding from being scraped along in the shale and shingle. He did not fancy any more of that. He poked a reflective finger up his nostril. He suddenly realised that this was where he missed Simon. He himself could shoot and kill well enough. But Simon could *think*. So, what would the Lieutenant – no, Captain now – do? He weighed the odds again. It looked like two against two. A quick glance at W.G. showed that the Sikh had wriggled round on his ledge to face the threat from the man on his right, so leaving the Pathan opposite to Jenkins. A frontal charge? Why not? These buggers took ages to reload their old guns. It was worth a chance that the first shot would miss; they hadn't hit anything yet.

Jenkins wiped his moustache, raised himself into a crouch and then, like a sprinter at the starting gun, was off, jumping from rock to rock, keeping low and running hard. But to where? He was well on his way before he realised that he had no firm idea where his target was: somewhere ahead, but behind which rock? To clarify matters he let out a high yell. Immediately, a long musket poked out about fifty yards to his right down the hill, and he saw the puff of smoke and heard the report simultaneously. The ball took him in the right thigh and sent him rolling down the slope – towards his assailant.

Jenkins's rifle clattered away across the shale and the

Pathan leaped from behind his rock, running at the crouch as he tugged a curved knife from the sheath at his belt. Despairingly, Jenkins clutched at his thigh and shot a glance towards W.G. But a low saddle of rock now screened both him and the Afghan from the Sikh on the other side of the track.

Jenkins was on his knees when the Pathan reached him. He bought himself a second or two of time by hurling a handful of stones at the Ghilzai. The Pathan flinched for a moment, then kicked Jenkins, leaped astride him and raised his dagger high in the air.

The shot took him in the back, neatly between the shoulder blades. Jenkins saw the look of astonishment on the man's dark, high-cheekboned face before he collapsed with a sigh across the Welshman's midriff. Jenkins looked around wildly and saw the last remnant of blue smoke wafting away from the cave's mouth.

'God bless you, bach,' he muttered. 'What a time to discover you're a good shot.'

Then another shot sent echoes answering from the valley below. It was the sharp crack of a second Snider, this time from across the track. There was no answering cough from a *jezail* and silence settled on the peaks again.

Jenkins lay for a moment, his hand gripping his thigh, and watched as his blood mingled with that of the dead Pathan in a little scarlet stream that slid slowly between the stones down the hill.

He raised his head. 'Gracey.'

'Yes, Sergeant bach.'

'Did you get 'im?'

'Of course. Between the eyes, I think. He made mistake of looking too long, too long.'

'Is that the lot, then?'

'Yes, five. I outdistanced the rest. But these followed me through the night. Very disconcerting and annoying. I am glad I have found you. Where is the Captain, lord?'

'In a cave just across the way. I've been hit. Come and help me.'

In a moment the tall Sikh appeared, his face smudged darker by cordite marks. Contemptuously he turned the Pathan over with his foot. 'Ah. But he was shot in the back. How did you . . .?'

Jenkins, grimacing with pain, nodded towards the cave. 'The Captain. Bloody good shot. Particularly as 'e was shakin' with the fever the last time I saw 'im. This feller put a ball through me thigh. That was good shootin' as well. I lost me rifle an' 'e was about to cut me throat, look you, when the Captain got 'im. Saved me life.'

The Sikh gathered up Jenkins's rifle and, putting his arm around the Welshman, helped him limp back to the cave. There they found Simon staring down his Snider barrel, shivering violently. He gave no sign of recognition as the two men approached but looked beyond them to where the Pathan's body lay. W.G. was visibly shocked at the young man's appearance: the blood from his broken nose and from the various head wounds had congealed but the fever's perspiration had now streaked through it, giving him a bizarre, striped appearance, as though war paint had been applied. The wildness was emphasised by his red-rimmed, wide-eyed stare.

The Sikh drew in his breath. 'You must stay warm, lord. Please get back under the cloak.'

Simon paid no attention. 'I know that you are not supposed to shoot men in the back,' he murmured, as though to himself. 'But these are very evil people.' He looked up appealingly. 'Aren't they?'

Jenkins sat down beside him awkwardly, his wounded leg stretching out straight. Gently he removed the rifle from Simon's grasp and helped him back into the cave and beneath the folds of blanket and cloak. 'Well, they don't seem to like us much, that's a fact. That was a bloody good shot, bach sir. If you 'adn't 'ave picked 'im off, 'e would 'ave slit me throat, as sure as God made little apples.' He took the young man's hand. 'I'm very grateful, see. Now try and sleep a bit more, eh?'

Like a child, Simon nodded and, closing his eyes, turned his head. He seemed to slip into sleep immediately.

W.G. looked down at the pair and a smile lit up his face. 'You and the captain sahib are close, Sergeant bach. I can see that. It is good. It is good to be brothers. It makes the team better.' The smile disappeared. 'Now I must get the horses because we must travel on. The rest of the mullah's men will not be far behind and they will have heard the shooting. When I come back, I must take that ball from your leg.'

Jenkins looked up in surprise. ' 'Ang on, Gracey, the Captain can't travel now. An' I'm not up to much. Why can't we stay in the cave till we're a bit better an' then move, eh?'

The Sikh stood erect and slowly shook his head – everything he did had dignity, it seemed to Jenkins. 'I hope that the Sergeant does not think me disrespectful, but no. That would not do.' He gestured inside the cave and laid a long finger on the palm of his other hand. 'Fact number one. There is hardly room for two in there and certainly not for three. Fact number two. The horses are our only means of reaching Lord General Roberts – you cannot walk all that way – and,' he shrugged his shoulders and looked around theatrically, 'where can we hide them? These men of the hills can smell a good horse at two thousand paces. They have found the horses once and assuredly they would find them again. No, Sergeant bach. However difficult, we must ride.'

Without waiting for a reply, the Sikh turned and trotted down the track, rifle at the trail, in the direction the horses had disappeared. Jenkins shook his head resignedly and, for the first time, took a close look at the wound in his leg. The ball had lodged in the fleshy part of the under-thigh and, by the feel and look of it, had not penetrated far. Gingerly he bent his leg at the knee and felt around the wound. Certainly there were no bones broken and he thanked his stars that the Ghilzai had not been armed with a modern rifle. At that range, his leg would have been shattered. The wound had stopped bleeding and he cleaned it as best he could. Then, taking the water bottles, and the handkerchief from Simon's head, he limped to the stream, refilled the canteens and cleaned and soaked his handkerchief. Back in the cave he gently wiped Simon's face and head and, when his eyes opened, gave him water to drink.

The young man sat up. He was no longer perspiring although his face, under what remained of the congealed blood and the dye, had paled perceptibly. 'Thank you, 352,' he said, taking another deep draught from the bottle. 'Listen, did I . . . did I dream it or did I shoot someone?'

'No, bach sir, you didn't dream it. You shot the feller who was tryin' to top me, and I'm grateful to you, see.' Quickly Jenkins explained to Simon what had happened from the time they had left the Pathan camp, and the need now to keep moving. 'Can you ride now, d'you think?'

Simon nodded, although without enthusiasm, and Jenkins, wincing from the pain of his leg, unwrapped the turban he had wound round Simon's loins and inspected the wounds.

He sniffed. 'I'm no doctor, bach, but I think that fat has done a reasonable job.'

They were interrupted by the return of W.G., who came loping up the trail leading the two horses. Hitching them to the bush, he knelt down to look at Simon's wounds, as Jenkins explained their history. The Sikh nodded and spoke softly to Simon. 'The sergeant bach could not have done better. We will not disturb the fat. It should keep away germs, lord. But now we must remove ball from the Sergeant's leg. And we must risk making fire.'

Quickly W.G. built a small fire in the interior of the cave. The smoke made them cough and their eyes water but it was better than letting it curl up straight outside like a signal column. The Sikh let it remain a flame only long enough to heat the blade of his knife to a dull red. Then he extinguished the blaze with dust and turned to where Jenkins waited, sucking his moustache.

'The ball is not far beneath the skin,' he said, waving the blade to cool it. 'I shall flick it out like I dispatch the red cherry to fine leg boundary.' He gestured, using the knife as a cricket bat, rolling his wrists to demonstrate the leg glance. 'Little pain, Sergeant bach, I am assuring you.'

'Oh bloody 'ell,' said Jenkins, closing his eyes.

In fact the Sikh was as good as his word and the operation took only seconds. Then, tearing fine cotton from Jenkins's only other shirt, he bandaged the wound tightly and a perspiring Jenkins got to his feet, albeit with caution. Simon was tightly wrapped in whatever their packs could provide and the three men shuffled to the waiting horses. Simon mounted the Balkh stallion with W.G. seated behind him, holding him around the waist, while Jenkins, grimacing with pain, brought up the rear on his original Herat mount. They set off to the south, still climbing.

After half an hour, Jenkins urged his horse forward so that it was almost alongside that in front. He looked carefully at Simon, who was sitting well enough in the saddle but with his

eyes closed. 'You all right, bach sir?' he enquired. Simon
opened his eyes and nodded. 'Ah, good,' said the Welshman.
'Look, see. I forgot to ask in all the fuss. Was it worth it? Did
you learn anything back there, then?'

Simon gave a half-smile as his head nodded with the gait
of the horse. 'Oh yes. I learned all sorts of things – even some
things which might help the General.' Then he closed his eyes
again and pain crossed his face. 'Don't ask me now, because
my brain's in a muzz. I'll tell you when I've got my thoughts
straight.' He grimaced and his head fell forward again. Jenkins
had to bend close to hear his last muttered words: 'But whether
it was worth it I don't know. I just don't know.'

Chapter 7

It took the little party two more days to reach the Shutargardan. The Kabul road was far too dangerous to use, which meant that the three men had to pick their way by compass through the mountains, using goat tracks where they could find them and always, always climbing. Simon lapsed into a state of semi-consciousness and only the arm of the Sikh kept him in the saddle. The first night after leaving the cave they found shelter and blessed hot food – gruel, mutton and sweet tea – with a nomad goatherd and his family. Not Ghilzais, said W.G. There were signs that Simon's fever was returning and the two rough blankets they purchased to wrap him in were as welcome as was the lean-to that protected them all to some extent from the bitter wind and cold.

Nevertheless, Simon's condition deteriorated the next day. He became delirious, shivering, his eyes half closed, mouthing meaningless phrases through which only 'the Zulus move *fast*' and 'twenty thousand Russians' were understandable. It was becoming more and more difficult for W.G. to hold him in the saddle as the horses slithered and stumbled on the shale.

It was Jenkins who insisted that they risk taking the road, the better to make progress: 'Look, Gracey, look at 'im. He'll die if we don't get 'im to a doctor soon. Use that compass thing to get us down to the road. Come on. I'm pullin' rank, look you. It's the sergeant speaking, see.'

The Sikh turned Simon's face round so that he could look into the young man's eyes. Wordlessly, W.G. nodded and pointed to their right. An hour later they hit the road just before it crested the range at Shutargardan, both the wind and the pass's eleven-thousand-foot elevation taking their breath away. Just below the crest they met a patrol of British cavalry, lances held high, carbines slung at their saddles, and they were escorted down over the battle-scarred ridge of Peiwa Kotal, into the Kuram valley and, eventually, as the shadows lengthened from the mountain peaks, into the British forward encampment of Alikhal, twelve miles from Kuram.

It was clear that Simon could go no further but a doctor was with the forward post and he bustled in to take charge as the young man was lowered from the saddle by Jenkins and W.G.

'What's wrong? Dysentery?'

Jenkins shook his head and slowly explained what had happened to Simon. The doctor, a short, red-haired Scotsman, wrinkled his nose in disgust and looked with concern at the half-dead form that Jenkins carried in his arms. He put a hand to Simon's forehead.

'Right,' he said. 'Warmth. The fever's the main problem at the moment. We must keep out pneumonia, though . . .' he gazed pityingly at Simon's lower half, 'God knows what we do about down below. This way. Quick as you can.'

For three days Simon lay in a semi-coma, sweat plastering his hair and his broken nose making his breathing even more laboured. On the morning of the third day, General Roberts and Colonel Lamb rode into camp and to the tent where he lay. The two little men, their faces inscrutable, stood for several moments looking down at the unconscious man. Eventually Roberts turned to the doctor. 'Will he live?'

'I'll know soon, General. I'm hoping the fever will break tonight. I think we've caught him just in time.' He shook his head. 'Though whether the laddie is ever going to be able to enjoy married life is in the hands of the good Lord above. There's not much I can do in that department, except keep stickin' on fresh dressings.'

Colonel Lamb frowned and blew his nose, but Roberts's expression did not change. 'Has he regained consciousness to say anything – has he talked at all?'

'No, sir. Only blatherins that we can't make head nor tail of.'

Roberts tapped his thigh with his riding crop. 'I shall stay here overnight. I want to be told as soon as he regains consciousness or . . . er . . . gets worse. Understand?'

'Aye, sir.'

The two men strode out of the tent. Roberts, in fact, had already known about the Kabul massacre when Simon and his companions rode into Alikhal. Five days earlier, he had been with his wife in attendance on the Viceroy at Simla, the summer seat of Indian government, when a telegram had reached him to tell him of the rumoured death of Cavagnari and the embassy staff. Immediately, the little officer had metamorphosed from polished courtier to man of action. With the two other British columns long since withdrawn from Afghanistan, his Kuram force was the only one in the field, and he instantly resumed his command and prepared to march on Kabul before winter snows closed the passes. Within days he had assembled a force comprising two infantry brigades (Indian and British regiments), a brigade of cavalry, a brigade of artillery with twenty-two guns, and a force of engineers. (The Mullah Mushk-i-Alam's intelligence was impeccable.) Even as Simon lay in his tent, one of the infantry brigades was moving up past Alikhal to occupy the Shutargardan and so keep open the door to Kabul.

It was clear that the invasion would be opposed. But to what extent, and what role would the Amir play? Roberts knew that the disenchanted Herat troops from the west had been at the heart of the insurrection and that the people of Kabul had supported them. But what of the hill tribes? Would they attack his small force – he had only seven and a half thousand men – as he advanced? And if they did, how many men could they muster? Not for the first time, his intelligence was sketchy and contradictory.

At the door of the hut that served as his headquarters Roberts turned to Lamb. 'Baa-Baa, fetch me the two men who were with Fonthill. I am sure they can tell us something.'

Jenkins and W.G. filed into the dark little room and stood before Roberts, who was joined by Colonel Lamb. The Welshman and the Sikh made an incongruous pair, their disparity in height and dishevelled native garb giving them an air of the bazaar that was dispelled abruptly by the guardsman-like rigidity with which they crashed to attention.

The General – he was now Sir Frederick, the knighthood quickly recognising his victory at Peiwa Kotal – examined each man with care, his eye taking in the bloodstain on Jenkins's trousers and the slight wince with which the Welshman stamped to a halt. His gaze, however, betrayed no sympathy. It was that of a man weighing up the pair's usefulness – and their credibility.

'Now,' he said. 'Stand easy and tell me exactly what happened to you. You first, Sergeant.'

So Jenkins took a deep breath and began their story, hesitantly at first but gaining in confidence as the tale unfolded and his Welsh loquacity took over. The General occasionally interrupted to ask a question but mainly listened in silence, while Colonel Lamb took notes steadily.

Eventually, Jenkins tailed off, taking out a rag and blowing his nose noisily, as though to mark the end of a tale well told. Roberts frowned and drummed his fingers on the table top. 'How many men did the mullah have in the valley?'

'Don't know, sir. Couldn't really see, was the truth of it.'

'Dammit man, you must have seen *something*.'

Jenkins's eyes narrowed and held the pale blue gaze of the General. 'Oh aye. I saw that cow of a woman tryin' to burn Mr Fonthill's privates. But it was a bit dark, see, to take in much else . . . sir.'

Roberts snorted through his moustache, his mouth pursed and he took a deep breath through his nose, as though to issue a rebuke, but then thought better of it. Instead, he turned to W.G. 'When you were in the north with Cavendish last year, was the area teeming with Russian troops?'

The Sikh looked slightly puzzled. 'That, sir, was in Mr Cavendish's report, sir, undoubtedly.'

'Yes,' the General spoke impatiently, 'but I want to get your impression. You were there. I know you have good eyes and a good brain.'

W.G. beamed. 'The General is very kind. No, sir. No troops teeming, sir. Not teeming at all, sir. What there were looked to me very much like second eleven, sir.'

'What, what? Second what?'

Lamb leaned over. 'Cricket, sir.' He gestured almost imperceptibly to W.G. with his pen. 'You will remember, sir, I think. Cricket.'

Roberts frowned. 'Oh yes. Cricket. I had forgotten. Bloody game. Hated it myself. But never mind.' He turned back to Jenkins. 'Did you – did either of you – get the impression that Captain Fonthill had gathered information of any useful kind as a result of his . . . er . . . experience in the mullah's camp?'

Jenkins wrinkled his nose so that his moustache almost

met his eyebrows. 'We don't know, sir. Mr Fonthill wasn't able to talk much once we'd got away. But you can be sure of one thing: he will have tried. Oh yes, sir. He will have tried.'

At this Lamb smiled and nodded but Roberts's expression of thinly veiled irritation remained. 'Very well, Sergeant. We shall have to wait and see. It could be quite important. Now,' he stood up, 'that will be all. You will not return to general duties because I want you to stay with Captain Fonthill until he recovers. I don't want to break up the team, so to speak.' He shot a glance at the Sikh and smiled for the first time. 'There will be plenty for you to do, once we start our advance. You have both done well. Now dismiss.'

Both men sprang to attention – no salute, for they were not wearing regulation caps – turned and marched out of the hut. Outside, they stood and looked uncertainly at each other.

'Well,' said Jenkins. 'Excused duties for a bit. That's the best bit of news I've heard on this postin'.'

W.G. looked around him, his eyes taking in the bell tents pitched unevenly on the sloping ground, their guy ropes weighed down with stones where stakes would not penetrate the rocky terrain. 'No chance of pitching stumps and playing a game though, Sergeant bach,' he said glumly. 'Pity.' He emulated a flowing off drive. 'I am being a little out of practice, you know.'

Jenkins's eyes went heavenwards. 'Bloody 'ell, Gracey. Give it a rest for a bit, there's a good feller. Let's go an see the Captain.'

But an orderly shooed them away at the tent opening. The doctor knew that Simon was facing his crisis point and that he had to fight his battle alone. In fact, it was little more than an hour later that Simon regained full consciousness. For him, the last few days had been a tumble of pain, discomfort – he had vomited several times from his precarious seat on the horse – and a mess of nightmarish fantasies: surrealistic dreams of fire, burning, dark, wild-eyed faces and always heat, heat, heat. He had been vaguely aware of being lifted from the horse at the camp and of the doctor's ministrations to the centre of his burning. But what was left of the rational part of his mind had become more and more consumed with torture and the great question of whether he had given away vital information.

As he opened his eyes and concentrated on the white canvas of the tent wall above him, he was aware that he had passed a climax in his illness and had survived it. Although perspiration still trickled from his hair on to the sodden pillow, he was no longer on fire. He felt utterly exhausted, but the arm which hung down from the bed to touch the beaten earth was cold, healthily cold. He wiped the perspiration away from his eyes and then tucked the arm under the welcoming bedclothes and concentrated on the tent pole while his mind went back. No. As best as he could remember, he had told the mullah nothing. That was a relief.

Then a flicker of pain from his genitals – not a stab of anguish, more a gentle reminder that all was not well after all – took his mind on to the agony of the fire and the burning brand. He groaned involuntarily and explored with his hand. He was tightly trussed but, apart from that gentle reminder, there was no pain now, just a dull background ache, like that from the sensitive scar of a once open wound. He moved slowly on to his side. That little jar of pain again, but nothing more. He lay quite comfortably, yet his mind was far from tranquil, even though the demons of betrayal had been banished. He had never made love in all his twenty-four years. He had bought a glass of the then fashionable port and lemonade mixture for a tart in a pub near Sandhurst when he had been a cadet, but had found himself unable to go through with the act with someone who smelt of stale tobacco and God knows what else. Would he even be capable of it now? Had that hag, with her fire-stick, robbed him of the gift of fatherhood? Quietly, his mouth half stifled by the pillow, he moaned.

The medical orderly found him lying, eyes wide open, breathing regularly, and doubled away for the doctor.

'Good man. You've passed the worst.' The young Scot put his hand to Simon's brow. 'I've broken the only bloody thermometer between here and Simla but there's nae doubt that yer temperature is way doon.' He took Simon's pulse and nodded approvingly. 'Good. Would yer like some porridge?'

Simon forced a smile. 'Does it have to be either porridge or haggis? Can't I have something English, like a cup of tea?'

The doctor grinned back. 'I don't approve o' the sentiments but I applaud the spirit. Aye, I'll get yer a cuppa.' He made to go, but Simon restrained him.

'Sorry, I know you must be busy, but could I ask you something? Am I . . . am I permanently hurt down there? Will it be possible for me to . . . you know . . .?'

The doctor frowned. 'You'll want an honest answer, and I wish I could could gi' yer one, but I can't. I'm just an army doctor wi' two years' service under his belt, and while I can cut off a leg wi' gangrene in five minutes an' hae the laddie fit an' well within five weeks, I ken very little about what a burn will do to an erection. An' that's a fact.'

He perched on the edge of the bed. 'Look, laddie, it's like this. It could be you need a skin graft but there's no way we can do that here – in fact, I doubt if there's anyone in India who can do that to a penis – and by the time we got you back to England, I should think there'd be no point tryin'. So it's a question of waitin' and seein'.' He ran a hand through his red hair and gave a lop-sided smile. 'There'll not be much of a chance of you exercisin' yer wee winkie in that way here, in any case. But no.' The smile disappeared. 'As yer know, when a chap gets . . . er . . . excited, blood rushes into the penis and the dear wee thingy expands. This means that the skin on your johnny stretches – that's what a foreskin's fer. Now, you've taken a bit of a burnin' there, and whether what's left of yer skin can recover to the point that it can manage a bit o' stretchin' remains to be seen.'

He stood up. 'But it's no' all gloom an' doom, by any means. There's no infection there, as far as I can see – that's what was worryin' me about yer fever. You owe a lot to the chappies who brought you in. They dressed you rough but proper. Lookin' at yer, it seems yer all skin an' bones, but if there's nae fat on yer, there's plenty o' muscle, an' I'd say you've got the constitution of a Highland buck.' His blue eyes smiled again. 'You've turned the corner now, laddie. You're awful bruised still about the ribs but that'll soon go. The swellin' on that broken nose is goin' doon quickly and your breathin's all right, so it's best to leave the nose well alone. The General will surely send you back doon the line. Just keep takin' good nourishment an I'd say you'll be fit again within a couple o' weeks. Now, the General and his wee colonel are hoppin' up an' doon to see yer. Are you up to it? We'll change your dressin' afterwards.'

Simon nodded.

With an answering nod, the doctor was gone and Simon was left with his thoughts. He had found nothing to reassure him in the Scotsman's prognosis and he had listened with growing dismay to the analysis of his injury. The evidence seemed to point to a future arid in every sense.

His gloomy thoughts were broken by the entry of General

Roberts and Colonel Lamb. Roberts looked down at him with an expressionless face.

'Ah, Fonthill. Good. Dr Knox says you seem to be better. How do you feel?'

'Not bad, sir, thank you.'

'Good. Now, we don't wish to tire you, but things are warming up a little, as I know you know. Do you feel fit enough to tell us everything that happened? I would like to know every single thing you can recall, from the terrible affair at Kabul to what . . . what happened to you in the mullah's camp. Are you up to it?' And then he added, almost – and uncharacteristically – apologetically, 'Time is of the essence now, you see.'

'Of course, sir.'

Colonel Lamb leaned across and took Simon's hand, resting on the coverlet, and shook it firmly. 'Well done, Fonthill. Well done indeed. Glad to have you back.'

'Thank you, sir.'

The General dragged up a camp stool and Lamb took out his notebook. 'Right, fire away. In your own good time.'

So Simon related all that had happened, from the time that the trio had entered Kabul to their flight through the hills and their pursuit by the Ghilzais. Both men listened carefully, without interruption, Lamb, as before, taking notes.

At the end, Roberts pulled on his silver moustache. 'Why did you not join Sir Louis and help to defend the Residency?'

'As I explained, sir, we arrived too late to get through the crowd. We felt we could help the defence best by shooting from the houses.'

'Humph. Now, tell me again about the mullah. There was no question, do you think, of him blustering a bit – adopting a negotiating position to get more rupees from us to help?'

Simon gave a half-smile – at the question, and at the memory of the hatred in the mullah's cold black eyes. 'No chance, sir. He doesn't like us much.'

'Hmmmn. Sixty thousand tribesmen, you say? And twenty thousand Russians on their way?'

Simon nodded. 'That's what he said.'

Roberts looked across to Lamb, who was scribbling away on the other side of the bed. 'Don't believe it,' he said. 'At least, don't believe that there is a Russian force in the offing. We would have heard about that, somehow. But,' he put his riding crop to his moustache and mused, 'given that the feller was exaggerating for effect, even twenty thousand tribesmen coming down at us from the hills as we advance could give us no end of a problem.' He looked down again at Simon. 'How many men, would you say, had the mullah got there in his encampment?'

'Oh, I saw comparatively few, sir. I wasn't in much of a state to notice anyway. I'd been beaten a bit, you see.'

Roberts evinced no sympathy. 'Indeed. But could a large force have gathered there, in that valley? I mean, did it look like a rallying point where the hill tribes could confederate against us?'

'Bit too small, sir, I should think. But I saw enough on the journey to know that there are plenty of valleys which *could* serve as such a meeting place, though the mullah talked about the tribes gathering at Kabul.'

'Right.' Roberts stood up. 'You've done well, Fonthill. I must confess that I was a little surprised that you couldn't force your way into the Residency to help Cavagnari more directly – perhaps it could have made a difference. But then I wasn't there.' His rosy face remained imperturbable. 'Letting yourself be captured was also a great risk and could have misfired. Nearly did. But,' he shrugged, 'I am grateful to you.

I shall see that you are moved back to India to recover from your wounds.'

'No, sir.' The force of Simon's response took both men by surprise. He raised his head from the pillow in emphasis. 'I do not wish to go down the line, sir. The doctor says that I am strong and that I should be able to get up and resume duties in about two or three weeks. It will take as long as that to get to India and back. I might as well stay here to recover.'

Roberts's face remained impassive and totally without sympathy. 'Look, sir.' Simon raised himself on one elbow. 'You are going to need all the intelligence you can get on the advance, and my men and I now know all the country from here to Kabul.' He winced inwardly at the lie. 'We know the city, too. Even if you began the advance tomorrow – and I know you can't do that – I could be with you well before you reached the walls of Kabul.' He lowered himself back on to the pillow and then spoke with slow emphasis. 'I am not going back, sir. There is nothing for me in India. I can be useful to you here.'

The General looked down at the young man, noting the truculent set of his jaw and the directness of his gaze, and then glanced across at Lamb. The Colonel nodded, almost imperceptibly.

'Very well, Fonthill. But there can be no room for invalids in an advance. This army will begin the invasion within a week. You will be riding by then, or I will move you back. Understand?'

'Very good, sir.'

'Very well.' Roberts nodded at Lamb, who rose and stuffed his notebook into a pocket and directed a smile at Simon. At the tent opening the General paused, like a schoolboy who had suddenly remembered his manners, and turned. 'Er . . . get well, then, Fonthill.'

'Thank you, sir.'

As the tent flap fell back, Simon mouthed the word 'bastard' and lay back on his pillow. Suddenly, he felt exhausted and realised how weak he was. The General's inquisition had taken what little strength he possessed after the passage of the fever. He knew that, whatever the worth of Colonel Lamb's friendship, the General was a ruthless man. He was as much a careerist as any politician and there was no way that Simon could rely on any indulgence from him. Lord, there had even been an intimation of disapproval that he had not led his team to certain death in the Residency! How worldly was this man who had led all his soldiering life in colonial India?

Simon studied the canvas above him and explored again the dressing beneath his coarse cotton nightshirt. Could he be fit to sit a horse again within a week? One thing was certain: he would *not* be dismissed back to India; jettisoned as a lightweight who had failed in his first mission; dumped back into the stiflingly structured world of army base camps. No. He clenched his teeth. He *would* ride within a week.

'There's no way you can do that, sonny,' said Dr Knox, when Simon told him. 'You'll no' get your strength back in time. Just possibly two weeks but not seven days. And if you do, which you won't, you'll have to ride wearin' a wee nappy.'

'Right, Mother,' sighed Simon. 'Let's start by changing this damned dressing down here.'

That night he slept like a baby, and the next day, refreshed, began a regime of gentle sit-ups in his cot, followed by crawling on hands and knees and, later, slowly walking around his bed. He was helped by the fact that he carried no weight and his 'constitution of a Highland buck', and although his appetite was poor, he forced himself to eat the porridge and light curries which were brought to him. Jenkins and W.G. visited him daily, and, with the Sikh's help, Simon traced on an old Indian Survey map the rough route they had taken in their escape from Kabul. The map had been borrowed from the General's ADC, and looking at it, Simon realised the extent of Roberts's problem. The map showed little of the detail of Afghanistan, tracing only the main roads between the border and Kabul and the larger cities and towns such as Kandahar and Herat. The mountains were only shaded in and no attempt had been made to delineate the tribal regions that were so important a part of Afghanistan's geography. Roberts was about to invade like a blind man feeling his way across a road riven with potholes.

On the sixth day, Simon mounted a horse again. He promptly became dizzy and would have fallen but for Jenkins's supporting hand. He sat astride the saddle for a while and found to his relief that no pain came from beneath the dressing that still wrapped his genitalia, only the familiar dull ache. And (was it wishful thinking?) even this seemed to be receding a little now. Once the horse was urged into a walk, however, the dizziness returned and Simon had to be helped down to sit on a rock for a while, his head between his knees.

Nevertheless, he did not miss the advance. If the march had begun on the day planned for it, then Simon would have been left behind, but Roberts's commissariat still lacked its full complement of supplies for the invasion and one more precious day was granted to the sick man. It was enough. When the bugles sounded the advance at five a.m. the next morning, Simon was ready, sitting erect, if a little gingerly, astride his Balkh stallion, Jenkins and W.G. flanking him on serviceable army mounts.

Colonel Lamb cantered up. 'How're you feeling?'

'Fine, sir.'

'And how's your leg, Llewellyn?'

'Jenkins, sir, 352 Jenkins. Fine, sir. Thank you, sir.'

'Ah, yes. Of course.' Lamb pulled in his rein to curb the friskiness of his horse. 'Now look, Fonthill. You are to take it easy this first day. Stay with the column until way after we have crossed the Shutargardan. Then seek me out for orders. We shall want some keen scouting then. I shall want the three of you to move out into the hills, above the column and beyond our cavalry patrols.' He looked down the line. 'Short of bloody transport, of course. Always are. By the time we get beyond the Shutargardan we shall be strung out along this track like washing on a line.' He sniffed and eased the chin band on his helmet. 'With six thousand men on the advance there will probably be half a day's march between the head and the arse of this column. So we will be very vulnerable once we're in Afghanistan proper and they'll be at us then. We shall want plenty of eyes and ears. Right?'

'Right, sir.'

Lamb ran his eye over the three of them. They were dressed in Afghan garb, what was left of their original disguise topped with drab, loose-fitting jackets and old turbans. Simon had lost all trace of the affluent Persian merchant. Gone was his gold braid and brocaded waistcoat. A scuffed sheepskin jacket now gave him the air of a nondescript tribesman and his illness had hollowed his cheeks and heightened his cheekbones so that his face possessed a sharpness characteristic of the Pathan. The scars of the broken nose were still livid, but the end of the bone was bent down and to the left, giving it the look of a talon. Simon's whole appearance now was that of an Afghan. The Colonel grunted approvingly.

'Look the part, anyhow,' he said. 'Don't get yourself shot

by our pickets.' He pulled on the rein and cantered off, towards the head of the column.

Simon glanced at W.G. and then at Jenkins. Both were watching him keenly. He smiled. 'Don't worry, gentlemen, I'm feeling better by the minute. Let's go and invade Afghanistan.'

The three men moved forward at a gentle walk and slipped into a gap in the column. Forward and behind, the thin line seemed to stretch for ever. Far ahead, Simon could just make out the silver and blue flashes of Punjab cavalry in the van, although the rocky terrain prevented them from fanning out into a screen. Behind them he could see the white helmets, crossed pipe clay belts and dark kilts of the 72nd and 92nd Highlanders, followed by the mules of a mountain battery, its guns broken down and lashed to the animals' backs. Immediately ahead jangled two squadrons of the Royal Horse Artillery, their cannon bouncing and banging from rock to rock behind the horses. Behind Simon and his companions marched a company of Bengal sappers and miners, dark little men in nondescript uniforms, their white teeth flashing in the early morning sunlight. Behind them, swaying in ponderous rhythm, walked six elephants in single file, their *mahouts* perched behind their ears, scratching their charges' heads with their sticks.

It was cold, but there had been no rain, and dust rose from the marching feet and wagon wheels: this could be no surprise invasion. The road, such as it was, allowed only about six men to march abreast, and despite its weaponry, the column gave off an air of vulnerability as it wound its way slowly and sinuously upwards, towards the Shutargardan, along the track which Simon and Jenkins had taken just a few weeks before.

To Simon it seemed a perilously sparse force with which to conquer a country, and his mind slipped back to a similar column, which had marched into Zululand with equally high hopes less than a year ago. He sighed and, with a touch of impatience, urged his horse forward, wincing as the familiar ache accompanied the action.

Chapter 8

Simon, Jenkins and W.G. cantered along the wide road of the Kabul valley past the two villages, Chardeh and De-i-Aghan, which fringed the outskirts of the capital. Their horses and garments were covered in ochre-coloured dust and they looked more like Saharan Touregs than Pathans, for they had wound cloths around their faces to protect themselves against the fierce December wind which rampaged up the valley. Only their eyes were visible, eyes that blinked and watered from the wind and dust. Ahead of them and to their right rose the ramparts of the Sherpur cantonment, within which Roberts had been forced to withdraw with most of his small army.

At the main gate, a massive, metal-studded affair which it took two men to open and close at dawn and dusk, the Highlander sentry challenged the trio. 'Captain Fonthill, Guides, for the General,' replied Simon and was waved through without ceremony. Many and varied were the men who had ridden down from the hills to have audience with Roberts since the army had reached Kabul two months ago; these dusty strangers evoked no surprise from the sentry.

The three dismounted – Simon gingerly, the others loosely but with obvious relief – and looped their reins over a hitching post outside the General's headquarters. They were on the edge of a huge square within the walls and Simon whistled as he looked around him. The fortress of Sherpur was vast. Enclosed on three sides by a high and massive loop-holed wall and backing on to the Bimaru heights, it stood about a mile and a half outside Kabul and near to the Bala Hissar, which Roberts had had destroyed in revenge for the attack on the Residency. It seemed impregnable, yet it had a perimeter of some four and a half miles: difficult to defend with a force as small as that under Roberts's command.

The Sikh caught Simon's gaze. 'A big pavilion, lord,' he smiled. 'Perhaps too big, I am thinking.'

'Do you want us with you to see the General?' asked Jenkins. 'If you don't, I could do with a cup of tea and a lie-down, see. Four weeks on that bloody horse has rubbed me bum raw.'

Simon shook his head. 'No. Look after the horses and then report to the Guides' quarters so that I know where to find you. And . . .' he frowned, 'I know I don't have to tell you to keep what you know to yourselves.'

Jenkins's eyebrows rose. 'Look you, bach, I am not sure that I know anything. And if I did know something I wouldn't know anyone to tell it to, we've been out so long. Come on, Gracey, let's find some *char*.'

Unwinding his turban and shaking some of the dust from his half-blanket, half-cloak, Simon walked through a succession of rooms to find the General's anteroom, where an infantry subaltern regarded him with interest. 'Captain Fonthill? Ah yes, sir, we've been wondering about you. The General is out, up at the back on the heights with Colonel Lamb. He shouldn't be long, so please wait. I know he will want to see you urgently. Take a pew.'

Gratefully, Simon lowered himself on to a canvas chair. 'Any chance of a cup of *char*? I've had nothing since last night. We ran low on fodder up in the hills.'

The lieutenant's eyes widened and he smoothed his

generous moustache. 'Good lord, sir. Right ho. Straightaway. This very minute.'

Simon stretched out and looked around him. The ante-room seemed as active as an anthill. Indian clerks scurried past him carrying files and boxes; a quick-striding colour sergeant of the 67th Foot made as if to kick Simon's outstretched feet out of his way, caught Simon's eye and thought better of it; two subalterns were writing intensively, at trestle tables; and, in a corner, a *punka wallah* was pulling his cord, quite unnecessarily, for the December weather was cool enough. It was a ritual. This was an Indian army, therefore there had to be a *punka wallah*, whatever the temperature. The atmosphere within the mud walls of the room was bustling but, it seemed to Simon, somehow uneasy. More that of a beleaguered garrison than a victorious army: tense and nervous.

It was now nearly three months since Roberts had invaded. At Charasia he had outflanked and dispersed a strong force ranged against him and had entered Kabul on 8 October. Two days later, the Amir, Yakub Khan, had abdicated and Roberts found himself in command of a sullen, resentful city and of a nation which had no acknowledged leader. He had been forced to bring to Kabul the force he had left behind at the Shutargardan pass keeping open his line of communication to India. Determined to punish the men responsible for the massacre at the Residency, he had placed under arrest the Amir's main advisers and set up two councils of enquiry. While the councils deliberated, it became clear to Roberts that he could not garrison the crowded, narrow streets of Kabul itself and he had withdrawn most of his army behind the ramparts of Sherpur. There, rumours reached him of tribesmen massing in the hills and of an imminent attack. But from where, and with what force? 'Friendly' Afghans brought him intelligence that conflicted and made him suspicious about its source.

It was against this background that Simon and his two companions had been ordered to scout into the hill villages and gather what information they could. In the initial stages of the advance, Simon, with the help of W.G., had negotiated with the *maliks* of the Logar valley and procured precious grain for the column, thereby establishing a relationship of grudging respect with the General. Now they had become the eyes and ears of the army. They had been away for more than a month. It was their true testing time.

Simon was woken by a hand shaking his shoulder. 'Tea's getting cold and the General is back,' whispered the young subaltern. 'Wants to see you right away. Door behind you.'

'Right. Thanks.' Simon took a mouthful of the still-warm tea and wiped his chin with the back of his hand, so depositing another layer of dust across his mouth. He knocked on the door and strode in.

Roberts was sitting behind a trestle table, tapping its top with a riding crop. On stools to his right and left were Colonel Lamb and someone unknown to Simon, a dark, tall European, dressed in an unseasonable summer-white linen suit. The General gestured to Simon to sit in the camp chair facing the desk. 'And bring your tea,' said Lamb, with a reassuring smile.

'Right.' The General showed no affability. 'You've been away a hell of a time. Thought we'd lost you. Why didn't you report?'

Simon thought it best to put his tea down. 'Sorry, sir. We were a bit busy. There was no chance of sending you a message and, anyway, until the last couple of days there was not much *to* report.'

Lamb leaned forward. 'Ah, but you have something for us now, Fonthill?' Simon noticed that the dark civilian was regarding him with a fixed stare. The tension in the room was palpable. These men, he thought, were like blindfold pugilists, put into a ring for sport and not knowing from where the next punch would come.

'Yes, sir.' He leaned forward and pointed to the map which hung on the wall behind Roberts – a map, he noticed, with the usual white spaces revealing the poor state of British cartographical knowledge. 'You are in the middle of a pincer movement. Here,' he rose, walked behind the desk and put his finger into one of the white spaces, to the south-west of Kabul, 'Mohamed Jan is advancing from Ghazni.' He moved his finger down and across. 'From the south there is a large force advancing with the object, as far as I could learn, of seizing the range of hills extending from Charasia, here, to the Shahr-i-Darwaza heights, including the fortifications of upper Bala Hissar. And here,' he pointed to the north, 'there is a comparable force marching south to occupy the Asmai heights. Once they are all assembled, they will have you virtually surrounded and will be joined by most of the people in Kabul and surrounding villages. You will, of course, be completely outnumbered. They will then launch an attack to re-take Kabul. The advance on the three fronts seems to be co-ordinated. Since you moved in here, the Afghans have been waiting for you to do what the British have always done when they have invaded before, that is,' he coughed apologetically, 'make a few pronouncements and then leave. But you seem to be staying, so the decision has been made to attack.'

The three men gazed in silence at Simon. Eventually, the General spoke. 'How many men?'

'Don't know, sir. Probably about forty, fifty thousand

181

or so. Maybe more.' The silence continued. Simon was unsure whether it was prompted by admiration for the detail he was providing or overall disbelief. Most likely the latter. He thought it a good time to bend down and retrieve his tea.

It was the white-suited man who broke the quiet. 'Don't believe a word of it,' he said. 'My information is that the tribes are scattered and leaderless. They have lost the Amir,' his lip curled, 'not that he could ever unite them, but he was a central, focal point of resistance. Now there's no one. They're still arguing the toss among themselves about what to do next. They are disunited.'

Roberts gestured. 'This is Mr Harding. Political officer.' The hostility with which Harding regarded Simon was obvious, a case of the professional despising the upstart amateur. Simon shrugged his shoulders. It was not for him to cross swords with this slim insider. If Roberts chose to disbelieve him, so be it.

The General pursed his lips and buried his riding crop deep into his moustache. 'Do you know who is leading them, Fonthill?'

'Not in the field, no, sir. But the man who has rallied the troops, so to speak, is this mullah chap, whom I ... er ... met, you may recall. I understand that he has been stomping the hills, denouncing us from every mosque in the country.' Simon shot a glance at Harding. 'Name of Mushk-i-Alam, Mr Harding. Means Fragrance of the Universe, I understand.'

'I am aware of that, thank you.'

'Ah. Just trying to help.'

Roberts seemed unaware of the look of pure hatred that Harding directed at Simon. He spoke more to himself than the others: 'If these forces *are* converging on us here at Kabul and they amalgamate, they could be too much for us. I must go out and knock off at least one of the columns, to destabilise them and prevent them all joining up.'

'And split your already small force in the face of the enemy, sir?' Lamb interposed quietly.

'Could be the lesser of two evils,' mused Roberts.

Harding's face took on a darker hue. 'With respect, Sir Frederick, you can't take that sort of risk on the basis of this .... this ....' he gestured towards Simon, 'sort of unsubstantiated report. It certainly doesn't conform with my concept of reliable intelligence.'

Lamb turned to Simon. 'I think, Fonthill, that you had better reveal the source of this information. You will see that much hangs on it.'

Simon looked at the three men facing him: one openly and contemptuously sceptical; Lamb solicitous and almost begging his protégé to impress; the General completely expressionless but fixing Simon with a gaze that seemed to bore through him.

'We managed to extricate this from one of the mullah's right-hand men, sir,' said Simon in a matter-of-fact tone. He gestured towards his broken nose. 'He was the chap who did this to me and I remember him well. He was certainly close to the mullah. He spoke good English and seemed to be well informed.'

Roberts frowned. 'Spoke. Where is he now?'

'He's buried under a pile of stones up in the hills, sir. We shot him. At least Sergeant Jenkins did. Remarkable shot. At a range of about one hundred and twenty paces in the semi-darkness. Got him behind the right ear. I couldn't have done it.'

Before Harding or the General could respond, Lamb spoke. 'Right, Captain. The whole story. From the very beginning, please.'

'Indeed,' snorted Harding. The General remained silent, but his bright blue eyes gazed unblinkingly at Simon.

'Very well, sir,' Simon sighed. Just as he had expected, this report was not going well. 'We spent our first three weeks in the hills visiting the small villages, talking to the herdsmen. That sort of thing.'

'Do you speak Pushtu?' snapped Harding.

'A bit, but not well. W.G. ... er ... my Sikh speaks it fluently and knows the hills and the people well. But we were getting nowhere. The villagers were much too cautious. Afraid of their own people and of us. So I decided that there was nothing for it but to go back to the mullah's den, so to speak: the valley where I was taken when I was captured.'

General Roberts's eyebrows shot up. 'You went back *there*, to where they did that ... to you?' He gestured vaguely to Simon; it could have been to his nose or his genitals.

'Yes, it seemed the only thing to do. It was a risk but I was fairly sure we would find someone who would know *something*. We went in at night down a fissure in the rock wall that Jenkins remembered, though,' and Simon smiled, 'he had a problem finding it. It was pretty well protected from view and away from the entrance to the camp, which I recalled was well guarded and so almost impenetrable. But the bird had flown. Well, almost flown.' He took another sip of tea, as much to aid concentration as give refreshment. 'The camp was virtually empty – certainly the mullah had gone and, it seems, taken with him all of his men and camp followers. But this one chap had stayed behind for some reason.'

Simon stared unseeingly at the map on the wall and frowned at the recollection. 'I remembered him well so he was quite a catch. We hit him on the head and bundled him up like washing. He was a dead weight, so we couldn't carry him up the rock face. Only thing to do was to go out the main gate, so to speak. So we slung him over a mule and led him out past the guards in the dark.' He smiled at his interlocutors. 'Funny thing about guards. They're always worried about people coming in, never those going out.'

'Quite so,' observed Roberts drily. 'What happened then?'

'We found our horses, rode back to our camp, which was pretty high up, just below the snow line, and persuaded our guest to cough up.'

There was another silence, broken only by the low murmur of voices from the anteroom. Harding spoke: 'So he just . . . coughed up?'

Simon shifted slightly in his chair. 'Oh no. He needed a bit of persuasion.'

'Persuasion?'

'Yes. We lit a fire between his legs. It worked quite well.'

The General lowered his riding crop slowly. 'You did *what*, Fonthill?'

'We spread-eagled him on the ground, sir, and lit a fire between his legs. Didn't hurt him at all really, because he began singing as soon as the flames got going.'

Harding rose, his face flushed with anger. 'Sir, you are a barbarian. You don't deserve to hold Her Majesty's Commission. Apart from the disgusting, uncivilised nature of your action, it will have set back our relationship with these people by years – a relationship I have spent a lifetime building.'

Simon took another sip of tea. It was cold now. 'Oh, I don't think so, Mr Harding,' he said. 'Firstly, as I said, this man is dead now, so he can't tell his story to anyone.' He turned to the General. 'We had him tied and were going to bring him here for interrogation, but unfortunately he somehow slipped his ropes while we were asleep. Luckily Jenkins

– our best shot – was on guard and spotted him and . . . . er . . . . potted him, as I said. Buried him in a shallow grave below stones, so it's unlikely he will be found.' Simon turned back to the political officer. 'But in any case, I was under the impression that this burning business – not that *we* actually did it, mind you – was a kind of national sport here.' His smile froze and his eyes were blank. 'They did it to me, you see – properly. I still hurt.'

Harding looked puzzled. 'What . . .?'

'Never mind that,' said Roberts crisply. 'If you obtained this information under torture, which is what you did, young man, then how do we know it is genuine? A man will say anything under pain, I would have thought . . .' Momentarily, the General's glance dropped to Simon's groin and his voice tailed away, in some embarrassment.

'Not torture, General. *Threat* of torture. There is a difference.' Simon's face had now resumed an expression of sweet reasonableness. 'But I thought of that, of course. W.G., our Sikh, that is, has travelled extensively through Afghanistan, as you will remember, sir. He knew that Mohamed Jan is from Ghazni and that it was logical that he should raise forces from his home ground. So that bit seemed true. We also asked our man the composition of the various forces in terms of their tribal origins. According to W.G., it was all accurate: Kohistanis in the northern army and so on. In any case, this man – never did get his name, but I remembered that he seemed to be in the mullah's inner circle – would not have worried too much about disclosing this kind of information. He felt that the British were trapped in Kabul and could do little to stop the trap being closed around the city. In fact he boasted of it.' Simon smiled. 'Of course, he may have been exaggerating the size of the columns, but our Sikh, having recently travelled through the country with a British intelligence officer, thought not.'

Harding opened his mouth to speak, but Roberts silenced him with a wave of the riding crop. The General turned to Lamb, who had been taking notes throughout Simon's account. 'Baa-Baa,' he said. 'What do you think?'

Colonel Lamb put down his pencil. 'Harding may well be right,' he said thoughtfully. 'I can't quite see from where a leader in the field will emerge. Ayub Khan, perhaps, a relation of the old Amir, but as far as we know, he is way off to the west. On the other hand,' he squinted at Simon, 'the problem remains that we haven't yet defeated the Afghan army. Oh yes,' Lamb held up his hand as Harding began to interject, 'we've had a couple of brisk engagements which we have won hands down. But we have not taken on a full Afghan force.' He gestured. 'They're out there, scattered all over the bloody place. Itching to fight. We're here, provokin' them. They'll have a go at us. Pride dictates it. They don't need the mullah to tell 'em. They'll unite somehow and come in. I think Fonthill's picked up the true stuff. 'Pon my word, I do.'

Harding leaned forward. 'General, you have had to leave units behind to secure your lines of communication so that you have fewer than six thousand troops here. It would be unwise to leave the comparative safety of these walls. Give me a week or two to get to my informants and see what I can find out.'

Slowly, Roberts shook his head. 'Haven't got the time, Harding. No.' He took a deep breath. 'I must take the risk. There is only one way to find out if Fonthill is right; that is to presume that he is and go out and attack one of these columns at least and destroy it before they unite. I shall send MacPherson to attack the tribesmen coming from the north and put Baker across the Ghazni road to cut off the retreat of that northern column and prevent their remnants linking up with Mohamed Jan's men coming from the south-west. The rest of the force will stay here to protect Kabul. Baa-Baa, tell Martin to come in and I will draft the orders.'

As Lamb went through the door, the General turned to Simon. His blue eyes were icily cold. 'Captain Fonthill, you may well have performed a signally important service to your Queen and Country. Time will tell whether that is so. But I want to make it perfectly clear that if you indulge in any further "persuasion", as you call it, of the native people here, then you will face a court martial. Do I make myself clear?'

'Perfectly, sir.'

'Very well. You and your two men will join Brigadier MacPherson's force, which will march tomorrow.' For the first time, he seemed to notice Simon's appearance. 'Do you all have uniforms?'

'No, sir.'

Roberts looked with distaste at Simon's dusty folds. 'Very well. Probably just as well. MacPherson will want to use you as scouts, no doubt.' For the first time his face softened somewhat. 'How are your . . . injuries?'

'Getting better, I think, sir.'

'Good. That will be all.'

At the door, Simon almost collided with the young, fresh-faced subaltern, who bustled in carrying a notepad. In the anteroom, Colonel Lamb was awaiting him. They exchanged gazes for several seconds, neither speaking. Simon did not lower his eyes, but allowed one eyebrow to creep up.

'I don't quite know what to say to you, Fonthill,' said Lamb, 'which is just as well because there is no time. I have to rejoin the General. You have changed, there is no doubt about that.' Then a half-smile crept across his face, although his eyes did not share in it. 'For now, I will content myself with saying just two things: well done – and I hope to God that you are right. That's all.'

'Thank you, sir.'

Simon loped to the door and, once outside in the huge courtyard, took a deep breath. Instinctively, his hand went to his loins and he rubbed to ease the ache, then spat into the dust. 'Bastards,' he swore. He asked a guard for directions to the Guides' quarters and as he slowly walked there he asked himself once again what the hell he was doing here, in this arid, windswept country, working for an army he hated – and once again he could find no satisfactory answer. Duty? No, he had left that behind in Natal. Fear that Lamb would exercise his threat of a court martial? Well, partly, but he doubted if the little man really meant it. Love of adventure? Possibly, but – and he frowned at the thought – he had had enough of that in the last six months to last a lifetime. Perhaps, and he paused for a moment in his stride, perhaps he was still somehow trying to redeem himself in the eyes of those whom he loved and respected: his parents, Jenkins, Alice . . .? Ah, Alice. How was she getting on with Gladstone? The question brought a better humour and his gait quickened.

Reveille was at three a.m., and the column was due to march at four thirty, so it was dark and bitterly cold when the three men, muffled to the eyes again, reported to Brigadier MacPherson at four a.m. The Brigadier, a portly, comfortable-looking man with sharp eyes, looked them over keenly.

'Heard all about you,' he said to Simon. 'Want the three of you to stay together and with me. You could be damned useful. Anyway,' he pulled his red nose and then grinned, 'don't know where else to put you. So stay close.'

Simon smiled. He had no wish to become a line soldier again. The three of them walked their horses in behind the

Brigadier's brigade major and his ADC and among his signallers and mounted messengers.

The column comprised slightly fewer than seventeen hundred men. As the bugles sounded the advance, two squadrons of the 14th Bengal Lancers jingled out ahead of the column and fanned out as the vanguard. Jenkins nudged Simon: 'Look you, bach. They're just like chocolate soldiers.'

And indeed they were. The Lancers were wearing their parade ground best: dark blue jackets and white buckskin breeches thrust into highly polished knee-high riding boots. Scarlet sashes adorned their waists under white pipe-clay belts that also criss-crossed their chests. The Lancers had fine beards and wore tightly bound turbans decorated with bright cotton thread. Each carried a high lance. It could have been the Queen's birthday parade at Delhi.

'It's for effect,' murmured Simon. 'A bit of pomp to show who's boss.'

'Indeed, lord,' nodded W.G. 'It is right that whoever opens the batting should be absolutely bloody dressed well. It is good for morale and all that sort of thing, you know.'

The rest of the force was less grand but, even so, it was clear that the column had been put together for business, not for show. Behind the Lancers marched four hundred rifles of the 67th Foot; then came four cannon of the Royal Horse Artillery and four smaller guns of a mountain battery, broken down and strapped to mules; followed by five hundred and nine rifles of the 3rd Sikhs, not quite as splendid as the Lancers but earning an approving nod from W.G.; three hundred and ninety-three men of the 5th Gurkhas, quick-stepping and smiling in the dark cold; and, finally, a squadron of the 9th Lancers. It was a column lacking only engineers to give it independence, but unburdened by heavy wagons or elephants: it was a quick-moving, manoeuvrable force, containing some of the best troops under Roberts's command. Yet, wondered Simon, was it strong enough to take on a full Afghan army in the field? And could Roberts afford to spare it from the thinly defended walls of Sherpur?

The column halted at eight a.m. for a quick breakfast. MacPherson, cradling a mug of tea in his cold hands, called Simon over. 'Right,' he said. 'We've not gone far, but if your story is true about millions of Pathans on the march from the north, we should have seen or heard something by now. Get out there,' he gestured with his mug to the head of the column, 'with your two ruffians. Get out beyond the screen of Lancers – this is no country for cavalry anyway – and find us your army. We will be doing little more marching today. The General wants me to wait at Kila Aushar,' he gestured towards a small collection of mud roofs that could be seen about a mile to the right, 'probably overnight to give Baker time to wheel his cavalry round on the Ghazni road to the west.' The Brigadier eased his considerable bulk in the saddle and his eyes twinkled in his round red face. 'Find us some sport, Fonthill, there's a good chap.'

'We'll do our best, sir.'

The three rode through the Lancers and then split into a trident formation: Jenkins to the right, Simon in the middle and W.G. to the left, spreading about three quarters of a mile. The country was broken and difficult for horsemen. Terraced for irrigation and fissured by *nullas*, it was studded with rocks and scrub. Although the route north lay through a valley of sorts, it undulated so that visibility for any distance was poor, and it proved difficult for Jenkins and W.G. on the flanks to keep Simon in view at all times. The cold of the winter morning soon gave way to midday warmth, which beat back from the boulders and slabs of rock and made perspiration run down from the riders' turbans into their eyes, stinging and making constant vigilance difficult.

It was a tiring, fruitless day and the three rode back into Kila Aushar despondently just before dusk. Ravens and eagles were all they had seen, and for the first time, Simon began to doubt the information they had drawn from the mullah's henchman. Had he been boasting? It would have been in character.

The Brigadier, however, was surprisingly reassuring. 'No,' he said. 'I feel in me water that you're on to something. Baker will be in position to the west probably soon after sun-up. So get you out well before dawn and flush the bastards out. I have to wait here for further orders.'

The next day they had put about ten miles behind them, picking their way cautiously to the top of each rise, before, to the right, Jenkins caught Simon's eye by waving a hand-kerchief from the muzzle of his rifle. Simon signalled to W.G. and rode to the Welshman.

'There they are, look you,' said Jenkins. Together they crawled to the top of a gentle hill. At first, Simon could see only a familiar vista of rocks, shale and scrub, stretching, it seemed, for ever. Then, a flash of light far to the right caught his eye. He focused his binoculars and the flash became a silver blur as the sun bounced from a thousand lances and then drew into his vision dozens of swirling banners. As he watched, small figures slowly moved over the hill and disap-peared from sight into the declivity below. But they kept on coming and coming.

'God,' whispered Simon. 'It must be the whole damned Afghan army.'

'Not quite, lord.' W.G. had noiselessly joined them and was squinting from under a shielding palm. 'Probably no more than ten thousand. Look.' He pointed with his other hand. 'You can see where they end, to the left, at deep long on.'

'Wish I had your eyesight, W.G.' Simon moved the glasses slightly to the left and then lowered them. 'Yes. But there's enough of them to keep MacPherson busy. Now, a body that strong will have patrols out front, between us and them, though I can see no signs of them. But we have to be careful, because they could be just a few hundred yards ahead of us now. Jenkins, you ride back to the Brigadier at Kila Aushar and—'

A look of quiet desperation came into Jenkins's eye. 'Where's she when she's at home, then?'

'It's where the Brigadier's camped. Where we slept last night. He won't have moved far, if he's moved at all. For goodness' sake, even *you* can find seventeen hundred men . . . oh, very well. W.G., you'd better go. Tell the Brig what we have seen and explain that we are shadowing the army. Wait.' Simon raised the glasses again and studied the distant ridge. 'Yes, I can see cannon, and they are marching, not just sauntering all over the place.' He turned back to the Sikh. 'Make sure the Brigadier understands that this is a well-equipped force, not a rabble. Tell him they have artillery and that they seem to be advancing on Kabul, directly towards Kila Aushar, but slowly.'

'Very well, lord.'

Jenkins watched the Sikh ride off and scowled. 'You should have let me go. I can ride better'n that.'

'Oh yes?' Simon raised his eyes heavenwards. 'And which way would you have gone? North, south, east or west? Never mind. Move out to the left – that's that way – about half a mile and watch to the front for patrols. Keep me in sight. We shall need to drop back a little every half-hour or so. Don't fire unless you have to.'

For three hours the two men observed the advancing host, retreating slowly to keep distance between them and whatever patrols were ranging out ahead of the army. Then, in the early afternoon, it became clear that the Afghans had stopped their march and were concentrating around and upon a steep, conical and isolated hill at the base of which sat a small village. Through his field glasses, Simon could just discern what seemed like earthworks being thrown up and cannon dug in. It was an admirable defensive position and, for the first time, it occurred to Simon that the Afghans knew of MacPherson's force and had decided to fight him there. Could it be a trap? He climbed a higher knoll and carefully searched the terrain to east and west, but it seemed empty. He was considering whether to risk sending Jenkins back with this latest development when a small cloud of dust to the south indicated the arrival of a troop of Lancers, led by W.G.

'Hear you've found the buggers!' The subaltern in command, the only European – and therefore the only beardless man – in the troop, was glowing with excitement. 'Well done . . . er . . . sir. I missed the show at Charasia but it looks as though I shall be in at this one. Where are they?'

Simon showed him. 'Good God,' the young man exclaimed. 'Millions of 'em. And dug in, by the looks of it. Oh, sorry. Orders for you from the Brigadier. Please will you and your men fall back to Kila Aushar – we haven't moved from the bloody hole since you left this morning – and report to him. We will stay and keep an eye on this lot.'

Ninety minutes later, Simon was giving his report to the Brigadier, who listened in silence throughout. At the end, he nodded in approval.

'Well done, Fonthill. It looks as though you've been proved to be right. Capital! We'll have a go at them first thing in the morning, unless for some unfathomable reason Bobs doesn't want me to – I have reported to him, of course.'

'Of course, sir.' Simon took a breath. 'Just a word of warning, Brigadier. It looks as though they are well positioned and waiting for you. You are, of course, outnumbered, I would think by about six to one – and they do have artillery.'

MacPherson rose languidly from his camp chair. 'So your Sikh said. But you forget, Fonthill, that our whole bloody army here in this godforsaken country is outnumbered by far more than that.' He stretched his arms above his head. 'Anyway, my job is to bring this lot to battle and beat 'em. Tomorrow I shall do that. Now get a good night's sleep.'

By four a.m. MacPherson's column was on the move, picking its way along the valley as fast as the infantry could march. Once again, Simon, Jenkins and W.G. rode with the Brigadier, who, now that the enemy had been located and battle loomed, was the soul of joviality. His orders from Roberts, he explained, were straightforward: he was to attack the Kohistanis (for so they were perceived to be) immediately and to put them to flight before they could join forces with the other formidable Afghan column that was approaching, it had now been confirmed, from the south-west. Any attempt by the remnants of the defeated Kohistani column to join up with the men from Ghazni would be foiled by Brigadier Baker's cavalry, positioned astride the Ghazni road.

'At last a chance,' he chortled to Simon, 'to beat 'em fairly and squarely in the field and then mop 'em up.'

Simon fell back slightly and exchanged glances with Jenkins. The Welshman, as always, was riding easily, looking every inch a Pathan: coal-black eyes, fierce moustache, swarthy countenance, his turban loosely wound and seeming as though it might topple at any minute. All very Afghan. Yet his legs were bent into unusually short stirrups and the width of his chest and shoulders told of an origin far from India's North West frontier. Jenkins nodded ahead.

'Looks as though we're goin' to be in another old-fashioned battle, then. Better stay close, bach.' His face was smiling but his eyes betrayed concern.

Simon frowned and turned to look at the column behind. 'No need to worry. This lot should be able to see off whatever is in front. But I agree. Stick together by all means. We'll probably be sent ahead with the skirmishers – I don't think the Brigadier will like us lowering the sartorial tone by fighting with the uniforms once the action starts. So watch your back. In this garb we're quite likely to be taken for the enemy by some young sepoy once we're out in front. Tell W.G. I'll ride on with the Brigadier.'

MacPherson had spurred ahead to join the head of the column now that they were nearing the enemy, and Simon pulled out to follow him. He was in no mood to exchange banter with Jenkins, for the riding was once again triggering that dull ache in his loins that told him he was not a whole man. Where once his mind would have been filled with apprehension about the fighting ahead, now it groaned once again with the thought that he was impotent. He was sure of that now. The days of riding in the hills had hardened his hide but not his sensitivity to the well-remembered ordeal and to what must be the result of his injuries. The pain had retreated and lost its sharpness so that he could stay in the saddle well enough, but the ache of doing so was a constant reminder of his loss. Try as he might in the privacy of his tent to conjure up exotic memories from the past, nothing stirred his reddened, scarred member. As he cantered forward to catch the Brigadier, he passed three subalterns of the 67th Foot, young men roughly his own age, sitting easily in their saddles, khaki-clad backbones as straight as rifle barrels, teeth flashing in sunburned faces as they laughed at some obscenity. They were fit and potent, without a care in the world. He cursed and spat into the dust. So Lamb thought he had changed! How little he knew!

Brigadier MacPherson at the head of the column had halted the advance and was standing in his stirrups staring at the conical-shaped hill through field glasses. As Simon quietly joined the little group surrounding the Brigadier, MacPherson swung the glasses and scoured the broken country to his left and left rear. What he saw made him lower the glasses and turn to the colonel at his elbow.

'The enemy in front is not waiting for *us*, George,' he said quietly. 'They're waiting to join up with that very considerable army that is on its way through the Paghman and Chardeh valleys there.' He nodded to his left. 'They must have got through Baker somehow.' He raised the glasses to the front again. 'If I don't send these Kohistanis flying quickly, we shall be caught between two fires.'

He lowered the glasses and turned to the colonel again. All traces of the jovial buffer had now gone and been replaced by a taut air of command – that of a professional who knew exactly what he wanted and how to get it.

'Right. You take one company of the 67th, five companies of the 3rd Sikhs and two guns and hold the ridge here to protect our rear. Arnold,' he swung to a lieutenant colonel of the Sikhs, 'go with the remainder of your Sikhs and harass the enemy's left flank. The bits of cavalry we've got will form a screen there to protect you and also threaten their line of retreat. The mountains will stop an escape to the right. I shall make a frontal attack now with what we have left.' He beckoned to a subaltern. 'Tell Morgan to advance with his guns in close order and shell that damned hill ahead as soon as he is able. Then, as we attack it, he is to direct his fire behind it to catch them as they run – as run they will.'

For the first time he noticed Simon. 'Ah, just the man. You heard all that?' Simon nodded. 'Very well. Gallop back with your two men – you may need them and your disguise if scouts from that lot on our left get behind us – and tell the General at Sherpur exactly what has happened. Explain that I have found the Kohistan army and am engaging it immediately. But tell him that I have glimpsed what I think is the advance guard of the column from Ghazni to our south-west. If all goes well I should be able to defeat this northern column and prevent the two forces joining together. Then I shall turn and face the other lot. Clear?'

'Yes, sir.'

'Good. Then bugger off. Bugler, sound the advance.'

As the clear notes of the bugle echoed from the surrounding hills, Simon spurred his horse, beckoned to Jenkins and W.G. and began the journey back down the now well-beaten trail to Kila Aushar and then Kabul.

It took three hours of hard riding to raise the familiar ramparts of Sherpur, but the journey, though difficult, was uneventful. If the Ghazni patrols were out, they had not advanced far enough to cut off the route back to the capital.

Simon found General Roberts conferring with Lamb and three other senior officers. His news was received in silence. If Roberts was disappointed to find that the two Afghan armies were near to joining, he showed little sign. He squinted at the darkening sky through his window. 'We can do nothing more tonight,' he said. 'MacPherson will have done the job by now, I am sure.' He pulled a piece of paper to him and began scribbling. 'Baa-Baa, make sure that Mac has this by just after dawn tomorrow. I want him to link up with Baker and I shall send Brigadier Massey to command the Horse Artillery and the cavalry left at Aushar and move them out to act with MacPherson in confronting Mohamed Jan. But timing is the essence. We don't want to be picked off piecemeal, we are outnumbered enough as it is. We must consolidate before we take on this Ghazni army.' He looked up at Simon, standing once again in that small, neat office, looking outlandish in his dishevelled, dusty garments.

'You were right, Fonthill, in your intelligence. You did well. I shall ride out to take command myself in the morning. I want you and your two men to ride with me. We will leave at dawn. Gentlemen, I have much to do. You will receive your own orders within the hour. Good evening.'

The early departure of Roberts's small party confirmed the imminence of the Afghanistan winter. It was bitterly cold and the breath of horses and riders rose to the dark, star-twinkling sky as the little column of some fifty men took the now familiar road to the north-east. Simon, Jenkins and W.G. took position on the left flank of the General's escort and once again muffled themselves against the keen air, even Jenkins riding slouched in contrast to the upright posture of the cavalry.

The Welshman sniffed beneath his scarf. 'I'll tell you what, bach sir. I'm gettin' a bit fed up with this bloody road. It'd be nice to see another part of this country, look you.'

Within the hour, he had his wish. A section of cavalry, their horses perspiring despite the cold, galloped in from Kila Aushar with a message from MacPherson. Roberts read it eagerly and allowed his face to crease into a half-smile. 'Good. MacPherson has broken the Kohistanis.' Then, as he read on, the smile disappeared. 'But Massey with his cavalry and guns has not linked up. Where the hell are they?' He looked to his left into the growing daylight. 'I hope to God he's not fighting Mohamed Jan on his own.' He turned in his saddle. 'Captain Fonthill.'

'Sir.'

'Can you find the Ghazni road across the country from here?'

Simon's heart sank. From the corner of his eye he saw W.G. give a brief nod of his head.

'Yes, sir.'

'Good. Gallop on. Reconnoitre the ground that way – but with care. Don't run into the Afghan cavalry. Look for Brigadier Massey's force. I have a feeling that he may have strayed to the west. If you find him, tell him to halt until I come up. On no account must he engage with the enemy on his own. I will follow as soon as I have sent messages to MacPherson and back to Sherpur. Now go quickly.'

Simon pulled a compass from beneath his coat, nodded to Jenkins and W.G., and the three set off to the west as fast as their horses could move across the broken ground. The Sikh pulled abreast of Simon. 'On this course, we should hit the road within the hour, lord,' he said. 'We should see in the dust if a column has gone that way.' Simon nodded, and the sun low behind them cast their shadows far ahead as they picked their way, galloping where they could, between the rocks and thorn scrub.

In the event, they had no need to scour the ground for tracks because they heard the sound of gunfire long before they found the Ghazni road. As they crested a small ridge, they looked down on open ground and a vista that brought a gasp of 'Blimey!' from Jenkins. Ahead of them, extending for about two miles across the plain, an unbroken line of Afghan infantry was advancing at a steady, disciplined pace, long green and white banners borne aloft and the early sunlight flashing and glinting from spears and the long, distinctive Pathan swords. On the left flank of the army a small group of Afghan cavalry was keeping pace. The mass seemed to extend back to infinity.

Facing them, no more than two hundred and fifty yards below, stood Massey's force. In comparison to the Afghan horde, it was pathetically small. He had two hundred of the 9th Lancers and forty Bengal Lancers, all dismounted, carbines at the ready. On the right, at a little distance, a mounted troop of 9th Lancers were watching the enemy's cavalry. Massey had thrown forward his four guns, which had unlimbered and were now shelling the Afghans – ineffectually in that, although it was impossible for the cannon to miss, the shells did nothing to halt the approach of the army. As each shell exploded in an eruption of flame, smoke and dust, the mass ahead simply absorbed it, like waves closing over a thrown pebble.

Simon turned to W.G., but his mouth was so dry he could only croak. 'Gallop back to the General and tell him that Brigadier Massey seems to be engaging the whole bloody army. How many would you say?'

The Sikh pulled at his beard. 'Perhaps twelve thousand, lord.'

'Nah,' said Jenkins. 'More like fifteen to twenty. That bunch o' lads down there will never stop 'em, see. Just like fartin' against thunder.'

'I agree,' said Simon. 'Get off quick, W.G., and find the General. Tell him he'll need every man he's got.'

As the big man galloped off, Jenkins turned to Simon, his eyebrows raised lugubriously. 'What about us, bach?' he asked. 'I don't fancy 'angin' about down there. Two of us are not goin' to make much difference, look you.'

Simon swallowed. 'Can't help it. We can't ride off. Come on.'

The two men dug in their heels and galloped down to join a small knot of officers grouped behind the second rank of kneeling soldiers. As they pounded down the slope, a carbine was fired at them and the officers tugged at their revolvers. Simon waved a cloth.

'Captain Fonthill and Sergeant Jenkins, Guides,' he shouted as they dismounted in a cloud of dust.

A small, bearded man, in faded blue uniform and wearing a conical pith helmet and green pugree, stepped forward. 'Good,' he said. 'You've come from MacPherson? He must be near.'

'No, sir. From Sir Frederick. MacPherson's force is at least five miles to the north-east. The General is not far behind us. He is looking for you. He had expected you to link up with Brigadier MacPherson's force by now.' Simon looked at the advancing Afghans and the gunners as they coolly reloaded and fired. 'My orders, sir, were to tell you not to engage the enemy but to fall back on MacPherson's column.'

The Brigadier puffed out his cheeks. 'That's all well and good but I couldn't find the damned column. I intend to delay the Afghans' advance as best I can.'

'But Brigadier,' Simon could hardly keep the disbelief from his voice, 'you will never stop that army with this small force. You will be engulfed . . .'

Massey slapped his breeches with his riding crop. 'I will thank you, sir, to keep your opinions to yourself. Now fall into line here and make yourself useful with your rifles.' He eyed the Afghan dress of Simon and Jenkins with disparagement. 'If you know how to shoot, that is.' He turned his back on Simon and eyed the Pathan army, the advance guard of which was now almost within rifleshot. Cupping his hands, he called: 'Limber up the guns there. Quickly now. Retire five hundred yards and recommence shelling. Colonel Cleland.'

'Sir.'

'Have your men begin volley firing as soon as the enemy is within carbine range. Four volleys from each rank in sequence. Then mount and retire to the guns.'

Simon felt a tug at his sleeve. 'Beggin' your pardon, bach sir,' said Jenkins. 'But I think that brigadier is fuckin' barmy. This is goin' to be as bad as that Zulu thing, at Ishandwinney or whatever it was. I don't want another bleedin' spear in me back. You told me we wouldn't 'ave to be in the army proper again, yet 'ere we are, standin' in line like bloomin' dummies.'

As he spoke, a native orderly came forward and took their horses to the rear. From ahead, the noise of the Afghan drums and long trumpets was becoming deafening and the long line was beginning to curl to take the little British force from sides and rear. There was an indefinable smell in the air: a combination of dust, heat, bazaar and perspiration, perhaps. He knew what it was – the fragrance of fear. The dryness in his mouth now made his tongue feel like a balloon. He was afraid, all right, but not, he reflected with gratitude, with that swooning fear which disconnected his brain and made his legs tremble. He could fight.

'Don't talk rubbish, 352,' he said. 'The Brigadier has done this before. We're all mounted. We can delay them and fall back. That's his tactics.'

Jenkins scowled and, with a thumb, deposited spit on to the foresight of his Martini-Henry for luck. But internally, Simon was far from sanguine. Fall back – yes, but to where? There was only Roberts with fifty men between them and an under-garrisoned Kabul. Unless MacPherson could bring up his column, there was no way to prevent Mohamed Jan from reaching the capital and combining with the other

Afghan forces approaching from the south. In any case, their fallback now relied upon being able to retreat faster than the Afghan infantry could advance; yet the Afghans had cavalry too, and as he watched, he saw them fan out to the right, their long curved swords sparkling in the sun, preparatory to an attack on the thin screen of Lancers which faced them.

The British six-pounders had now ceased firing and the gunners were busy limbering them up to their trains. As they saw the horses sweep round and begin to pull the guns, bouncing and rattling behind them, to the rear, the Afghans let out a great roar of derision and triumph and their van began to break into a trot. They were still out of range of the British cavalry carbines. But not of a Martini-Henry. Coolly, Jenkins nestled his cheek against the stock of his rifle and squeezed the trigger. The distance was all of eight hundred and fifty yards, but the waiting troops saw a white-robed mullah in the centre leap and fall as the bullet took him in the chest.

'Who fired that shot?' Brigadier Massey, now on horseback, was standing, purple-cheeked, in his stirrups. 'I said only volley firing,' he roared. 'Sergeant Major, put that man on a charge. Begin firing only when ordered.'

A huge Lancer warrant officer detached himself from the line and walked to Jenkins. He took out a small pad and a stub of pencil. 'Right, let's 'ave your name, you little black bugger,' he demanded.

Simon intervened. 'His name,' he said evenly, 'is Mazr Ali, rissaldar in the Punjab Light Horse. He is therefore senior to you and not a little black bugger. What's more, I am a colonel in the Royal Corps of Guides and nephew to the Commander-in-Chief, Major General Sir Frederick Roberts. If this man is put on a charge I shall see to it that both you and that arsehole of a brigadier of yours are court-martialled. Now let's get on with this war, shall we?'

The sergeant major looked down into Simon's thin face, with its hooked nose and burning eyes. He licked the end of his pencil and smiled. 'Very good, sir,' he said. 'Now 'ow would we be spellin' Mazr, then?'

Before Simon could reply, the command of 'Front rank aim, front rank fire!' rang out and a hundred and ten carbines roared into action. A second later a thud of hoofs from the shale behind them made all the officers whirl round. Roberts appeared on the rise, completely alone. He sat immobile for a second, taking in the scene below. He then trotted down the incline and, without expression, spoke to Massey briefly before whirling his horse round and disappearing over the crest again.

Immediately, all was action among the British cavalry. Massey barked orders, the horses were brought forward, one more volley was fired into the mass ahead and the small British force mounted and rode back up the hill and over the rise. Instinctively, Simon looked to the right, where the Afghan cavalry were now cantering towards the troop of 9th Lancers, who were outnumbered by four to one. As he watched, Roberts's own escort of forty Bengal Lancers, their lances held high, came into view from behind the ridge and trotted forward to join their British counterparts. As though on a parade ground, the combined force of fewer than a hundred men dressed their line, lowered their lances and charged at the Afghan horsemen ahead of them. Within less than ten seconds, the two forces had clashed in a storm of dust.

'I don't think we'd better stop and see the show, look you, because these fellers in the nightshirts will be at us in 'alf a minute.' Jenkins was standing next to Simon, the reins of their horses in his hand. The Welshman's face was beaming. 'I do like it, bach, when you're lyin', see. Nobody does it as well as you. But come on, Colonel Roberts, or we shall be skewered.'

The two mounted their horses. The Afghan infantry had now been launched into the attack and were only two hundred yards away. Bullets from rifles and musket balls from *jezails* thudded into the sand on the rise behind them. Simon and Jenkins dug their heels in and rode for their lives.

At the top of the rise, Simon could not resist reining in for a brief moment to look back at the cavalry clash. He saw that the Lancers had cut a great swathe through the Afghan cavalry, who were scattered in all directions. Some thirty or forty of the natives were lying on the ground and Simon counted nine or ten of the blue-coated Lancers among them. Riderless horses were prancing and galloping, and as he watched, the British troop re-formed, lowered their lances again and charged at the last group of Afghan riders still in formation, who broke and fled. Below him, however, the advance guard of the mass of infantry had reached the rise and were bounding up the slope.

'For God's sake, come on,' shouted Jenkins. Simon put his head down and galloped away.

The British troops had retreated, not directly east towards Kabul, but more to the north, and as the two men followed, Simon realised that Roberts was trying to lure the Afghan army towards MacPherson's force. Indeed, the four guns had been unlimbered and the six-pound shells began whistling over the heads of Simon and Jenkins as they galloped towards where Roberts's small force had dismounted and been deployed, once more, behind the guns.

But the route Roberts was following was taking them into ground which was much more broken and unsuitable for horses. Beyond their position, the ground was fissured by ditches and gullies leading to a small village fringed by low stone walls. Puffs of white smoke appeared from above the walls. The villagers were obviously determined to join in the fight against the foreign invader.

To Simon's left, as he and Jenkins rode back past the guns to Roberts's position, the detachment of Lancers appeared, some of them double-mounted carrying wounded, also returning to join the main force. This now numbered about three hundred men, plus the four guns, a pathetically small contingent with which to delay the advance of Mohamed Jan's army of twelve to fifteen thousand. In fact, the forward pair of guns was already in some difficulty, threatened by rifle fire from the forward line of the Afghan infantry, still advancing at a fast trot.

Simon and Jenkins dismounted near to Roberts, who was coolly watching the Afghan advance through his field glasses. He looked up. 'Glad to have you back, Fonthill,' he murmured, then: 'Massey, I feel we shall have to bring the guns back again. The enemy seems to be advancing rather quicker than I thought and our six-pounders aren't doing quite enough to stop them, I fear.' He spun on his heel and studied the village behind him. 'That's the place for 'em. Send a troop to clear out those snipers and put the guns behind those walls. Sharply now.'

A rider galloped forward to take the order, and once again the guns limbered up, with an unthinking smoothness born of hundreds of parade-ground rehearsals, as the troop of 9th Lancers who had performed so well against the Afghan cavalry cantered back to deal with the sharpshooting villagers. As before, the sight of the guns retreating brought a cry of triumph from the advancing Afghans, who broke from their loping trot into a run to attack the two ranks of riflemen ahead.

'Two volleys each rank, I think, Massey,' murmured Roberts, 'and then fall back on the guns. MacPherson should soon be here to take them in the flank and I've sent back to Sherpur for the 72nd Highlanders.'

Simon, standing close by, could not but admire the sang-froid of the little ex-quartermaster, now commanding with quiet confidence this small group of soldiers in the field. Jenkins had heard too, and he nodded to Simon in approval. 'But we've lost old Gracey,' said the Welshman, looking around. 'I suppose 'e'd say 'e was fieldin' in the deep outfield or somethin'. Funny old bugger.'

The guns swept by them with a clatter and a jingle and momentarily disappeared in a declivity in the ground, some two hundred yards away. After a brief pause, three of the carriage teams reappeared and continued their retreat towards the village, but of the fourth gun there was no sign.

'Damn,' said Roberts. 'They're probably stuck in that gully. Massey, send a troop to pull 'em out. Fonthill, go and lend a hand.'

As the volleys rang out again – showing that the Afghans were within two hundred yards or so – Simon and Jenkins grabbed their horses, mounted, and rode as fast as the terrain would let them towards the gully. In fact, it proved to be no gully but a deep, dry ditch, all of twelve feet down, at the bottom of which the team of horses was vainly endeavouring to pull up the steep slope a cannon whose wheels were buried up to the axles in sand. The team had chosen a part of the ditch where the sand was deepest and the horses could get no purchase on the slope. Two gunners were vainly trying to manhandle the gun out, while a third whipped the horses, whose hoofs kept slipping in the deep sand.

'That's useless,' cried Simon sliding off his horse. 'Unlimber, put a rein round the muzzle and we'll pull and manhandle the thing up.' If the gunners were disconcerted to be given orders by a Pathan in tones of crisp, authoritative English, they showed no sign, but set about slipping the traces from the cannon. The horses, freed of the weight of the gun, quickly scrambled up the side of the ditch and stood panting at the top. Within seconds other troopers arrived and put their shoulders to the wheels, but the gun had become even further buried in the soft sand and refused to move. Simon, straining and pushing with Jenkins at the right-hand wheel, was aware of many horsemen sliding down the gully and mounting the facing slope as the retreat continued.

A strong voice called out: 'Spike the bloody thing and leave it. The enemy are close.' Simon caught sight of the back of Brigadier Massey as he urged his horse up the steep slope.

'Who's got the spike?' shouted Simon. He caught the frightened gaze of a gunner.

'The Corporal, sir,' said one. 'He's gone.'

Simon became aware that only one artilleryman, Jenkins and he remained in the gully.

'Come on, bach,' said Jenkins. 'We're a three-man rear-guard. Let's get out of here.'

'No. We can't leave the gun to be used against us. Quick,' he turned to the gunner, 'give me your lunger.' He grabbed the long, triangular bayonet which hung at the man's belt and thrust the point into the priming hole of the cannon. Then he banged it in firmly with the butt of his rifle, and wrenched at the hilt until the point, still firmly embedded in the hole, broke off.

'Right.' Simon turned back to the gunner. 'Let's go.' But the man was standing, seemingly transfixed, and staring over Simon's shoulder. Protruding from his breast was a long throwing spear. With a sigh, he slid slowly to the ground.

Simon whirled around and heard Jenkins's rifle crack at

his side. One Afghan, with blood oozing from his stomach, his eyes wide as though questioning his fate, fell to the ground at the lip of the ditch and tumbled over. Two others then appeared and raised their *jezails* to shoot. Instinctively, Simon fired his Martini-Henry from the hip. The bullet flew wide, but the flash of the gun was enough to send both of the Afghans ducking back behind the edge of the ditch.

'Run,' shouted Jenkins. 'Along the ditch.'

The two ran for their lives along the sandy bottom of the ditch, which, luckily for them, twisted and turned so that momentarily they lost their attackers, who were uncertain as to which direction they had fled. Simon, whose light dressing under his pantaloon trousers had long since worn loose, now began to experience pain from his genitals, but he kept up with Jenkins until, rounding a bend in the gully, he crashed into the Welshman, who had pulled up short. 'Oh shit!' said Jenkins. They had rushed into the first line of the advancing Afghan infantry, which had slid down one side of the ditch and was now scrambling up the other. Immediately, black eyes turned to them.

Simon waved his rifle in the direction of the British line and a flash of dialect came back to him from those training days at Gharghara. '*Allah! Bismullah!*' he shouted. The Ghazni war cry brought an immediate response. '*Allah! Bismullah!*' And Simon and Jenkins joined the first wave of the Afghan attack, climbing up the yielding slope, over the edge of the ditch and charging towards the stone wall of the village, some two hundred yards ahead, where khaki topis could be seen, lining the parapet.

Running at Simon's side, Jenkins turned an anguished face to Simon. 'Fuck me, bach,' he puffed. 'We can't attack the British Army, can we?'

From the village, Simon heard the order: 'Volley firing.

Even numbers, first volley. Odd numbers, second. Pick your target. Take aim. F—' Immediately, he grabbed Jenkins and swung him to the ground as the volley crashed out. All around them men fell, most silently, as the bullets of the carbines and, more lethally, the soft-nosed Martini-Henry slugs crashed into their bodies, killing them instantly. Others, wounded, shrieked and crumpled, to lie moaning. Simon, one hand pressing Jenkins's back into the ground, the other still gripping his rifle, felt that awful, tongue-swelling, mouth-drying fear. He was experiencing what it was like to be on the receiving end of disciplined volley firing from the most experienced and best-trained troops in the world. It was terrifying. How could anyone have the courage to charge into that wall of fire? He pressed his cheek into a tussock of coarse grass as the order rang out: 'Odd numbers, fire,' and heard the bullets sing above his head.

He had no idea how long they lay there but he was conscious of Afghans running past him to the rear, one, indeed, treading on his back as he sprinted away from the dreadful firepower of the British behind the wall. Then the cry of 'Cease firing!' came, and Simon allowed himself to move his head very slowly towards Jenkins.

'You all right, 352?'

'Well,' replied Jenkins, almost conversational in tone but without moving an inch, 'I was just lyin' 'ere askin' myself whether the Afghanistanis give medals for brave attacks on the British Army. Do you think they do, then? And perhaps pensions, an' all?'

'Shut up. How the hell are we going to get out of this?' Very, very slowly, Simon lifted his head to look towards the British lines. At first, all he could see were the bodies of Pathans, lying in the contortions of death. Then, raising his head further, there was the wall, about a hundred and fifty yards away, lined by a row of rifle barrels pointing towards him. Where were the Afghans? With equal care, he turned to look behind him. More bodies and, just out of rifle range, the mass of the enemy infantry regrouping for another charge. As he watched, he saw that the Afghans were moving out to each flank, obviously intending to take the village from the sides and rear. They had more than enough troops to surround the small British force.

Then a cheer from the village made him turn his head again. From a break in the wall to the side, out rode an officer of the 9th Lancers, sitting as erect as his drawn sabre, the end of which rested on his right shoulder. He was followed by mounted troopers, until some hundred and fifty had assembled in a line, their lances erect. Then, to a command, their lances were lowered and they began trotting forward.

'My God,' said Simon, 'they're going to charge the whole Afghan army!'

'And right over us, look you,' said Jenkins, now staring in disbelief at the line of horsemen. 'Here they come. Heads down and pray.'

The two men, their eyes closed and cheeks pressed into the sand, dared not look at the charge, but they certainly heard it. The earth trembled as the Lancers broke into a gallop and thundered towards them. But it was far from ideal terrain for a cavalry charge. Apart from the broken nature of the ground, the Lancers had to pick their way over the dead and wounded lying in their path and the charge could not pick up the kind of speed and momentum demanded of mounted men attacking a mass of infantry. Simon and Jenkins, huddling close behind the dubious protection of two dead Afghans, put their hands over their heads and pressed into the sand and grass tussocks. They sensed rather than saw two horses leap over them, and then the thunder had passed. Turning, Simon saw the line of cavalry crash into the Afghans and disappear into the mass in a cloud of dust and flashing steel. The cannon and the carbines, of course, had stopped firing and, turning to the British position, Simon realised that the rifle muzzles and the artillery barrels had disappeared from the wall.

'Of course!' He grabbed Jenkins's jacket. 'We're retiring to avoid being surrounded. The charge was to cover the retreat.'

The two men stood and looked back at the Afghan lines. What real effect the heroic charge had had on the Afghan advance was difficult to see, but the flanking movement had stopped and the centre of the Afghan line was certainly in disarray, with men running to either side. As Simon and Jenkins watched, a number of Lancers began to re-appear and coolly trotted back towards the village. Perhaps half of the attackers seemed to have survived and they, with a number of riderless horses, began to canter back, seemingly impervious to the shots which came after them.

'Oh no!' Jenkins sat down again. 'Now we're goin' to be stuck by our own blokes.'

'No.' Simon pushed him flat. 'They won't be bothered with us. Just lie still. Then we'll run for it before the Afghans attack again.'

But there was no need. A horseman suddenly emerged from the village and made towards them; a tall, bearded man in native dress who gave a smart salute to the cavalry leader as he rode by him and then came on directly to where Simon and Jenkins lay.

'Blimey,' said Jenkins, peering at the horseman from behind the dead Pathan, 'it's dear old Gracey.'

'Sorry, lord,' said the Sikh, reining in, 'I could see where you were and what a bally predicament you were in, but was not allowed to come on to the outfield to get you till now.'

'Bless you, W.G.,' said Simon.

'The enemy are coming again, lord. I could not find horses for you, so I think you had better hang on to my stirrups and you must run if you can. The General has ordered a retreat to the gorge of Deh-i-Mazand but that is three miles back and they will not wait for you.' He looked towards the Afghans. 'These people are coming now. We must go.'

Simon's heart sank at the thought of running, but he and Jenkins hung on grimly as W.G. turned his horse and began to trot back towards the now deserted village.

They were overtaken by the survivors of the 9th Lancers' charge, who seemed to find nothing unusual in two Pathans stumbling towards the retreating troops, clinging to the stirrups of a British cavalry horse ridden by a Sikh. Staring at them, Simon realised why. They all seemed in a state of shock. Closer examination revealed that many were wounded: congealed blood on tight blue trousers showed where spear thrusts had gone home; some clasped their sides over deep knife slashes; one man slumped over the mane of his mount, one hand loosely grasping the reins, the other hanging down from an arm connected to his body only by sinew. The horses were blown, their eyes still rolling and breath steaming from their nostrils. Some had empty saddles.

They drew abreast of the officer who had led the charge. He was walking his horse and, though seemingly uninjured, he appeared to be dazed. His blood-stained sabre hung by a cord from his wrist and he stared straight ahead. Simon called to him. 'Colonel. Fonthill and Jenkins of the Guides. May we take a couple of these horses? We can't rejoin on foot.'

At first, the colonel seemed not to hear. Then he looked

down at Simon with a frown. 'What? You're what? Ah, yes. Yes. Help yourself. My poor chaps won't be wanting 'em.' He rode on unseeingly. The price paid to cover the retreat from the village had been a heavy one.

Simon, Jenkins and W.G. rode back with the Lancers to ensure that they were not fired on by the British. The three remaining guns had now resumed their cannonade and the six-pound shells whooshed overhead as the sad party rejoined the British lines. Once again General Roberts was a centre of calm. The little man was perched upon his large grey, looking at a distance like a child sitting his first thoroughbred. The gallant charge of the 9th Lancers had enabled him not only to retreat from the village in good order but also to regroup his small force and ensure that the retreat was orderly. Under his direction, the three guns retired in rotation, so that continuous fire was directed. The cavalry was re-formed and fell back slowly by alternate squadrons.

These tactics were sufficient to prevent the Afghans from making a full-scale attack, although they continued to advance in overwhelming numbers, firing as they came. On open ground, it would have been impossible for Roberts's small force to have delayed Mohamed Jan's advance on Kabul – there was still no sign of MacPherson's column – but by retreating to the gorge of Deh-i-Mazand, through which wound the Kabul road, he was luring the Afghans towards a position from which he could make a stand, for the narrowness of the defile would negate the Pathans' heavy superiority in numbers.

Roberts had noticed Simon's arrival. 'What happened to the gun, Fonthill?' he asked as he rode up.

'Couldn't get it out, sir. We were left with only three of us and the Afghans attacked. Had to spike it.'

'Damn,' said Roberts and pulled his moustache. He turned to the brigadier at his side. 'Massey, if we get a chance, we must send a team back to get it. Can't afford to lose it. Got few enough as it is. Carry on, Fonthill.'

'Sir.'

Roberts urged his horse forward, but Brigadier Massey lingered for a moment. 'Get off those damned horses,' he hissed at Simon. 'They're my Lancers' mounts.'

'Very good, sir.' Simon held the Brigadier's gaze, but made no move to obey the order.

'I said—' began Massey.

'For God's sake, Massey,' called Roberts, 'do come on. We must fall back again.'

'Coming, General,' then, to Simon, 'Get orf 'em, I said.' And he turned his horse and cantered after Roberts.

A hail of shots revealed that the Afghans were getting close again and Simon pulled on his rein and cantered towards the rear, Jenkins and W.G. behind him, but well away from the General's party.

'Let me 'ave a think for a minute, now,' said Jenkins to the Sikh, loud enough for Simon to hear. 'Already today we've pretended to be the General's nephew, been very, very rude to a warrant officer of the Lancers, changed sides and attacked the British Army, and now we've stolen two 'orses belonging to the very fancy Lancers. Do you think we will be shot, Gracey?'

'Oh, very likely, Sergeant bach.' W.G. nodded his head. 'It seems that you have had a very interesting day . . . er, isn't it?'

Ahead, Simon smiled, but only for a moment. His mind was considering Roberts's position. It was clear that the General's strategy had failed. Even if MacPherson had been able to halt the Kohistanis from the north, it was obvious that

216

Baker had not been able to link up with him – Mohamed Jan's force had been in the way. Without Baker, MacPherson had little cavalry. And without cavalry, the defeat of the Kohistanis could not be complete, for the remnants of the Afghan column could not be pursued. They would live to regroup and fight another day. As a result, the British had not been able to pick off the limbs of the Afghan army in sequence before they were able to coalesce into one mighty body. Once that body had formed, there was nothing to stop it advancing on and surrounding Kabul.

If Roberts's overall strategy had failed, however, it became clear to Simon that the General's tactics in the field that day against Jan's army were succeeding. Massey's small force, handled shrewdly by the little quartermaster, continued to fall back in good order, the three remaining guns and the carbine volleys doing just enough to stop a frontal attack by the Afghans. Nevertheless, it was a huge relief to find, when they reached the small village of Deh-i-Mazand, set amidst cliffs on either side, that the 72nd Highlanders had reached the gorge from Kabul in time and were lining the village walls and contiguous heights.

Their presence was enough to halt the Afghan force. Although they still outnumbered the British, it would have been suicide for them to have stormed the pass under the guns of the Highlanders. In addition, far to the rear could now be heard muffled gunfire. MacPherson had arrived.

Riding at the rear of the British force with Jenkins and W.G., Simon realised that Mohamed Jan, probably unsure of MacPherson's strength, was now disengaging his army and allowing the British to retreat unhindered to Kabul. The Afghan general knew they would be going nowhere. With the Afghan force from the south now nearing the heights surrounding the capital, the ring was closing. He could take his time about springing the trap.

It was after dark before Simon and his two companions entered through the archway of Sherpur. An hour and a half later, MacPherson's brigade rode in. The big gate clanged shut behind them all.

Chapter 9

Once inside Sherpur, the trio were told by Lamb to rest for a couple of days. 'There's a lot the General wants done,' he said. 'But it'll be the uniforms who will do it. You'll be needed soon enough.'

Simon could see how the situation now gave Roberts little option for manoeuvring. More or less safe within the walls, the General knew that he had insufficient men – Baker's column was still out on the plain to the north-west somewhere – to hold the city as well as the fortress, so he gave orders for the few detachments he had left patrolling the streets of Kabul itself to be withdrawn and concentrated all of his force within Sherpur. But he still retained hopes of preventing the concentration of the Afghan forces, now approaching the capital from north, west and south. Accordingly, over the next three days, he sent out troops in forays into the hills in an attempt to take and hold some of the key strategic heights. The actions were partly successful in that, in a series of brave and skilful attacks, the British were able to take most of their targets, but they were unable to hold them, so great were the numbers arrayed against them. Baker's force, fighting its way back to the citadel after having failed, by a sequence of misfortunes, to find MacPherson, took part in one of these actions. But it, too, suffered unacceptable casualties and had to limp into Sherpur. By the end of the third day Roberts was forced to

219

give up all attempts to prevent the ring closing around him. He barred the vast gateway to the fortress and decided to let the Afghans come to him there.

Two days later Lamb sent for Simon. The Colonel was perched on the edge of a chair in his small office and looked uncomfortable. Simon sensed trouble. 'Got a job for the three of you,' said the little man. 'A job – and then a bit of . . . ah . . . news for you. The job first.' He stood to join Simon, there being no other chair in the room. 'You know we're surrounded?'

Simon nodded.

'Right. Bobs wants to know when the attack is coming. Harding seems to think that it won't be until the New Year – what's it now? Twenty-first of December, or something like that. Well, Harding believes they'll sit and wait a bit – two or three weeks or so – and tempt us to make sorties. They will knock us about a bit as and when we come out and so reduce our force further before storming the walls. What do you think?'

Simon half smiled at the compliment. His opinion was being asked, as though he was an experienced frontier man. Well, he would play the part! 'Don't think so, sir. It's biting cold and the snow will be here very soon, maybe tomorrow. Mohamed Jan won't be able to keep these men sitting about in the snow, far from the comfort of their villages. He knows exactly how many men we've got, and he knows the General will be hard put to defend every yard of these walls. He won't hang about. He will come soon, is my guess.'

Lamb nodded his head. 'Agree completely. Right. Now. Bobs wants you and your men to slip out there, up to the heights somewhere, and try and pick up information as to when the attack will come. As you know, we haven't got enough men to guard the perimeter walls continually. We can't stand to all the time. Knowing roughly when they're coming will be vital. Think you can do it?'

Simon felt the room go colder. 'Well, we can try, sir. The trouble is, only our Sikh knows the language. Jenkins and I will be in trouble as soon as we open our mouths.'

'Thought about that. Cigar?'

Simon shook his head.

'I know you've got some Parsi. If you're in trouble, gabble fast in that.' Lamb waved his cigar dismissively. 'The Afghans out there are a polyglot lot. They're a mixture of the Duranis from the plains in the west and the Ghilzais from the hills, churned up with Hazaras from the central highlands, the Tajiks from around here and the Chahar Aimaks from everywhere – they're nomads. Then there are the subordinate tribes, all with their own lingo and vernacular. They will all have answered the call in the hope of getting in on the spoils if they knock us over. Half of 'em won't know what the other half is saying.'

The Colonel put his hand on Simon's shoulder. 'In other words, it sounds worse than it is. They're not a standing army. Oh, yes, yes. There is a hard core of good professionals there who are regular soldiers. But around them Mohamed Jan has gathered tribesmen from all over. They're not – what's the word – homogenous. You won't stand out. Sit, metaphorically speaking, on the edge of the campfire. Let your Sikh do the talking and the listening. Your Welshman will just have to pretend he's dumb, but you will need him if you get in a scrape.'

Simon nodded. 'I wouldn't go anywhere without him. But won't our Sikh stand out like a sore thumb? You can tell his origins at a glance.'

Lamb shook his head. 'You're forgetting that it's less than

221

thirty years since we beat the Sikh nation in the Punjab. Half of them are now in the British Army and the rest still hate us and take up arms against us whenever they can. That lot out there,' again he gestured with his cigar, 'will have plenty of Sikhs with 'em. Your chap won't seem strange. But there is one thing . . .'

'Yes?'

'You'll have to leave your Martini-Henrys behind again. They *would* stand out. And Sniders would be a risk. Afraid it will have to be *jezails*.'

'Oh lord.'

'Sorry, it can't be helped.' Lamb dropped his gaze for a moment and, untypically, addressed the floor. 'I'm also sorry that we've had to ask you to do this. I am well aware of the risk.' He looked up again. 'Trouble is, that arrogant political officer chap, Harding, has been wrong before and Bobs now can't bring himself to trust him and his native informants. Anyway, this is the sort of work you came out to do. So,' he slapped a forefinger into the palm of his hand, 'one, give us some indication of when they are going to attack us, and two, where – a full frontal or round the back from the heights. Anything else will be a bonus.'

'Very good, sir. We will leave now.'

'Ah . . . there is one other thing.' The faint air of embarrassment had returned to Lamb. 'I spoke of some news for you.'

'Sir?' Simon knew that he would not like what was coming. Lamb did not embarrass easily.

'Yes. I am being promoted to brigadier general and am taking over a brigade. Bobs has not been entirely happy with one or two of his senior men in the field, so he is making some changes.'

'Congratulations, sir.'

'Yes, well, thank you. My replacement as Chief of Staff and head of intelligence is on his way here, together with a reinforcing brigade from Gandamak – and, by the way, a gaggle of journalists from home, which none of us likes but we can do nothing about that. The brigade has got about thirteen hundred men, just what we need here. The trouble is that they are not strong enough to fight their way through to us. Bobs has ordered them up, but they won't be able to get through. We are on our own for this fight.'

'Quite, sir. And . . . er . . . may I ask who your replacement is?'

'You may, as long as you don't fly off the handle when I tell you.' Lamb pursed his lips and braced his shoulders. 'It is Lieutenant Colonel – now full Colonel – Covington, of your old regiment, the 24th Foot.'

'What!' Simon stared at the little man before him, whose back was now artificially straight as though he was about to resist a physical attack. 'Do you mean,' said Simon slowly, 'that Covington is coming here and that I shall have to report to him again?'

'I do. Can't be helped. It's the bloody Horse Guards at home.' It was the turn of Lamb to look angry. 'The army command seems to think the Indian Army can't handle trouble on its own territory. Garnet Wolseley, the Adjutant General in London, believes that we should be – "stiffened", I think is his word – by officers from British line regiments. And Covington, of course, served with him in Ashanti. So he was ordered here from South Africa, just after we left. He was given my job on his way here from Gandamak. In fairness, Roberts was happy to take him. He has the reputation of being a good staff man.'

Simon stared over Lamb's shoulder. 'I shall undertake this job, Colonel,' he said, 'but it will be the last one. On its completion, I shall resign and, somehow, find my way back to India. I refuse to serve under this man.'

'Can't do that, Fonthill. You forget that you are on active service. You can't walk out in the face of the enemy. That would be construed as cowardice. If you desert we shall find you and I will have you shot.' The little man's eyes were quite cold as he held Simon's gaze. 'You have no choice.' Then, for a moment, he relented. 'Oh for God's sake, man. You have done good work here. Don't spoil it all because of your hatred of a serving officer. I promise that Covington will be told of what you have done on the Frontier. I can't and won't promise to protect you. I shall have enough to do elsewhere. But I shall see that he understands that you are respected here. Now, push off and get on with it.'

'Sir.' Simon wheeled and left the room. He felt tired and sick. His loins, which had gone unbandaged since his return to Sherpur, now throbbed anew. The thought of impotence, which had been deliberately pushed into his subconscious during the days of action, now returned to him. Even if he survived this latest, ludicrously dangerous mission, what awaited him on his return? Persecution and constant undermining from his old enemy – and the ever-present thought that he was only half a man. It all seemed too much.

Snowflakes were falling into the compound and he strode for a while, taking in deep draughts of the teeth-achingly cold air. Along the top of the wall, sentries walked, stamping their feet and blowing on their hands. The snow had already mantled the beaten earth of the huge compound, but few footmarks had violated the gentle white. Only those who needed to be about had left the comfort of barrack room and mess. Simon could see why Roberts did not wish to have large numbers of his force standing to. There was no sign of afternoon sun, it was grey and bitterly cold. Standing and waiting on the ramparts in these conditions for an attack that showed no sign of coming was a recipe for destroying morale.

Except for the thin screen of guards atop the wall, the fortress seemed almost deserted. Simon was glad of the solitude and he walked firmly along at the base of the wall as he considered his position. After a while, he felt better. What the hell! He had defeated Covington once before and he could do it again. He turned on his heel and went to find Jenkins and W.G. He had decided against mess life with the officers of the Guides and the three of them had found a room where they could lay out their mattresses and eat. It was easy to find space in that warren of a citadel and no one seemed to miss them. They were truly irregulars.

Quickly, he told the other two of the task before them. W.G. seemed unperturbed. Nothing seemed to disturb the measured way of the big Sikh. Jenkins, however, was furious at leaving behind the modern rifles in favour of the old Afghan muskets. 'I'll not bother, look you,' he said. 'I couldn't 'it a mountain with one of them. I'll just take me penknife, see, and Gracey can take a cricket bat.'

W.G. shook his head in disagreement. 'We must look the part, Sergeant bach. No Pathan would go to war without his *jezail*. And I am thinking that they will be better than nothing if we have to shoot and run. Am I making my meaning absolutely quite—'

'Very clear,' Simon interrupted. 'Now we need some basic provisions and these bloody muskets. I want to be out of here as soon as it's dark.'

In those minutes after sunset and before the moon had risen, when the eyes found difficulty in adjusting to the darkness after the brightness of the day, the three slipped out of the defences on the far slopes below the Bimaru heights, which were contained within the overall Sherpur cantonment. Here, trenches and wire had been thrown up on the slopes of the ridge. The heights commanded the approach and it was thought that the Afghans here would be thinner on the ground, and that an attack would not be made from this quarter. It was also easier to leave across the broken ground than from the walls, but the exit remained potentially the most dangerous part of their mission. Nevertheless, although camp fires could be seen flickering only a few hundred yards below them, showing the presence of the besieging force, they were not challenged as they scrambled along a ditch, keeping away from the fires. Snow was now falling heavily and it blanketed their passage and also further restricted visibility. Simon was anxious that they should work their way round to the south-west of Sherpur, to the Asmai heights, which commanded a view of the fortress and the valley between and where he suspected that Mohamed Jan's headquarters might be situated. So, following a compass bearing, they walked through the night, all of them muffled against the cold, with W.G., as the linguist, leading.

Simon had worked out a rough strategy. They would walk – urgently, as though on a mission – round the periphery of the besieging Afghan army to establish where the main groupings were and how strong were the forces opposing Roberts. If challenged, W.G. would say that Simon, with his dumb brother, was a Persian from the Afghan border who had walked to Kabul to join Mohamed Jan in his holy crusade against the invading infidel. They were looking for his headquarters. Then, at the heart of the army, they would just have to use their eyes and W.G.'s ears to pick up what they could.

That first night they moved unmolested west and then south, through the valley below the heights. There appeared to be no established front line, or at least no fortifications. Nevertheless, they were conscious that they were in the midst of a host, for camp fires glowed through the falling snow and they exchanged gruff greetings with a series of patrols, who moved slowly and disinterestedly in the cold. It was clear that the Afghans expected no sorties from the defenders in darkness and weather like this, nor did they suspect for a moment that spies might be afoot. After stumbling for a couple of hours in the darkness, Simon realised that further progress was impossible, so the little party holed up in a copse of birch trees between the canals which criss-crossed the ground below the Asmai heights. They were near enough to a picket of cavalrymen to see their Turkoman caps and know they were from the north, yet secluded enough to avoid awkward questions. Nevertheless, Simon decided against lighting a fire, so they built a rough shelter of birch boughs, wrapped their cloaks about them, huddled together for warmth and grabbed whatever sleep they could.

The dawn took its time to arrive, for the light had to fight its way through the dark clouds that continued to deposit snow on the besieging army. When it came, it brought a shock. Peering from the edge of their rough shelter, Simon realised that, somehow, they had blundered through to the heart of the Afghan cavalry. The falling snow had concealed not only the rough sheepskin shelters under which the cavalry were sleeping, but also the noise of the Afghan ponies as they moved on their hobbles, searching for tussock grass. The snow had been their saviour, for otherwise they must have been challenged as they approached the lines.

His teeth chattering, Simon shook the others awake, his finger to his lips. 'Now we've done it,' said Jenkins, looking around at the figures who were beginning to emerge from their shelters, bringing with them precious scraps of dry wood and moss with which to light fires. 'They'll 'ave us for breakfast.'

'No,' whispered Simon. 'We must just play our roles. Is there enough dry wood under here to start a fire?' They had brought with them scraps of paper for that purpose but they would need kindling wood. A little was found within their primitive shelter – too little.

'Right,' said Simon. 'W.G., go over there and ask if they could spare a burning brand to light our fire. Also ask them if they can give us some tea – and where Mohamed Jan's headquarters are, for we need to report to him.'

The Sikh smiled. 'The Captain is taking a risk with his field placement, I am thinking, but golly, it is good we should take the game by the throat, isn't it?'

As the others affected to lay their fire, W.G. crawled out of the shelter, stretched himself and ambled over to the nearest group of cavalrymen. Neither Simon nor Jenkins could hear what passed, but, under lowered brows, they could see the Sikh talking with a short Afghan, who wore long kid riding boots and a black sheepskin cap, the fringe of which hung over his eyes and cheeks. He seemed to be in authority, for he made no effort to help his companions, who were bustling to light the fire and beginning to cook something within a large and blackened earthen pot. He gestured up behind him with his riding whip and looked across without too much interest at Simon and Jenkins. Simon inclined his head and the Afghan nodded. Then W.G. bent, picked up a couple of burning sticks from the fire, accepted the gift of a little leather pouch from one of the cooks and ambled back to his companions, blowing to keep the brands alight.

The Sikh squatted and shook the snow from the edge of his turban. Without speaking, the others helped him light the fire, and Simon poured water from his leather skin into a small kettle and set it on the flames.

'There is nothing,' said Jenkins, 'but nothing, like a nice cup of tea to start the day.'

'Keep your voice down,' hissed Simon. 'Now, W.G., what news?'

'Lord, I think that we have come out here just in time. That man is a *rissaldar* of cavalry in Afghan army. It is good that we talked to him because it means that everyone else thinks we know him and he is very important. He says that we have arrived just in time to take part in attack which will be launched at dawn tomorrow. Signal will be lighting of great bonfire by His Holiness the Mullah Mushk-i-Alam himself.'

Simon's eyes widened. 'The old man himself is *here*?'

'Ah yes, lord. He is with General Mohamed Jan up on the top of the Asmai mountain just behind us here. The bonfire will be lit up there. The rissaldar compliments you on making such long journey to fight the British.'

'That's kind of him,' said Simon. 'When you return the tea pouch, thank him and give him my hope that Allah will be with him through the fighting.'

The kettle boiled with a hiss and Jenkins emptied out the tea leaves into the kettle, added a sprig of mint from his pocket and produced three small earthenware gourds. He poured the tea and looked up at a silent Simon. 'I know just what you're thinkin', bach sir,' he whispered. 'We mustn't do it. We would be bloody barmy to go up there to this Jan chap's camp. We've got what we want to know. So let's get out of here while we're lucky. Back to the fort, tell the General, an' pick up our Victoria Crosses.'

Simon shook his head. 'We must have confirmation,' he said, half to himself. 'We can't report back just on one man's word. There has to be a reason if they've picked tomorrow morning for the attack. We must have proof. And we must try and pick up some indication of where the attack will be directed. The General can't man all of the perimeter with the troops he's got. No. We've got to go on up. Sorry, 352, but, please, do finish your tea first.'

Jenkins sniffed and sipped his tea with care, his little finger raised high in contempt. Awkwardly, the three men stretched their cramped limbs, kicked snow on to the fire and gathered their meagre belongings together. Then, scarves round their necks to protect themselves from the cold – as well as to conceal their features – they began to scramble up the slopes of the Asmai heights. It was more of a hill than a mountain, turning into a ridge that stretched for some one and a half miles west to east, before forking into two crests, like the top of a Y, which loomed over the River Kabul below. The eastern side of the ridge commanded Sherpur as well as the flat plain which fronted the western, southern and eastern walls of the fortress. The three were climbing the slopes of the longer of the two arms of the Y, and as they rose higher, Simon could see the other hills which curled round the southern and eastern aspects of the citadel: the Shahr-i-Darwaza heights and the Siahsang. It was here that Roberts had tried to establish positions during the last few days and it was from here that he had been repelled.

It was not only the cold and the altitude which took Simon's breath away, however, as the full panorama came into view. These hills and the declivities between were crawling with Afghan tribesmen. The snowfall had stopped, throwing the whole of the Kabul valley into perfect relief as the three paused for breath on an outcrop of rock and watched the Pathan army come to life below and all around them. Blue smoke coiled into the air from under a myriad cooking pots, the weak sunlight glinted from sword, spear and knife blades, and everywhere, tiny dun and white figures scurried about, starting their day. There were thousands of them, stretching into the blue morning mist, straddling the river and curving round behind Sherpur to the hidden Kohistan road behind. From their own hill, on Asmai, the noises of a stirring army were all about them: the harsh grunts of mules, the clink of harness, the hiss of food being prepared, the occasional scrape of a knife being sharpened and the muffled hum of guttural voices.

'Must be thousands and thousands,' muttered Simon, staring into the morning sun from under his hand. 'How many would you say, W.G.?'

'Between thirty and forty thousand, perhaps more, lord.'

'How many has the General got, then?' asked Jenkins.

Simon still scanned the distance. 'With the few reinforcements that came through before the Khyber road was closed, and the detachments that came in from the city,' he said, 'I would guess between six and seven thousand.'

'Right,' said Jenkins. 'That settles it. General Bobs needs us. Let's get back quick, then, and make it seven thousand and three. Even the odds, like.'

'Rubbish. Come on. Onwards and upwards.' It was as well that they recommenced their climb, for, by standing gazing, they were beginning to attract attention. As they trudged upwards, they were now forced to push their way through Mohamed Jan's infantry, who were resting in loose ranks on the terracing of the Asmai heights. Looking covertly around him, however, Simon realised that he and his companions looked indistinguishable from the multitude of loosely swathed Afghans all about them. He had long ago cultivated the long, lissom stride of the Pathan, and Jenkins's short, squat carriage was more than compensated for by his sharp coal eyes and fierce black moustache. Even W.G.'s height and distinctive, tightly bound turban were matched by those of several tall, bearded warriors they passed who might – or might not – be Sikhs. No one challenged them. The urgency with which they climbed showed to those around them that their passage had some purpose. It was enough. This was no army of movement orders and counter-signed chits. Yet, as he climbed, Simon sensed it had a dynamism and purpose of its own. There was a feeling, even this early in the morning, of suppressed excitement. Everyone, it seemed, was looking down at Sherpur. The attack must be near – but when?

As they approached the summit it became apparent that they were nearing the command centre of the Afghan army. Most of the Pathans around them now wore nondescript khaki uniforms and carried modern rifles, although not of a make Simon recognised. Were they Russian? The crest of the hill revealed a flat plateau, no more than a football pitch in area, but upon which many low tents had been pitched. Outside them, long banners flew from spears thrust into the ground. Simon felt a nudge from Jenkins. At the lip of the plateau, on the edge directly overlooking the valley and Sherpur, tribesmen were laying a huge bonfire from wood that had been piled nearby and covered by layers of sheep-skins to keep it dry.

The three men exchanged glances. The signal bonfire was being laid. Simon frowned. Today? No. It was too late. The attack would surely come just before dawn, as the cavalryman had said, before daylight gave the defenders the advantages of a clear view for firing across the open ground below the walls. So it was almost certain to be tomorrow. But where? Would Jan surprise Roberts and attack up the slopes of the Bimaru heights, behind Sherpur? This option had been discounted by Roberts and his staff, for it would be difficult for the attackers to charge the wire and the trenches up the steep hill. But there would be no walls to scale that way and it would have the advantage of being unexpected. Jan would know that the British could not defend every sector in depth.

Simon whispered to W.G., 'I think we are at the army headquarters. See if you can pick up any information about the timing of the attack and where it will be delivered. But,' he put a hand on the Sikh's sleeve, 'don't make yourself conspicuous. If questioned, say again that you have just arrived and have come to report.' Simon nodded to where a number of Afghans seemed to be collecting behind one of the tents. 'We will join that crowd there. Come to us as soon as you can. Don't hang about.'

The Sikh nodded and walked away towards where guards were stationed at the entrance to one of the larger tents, outside which flew two long white and green banners. Simon and Jenkins ambled towards the crowd, which spilled over the lip of the plateau to form a large semi-circle on a wide, flat area of ground. The crowd's attention was fixed on a black-robed figure, bent over a staff, who was haranguing them with a force that belied his elderly frame.

Simon's eyes narrowed and he felt his stomach contract, as, across the heads of the Afghans, his gaze again met that of Mushk-i-Alam, the Fragrance of the Universe. The distance was about a hundred yards. Simon drew in his breath. Could the old man see that far? Would he be recognised? He forced himself not to lower his gaze, and as the soldiers roared approval and waved their *jezails*, he nudged Jenkins and the two men followed suit. The mullah fell silent for a moment but his eyes remained fixed on Simon. Then, slowly, he turned and spoke to two attendants at his side.

'Quick,' whispered Simon. 'I've been spotted. Let's go. Don't run, but walk quickly.'

'Bloody 'ell,' said Jenkins. 'I knew it couldn't last. Tell me if I'm runnin'.'

The pair thrust their way through the edge of the crowd, which had thickened behind them as they stood, and joined a stream of Afghans, not in uniform, who were making for a copse at the far side of the plateau. Simon turned and saw W.G. deep in conversation with one of the guards at the big tent. Their eyes met and Simon nodded towards the copse and then lowered his head and lengthened his stride.

The trees proved to be but a thin screen, but a path led through and immediately plunged down towards the valley. At the edge of the trees, Simon pulled Jenkins behind a thicket. 'Take off your turban and throw it away,' he said. 'Pull out a scarf and wrap it loosely round your head, like this. It's the best we can do. They'll be looking for us in turbans.'

The destination of the tribesmen became clear as, on a patch of level ground to the right of the path, uniformed soldiers were leading the men off to huge piles of roughly bound crude ladders, some twenty feet in length. Each man shouldered a ladder and shuffled off, down the hill.

'Scaling ladders for the attack,' murmured Simon, as they fell into line.

'Oh shit,' said Jenkins. 'Don't tell me we're goin' to attack the bleedin' British Army again.'

'Voice down, for God's sake. No. But it means that it will be a frontal attack. They will only need these for the walls. And there are far too many just to make a diversion.

234

Grab one and walk on down. They will make excellent cover.'

'Bloody 'eavy, though. An' my leg's playin' up.'

The two men shuffled forward in the line and, without so much as a questioning glance, were each handed a scaling ladder. They balanced them awkwardly on their shoulders and began walking, with the rest, down into the valley below.

Simon stole a glance behind him. Up above, he saw a group of khaki-clad soldiers emerge from the trees, pause there for a moment while they looked around, and then engage in conversation. It was clear that the pursuers, if that was what they were, had no idea in which direction to continue their search. They would only have the mullah's description of Simon, and there were dozens of look-alikes all around: turbaned, slimly built Afghans, dressed in nondescript sheepskin and duffel. As Simon watched, the party of soldiers split up; some retreated back into the woods, some turned right, some left, and the residual half-dozen came down the slope just above Simon, out of his sight, to where the ladders were being issued. Then the unmistakable figure of W.G. appeared from the trees, looked down, gave an almost imperceptible nod of the head on seeing Simon and followed, at a leisurely pace.

Simon felt suddenly elated. Gone was the depression of the Sherpur compound, the sense of frustrated hatred of the army and that lurking fear of impotence. In their place sat an excitement which he did not remember experiencing before – a thrill of the sheer adventure of it all, a feeling of achievement at penetrating the enemy camp and of elation at holding the black-eyed gaze of the mullah himself, of gaining his recognition and then slipping away. The ladder that he gripped so firmly was proof, if proof were needed, that Jan would target the walls and not the entrenchments on the Bimaru heights, for he would need no ladders to attack trenches and wire. The heights constituted about forty per cent of the total perimeter of the fortress. By guarding them lightly, Roberts could concentrate most of his force on the walls to meet the main attack. If they could reach Sherpur soon after darkness they could give the General all the intelligence he needed and allow him to deploy his forces in plenty of time. *If* they could get back . . . He turned and grinned at Jenkins. *Of course they could.*

And they did. It took most of the day by the time they had wound their way through the Afghan army, heading east-north-east, between the river and one of the many canals which bisected the plain before Sherpur. There was no sign of pursuit and W.G. caught them up at the foot of the Asmai heights. He told them that he had been able to confirm that the attack would indeed take place at the next dawn, which was the last day of the Moharram, when religious exaltation among the Musselmen would be at its height and which was, therefore, a propitious time to drive out the infidels from the capital.

Simon and Jenkins held on to their scaling ladders as long as others about them were carrying theirs, so merging happily into the crowd. By late afternoon, however, when the long shadows of the mountains were spreading along the valley, the three men reached the north-eastern face of the fortress and quietly jettisoned their burdens in a ditch and turned to walk, at a distance, along this wall of Sherpur. This was the shortest of the ramparts and, just before the ground rose to become the Bimaru heights, the wall was broken and barbed-wire entanglements had been erected by the defenders to bridge the gap. Less than two hundred yards away a small hamlet called Kurja Kila threw its outbuildings close to the fortress, and Simon saw that a considerable body of Afghan troops was already massing behind the cover of the buildings. It posed a threat, he noted, to what was obviously the weakest part of the defences.

As darkness fell, the three men began to edge their way round the Bimaru heights and then turned west and began climbing to find the little hollow through which they had exited from the fortress. Once again they had to pick their way with care between the Afghan posts, but these were signposted by camp fires, which made their passage easier, and the thinness of the besieging screen confirmed to Simon that no real attack would be launched up the mountain. By six p.m. they were hissing the password to a Highland sergeant and had slipped through the wire back to safety.

Lamb was absent from the General's HQ, away on the wall somewhere, so Simon asked to see the General himself. This time he insisted that Jenkins and W.G. should report with him, although the fussy major in charge of Roberts's office raised his eyebrows.

Roberts – now promoted to Lieutenant General – was alone. He showed no surprise at Simon's quick return nor at the presence of his companions. He gestured to them to stand at ease. 'Report,' he barked.

Simon told their story.

Roberts rose from his desk and paced around the little room. 'Tomorrow at dawn, eh?' He spoke half to himself. 'Good. Don't want to wait much longer. Thought they'd come at us on Christmas Day, thinking we'd be full of Christmas pudding.' He turned to Simon. 'Tomorrow? You're sure?'

'Yes, sir. It's damned cold on the hills. There's a hell of a lot of activity out there. The scaling ladders have been distributed and it's the last day of this religious festival. It all adds up. They'll come at dawn.'

Roberts turned his blue eyes to each of them in turn. 'Right. You've all done well. I am grateful. We shall stand the whole garrison to just before dawn. Now, you've spent much of the day walking through the Afghan army. How many men has Jan got, d'yer think?'

Simon frowned. 'The three of us have been trying to calculate that. From the hilltop we felt no more than, say, forty thousand. But we all now feel that a more accurate figure would be sixty to seventy thousand, maybe more.' He turned to the others. 'Yes?'

The Sikh nodded. Jenkins could not resist contributing. 'About that, General bach,' he offered. 'Oh, sorry, sir.'

If Roberts noticed the familiarity, he did not react. It was clear that the size of the enemy army was of some concern. He turned his back on the three and slapped his calf with his ever-present riding crop. 'Where are they mainly massing?' he asked.

'It looks as though the main attack will be on the south-west wall, sir,' said Simon. 'But there is no doubt that the fault line where the wall ends on the north-east side by Kurja Kila will come under pressure. There are many troops gathering there.'

'Good. Thank you again. Now, go and get something to eat and some sleep. Brigadier Lamb is in charge of the south-west sector. From what you say he will need good shots. Change those *jezails* for Martini-Henrys – you'll get a chit outside – and join him when the attack starts. Good night.'

The three men sprang to attention and filed out of the little office and through the anteroom beyond, under the keen gaze of the officers and clerks busying themselves there. Simon obtained his weapons chit, and once outside in the cold air of the square, they relaxed.

'Well,' said Jenkins, 'I'm not sure that he seemed all that grateful for what I'd call a fair bit of spyin', like.'

W.G. pulled his beard. 'Generals, Sergeant bach,' he said, 'are not put among us to be grateful, I am thinking.'

'Absolutely,' said Simon. 'And they're not used to being called bach, either. Come on, let's get rifles and food and go to bed.'

Seven hours later, the stamp of running feet awoke Simon and told him that reveille had been called – no bugles – and the three men made quick toilets, gulped down sweet tea, grabbed their new rifles and trotted towards the south-west corner of the fortress. The sky was deep blue velvet through which bright button stars twinkled, and although no snow now fell, its promise was evident in the eye-watering coldness of the night. The breath of the garrisoning soldiers rose like steam as they doubled across the compound and began climbing the walls to take up their positions.

'Sit with yer backs to the wall an' don't show yerselves till the bugles sound,' hissed a large warrant officer. 'It's supposed to be a surprise party. Only the guard to show. Anyone sticking 'is 'ead over the top's on a fizzer right away.'

Simon found Lamb pacing the wall at the south-west corner, immediately facing the looming edge of the Asmai heights. He looked at the three men quizzically. 'Well, Fonthill my boy,' he said, with that smile which never quite reached his eyes, 'you've turned us all out. I hope you know what you're doing. We've got every man on the walls but the reserve. If they don't come we shall all have frozen balls for nothing.'

'Oh, they'll come all right, sir.' Simon looked up at the heights and pointed. 'The signal will come from just up there and,' he gazed to the east, where the first, hardly perceptible fingers of yellow light were creeping above the mountaintops, 'I should say any minute now.'

Almost as he spoke, the beacon on the edge of the longest tip of the Y of the heights above them flared into light and the valley boomed with one great universal yell as seventy thousand Afghans shrieked their relief that the waiting was over. Simon would remember the noise that followed for the rest of his life. It was an eerie, rhythmic, high-pitched sound, like many trains trundling over points, and it grew louder by the second. From Roberts's command post in the centre of the compound a bugle sounded, and the defenders sprang to their rifle ports. Simon peered into the darkness but could see nothing, although the deafening trains seemed almost upon him. Then, with delicate precision, three star shells from equidistant points along the Sherpur walls burst into life overhead, throwing a surreal orange glow over the plain below and solving the mystery. The noise was that made by thousands of slippered feet slapping on the frozen ground as the Afghan army raced towards the walls. As the star shells hung in the sky, the attackers yelled their defiance at the infidels and brandished their weapons. They were still well out of rifle range and the defenders on the walls could only stare at the multitude that poured from the blackness, into the light of the flares hanging over the valley.

Despite the cold, Simon found that beads of sweat were running down his nose and trickling into the corners of his mouth. He put his hand to his chin and found that his jaw had fallen. There were so *many* running towards the fort! From the blackness of the mountains, beyond the lit stage of the plain, more and more Afghans poured into view, hundreds upon hundreds and then thousands upon thousands of them, yelling and waving their swords, spears and banners. It seemed as though the fort must be engulfed.

Simon swallowed hard, wiped the perspiration from his brow and looked at Jenkins and W.G. Their faces were a ludicrous yellow as the shells began to sink and change colour, but they seemed quite unperturbed. The Sikh's eyes were narrowed as he estimated the range between the walls and the leading wave of attackers . . . perhaps eight hundred yards? Still too early to fire. Jenkins, sucking his moustache, was picking his nose as he surveyed the scene. Their nonchalance was reassuring and Simon realised, with relief, that he was not afraid. He cleared his throat. 'Right,' he said, nodding to three vacant rifle ports on the castellated walls – there were plenty of them – and they took up their positions, the smooth stocks of their rifles nestling against their cheeks.

'Just like old times, eh, bach?' said Jenkins, but his raised eyebrows belied the smile and there was a question behind it.

Simon smiled back. 'No, 352, it's *not* like old times. I'm fine, look you, bach.'

'Nah then.' The cool voice of a sergeant in the 67th Foot came from behind them. 'No chattin' from you black buggers. Look to your front. Pick out your target. But don't fire till you 'ear the order, or I'll 'ave yer bollocks off an' served for supper.'

'There's charmin', isn't it?' said Jenkins, pushing his trigger guard down and up to cock the rifle.

The sergeant whirled. 'Eh, wot the 'ell—' he began, but was interrupted by the shout of 'Fire!' which echoed all along the wall. Instantly the embrasures exploded with flame and the familiar smell of cordite engulfed the defenders. Simon, shooting at the very limit of his range as a marksman, had no idea if he had scored a hit, but a satisfied grunt from Jenkins at his side showed that the Welshman had killed. As the rifle smoke cleared, Simon saw that the volley had done nothing to stop the advance.

The shrill voice of a young subaltern rose above the tumult. 'Begin rapid firing,' he shouted. 'Pick your targets and look to your front at all times. Fire at will!'

Simon dug a handful of cartridges from the box beside him in the embrasure, inserted one in the slot behind the backsight, cocked the action by pushing down the trigger guard, squinted down the long barrel and fired into the mass ahead and below him. This time, he saw his man fall, as did others in the front of the running tide. It was impossible to miss, but rifle fire alone, it seemed, could do nothing to halt the attack. Roberts had no Gatling guns and he had found it impossible to mount his cannon on the high walls. His artillery sat in the compound, below the walls, waiting for an opportunity for the gates to be opened so that it could be deployed. For the moment, it was the Martini-Henry rifles of seven thousand British and Indians against the speed and courage of seventy thousand Afghans – and the problem was that those rifles, accurate and lethal as they were, could be loaded with only one cartridge at a time. It took perhaps ten seconds to fire, open the ammunition chamber, pick up and insert another bullet, cock the gun, aim and fire again – perhaps longer as the rifles heated. In that time, the Pathans could sprint some fifty yards.

The front line was now only a hundred yards from the bottom of the wall, and Simon noticed, for the first time, that the assault was being led by the khaki-clad soldiers of Mohamed Jan's regular army. Then, suddenly, the attack stopped. With impeccable discipline, and despite the fire being rained on them, the front ranks knelt, elevated their rifles – there were no *jezails* in sight – and opened up a cool fire upon the defenders at the embrasures. Jenkins drew back with a curse as a splinter of stone sprang from the castellated top of the wall and tore a wound in his cheek.

Fifteen yards to Simon's left, a private of the 67th Foot crashed to the ground, a neat blue hole beginning to seep blood from his forehead.

'Eh, this is getting' 'ot,' said Jenkins, wiping his cheek.

'Yes.' Simon fumbled in the ammunition box. 'W.G.'

The Sikh withdrew behind his castellation. 'Lord?'

'Look,' said Simon. He gestured towards the unoccupied embrasures on either side of them. 'Spread the ammunition out and the three of us will keep moving between these ten firing positions. It will unsettle their snipers. But we have to keep firing as quickly as possible, or the scaling ladders will be up.'

He risked a glance outwards and along the face of the wall. It was clear that their section was taking the main brunt of the attack, for the masses fronting the wall towards the north-east were distinctly thinner than those opposite Lamb's defenders. A bullet hit the wall just below him and pinged away. He fired, ducked, reloaded and fired again from the next embrasure. To either side of him, Jenkins and W.G. were doing the same.

Then the firing from below relented for a moment and Simon saw the ranks of Afghans part to allow scores of tribesmen – no uniforms here – to run through and lean their scaling ladders against the wall. Immediately, the firing recommenced to cover the Pathans who lined up, curved swords glistening, to mount the ladders.

'Wait until the firing stops,' shouted Simon, his back to the wall. 'Then fire down on to the ladders.'

'We'll never stop 'em all,' Jenkins shouted back. 'There's too many 'oles along 'ere without a gun at them, look you.'

'Never mind. Keep dodging one to the other. While their men are climbing the ladders the snipers can't shoot. Just fire at the leading man and he could bring down the rest.'

Immediately, the firing from below stopped again and Simon realised, with sinking heart, that the leading attackers must be near the edge of the embrasures. He pushed his rifle barrel out, only to have it seized from below by the white-turbaned Afghan at the head of the ladder. The effort of seizing the gun, however, unbalanced the man, and Simon brought up the rifle butt, hitting him in the stomach so that he fell from his perch, crashing into the men on the rungs below him and bringing down the ladder itself. Twisting, Simon shot at point-blank range the top man on the ladder to his left, and caught a glimpse of W.G., on the other side, half leaning over the wall, the shafts of a ladder in either hand, slowly toppling it backwards into the mob below.

But everywhere along the line the ladders were being climbed, and although the men on them were easy targets, the thinness of the line of defenders along the wall meant that sooner rather than later the attackers would spill on to the ramparts and overwhelm the soldiers on the top.

Simon, Jenkins and W.G. had now given up scurrying between the unoccupied embrasures and were leaning out, firing as fast as they could at the tribesmen below. It was dangerous work because the marksmen of the Afghan army had now returned to their task, regardless of the danger of hitting the leading ladder men. The flares had long since sunk to the icy ground and been extinguished and the half-light of dawn impaired the marksmanship of the Pathan riflemen, firing as they were towards the dark sky above them. Fewer of the defenders were now reeling back from the embrasures with wounds or slumping over their rifles with those fatal bullet marks in their heads. Yet the ladders remained full, and every time one crashed to the ground, another was erected. Still the tribesmen crawled upwards, striving to get close enough to swing their swords at the riflemen above, some of them doing so and pulling their adversaries through the embrasure, only to be shot by the sepoy or infantryman at the next position. It was desperately close work, with the advantage going to neither side.

Suddenly Simon heard the thud of running feet along the top of the wall and swung back from his embrasure in despair, realising that the defending line had been broken and cursing that they had forgotten to draw bayonets – vital for close-quarter work – from the armoury. But the attackers had not cleared the wall. Doubling along the parapet, revolver in hand, his pith helmet askew, was Brigadier Lamb, leading a column of sepoys from the 28th Punjab Infantry, each of whom peeled off as he reached an unmanned embrasure and immediately began firing.

'You all right, Fonthill?' the little man panted.

'Yes, sir, but you're only just in time. Another couple of minutes and I think they would have been over.'

The Brigadier leaned beyond Simon and fired his own revolver. 'Sorry about that, but Bobs wouldn't release this reserve until he was sure this was where the main pressure was. More ammo is on its way.' He turned to Jenkins, whose face was hideously bloodstained from the cut on his forehead. 'You've been hit, Llewellyn. Get down below to the first-aid post.'

Jenkins grinned through the red mask. 'Jenkins, sir, 352. Llewellyn is me brother-in-law, as it 'appens. Taller than me, see. But then everyone is, isn't it?'

'Eh? What? Ah yes, I see. Well, well done, 452. Stay if you can. We need every man.'

Simon aimed, fired and then turned quickly to Lamb. 'Is it as hot as this all along the perimeter, sir?'

'Not quite, but they are probing our weak spots. This corner is one of 'em because the wall is a bit lower here, but I know

245

we can hold them. Bobs is only committing his reserves when he has to, because we are so thinly stretched. They won't keep this up for long. They'll come in waves.' He leaned over the parapet, nearly losing his helmet. 'Thought so. Look. They're pulling back.'

A ragged cheer came from the defenders along the wall. Sure enough, the stronger light now showed the Afghans moving away, firing as they went. At the foot of the wall, and for about a hundred yards back, bodies littered the white ground, showing how effective the fire of the Martini-Henrys had been. And yet, as Simon narrowed his eyes to focus in the growing light, the retreating mass still seemed as large, as impenetrable, as when it had first attacked. To their left, along the line of the fort, continuous rifle fire could be heard, showing that the attack was unrelenting elsewhere.

'Phew.' Lamb took off his wayward helmet and wiped his face and head with a red handkerchief. 'That was hot work while it lasted. But they'll be back.' He spat on his handkerchief and walked over to Jenkins. 'Here, Lloyd.' Gently he began wiping the Welshman's face until he had revealed the wound made by the flying masonry chip. 'Ah, just a scratch. My God, we Welshmen do bleed, don't we? Eh, eh?'

For the first time in their relationship, Simon had the satisfaction of realising that Jenkins was embarrassed, as, like a mother with a grubby child, the Brigadier wiped the blood from round his eyes and cheeks. 'Very kind, sir, I'm sure,' murmured the Welshman, 'but I can manage now, see. No, I can manage all right, sir, thank you.'

'Very good, Sergeant.' The Brigadier inspected his handkerchief for a moment, sighed and pocketed it. 'Right, Fonthill.' He smiled. 'We're not out of this yet, by any means. But I must congratulate you. Your intelligence was accurate and you and your three-man army,' he nodded to include

W.G., who was leaning on his rifle at a respectful distance, 'have done extremely well. And I shall tell the General so. Now,' he leaned over and took in the bodies at the foot of the wall, 'your shooting has also been exemplary, and I feel inclined therefore to include you all in our mobile reserve. Need good shots.' The little man nodded towards the recently arrived Punjabi infantry. 'So attach yourselves to this lot. I'll tell their CO. I fancy that sooner or later we're going to have a crisis up at the north-eastern end, by Kurja Kila. No wall there. Only got bags and wire entanglements. So when they move, you join 'em. For the moment, stay here. There will be more attacks.'

He was right. There was only time for the ammunition bearers and the water *wallahs* to distribute their precious supplies to the defenders before a wailing cry and the beating of drums heralded the next wave of attack. The tactics were the same: a massed charge across the icy plain until, heedless of the heavy fire from the embrasures above, the marksmen knelt and fired in their turn, enabling more scaling ladders to be erected and the attackers to climb the walls. This time there were more ladders – but this time there were more defenders too, and the attacks were repelled more decisively than in that first, hard-fought battle in the half-light of dawn. And so it went on through the morning, with the defenders standing to at what seemed like half-hour intervals and firing until their rifles were almost too hot to touch.

By noon, it became clear that the attacks on this south-west face of the fortress were diminishing in intensity, although a strong fire was being maintained by the Afghan riflemen. At this time a young subaltern of the Punjabis came along the parapet and, hesitantly, approached Simon.

'Captain . . . er . . . Fonthill, is it, sir?'

Simon grinned. 'Yes. Sorry about our number one dress. We had to leave our dungarees at a ball in Simla.'

The lieutenant grinned back. 'My word, it becomes you, sir! Very fetching, I'd say. Anyway, our CO, Colonel Brookes, sends his compliments. We are being called to the gap in the north-east wall right away. He wonders if you would care to join us.'

The formal wording took Simon back to a more leisurely, mannered world. The young man gestured over his shoulder and Simon saw the Punjabis peeling away and doubling, heads down, along the parapet before descending to the compound below. He nodded. 'We'll be right with you.'

Touching the shoulders of Jenkins and W.G., Simon picked up his rifle, and the three followed the subaltern down the steps and joined the tail end of the Punjabis, who were marching in quick time across the vast space towards distant heavy firing. As they loped along, a strange trio in their Afghan garb behind the smartly accoutred sepoys, they could see, in the distance, a line of infantrymen crouching behind sandbags, which seemed to be the only obstacle preventing the Afghans from pouring through the gap between the end of the broken wall to the right and the mountain climbing to their left. Simon knew that the new American invention, barbed wire, had been stretched between crossed timber stakes out ahead of the bags, because he had seen it yesterday. Roberts had brought samples of the wire with him from India, under great protest from his transport officer, for the stuff was hell to coil and carry. Its use in battle was unproven, but the little ex-quartermaster had a nose for innovations and he sensed the potential worth of the wire in defensive situations. It was to be tested now. At least light cannon could be fired through it, and Roberts had placed three field guns at intervals in the gap. The noise of this artillery intensified as the Punjabis neared this corner of Sherpur.

Simon realised that the guns must be firing over open sights, for as the Punjabis ahead of him broke ranks to spread along the line, he could see that Afghan bodies were strewn ahead, extremely close to the defenders, and that some of them were hanging in grotesque postures on the wire. The bravest of the attackers, however, had pulled part of the wire fencing – which was free-standing – to one side, and it was through these gaps that the attackers had poured and were now engaged in hand-to-hand fighting with the kilted men of the 92nd Highlanders.

Despite the cold, Simon once again found himself perspiring. His mouth had gone dry, and although he lengthened his stride, his legs seemed insecure and he felt that they were trembling. Fighting from the top of the wall had been different: then there had been the advantage of height and distance from the enemy to lend protection in the fight, however illusory. The shooting was impersonal. The bullets hitting the wall all around him were a lottery; it was in the lap of the gods whether one found its target. He could do little about that. But hand-to-hand fighting was another matter altogether. The confrontation would be between spear and sword – savage, brutal weapons – and a bayonet-less rifle; it would be about ferocity and strength, and he doubted whether he possessed either. Oh God, was he going to freeze, as he had looking down that stairwell in Kabul? He stole quick glances at Jenkins and W.G. on either side of him. As usual, they showed no sign of fear, or even concern. Oh, how he envied them! Not for them this crippling imagination, this vision of sharp steel cutting through flesh, the pain . . .

'Bloody 'ell.' Jenkins interrupted the reverie. 'I'm puffed. Why didn't we join the cavalry? Them pretty boys,' he gestured to where lines of horsemen were standing by their mounts, reins in hand, ' 'aven't fired a shot in anger since Waterloo. Not exactly fair, now, is it?'

Jenkins's magnificent, typical indignation and the sight of his short legs stumping into the ground to keep pace, his turban askew, his cheeks blowing out and his moustache, as ever, bristling, brought a smile to Simon's lips, despite his fear. How could anyone be afraid with a companion like this! The indomitable, the nonpareil Jenkins. Five feet four inches of matter-of-factness, courage and strength. Once again he had come to the rescue.

The Punjabis had now broken into a run. Taking a deep breath, Simon ran forward too, leading Jenkins and the Sikh towards the gun in the centre of the line. As they neared, they saw a tableau that would remain with Simon for the rest of his life. Around the gun lay the bodies of artillerymen and kilted infantrymen. In front of it, a huge major of the Highlanders stood on a sandbag, his tam-o'-shanter askew, his kilt blood-soaked and both stockings hanging over his boots, swinging a giant claymore and hurling Gaelic oaths at the line of Afghans who hesitated before him, some attempting to dodge beneath the terrible arc of the blade to stab him, others fumbling to reload their muskets.

Simon lost his fear immediately. The three men fired simultaneously into the line and saw three Pathans fall. W.G. stooped to pick up a discarded Martini-Henry to which a bayonet was fixed and jumped into line beside the major, thrusting and parrying, his great height almost matching that of the man beside him. Of the gun crew, only an exhausted corporal was left. He was attempting to swab the heated barrel. Simon grabbed his arm. 'Tell me what to do to reload,' he shouted.

The corporal looked up wide-eyed, but nodded. If he was surprised to hear a Pathan speak in the tones of an English officer, he showed no sign. 'Shells, mate,' he said, and pointed to an ammunition box behind the limber. 'No, the others, the shrapnel.' Simon lifted a shell while the corporal opened the breech. The six-pounder slipped in easily. 'Stand away, Major – and you, W.G.,' shouted Simon.

'Watch the recoil,' screamed the corporal, and pulled the lanyard. The noise was deafening and the gun sprang back, its right wheel nearly hitting Jenkins, who was kneeling, systematically firing into the mob before him. At such close range it was impossible to miss and the shell, bursting horizontally from the barrel, which had been depressed to its lowest point, carved a dreadful swathe through the massed ranks of the Afghans before exploding on a short fuse. It was as though a fireball had bounced through a crowded street. A lane some four feet wide was opened through the attackers, and the shock of this, plus the firepower of the newly arrived Punjabis, caused the Pathans to fall back – at first slowly, and then running for the protection of the outbuildings of Kurja Kila several hundreds yards away.

'Well done.' It was a familiar voice and, turning, Simon saw that General Roberts had ridden up, astride his familiar giant grey. Behind him rattled four field artillery pieces and a squadron of the 5th Punjab Cavalry, splendid in lances and high black boots. The little man stood in his stirrups. 'Double forward and move the wire,' he shouted. 'Let the guns through. Quickly now, before they can re-form.'

' 'E must be mad,' said Jenkins, looking up at the General. ' 'E'll lose them guns if 'e sends them out there, look you. 'E's barmy.'

'What on earth is he doing?' murmured Simon. It would only take a moment for the Afghans to form up again and surge forward – he could see them behind the walls and in the street of the little hamlet, still in formidable numbers. If they attacked quickly before the guns could be deployed, they would engulf the gunners and their thin screen of cavalry. Then they would surge forward again, before the wire screen could be replaced, and they must surely break through the gap.

Their opinion was supported by the Highland major, now leaning on his sword, gasping for breath through a tobacco-stained beard. 'The wee mon's gone off his rocker,' he panted. ' 'Tis against all the rules.'

Seemingly to defy them, Roberts coolly urged his mount forward and took up a position behind the leading gun as it swung about. Looking at the little man, sitting so erect on his large horse, Simon was reminded that, as a young subaltern twenty-four years before, Frederick Roberts had won the Victoria Cross for supreme bravery in the Indian Mutiny, in hand-to-hand combat. Whatever he lacked, it was not courage.

As though on parade in Hyde Park, the gun teams unlimbered their pieces with precision and at great speed. 'Very well,' called Roberts. 'Direct your fire at those houses ahead. I want that village cleared immediately.'

The gunners then gave a demonstration of rapid fire at short range that Simon had never seen in all his years of training on manoeuvres in support of artillery. The fragile mud walls of Kurja Kila could not withstand a bombardment of this ferocity at such close range and they crumpled in dust and flame. Within minutes the whole village, save for a few houses, had been levelled. The mass of Afghan warriors who had taken refuge there seemed to have miraculously disappeared and only white-swathed bodies, lying amidst the rubble, showed that this had been a key strategic position in the Afghan plan of attack.

The General rode forward a few paces and then turned. 'Cavalry,' he called, his voice high-pitched against the background noise of the attack that continued along the front of Sherpur, 'go forward and screen the movement forward of the guns. Now, Craster.' He gestured with his riding crop to the officer in charge of the guns. 'Limber up and set up position down there on the flank of the main attack on the walls. I want you to direct a steady fire into the Afghan army. Don't worry about being exposed. The natives on this side are finished and the 5th Cavalry will protect you while you set up. Quickly now. We can turn this affair in the next ten minutes.'

As quickly as they had dismounted, the gunners limbered up and clattered forward to the turn of the wall, where they deployed once more and began to send their shells into the main body of the Afghan attackers, raking their ranks with a deadly fire.

'Good Lord, I think he's done it!' exclaimed Simon. The blood-stained patch of ground between the wire and the shattered remains of the village was now empty, except for the bodies of the dead. Simon turned. Behind him, ranging deep within the compound, stood rank upon rank of cavalry, lances couched, ready for the order to advance, pennants fluttering in the cool midday breeze which had sprung up. 'He's planned it all, the clever bastard,' said Simon to the Highlander.

'Aye, I think yer right, mon,' replied the giant, wiping the edge of his blade on his kilt. He looked at Simon through narrowed eyes. 'I dinna ken who you are, dressed up like a savage. But I'm grateful for your intervention back then. It was a wee bit awkward for the minute. Nevertheless, if you are British, then you shouldna be calling a British lieutenant general a bastard, even if he is an Englishman.'

'Sorry, Major,' said Simon. He turned to Jenkins and W.G. 'Come on, you two. We've got to see this.'

Simon felt as though a huge weight had been lifted from his mind. Whatever the cause of his exhilaration – relief that his fear had been banished, satisfaction that he had played his part in repelling the enemy, or just excitement that the battle was swinging their way at last – he knew that he was happy: happier than he had been since entering Afghanistan so long ago. He bounded up the broken wall of the fortress, the others behind him. On the ramparts they ran until they came to the south-facing wall, the longest part of the perimeter, where the attack had ebbed and flowed for five hours or more. Now, however, the Afghans could be seen in full retreat, streaming across the plain, back towards the slopes of the mountains, the four guns still sending crimson-tinged eruptions of earth and stones among them. The sepoys on the battlements cheered derisively and sent a scattering of parting shots after the retreating army. Then a bugle sounded, and around the corner of the fortress, in perfect order, trotted the squadrons of cavalry. The trot became a canter, the canter a gallop and, lances now lowered, the horsemen fanned out across the plain. There were about a thousand yards to be covered before the retreating Afghans could reach the comparative sanctuary of the canals and the banks of the river, so it was ideal territory for pursuing cavalry. The tide of the battle had been turned completely and no broken army – particularly one without formal training – could stand against the lances of trained hussars. Under the eyes of the watchers on the wall, several bands of extremely brave men tried, but they were stuck on the lances like pigs or slashed down by the heavy sabres. The retreat of the Afghans had become a rout.

The three men on the rampart fell silent. W.G. was the first to speak.

'That, lord,' he said, 'will surely be a revenge for the

cowardly attack on the Residency. I am thinking that the match is over now.'

'Yes, Gracey,' agreed Jenkins, 'I'd say that that's a battle well and truly won.'

Slowly, Simon nodded. His eyes followed the horsemen disappearing towards the foothills, now mercifully too far away for the details of the slaughter to be apparent. 'Aye,' he said, 'the General has had his wish. At last, without a doubt, he has beaten a full Afghan army in the field.' He turned away. But all his exhilaration had ebbed away. He just felt tired, tired, and somehow sad.

Chapter 10

The relieving column under Brigadier Gough had fought its way towards Kabul through to the defended staging post at Lataband, but there, threatened with tribesmen on all sides, it had been forced to wait and to replenish its supplies, which had been sorely reduced on the journey from the Frontier. As the brigade sat and licked its wounds, it could hear, from the direction of Kabul, the sound of musketry and, later, the deeper boom of cannon. Hearing the far-off noise of battle and not being able to thrust through to help determine the result was frustrating for everyone in the column, but for none more so than Alice Griffith. She suspected that not all of the small band of journalists with the column shared her sense of frustration at not being able to press ahead to take part in the relief of Kabul and to file back to London the story this would make. Some of them, she believed, would far rather write at a safe distance of the horror and dangers of battle. But from this charge, of course, she excluded John Campbell.

She looked across at him now as she sat warming her hands at a pathetic fire of damp brushwood and dried animal dung set between their tents. His head was down as he scribbled in his notebook and she noted again, with approval, the way that the cold, wintry sun brought out the highlights in his sun-bleached hair and the grace with which he sprawled on his top-coat, one jack-booted leg curled under the other. Her gaze travelled to their other companion around the camp fire, the very different but no less elegant figure of Colonel Ralph Covington, the newly awarded insignia of a Commander of the Bath glowing on his breast as he lounged back on his campaign chair, eyes half closed, his head back, a thin spiral of cigarette smoke drifting into the cold air. This was their sixteenth day on the trail since leaving India, but Covington's boots glistened as though he was on parade and his brown face, so carefully shaved around his long side-whiskers and full moustaches, glowed with health and self-confidence.

Alice's gaze travelled back again to Campbell. Two ardent admirers: the boy-man and the mature man. Each caring and attentive in his own, very different way. Each had declared his love. Each detested the other. Each, she sighed, so damned attractive!

Covington caught her eye. 'Well, whatever Gough decides,' he said, flicking cigarette ash, 'I'm damned if I'm going to wait around here much longer. If I had had my way, we would have fought through to Kabul by now and lent Roberts a hand. If we don't move on this afternoon, I shall take a platoon and go through on my own.' It had become clear for some days now that despite Covington's delight at being thrown together with Alice on this march – as a relieving officer, he had few duties to perform with the column, and was free to ride with the journalists – he was becoming increasingly restive at having so little to do.

Campbell looked up and smiled. 'If you have a platoon, you won't be on your own, will you, Colonel?'

'Don't be a pedant, Campbell.' Covington turned to Alice. '*You* know what I mean.'

'Of course,' said Alice. 'But you forget, precision of language is important in our trade. Anyway, if Roberts and the garrison are still fighting, one platoon won't help him much. If he is not, you will be killed and will have done no one any good. Besides which, if Gough and his brigade can't get through, I don't see how a platoon can.'

Covington snorted. 'Go over the hills, off the track, go fast. I could do it.'

Alice regarded him silently. Yes, she thought, you probably could. He was a handsome man, this soldier who had, with her compliance, removed her virginity so deftly and satisfyingly a year ago in Zululand. She tingled again at the memory. Alice had decided years before that she would have no hesitation in losing her virginity when the occasion was right and the man was acceptable. She would not demand love. For her, maidenhood had been a matter of, well, irritation, a state which would have to be left behind sooner or later – so why not sooner? She had no patience with the conventional view that she should preserve herself, in some kind of physical and intellectual aspic, until she entered into marital servitude with 'the right man'. Sexual intercourse was, obviously, interesting, to say the least. It should be experienced and got out of the way, and even indulged in again later, not flagrantly, but under appropriate circumstances.

Looking at Covington now, Alice thought he seemed even taller than his six foot two inches as he thrust in his heels and pushed back the chair, so that his head hung down over the canvas back rest. At forty, he was beginning to show a touch of corpulence, but his height and energy carried that well enough and he was always, always well dressed, even here in the dust and discomfort of Afghanistan. The air of command, of certainty, never left him, and Alice liked that. She admired men who took life by the scruff and fashioned it for themselves. There were plenty of officers of senior rank in the Indian Army who had never married, who had never, for one reason or another, stood a chance of selecting from the breathless girls of the 'fishing fleet' that came out annually on the P & O steamers. But Covington was British Army, home-based, and it was unusual, then, to find him still unmarried at his age and with his charm. She liked that, too. A man of discrimination. Covington had proposed to her in South Africa, and it was a tribute to his attraction that she had hesitated before declining, explaining that she wished to pursue her career and had no intention of marrying anyone – or at least not yet. 'Then I shall wait,' he had replied.

Campbell's proposal, on the other hand, had been diffident and rather unexpected. They had travelled together from Bombay. Campbell had sailed by an earlier steamer, but had been forced to wait in the port while some confusion about his accreditation to the army was cleared up. He and Alice, therefore, had travelled north together to the frontier, sharing a railway compartment, talking all the way and delighting in the colour and contrasts of this new country. The honesty and directness which had first intrigued her in Edinburgh, his professionalism (he had filed fascinating feature pieces from various stages of the journey, where Alice could see little to write about) and his youthful enthusiasm about everything had impressed her. And he had that delightful crooked smile! Alice knew she was attracted to him and had idly toyed with the thought of how she would react if he propositioned her.

But no such approach came. Instead, while they were waiting in Kohat for the other four members of the press party to join them before moving into Afghanistan, he had seized her hand, in the middle of the bazaar, and said, 'I love you very much. I know what the answer will be, but I must ask you: will you marry me?' He had taken her gentle but quick refusal well – because, he said, he had expected it – but Alice had experienced an immediate wave of remorse as she looked into his earnest blue eyes. That evening, for the first time, she doubted if she was right to dedicate herself so completely to her exacting profession. She knew she had an intellect the equal of if not better than most men, but did she *have* to sacrifice her womanly instincts, her awkwardly strong sensuality, for its sake? The answer came in the morning, when the others arrived and they joined Gough's brigade and began the ride towards the Frontier. The dust, the jingle of harness and the smell of cavalry leather brought an excitement that could not be matched by the chintz of a nursery. Nevertheless, she astonished and delighted Campbell by kissing him warmly the next evening.

Covington had joined the column shortly after it had crossed the Frontier, and he had slightly disconcerted Alice by riding with her and Campbell every day, when his duties allowed it. Nothing was said, but the two men quickly sensed that they were rivals and there had been an air of competition between them ever since. Now, they all waited, as though in suspended time, while the battle some fifteen miles away was being waged.

Gough had had to fight his way through to Lataband because, as he was fond of telling everyone, 'the whole country's up'. But his force was too strong to be confronted directly and the enemy had contented itself with regular sniping and the occasional night raid on the baggage train and rearguard. Several times horses had been stolen and parties had to be detached to recover them. As a result, the brigade's progress had been slow and it had run so low on provisions that, before the telegraph link had been severed, Gough had been forced to ask Roberts to send supplies forward to Lataband for him. Once in the post, while the quartermaster restocked and the column listened to the distant gunfire, the local sniping had died away, and the Brigadier sensed that the tribesmen harassing him might have with-drawn. Accordingly he had sent a patrol forward to probe the extent of the enemy's presence on the last lap to Kabul. It was for the return of this patrol that they now all waited.

It was Covington who brought the good news. Tired of sprawling before Alice's meagre fire, he had strolled forward to the edge of the camp, where he could view the road to Kabul. Standing by a sentry, he shielded his eyes from the glare of the setting sun and squinted down the track. Then he spun on his heel and strode – he never ran – towards Gough's tent. 'They're back,' he said. 'And they've got a messenger from Roberts with them.'

That evening the little outpost, swollen by the relieving force, celebrated the successful defence of Kabul and the rout of the Afghan army. It was too late for the brigade to advance to the capital and so the officers' mess broke open the champagne and toasted the defenders.

'Only Roberts could have done it,' exulted Gough, an Indian Army man.

'Oh, I don't know,' murmured Covington, gently sweeping upwards the end of his moustache with a forefinger. 'Wolseley could have seen 'em orf equally well.'

The story of the defence had been brought by a captain of the Guides, and after dinner Covington made it his business to befriend the officer, plying him with champagne, then port and brandy – the column's advance had also been slowed somewhat by the need to transport essential elements of comfort – and encouraging him to talk freely about all that had transpired in Kabul since the General had fought his way in, nearly three months before. Covington was to be Chief of Staff *and* head of intelligence, and he always felt happier, when taking up a new position, to discover as much as he could about the background to the situation. Gossip about events and personalities, he maintained, was as important as the facts delivered to him from formal briefings. After all, it was all intelligence.

So it was that he was able to give Alice news of Simon, as they rode together on the advance the next morning. He did so with studied nonchalance – and more than a little concealed pleasure.

'Ah, you remember your little friend Fonthill . . .?'

'What?' Alice twisted in the saddle. The mention of his name made her realise, with a small pang of guilt, that she had thought little of him in recent months. There had been so much to do and so many new sensations and experiences to absorb, not least emotionally, that he had slowly but irrevocably fallen from her thoughts. *Of course!* Simon had come out to do some sort of intelligence work. He would now be under Covington's command again. How awful for him! Her guilt made her stammer out the questions without thought. 'Simon Fonthill?' she asked. 'Is he here? In Kabul? Is he all right?' She cursed herself for sounding like a schoolgirl.

Campbell, riding as usual on her left, as Covington rode on her right, turned interestedly. This name was new to him. Alice sounded concerned.

'Now, Alice, do calm yourself,' murmured Covington, looking straight ahead but with a faint smile on his lips. 'As far as I know he is all right, and indeed, it sounds as though he has been quite busy. But, inevitably, he has made a bit of a fool of himself. To be expected, of course.'

Alice regained her composure and turned to Campbell. 'We speak of a family friend of mine, from the border country, back home.' She smiled. Although she addressed Campbell, she was speaking as much to Covington. 'We were almost brother and sister at one time, but I have not seen him for months. I had forgotten he was here.' She turned to Covington. 'What do you mean, made a fool of himself?'

'Ah yes. Well. It seems that he was in Kabul when the Residency was burned. Of course, he took no part in the defence.' He looked across at Campbell. 'This young man earned a reputation in South Africa for not *quite* being wherever the action was, you understand. In fact—'

Alice interrupted. 'That is most unfair. You know very well—'

Covington held up his hand. 'Yes, yes, yes. Very well. We won't go into all that again. Anyway, he observed the fall of the Residency from, it seems, the besieging crowd, and then escaped, only to fall into the hands of this mullah chap who has raised the whole accursed country against us.' The Colonel eased himself in the saddle and smoothed his moustaches. 'Then, would you believe, he was put through the wringer by some Pathan woman or other – only Fonthill could be tortured by a woman, don't you know—'

'Tortured?' Alice put her hand to her mouth. The thought of Simon, shy, sensitive Simon, being tortured was horrific.

'Well, so *he* says. Nobody else saw it, except his man, some ranker chap – a wild Welshman – who is always with him and is alleged to have seen something messy and interrupted it.'

Ah, thought Alice, the splendid Jenkins, 352. It would have been all right if he was there.

'Anyway, it's significant that he seems perfectly all right now.' Covington enveloped them both in a wide smile of mock surprise. 'A magical recovery you might say, except that he claims to be impotent, it seems. Though – saving your presence, my dear Alice – how he has had the chance to prove or disprove that in these damned mountains, I really wouldn't know. If you ask me, this young man was using his imagination again.'

Alice frowned. 'Impotent. Impotent? What do you mean? What did they do to him?'

For the first time Covington looked slightly uncomfortable. 'Look,' he said, fixing his gaze firmly ahead again, 'I don't know the details, but I am sure the whole thing is another cock-and-bull story, invented by Fonthill to excuse the fact that, once again, he wasn't doing his duty. Anyway, it will be, ah, interesting to have him in my command again. Now, if you will excuse me, I feel I should ride with Gough for a while. As a courtesy, you understand.' He raised a languid hand to his pillbox hat, kicked his heels into his horse's flanks, and cantered ahead.

'What on earth was all that about?' asked Campbell.

Alice pulled her wide-brimmed hat more firmly on to her head and thrust her jaw forward. 'Oh, it doesn't matter, Johnny. It doesn't matter.'

As the column moved down on to the plain beside the river, leading to Kabul, it passed between burning villages where Roberts's cavalry had put homes to the torch, partly in revenge for the assault on the fort and partly to ensure that no cover would be provided for further attacks. Alice wrinkled her nose in disgust as the smoke spiralled upwards to the cold blue sky, and reflected, once again, that this invasion by the British Army seemed a deliberately brutal act of revenge, a punitive expedition on a grander scale than ever before. She stole a glance at Campbell, who was looking around him with ingenuous interest. He seemed to keep an open mind on these things – indeed, he had always argued that it was wrong for a journalist to take sides: it put pressure on accurate reporting. Alice had now learned to keep her opinions to herself, particularly when in the presence of the army and, for that matter, of the other members of the press corps with the column. Nevertheless, she looked away in disgust as the brigade picked its way towards the fortress, between the burial parties who were disposing of the human detritus left by yesterday's battle. She rode in silence through the massive archway of Sherpur.

The arrival of a relieving column that had, in the event, nowhere to relieve was something of an anti-climax to the garrison, which had already celebrated the defeat of the Afghan army. Nevertheless, Roberts set about 'tidying up', as he put it, with characteristic energy. He re-opened communications with India, re-laying the telegraph and occupying key defensive positions along the route; a military governor of Kabul was re-established; all walled enclosures within a thousand yards of the cantonment were razed to the ground; roads fit for guns were made all around the outside walls; and two bridges, strong enough to take artillery, were thrown across the Kabul river. More ambitiously, towers were built on the Shahr-i-Darwaza range, and three forts were established: on the Asmai heights; on the south-west point of Siah Sang, which commanded the Bala Hissar and the city; and on the river crossing. The Bala Hissar itself was partly reconstructed to provide accommodation for Brigadier Gough's arrivals and to give a continuous line of fire.

Roberts had won his battle, but he was also determined to show that he had won the war and that there could never be another uprising in the capital. He turned his attention to the peace, however, as well. He issued a proclamation to the people of Kabul and surrounding territory, announcing that 'at the instigation of some seditious men, the ignorant people, generally not considering the result, raised a rebellion. Now many of the insurgents have received their reward and, as subjects are a trust from God, the British Government, which is just and merciful, as well as strong, has forgiven their guilt.' All those who came in without delay, continued the proclamation, would be pardoned, excepting only Mohamed Jan and . . . here Roberts listed a number of leading Afghans whom he suspected of being involved in the insurrection. The aim, of course, was to rebuild the commerce of the city and to restore some sort of stability to the capital.

The proclamation worked. Slowly at first, and then more quickly, families who had fled from the fighting came down from the surrounding hills and the streets of Kabul began to throng again. But Roberts also had an agenda of revenge. The British Empire could not be seen by the world to have shrugged off the violation of its Residency in Kabul, and the General reinstated his two commissions of enquiry into the causes of the insurrection and the identities of the people behind it.

The atmosphere within the citadel, however, was not one of complete sanguinity. Despite, or even perhaps because of, the establishment of the two commissions, there was an underlying current of unrest of which everyone – from Roberts downwards – was aware. The battle had been won overwhelmingly, but was the war *completely* over? The people in the bazaar were surly and there were rumours of forces out in the country, particularly to the west, who refused to be cowed. Accordingly, Lamb took his brigade out to the north, at first, and then to the west, in a show of authority, while Roberts continued rebuilding the defences of the capital.

Simon was detached from all of this activity and was unaware of the underlying tension in Kabul. In fact, he did not know at first of the arrival of the relief column and of Alice and Covington. On the evening of the successful conclusion of the battle, his temperature suddenly rose and he relapsed into a fever. It was not as severe as that he had suffered four months before, but it was enough to cause concern to Knox, the young Scotsman who had first treated him. Jenkins – a willing nurse – was assigned to attend to him and Simon was put to bed in the small room he had found for the three of them, out of the way of the main complex within the fortress. It was so secluded, in fact, that it was as though he had been forgotten by the Sherpur command. The demands on Covington's time were those of Chief of Staff rather than head of intelligence, and indeed, the responsibility for intelligence had seamlessly reverted to the political officers, who now attempted to resume their cordial relationships with local chiefs. Simon's illness, it seemed, was the perfect excuse for the Kabul hierarchy to forget the three of them completely.

The fever left Simon by the fourth day, but despite the cheerful care of Jenkins and W.G., it was replaced by the onset of lassitude and depression. The bare brown mud walls of the little room pressed in on him, but he could not summon sufficient energy to leave his bed. The future stretched before him as an empty waste. He was tired of killing, completely disenchanted with what he considered to be the brutality of the British Army and devoid of ambition, except that of extracting Jenkins and himself from their involvement with the army. At the same time, his fear of impotence grew stronger. Dr Knox still could offer neither comfort nor practical help, except to pass him along to his superiors in Delhi. There was little pain now from the injuries, just the familiar dull ache. But there was no sign of life, either.

It was in this depressed condition that Alice eventually found him.

She bustled in, on the fifth day after her arrival, looking spring-like in a patterned cotton blouse and light woollen skirt, her hair tied back with a familiar lime-green scarf. 'My dear, I've been looking everywhere for you,' she began. 'No one seemed to . . .' Her voice tailed away, as Simon levered himself into a sitting position, his eyes wide and startled.

For a moment Alice stood quite still by the door, looking down at Simon. She had had no idea, of course, that he had spent the last six months dressed as and looking like an Afghan, nor had she wished to enquire from Covington exactly what role Simon had played during the recent campaign. Jenkins had been relieved as nurse for an hour by W.G., past whom she had swept with hardly a word, so there had been no warning of the change in Simon's appearance, nor of the marks left on his face by his injuries. She observed now a thin, hawk-faced, broken-nosed Afghan, his brown eyes staring unusually brightly from a face that appeared even darker in the shadows of the little room. His black hair hung down, native fashion, to his shoulders and the hand stretched towards her, half in surprise, half in greeting, extended from an equally brown wrist, whose bones protruded like that of an invalid. But if Alice, for one brief moment, thought she had stumbled into the wrong room, she was immediately reassured by the familiar shy smile that immediately lit up the young Pathan's countenance.

'My dear Alice,' Simon said, struggling upwards, 'I am so sorry . . . You find me in a terrible mess here, I'm afraid. I've been a bit unwell, you see. How wonderful to . . .'

'Oh Simon.' Alice sat on the bed, put her arms around him without hesitation and warmly kissed his cheek, before gently pushing him back on to the pillows again. 'My dear . . .' She tailed off again, as tears came into her eyes.

Simon looked away. 'Sorry about all this.' His gesture this time took in his face as well as the tumbled bedclothes around him. 'I must look a bit strange, I suppose. Had to go native, you see. Skin and hair dyed and all that.' He looked up at her again and smiled, half apologetically. 'I heard that you had arrived, but I've had a bit of a fever so that I couldn't get to see you. Much better now, though.'

He made to throw off the bedclothes but Alice restrained him. 'No, don't get up. I can't stay long and I just came to find where you were, but now that I know, I shall be back. Though I must have your story. Tell me what happened, please.'

Simon shook his head. 'Not much to tell, really, but what there is would take too long.' He lowered his gaze again, then looked up at her sharply. 'I hear that Covington arrived with you. You know that I am supposed to report to him?'

Alice nodded.

'Well that would be intolerable for me, of course. I shall have to find some way of resigning and taking Jenkins with me. But it's difficult if the enemy is still in the field.' Simon looked away for a moment. 'I can't have them saying that I'm running away, you see.'

Alice gripped his hand. 'I don't think there will be any question of that. In fact, I think that we have all arrived too late. The Afghan army has been defeated and there's no story any more, although there are one or two rumours about trouble in the west. I don't see how they can stop you resigning now that the campaign is virtually over.' She scowled. 'From what I've learned, Roberts is about to hang Afghans by the dozens, to close the book, so to speak. So it must be over.' Her expression softened. 'But I hear that you have been ... wounded. Are you all right?'

Simon shook his head and avoided her eyes. 'Good Lord, yes. Broken nose and a couple of hurt ribs, that's all. I'll be perfectly all right once I've shaken off this fever. And that's almost gone now.' He smiled again and this time held her gaze. 'Matter of fact, I've been lying here feeling a bit sorry for myself. I'm something of a sham at the moment, dear

Alice, so it's a good thing that you are here to shake me out of it.' He squeezed her hand.

'And dear old Jenkins, 352, is he still with you?'

'Couldn't get by without him.'

'Very well, my dear.' She stood up. 'Now I must go. The General has received the recommendations of his two courts of enquiry and is, I understand, about to announce judgement on those whom he believes are responsible for the attack on the Residency and who have had the audacity to defend their homeland and oppose this invasion.' She smiled. 'So I must somehow report all of this factually but also attempt to show the Tories back home who read the *Morning Post* what an old barbarian their wonderful Bobs really is.'

Simon frowned. 'Alice. Do be careful. He is a very powerful man – particularly out here – and I have the feeling that he is the sort who strongly resents criticism. It happens to generals, you know: particularly successful ones.'

Alice bent down and planted a kiss on Simon's forehead. 'Don't worry about me. I'll be careful – and I will be back to see you soon.' At the doorway she turned and smiled at him, but she was frowning as she left.

Simon lay back on the bed and examined the ceiling. He had dreaded her visit. Only yesterday Jenkins had brought the news that the relieving column included Alice in the small party of journalists travelling with it. The Welshman's black button eyes had gleamed with pleasure: 'You'll never guess, bach, who's waltzed in with the new brigade – this'll cheer you up, see.' But it hadn't. In fact, Simon's despondency had increased at the thought that Alice, pure, virginal Alice, might hear what had happened to him in the mullah's camp. He had squirmed with embarrassment at the thought of her knowing of his injuries. It somehow seemed a weakness – and one consistent with the misfortunes that had dogged him since leaving England so long ago. To Alice he must seem like a loser.

Now, he shrugged deeper under the blanket, like a small boy hiding from the dark, and switched his gaze from ceiling to wall. He had always been certain that he was not in love with Alice; there was a huge well of affection for her within him, but it was not love. Yet as he lay and traced with a finger the crusty mud pattern on the wall, he realised in a rare moment of truth that he had always regarded Alice as being part of his long-term future: that, without being precise, somehow, somewhere, she would be a close part of his life. Impotence, however, had crushed that dream completely. No woman would want a man who could not ... Damn! He clenched his fist and rammed it hard into the wall, making blood spurt from the knuckles.

Alice came back that evening, although Simon did not see her. He had remained in his bed, churlishly refusing to eat and drinking only a little milk. Jenkins was sitting in the outer room, despondently darning a shirt, when Alice slipped through the door. She put a finger to her lips and beckoned the Welshman to follow her out into the corridor.

'It's lovely to see you, miss,' said Jenkins, his face cracking into a beam that brought his moustache almost up to his ears. 'I hope you've come to cheer 'im up, 'cos 'e needs it, look you.'

'Yes, I know. I saw him earlier.' She pulled Jenkins away from a group of soldiers who walked by, gazing curiously at them. 'Can we go somewhere where we can talk quietly? No, not in your room. I don't want Simon to hear.'

Jenkins frowned. 'It had better be in the compound then, miss. I'll get me coat.'

Once outside, Alice thrust her arm companionably through that of Jenkins and they walked in the semi-darkness, their breath rising like steam. 'Now,' she said, 'I know, 352, that you are his very best friend, so I want you to tell me exactly what happened to him when he was captured and why it seems to affect him so.'

Jenkins sucked in his moustache and looked at his feet. 'Well, miss,' he said. 'It's not very nice, like. In fact, it's a bit embarrassing and not exactly for a young lady to know about, if you see what I mean. Anyway, I'm not sure that the Captain would want me to—'

'To hell with that.' Jenkins's eyes widened at her vehemence. Alice frowned and then smiled at him. 'Sorry about that. But you know, I'm not a schoolgirl, Mr Jenkins. I have been with the army throughout the Zulu campaign, I was at Ulundi and saw what our cavalry did to surrendering natives; I have travelled through India and half of Afghanistan to get here. I know that the world is not a pretty place. Please tell me what happened to Simon. You see . . .' She stopped, and gently pulled Jenkins round so that she could look directly into his eyes. 'Perhaps – I don't know, but perhaps – I can help him. But I can't do that until I know what happened to him.'

Jenkins held her gaze. It was a long time – a very long time – since he had looked into so fair a face. Alice had wrapped a woollen scarf around her head to keep out the cold, but her hair peeped out to frame her face, and this softened the hint of masculinity that came from the square jaw. The grey eyes which looked so coolly into his displayed the kind of self-confidence and breeding with which he was familiar from people of her class. He had grown up with it as a boy in Wales, grooming the horses for the family at the manor, and he had seen it so many times displayed by officers in the British Army. He knew it came with money and education. But this combination of determination and beauty, presented to him in this savage place, so closely and personally, was a new experience, and he found it disconcerting.

'All right, then. But don't tell the Captain it was me who told you.'

Alice nodded and they recommenced their walk. Slowly, but then with growing volubility, Jenkins related all that had happened to them since their arrival in India. When it came to Simon's capture, he paused for a moment, took a deep breath and related Simon's ordeal in a matter-of-fact way, looking straight ahead so that he picked up no reaction from Alice. But she did not speak, merely gripping his arm a little tighter.

'So there you are, see. 'E got better all right, physically that is, though 'e's as thin as a rake. But I know 'e thinks 'e's 'urt permanently down there, look you.' For the first time, Jenkins sounded embarrassed. 'You see, 'e doesn't talk about it, but I know 'e thinks 'e can't produce babies an' that. So 'e thinks 'e's only 'alf a man.'

'And what do the doctors say?'

Jenkins sucked in his moustache. 'I've 'ad a word with the doctor who's treatin' 'im – a nice Scottish bloke – but 'e doesn't seem to know. Says the Captain will 'ave to wait until 'e gets back 'ome to find out. It's depressing 'im, see.'

Alice nodded her head and spoke slowly. 'Yes, I do see. I thought it might be something like that, but I couldn't be sure.'

They walked ahead in silence for a while, their feet crunching on the frozen snow. Then she stopped. 'Can't he find out? Aren't there any women here?'

Jenkins's jaw dropped. 'What? Blimey, no, miss. The General's made it a court-martial offence to go into the bazaar and 'ave it off, so to speak, with the women there. An' anyway,' his voice took on a note of scorn, 'the Captain's not that sort of bloke, see. No, miss, not 'im.'

Alice smiled. 'Don't be offended, Mr Jenkins. I know it happens. But thank you for telling me. I am very grateful. Now perhaps you had better get back before he misses you.'

Alice retraced her steps to the Bala Hissar, where the press were quartered with Gough's brigade. She was glad of the walk through the dark night, for she had much to think about. Jenkins's story was remarkable in itself. Could she use it for the *Morning Post*? The journalist in her weighed the issues coolly. It was magnificent copy: a first-hand, eye-witness account of the massacre at the Residency; the escape across the rooftops; Simon's deliberate sacrifice in putting himself into the hands of the mullah; the . . . No. She could not use it. For Simon's sake. Anyway, it would probably be censored by Roberts. The General was already proving himself to be no friend of the correspondents with him. All copy had to be sent by government telegraph to London via Tehran, and Roberts had insisted that stories filed had to be read by him personally and approved before dispatch. She could not – she would not – expose Simon's story, his very personal story, to the Commander-in-Chief's pen.

Alice turned her mind to Simon himself, for whom she felt such warm affection and maternal concern. Was he hurt irrevocably? Was he to be another casualty of this heartless piece of colonial adventuring – just as much a victim as those homeless villagers Gladstone had spoken of and whom she had now seen for herself? There had been too many broken men left behind in this campaign as the banners and the drums had moved on. She damned the empire-builders once again, and pulled her cloak more tightly around her and shivered, not entirely from the coldness of the air.

Twenty minutes later, as she acknowledged the greeting of the sentry at the partly ruined entrance to the Bala Hissar, she had made a decision.

The next evening Alice returned to Sherpur and to Simon's quarters. This time she found W.G. on duty in the anteroom and she immediately endeared herself to the Sikh by stretching out a hand and enveloping him in a warm smile. 'You must be W.G.,' she said. 'I have heard all about you from Sergeant Jenkins and I am so grateful for all that you have done for Captain Fonthill.'

Awkwardly, the Sikh took her hand – it was the first time he had touched a European woman. 'It was nothing, memsahib. Nothing at all.' Gravely, he bowed, the end of his long beard brushing the back of her hand.

'W.G. W.G.,' Alice mused, retaining his hand. 'Do you know, I saw him play once, at Gloucester.'

W.G.'s eyes widened. 'You saw the great Dr Grace play, miss?'

'Oh, yes. Not so long ago. It was so disappointing. He was out second ball – and he made a great fuss about it.' She laughed. 'Grumbled all the way to the pavilion. Not a good sport at all, I fear.'

The Sikh relinquished her hand and straightened up, his face shocked. 'Oh,' he said, 'I am sure that the miss is mistaken. Dr Grace is great sportsman who always plays with a very straight bat.'

'Well, he missed the ball that time. Bowled middle stump, I fear. Now, is the Captain inside there?'

Speechless, W.G. nodded. 'Good,' said Alice, feeling her colour heightening. 'I want to have a long talk with him, so perhaps you would be so kind as to see that we are not disturbed? Thank you.' She gave him another radiant smile, knocked on Simon's door and stepped into his room.

Simon rose from where he had been sitting on the edge of his bed and smiled, in embarrassment as much as welcome. 'Oh, Alice, it's you. I heard voices.' He was wearing only his nightshirt, and he gestured at it deprecatingly. 'I am sorry, I am still not quite ready to receive visitors, you see.' He looked round the room. 'Still in a bit of a mess, I am afraid, though I was going to tidy up and get out tomorrow. The doctor said that the fever has gone and I can report for duty again then. But do sit down. Would you like some tea?'

'No thank you.' There were two bright spots of colour on Alice's cheeks as she shook her head, unwound her scarf and slipped off her cloak. Turning her back on Simon, she hung the cloak on a hook on the door and, under cover of doing so, quietly slipped the bolt across. 'Now,' she turned back with a smile and pulled up the only chair in the room, 'how are you really feeling?'

Simon ran a hand through his tousled hair and sat back on the bed. 'Oh, I am much better now, thanks. Jenkins and W.G. are really taking care of me. I have made up my mind that I must report to Covington tomorrow. I'm a bit surprised he hasn't been after me by now. It's time we all went back to work.'

Alice tossed her head and slowly began unbuttoning her dress. 'Oh, I shouldn't worry about him. He's got enough to do getting to know Roberts. He doesn't really like him, you know. He's a Wolseley man.'

'Er . . . is he? Alice, what . . . what are you doing?' Simon watched as though hypnotised as Alice stepped out of her dress, pulled her slip up over her head, unhooked her bodice and threw it to one side, then sat down and unrolled her stockings. She slowly wriggled her light blue knickers to the floor and stood, quite naked, facing Simon as she ran her hands over her body. The room was lit only by an oil lamp, which sent darting shadows across her skin and made it seem golden in that half-light. She cupped her breasts unselfconsciously, and turned to see her shadow on the wall. Her nipples, enlarged by the projection, stood out clearly, and she moved slightly so that they protruded more provocatively. To Simon's astonished gaze she seemed an apparition: some houri, perhaps, summoned from the mystical past of this strange sub-continent by his fever, conjured up to taunt him about his departed manhood.

Then the apparition spoke: 'Golly, it's cold in here. Come on. Move over.' And it pushed Simon quite hard, so that he rolled against the wall. Alice slipped into the bed, pulling away the rough blankets and throwing them over both of them.

From a distance of four inches, Simon found himself looking into the greyest and most beautiful eyes he had ever seen. He gulped as Alice ran her fingers through his hair. 'Alice,' he began. She kissed him softly on the lips. He tried again. 'Alice. Don't, don't do this. You don't understand. Whatever it is . . . What are you doing? Please, please. You see, I can't.'

Alice kissed his broken nose. 'You know, Simon, I think this new nose suits you.' She kissed it again. 'It's got a sort of hook to it now. Makes your face seem thinner. I quite like it.' She stroked his ear. 'But my dear, your hair is filthy. I don't think you need to have gone quite as native as this, you know.'

Simon closed his eyes and breathed deeply. 'Alice, I am *not going to* . . . Oh, Alice. Please . . .' She quietened him by kissing him again, then gently inserting her tongue into his mouth and running her hand down his back so that she pressed his body against hers. He pulled back.

'I don't know why you are doing this,' he said. 'But you should know that I have been hurt and I cannot—'

Alice put her hand on his mouth. 'I am doing this, my dear, because I want to. And, anyway, how do you know that you cannot until you try . . . eh?' She slipped her hand down the bed, pulled up his nightshirt and, with infinite care, touched him. 'There, there . . . how's that? Yes. Ah, good. Now, kiss me again.'

'No. That will hurt. Oh . . .!' His voice became softer. 'Oh God!'

Slowly, gently, Alice stroked and encouraged until the body arched close to her gradually lost its rigidity and began to writhe rhythmically in response to her caresses. She gently kissed her way to his ear, inserted her tongue there for a moment and then whispered to him, 'There, there, my dear. That seems fine now, doesn't it?'

He groaned in incoherent acquiescence.

'Yes, well then. Now, Simon. Listen to me. We have no form of contraception here and I have no desire to become pregnant. So we must try something else. Something perhaps . . . er . . . a little softer. So just you lie quietly. I shall be very, very gentle.'

Kissing his ear again, Alice moved her lips down his neck and on until she reached her destination. A minute later she withdrew, inched her way back until her head was once again on the pillow and reached for a handkerchief. She wiped her lips and then, tenderly, mopped the perspiration from Simon's forehead as he lay, his breast heaving, staring at the ceiling.

'Well, my dear,' she murmured, 'that's the first time I've ever done that, so I'm no expert. But I would say, with absolute certainty, that you are not impotent.'

Simon turned his head and looked into her eyes. 'My

darling Alice,' he breathed. 'I . . . I . . . I just don't know what to say to you. I thought I could never—'

'Well,' Alice sat up, 'you *can*, so that's that. So stop feeling sorry for yourself.' She sprang out of bed and pulled on her knickers.

Simon sat up too. 'But darling . . .'

'Don't darling me, Simon.' Alice continued to struggle into her clothing. Her voice came now from underneath her slip as she pulled it over her head. 'What has just happened doesn't mean that I love you or that you have to love me.' Her head, hair tousled, appeared from the slip. 'And it doesn't mean that I have to marry you. As a matter of fact, my dear, I don't love anyone and I am not getting married to you or to anyone else. I am far too busy.' She thrust a toe into her stocking and began to roll it on.

'Alice.'

She caught his anguished eye and relented, leaning across the bed and kissing him lightly on the mouth. Stroking his cheek for a moment she whispered: 'Simon, I am and always will be your friend. Your very dear friend, but that's all.' She brushed her lips against his cheek and sat back on the chair. 'We had something to prove, you and I, and we have just proved it, and I am glad we did.' She began buttoning up her dress and smiled at him, a little roguishly. 'As a matter of fact, if you must know, I quite enjoyed it.'

Then she frowned and looked into his eyes with that old intensity. 'But I am not a whore. I thought about all this carefully before I came to you and it seemed the only thing I could do to help you. I am glad we were successful. But I shan't be cavorting around the regimental messes here, I assure you. What I did, I did to help my dear friend, who is now . . .' she swept a hand through her hair, 'quite whole again, I am glad to say.'

Simon lay back on the bed and summoned up a smile. 'Alice, I don't quite know what to say to you.'

She pouted. 'Well, you could try thank you, for God's sake.'

'Very well. Thank you.'

'Don't mention it.' She came and sat beside him on the bed for a moment and took his hand. For the first time since she had entered the room she looked at him uncertainly, and what could have been a flush came to her cheek. 'In fact, my dear, I don't think either of us should ever mention it to anyone, if you don't mind.'

Simon shook his head. 'Of course not.' He spoke quietly. 'Alice, you will hate me saying this, but I think I shall love you always.'

'No you won't. Life's far too short. Good night, my dear.'

She slid back the bolt noiselessly and stepped into the anteroom. Thankfully, it was deserted. She closed the door behind her and, for a moment, leaned against it, closed her eyes and sighed. Then she blew her nose, swung her cloak tightly around her and strode away, down the corridor and out into the compound, crunching the ice underfoot.

The next morning Simon – a *new* Simon, a man who astonished and delighted Jenkins and W.G. with his clearness of eye and his energy – rose early and donned the best clothes he could find in his very depleted Afghan wardrobe (they all still lacked formal uniform) to find Lieutenant Colonel Covington and report for duty. But Covington was nowhere to be found. Neither were the Commander-in-Chief, Brigadier Lamb or any of the senior officers. For that day, Simon learned, Roberts was hanging forty-nine Afghans.

They had all been named by the military court set up under the presidency of Brigadier Massey as being the ringleaders of the attack on the mission, and the executions were to be public and to take place, within the hour, outside the ruins of the Residency – a typical piece of Roberts symbolism. The whole garrison was ordered to be there, and Simon decided that Jenkins, W.G. and he must attend. They could not stay hidden, so to speak, for ever. Accordingly, they walked the mile to the city and joined the edge of the silent crowd which filled the square and lined every wall, balcony and vantage point overlooking it.

Facing the Residency was a grim row of gallows, under which, closely guarded, stood the prisoners, their hands bound, their heads hanging down. They made no attempt to protest. They merely stood, studying the ground, accepting their fate. Simon turned his head to see the windows from which he and his companions had fired on the day of the attack, and wondered how many of these bound men had fired back at them. He looked at Jenkins. The Welshman wrinkled his nose in distaste and slowly shook his head. W.G. was expressionless, his eyes fixed on the doomed men.

In the centre of the square stood a small group of officers. Simon recognised Roberts, MacPherson, Massey, Lamb and, with a little start of surprise, the tall figure of Covington. He seemed larger, somehow, than Simon remembered him. Away to the right, in a discrete group, stood a group of civilians whom Roberts presumed to be journalists from the way that several were scribbling in notebooks. Of Alice there was no sign. To the left of the officers, one man – a colonel, perhaps, from his uniform, age and bearing – was reading aloud from a large piece of paper. It was difficult to hear what was being said but it was of no matter. No one listened. The death sentence was immutable and the justification was irrelevant on that day. Above everything arched a metallic-grey sky.

'Nice day for it,' murmured Jenkins.

Eventually the officer was silent. Slowly, he rolled his document, turned and nodded to a subaltern, who, in turn, barked an order. From behind the gibbets a drum rolled, increasing the beat until, with a suddenness that was startling, it stopped. At that moment, the rickety platforms on which the prisoners were standing were kicked away and the forty-nine men dropped and jerked spasmodically. A low sigh came from the crowd, but there was no other noise or movement. After a few desultory kicks, the figures swung slowly in the windless air, like dolls on a string. As theatre, it had been impeccably produced and professionally performed. All that was missing was applause from the audience.

'Poor bastards,' said Jenkins.

'Yes, Sergeant bach,' muttered W.G., keeping his eyes on the hanging figures, 'but they broke their word, you know. They did not play the game.'

'They're still poor bastards, all the same.'

'Come on, let's get back before we're detailed to bury 'em,' said Simon.

The three men turned and began walking quickly back to Sherpur. Simon had taken a decision of his own and wished to discuss it with them, but not while the picture of those swinging dolls was so fresh in his mind.

In his little room he sat on the edge of the bed, Jenkins took the chair and W.G. stood, deferentially, until Simon gestured to him to sit beside him on the bed. It was to the Sikh that he spoke.

'W.G., I am afraid that I never did know your regiment. Which is it?'

'Ah, lord, I serve with one of the Punjabi infantry battalions, though I have been seconded to Guides. But battalion is

283

not here. When last I am hearing, it was on garrison duty on the Frontier in India.'

'When last you heard?'

'Yes. You see I have been away on special duties for so long that I am losing touch with them.' He frowned in concentration. 'Let me see, I have been with you for nearly six months now. Before that, with Lieutenant Cavendish I was away for more than a year.' He shrugged. 'I am not being in touch very much, you see, lord.'

Simon smiled. 'Long time since you hit a four through the covers, then?'

The Sikh leaned forward confidingly. 'You are hitting the ball precisely on the head, sir. I am becoming a little worried that I will lose talent, you see. It is important to keep in practice. Even the great Dr Grace can be losing his eye, so to speak, sir. I heard last night—'

'Yes, yes, I follow you.' Simon stood and stretched his arms above his head. Jenkins looked up at him and wondered again at the change that had taken place within just twelve hours. Today there was no sign of melancholy, no lack of confidence: the Captain seemed at ease with himself for the first time since his capture in the hills. It was reassuring and puzzling, but so welcome that Jenkins did not wish to waste time on pondering the cause. It was enough that it had happened. Now he sensed that some new change was in the air.

Simon took four paces around the small room and then addressed them both. 'I think our work is done here,' he said. 'The campaign is almost certainly over and I cannot see that we shall be needed further. I undertook to do a specific job for Colonel Lamb, and as far as I can see we have done it and no one can now hold us here if we wish to move on. Do you agree, 352?'

Jenkins nodded. 'Let's get out of this bloomin' place as fast as we can, says I.'

'Would you be happy, W.G., to go back to your regiment and practise your cover drive?'

The Sikh's face broke into a grin. 'Oh, absolutely, lord. I would very much like to see my wife and children again, isn't it?'

Jenkins looked at the Sikh in amazement. ' 'Ere, Gracey, you're never married, are you?'

'Oh yes, Sergeant bach. I have wife, two boys and two girls.' He smiled proudly. 'Biggest girl is good fast bowler.'

'Well I never. An' there's me thinkin' that you was a bachelor for life, like the Captain an' me.' Jenkins leaned forward. 'Gracey, I've bin meanin' to ask you. Are you a Hindee or a Musselman?'

The Sikh looked shocked. 'Neither, Sergeant bach. We Sikhs follow teachings of first guru, Guru Nanak, which means that we are not holding with caste and class but live by principles of truth, justice and freedom. All our women are called Kaur, meaning princess, and all men Singh, meaning lion—'

'And is that why you never cut your 'air, then, 'cos you don't, do yer?'

W.G. nodded gravely. 'That is so, Sergeant bach. Our signs of the Rehatnama, our code for life, are the five Ks: *kesh*, or uncut hair, *kirpan*, the sword, *kanga*, our wooden comb, *kachera*, the breeches, and *karra*, our iron bracelet. They were introduced in your year 1699 by Gobind Rai, our tenth guru. He—'

Simon interrupted. 'Well thank you, W.G., for that potted history. We are both grateful, but we must get on.'

Jenkins looked hurt. 'No, bach sir. But it *is* interestin', look you.' He turned back to the Sikh with a solemn face. 'I

285

suppose that if you spelled cricket with a 'k' that could be your sixth code thingamijig, couldn't it?'

Simon coughed quickly. 'That will do, Sergeant. Now, I propose that I will submit my resignation to Colonel Covington.' He turned to Jenkins. 'I shall have to buy you out again . . .'

'I'll pay you back.'

'What with?'

'Money you can lend me.'

'I see. I think we've had this conversation before. Anyway, I will buy you out. W.G., I have no power to order your return to your regiment, but I will submit a report to the General explaining how splendidly you have performed while with us and recommending that you now go back to India and receive a long leave, so enabling you to return to your family for a while.' He extended his hand to the Sikh. 'I can't tell you how much you have earned my admiration, my gratitude and my respect.'

The big man rose to his feet and looked embarrassed. 'Oh, it was nothing, lord.' He shook hands with Simon. 'I have learned much from you and the sergeant bach.' He turned to Jenkins. 'Though I am still not understanding why they do not play cricket in Wales?'

'Oh, but they do, Gracey. Trouble is, it's the mountains, see. Because of the slopes, all the teams 'ave to be picked from blokes with one leg shorter than the other. That's all right when they're facin' all the same way, but when the ball—'

'Oh for God's sake, 352,' said Simon. 'Do shut up. Now, out of the way. I must go and see Covington.'

The Chief of Staff's office was empty. Simon borrowed pen and paper, sat down and scribbled his resignation. Briefly he explained the terms under which he had accepted

Brigadier Lamb's offer of a commission in the Guides, and stated that the task he had undertaken had been completed and that it was now his intention to return, with Jenkins, to civilian life. He felt it necessary to add that Brigadier Lamb would confirm all that he had written and that it was his intention to explain the circumstances of his resignation to the Brigadier personally. His cheque for Jenkins's buy-out would follow.

He had been back in his room for less than an hour when an orderly called and requested that he return to see Colonel Covington immediately.

'Ah, good,' said Jenkins. 'You're goin' to get your Victoria Cross at last.'

'I doubt it very much. Smells like trouble to me.'

But the Colonel was surprisingly accommodating. As Simon entered the door, Covington looked up with a smile and, in a well-remembered gesture, put both hands behind his head and leaned back so that the chair balanced precariously on its back legs. 'Well, well, well,' he said. 'My God, you've gone completely native.'

'That was my job.'

'It seems that you have entered into it so completely that you now omit to address senior officers as sir.'

'That was my job, sir.'

'Hmmn.' Covington picked up Simon's letter. 'Running away again, I see, Fonthill.'

'My job is done, Colonel. My arrangement with Brigadier Lamb was that my commission with the Guides should be a short-term one. I have the right to resign and to take my man with me, as you know. Should you attempt to stop me, I shall take the matter up with the General and—'

Covington held up a languid hand. 'Stop you? Stop you? Why on earth should I want to stop from leaving a man who, when last I saw him, was threatening to put an assegai in my back at our next meeting?'

'No, not your back. I didn't specify where.'

'Ah, chest, was it? How very untypical of you. But to return, I won't stop you leaving the army. I certainly don't want to have a man like you working for me.' He let the chair come crashing forward. 'And from what I hear from . . .' he paused theatrically, '*journalistic* sources, not much of a man at that. So you can go, Fonthill. And good riddance.'

The words stung Simon like a slap across the face. *Not much of a man . . . journalistic sources . . .* Could Alice have . . .? He knew that she had been somehow close to Covington in South Africa. Could she have told him of his injuries and – even worse – of her treatment of them? Of course not. There could be no question of Alice betraying him in this way. No, Covington must have heard a rumour about the way he had been hurt; there had been plenty of gossip in Sherpur about it, he knew that.

The thoughts were racing through Simon's brain, but he kept his face completely impassive. He would not give this man the satisfaction of knowing that his words had wounded.

'I think my record in Afghanistan will show that I have performed my duties creditably . . . sir.' Simon's voice was quite emotionless.

Covington's urbanity now disappeared in a flash. His face scowling, he waved his hand dismissively. 'Oh, get out of here, Fonthill. I want to have nothing more to do with you. The sooner you go back to India the better. Get out.'

Simon gave a curt nod of his head, leaned forward and pushed his letter forward as a reminder, and turned on his heel.

His heart felt lighter as he walked through the labyrinth of passages that led him to his tucked-away quarters. Once there, he penned another letter. This one was to General Roberts, informing him of his decision and putting into words his commendation of W.G. and his recommendation for leave for him.

Then he sealed the envelope, leaned back in his chair and considered his position. Resigning, he knew, had been an emotional reaction to the hangings outside the old Residency. Part of him realised that Roberts's brutal action had been necessary and, indeed, proper. It was right that those who had broken the terms under which the mission had been accepted at Kabul and who had killed Cavagnari and his staff should be punished and seen to be punished. Nevertheless, the act of judgement had been military, not judicial, and the mass public hangings, with their elaborate ritual designed to impress the crowd, had been almost as barbarous as the events that had prompted them. The British were supposed to be a civilised race, for God's sake!

At the same time – and Simon frowned at the recognition – his resignation had also been a reaction to Alice's breathtaking initiative in demonstrating that he would not have to live with sexual impotence for the rest of his life. He shivered at the recollection: Alice holding him, Alice pressing her delightful breasts against him, Alice kissing him and sliding her mouth . . . ah! Surely she could not have done such a thing out of pure altruism? There must, there *must*, be some feelings of love for him, however deeply buried they might be beneath her woman-of-the-world demeanour and her protestations of only platonic affection.

He sighed. His mind had taken this path so many times over the last few hours that he felt exhausted at facing again the conflicting evidence his memory provided. No. He definitely had to go. To be away from her, to let her live her own life and allow him to sort his out once and for all. So . . .

what to do? There would be plenty of back pay in his account at Simla, plus an accumulation of his allowance from home. There would be sufficient funds for him and Jenkins to live well for a time, before deciding on the next move. Tea-planting in India, perhaps? Ranching in America? He stretched his hands above his head, interlinking the fingers. Plenty of time. But, oh, Alice, Alice . . .

The next morning, surprisingly, there came a message to report to Lieutenant General Roberts. Simon did so with some trepidation. Was this some last order or trick to keep him in the army? He entered the well-remembered room and saw, to his relief, that Covington was not present, only the General and Brigadier Lamb. Roberts gestured towards a chair. Ah, a good sign!

'I have your letter, Fonthill,' said the General, stroking the end of his silver moustache, 'and I have seen the letter of resignation that you have submitted to Colonel Covington.' The blue eyes held Simon's. 'Now, tell me, pray, why you want to give up what is a promising career serving Her Majesty. Neither of these letters is clear on this matter.'

Simon cleared his throat. How far to go? 'Well, sir, as Brigadier Lamb knows, I do not feel cut out to be a regimental officer and I don't suppose I can continue to serve in this . . .' he gestured down to his Afghan garb, 'irregular manner – and nor would I want to. I therefore believe that I should submit my resignation and return to civilian life while I am young enough to carve out some other career.'

'What sort of career?'

'I am not sure yet, sir. Perhaps tea-growing in India or something of the sort.'

'Wouldn't you find that rather dull after the kind of life that you have been leading lately?' For the first time a smile –

almost kindly – had been allowed to steal across Roberts's features.

Simon allowed himself a half-smile in return. 'It would probably be a welcome relief, sir. As a matter of fact, I don't take easily to fighting and I am not sure I have the qualities that are needed to lead men in action. Although I don't think that I am a coward, exactly.'

'Look here.' The General leaned across his desk. 'Lamb has filled me in on your background.' He coughed. 'South Africa and all that. It could be that the army has been a little . . . harsh with you. But life is not always easy and I am not going to apologise for that. The point is that you came through in a capital manner. I can assure you that there is not the slightest doubt about your character. You did an extremely brave thing in allowing yourself to be captured and . . . er . . . so on. Your work here has been outstanding and I shall always be grateful that, thanks to you, this garrison was prepared for the attack when it came. Eh, Lamb?'

The Brigadier nodded vigorously. 'Quite so, sir.'

'Now.' The General leaned back. 'We don't want you to go. As a matter of fact, we both think that you are extremely well suited to this . . . er . . . irregular work, and I want you to stay with us in India, here on the Frontier, and continue with it. If you will withdraw your resignation, I intend to recommend you for a decoration – can't say what yet, but I can say that you will receive an immediate majority and we can make your Welshman a warrant officer. Oh, and yes, I have already promoted your Sikh to the rank of *subaldar*, long overdue anyway. Now, what do you say?'

Simon's heart sank. Whatever he had been expecting, it was not this. Confident smiles were playing across the features of both the General and the Brigadier; they were men not accustomed to having their largesse refused. They were expecting gratitude, not rejection. Simon shifted on his chair.

'That is extremely kind of you, General,' he said. 'I appreciate it and I am grateful. But I still feel that I must go. You see, I am not in tune with life in the army – I don't always agree with the things which, I suppose, we have to do in places like this and I do not wish to be part of them.' His voice tailed away rather lamely. 'That's how I feel, sir. I am sorry.'

'Right.' The General's eyes had become cold again. 'Shan't argue with you. Not going to plead. I am afraid that there will be no question of a decoration now. Can't give one to a man who's resigned. Your back pay will be waiting for you at the Guides HQ at Simla. You may keep your weapons until you get back there. I'm afraid you won't be able to go yet. The passes are still not safe for small parties and it will be some time before we shall be sending back larger units. When we do, you shall join them.' He nodded. 'That will be all, Fonthill.'

Chapter 11

Simon had established that the small party of journalists was quartered at the Bala Hissar, but he made no attempt to go there and seek out Alice, and he saw nothing of her, although he did meet a newspaperman one day, as he and Jenkins were walking in the Sherpur compound. A young European in mufti – not a particularly unusual sight in Kabul, where many ethnic types now intermingled – passed as he and Jenkins were deep in discussion. On hearing fluent, colloquial English spoken by two seeming Pathans, the young man paused, turned and overtook them.

'Excuse me,' he said. 'You must be Captain Fonthill and Sergeant Jenkins.'

Simon regarded the man with interest. He was wearing a dark top-coat and astrakhan hat, riding breeches and boots – standard wear for a civilian in Kabul. But the hair that hung down from the fur hat and the moustache and beard were golden, and the eyes blue and alive with an open curiosity. The stranger held out his hand.

'John Campbell, the *Standard*. How do you both do?'

Simon nodded and gripped Campbell's hand. Jenkins did the same, bestowing on the young man one of his wide, life-enhancing grins.

'I'm afraid that you have the advantage of us,' said Simon.

'Oh, Alice told me all about you both.' Simon's face

hardened. How many people had Alice spoken to of him? Would this young man, too, know about his injuries? Campbell's smile turned into a frown. 'You know – Alice Griffith of the *Morning Post*.'

'Ah, yes, of course. She is a colleague of yours.'

'Very much so.' Campbell's warm manner returned. 'She's a very good friend. We came up here together. We got here too late for the fighting, alas, but Alice told me a little about you and the Sergeant here.' He turned and directed his open smile at Jenkins. 'I gather you've had a rare old time of it.'

'That would be very true, sir,' said Jenkins. 'Very true indeed. But the Captain 'ere and me,' he grew expansive, 'are quite used to that sort of thing, look you.'

'Well, you certainly look the part – whatever part it was.' Campbell put his hand on Simon's arm. 'Look here, Fonthill, I don't want to pinch Alice's story, nor to intrude into what's forbidden to know, but I would welcome the chance to chat with you about your experiences here.' He smiled disarmingly. 'Fact of the matter is that we've not much to write about now that the war is virtually over, and I would most appreciate the chance of telling of your experiences behind the lines, so to speak. If Alice has not already done so, that is.'

'Oh, we've got a right old story to—' began Jenkins. But Simon cut him short.

'What did Alice tell you, Mr Campbell?'

Simon's coldness immediately put Campbell into a mode defensive of Alice. 'Oh, nothing at all, really. Only that you and she were old friends back home and that you had spent some time up in the hills during the uprising and that you had been wounded . . . but nothing serious, I understand.' His voice had tailed away and then recovered, but the momentary flash of embarrassment told everything to Simon. So Alice *had* been talking! But had she? Like

Covington, Campbell could have picked this up from the scuttlebutt of garrison life. After all, enough people knew of his injuries. Simon shrugged his shoulders.

'Well,' he said, 'I don't think you should believe everything that you might read one day in the newspapers. I am afraid that we have nothing very interesting to say and the little that we could say is, of course, privileged. I am sorry, Mr Campbell. Please excuse us.'

Simon and Jenkins walked on in silence for a moment. Then the Welshman spoke.

'If you don't mind me saying so, bach sir, I thought you were a bit 'ard on 'im. 'E seemed a nice enough bloke. And I wouldn't 'ave minded 'aving a nice woodcut of me appearin' in the *Standard*, like.'

'Don't talk rot. We can't talk to newspapermen. We're soldiers.'

'I thought we were ex-soldiers now. Unless, that is, you've gone an' joined us up again, like you did before. Anyway, W.G. tells me that you an' Miss Alice 'ad a nice long talk the other night. An' she's a newspaperman . . . or woman, isn't it?'

'That's different. We're old friends. And anyway, I didn't tell her anything.'

At the mention of Alice's visit, Simon's face had coloured slightly under the dye – slightly, but enough for Jenkins to notice. The Welshman lifted his eyebrows and then smiled, but decided to say nothing. They walked on.

New excitement hit Kabul a few days later, when the news spread that a column was about to arrive from Kandahar, led by Sir Donald Stewart, a general senior to Roberts, who was coming to take command at Kabul of all of the British forces in Afghanistan. The word was that this would leave Roberts free to return home, while the future of Afghanistan – and in particular of who would replace the departed amir as ruler of the kingdom – would be settled. Simon, whose mind had been set seething again with speculation about exactly how close a friend Alice Campbell had become, was relieved to hear the news. This must mean that troops would be sent back to India and that Jenkins, W.G. and he could accompany them. Would Alice and her journalist friends go too? he wondered. He did not know whether he wished for this or not, but he resolved anew to put Alice from his mind.

For her part, Alice had been busy enough. She had, in fact, observed the hangings. She had done so from a balcony discreetly overlooking the square, a privilege for which she had paid a Kabul merchant handsomely. She had wished to be out of sight because she was unsure how she would react to the spectacle: not that she was worried that she would collapse at the horror of it all, but rather that her indignation would express itself too publicly. Accordingly, she stood behind a column on the balcony, stonily making notes, even as the bodies swung. That evening her dispatch, along with those of her colleagues, had been submitted to the General to be read and approved before they were all handed to the signaller for sending down the telegraph line to London.

Usually, the Commander-in-Chief made few alterations to the copy. There had been little need to do so with the writings of the others. With one exception, they had all been satisfyingly eulogistic in conveying to the Empire the success of Roberts in avenging Cavagnari and in subjugating the tribes of Afghanistan. That exception had been Campbell, who had had his knuckles rapped for questioning Roberts's estimate of the size of Mohamed Jan's army. Realising that he would have to accept censorship if he was to be allowed to continue to use the only way of communicating with his newspaper,

Campbell had shrugged and toed the line. Not so Alice. The General had found something to query or reject in every story written by her since her arrival in Kabul. Her narrative of the burning villages, seen as she approached Sherpur, had been deleted completely. So, too, had her emphasis on the absence of the judiciary in the make-up of the military tribunal set up to try those accused of leading the attack on the Residency. Her fulminations had been coolly rejected by Roberts's ADC – her interface with the command, for no journalist saw the General personally.

Accordingly, when she received back her copy for the hangings – initialled by Roberts on every page and therefore approved – she sat down and wrote a separate page, inserted it in the text and forged the General's initials at the bottom. This page painted the scene of the execution in cool, objective terms, and yet no one who read it could fail to comprehend the writer's disgust at the ritual and at the less than judicial methods used to try and then sentence the hanged men. The story winged its way back to London, via Tehran, and Alice sat and waited for the repercussions. She had no illusions about the fuss that would be caused if the story was used in its original form – and, knowing her editor, she was confident that it would not be suppressed back home. She realised that, for breaking the rules, Roberts would probably banish her from Afghanistan, but she was prepared to take that risk. The war was over and there was little more to say anyway. The important thing was that she had not betrayed her principles.

Events, however, did not quite work out the way that Alice had expected.

Afghanistan's short spring had slipped into hot summer, and Alice was in the tiny room allocated to her in the Bala Hissar, avidly reading two newspapers that had reached her from India in the supply column which had recently made its way safely through the passes. They gave her just the information she needed and she smiled as she read the prose – rather too purple for her taste, but useful ammunition nevertheless. She was busy sidelining various passages when a heavy smash on the door heralded the arrival of John Campbell.

'Open up,' he thundered. 'Open up, in the name of Lieutenant General Sir Frederick Roberts, Lord High Executioner.'

Alice carefully put away her newspapers – friend or not, Campbell was still the opposition – and pushed up the latch. 'For goodness' sake, Johnny, you will have us both arrested.'

But the happy crooked smile she expected was missing. Campbell, despite the fooling, was frowning. 'Bad, bad news, I'm afraid, Alice.'

'What?'

'A whole British brigade in the field out in the west at Maiwand has been attacked and defeated. There have been over a thousand killed and wounded, and what's left is scattered over the fifty miles between Maiwand and Kandahar.'

'Oh God! Then the war's back on again.'

'Seems like it. It's been a terrible defeat for us – almost as bad as Isandlwana, by the sound of it. Our force in the south-west is holed up in Kandahar, frightened to come out, and Ayub Khan – he's the son of the old amir, you know, the one before this cove who betrayed us at Kabul and then bolted to India . . .'

Alice nodded.

'. . . he's cock-a-hoop with his victory, naturally, and is either going to besiege Kandahar or advance directly on Kabul. Anyway, the rumour is that Stewart will remain in command here and Bobs will raise a special fast-moving force and march on Kandahar to relieve the garrison there and, hopefully, knock Ayub off his perch before the whole country is ablaze again. Obviously, the press corps will go with Bobs and we are to prepare to leave within, probably, a couple of days.'

'Oh no!'

Campbell frowned. 'What's the matter? Roberts can't forbid a woman to go, however hard the terrain. You have accreditation. He won't upset the *Morning Post*, surely?'

With a groan, Alice sat on her camp bed and gestured Campbell towards the stool, the only other form of seating in the room. 'No,' she said, 'but I know I've upset *him*. I know he won't let me go.' And slowly she told Campbell of how she had avoided censorship by forging Roberts's initials and telegraphing her critical story of the hangings. 'He will use this as an excuse to get rid of me. I know he will. I will not be allowed to cover the best story of the whole campaign. Damn! And damn again!'

Campbell gave a rueful smile. 'Oh dear, Alice.' He reached across and took her hand. 'I have to say, my dear, that perhaps you *have* over-reached yourself this time.' He shook his head. 'You can't just go around forging the signature of a commander in the field, you know, and expect to get away with it.'

Alice withdrew her hand. 'Oh, I know that, dammit. But it was a risk worth taking. I thought the war was over, for goodness' sake, and I wasn't worried about being thrown out. There was nothing more of importance to report – or so I thought. I wonder if Covington can help—'

Their conversation was interrupted by a knock on the door. A young subaltern entered. 'General Roberts's compliments, miss . . . er . . . ma'am. He would be grateful if you could spare him a few moments in his headquarters as soon as is convenient,' he gave a bashful smile, 'but I think he means right away.'

Alice nodded. 'Very well. I shall come directly.'

She closed the door behind the young man and turned back to Campbell. 'Well, here it is. The sack. Give me a minute, Johnny, will you?'

Campbell stood. 'Of course. But would you like me to come with you. Perhaps I can help?'

'You are very sweet. But no. I shall go alone. Please push off now.'

Campbell stood uncertainly for a moment, then leaned forward, kissed her on the cheek and left. Alice sat on the stool, looked in her travelling mirror and combed her hair. She applied a little face powder, tucked a scarf around her neck and pulled her cloak around her shoulders. At the door, she paused, turned and then rescued from a drawer the two newspapers she had just received from India. She slipped them under her cloak and stood for a moment. Then, her cheeks slightly flushed but her head held high and her jaw thrust out, she strode off to meet the General.

As soon as she was ushered into Roberts's office she could see that it was a hanging party waiting for her. Behind his desk Roberts stood stiffly. To his left was Brigadier Massey and to his right Brigadier Lamb. Covington – a furious-faced Covington, who regarded her with frowning, hard blue eyes – glowered in a corner, behind Lamb.

Roberts did not invite her to sit. The four men remained standing as he addressed her without preamble. 'Miss Griffith, I have asked you here to—'

Alice looked around and drew up a chair. 'Oh, do sit down, gentlemen,' she said. 'I certainly shall.'

Roberts was thrown for a moment. 'What? Oh . . . er . . . yes, do, of course.' Awkwardly, the four men sat and Roberts began again. 'Miss Griffith, I have asked you here today because I have just received a telegram from the Horse Guards in London which relates that a story has been published in the *Morning Post*, written, it would seem, by you, which implicitly criticises the action I have taken to punish those responsible for the cowardly attack on our Residency. There are to be questions asked in the House about it and I am being requested to provide answers.'

'Oh yes, General.'

'There is one particular passage in the story – that, indeed, which contains the criticism – which I certainly do not remember reading in the draft of your dispatch which you submitted to me for censoring.'

Alice smiled and shook her head. 'Oh no. Certainly not, Sir Frederick.'

Roberts looked puzzled. 'I don't quite follow.'

'I certainly did not submit my story to you for censoring, General. I did so because you have ordered that every dispatch from the correspondents here had to be given to you for reading before being telegraphed. But I did not submit my story to you to have it censored.' She smiled again and continued, keeping her voice level and without heat, as though she was explaining something self-evident to a small child. 'Censoring, of course, is anathema to any journalist worth his – or her – salt. It is regarded by us all as the action of a command which is unsure of itself and uncertain of the reaction of the public back home to the course it has taken; as an attempt, in fact, to prevent the public from knowing the true facts of any, shall I say, contro-versial development in the field. How can it be regarded as anything else?'

'Paw!' The exclamation came from Massey, whose face glowed darkly red in the poor light of the little office. But

Roberts held up a hand to cut short his interruption. He leaned forward.

'My dear young lady. Since *journalists*,' he emphasised the word slightly, as though it was distasteful to him, 'have begun to accompany armies in the field, it has become very necessary to vet their writings to make sure that, however inadvertently, they do not contain facts which might give information or comfort to the enemy. It has become essential, in fact.'

'But General,' Alice leaned forward in turn, 'there are at least three reasons why this is not so.' She slapped a forefinger into her palm. 'Firstly, you are surely not saying that my quite objective description of the elaborate proceedings you created to bring about the death of forty-nine members of the army which opposed your invasion of their country would have given essential information or succour to the enemy. Secondly, it is right that the people of Britain should know that you feel it necessary to burn villages here for miles around – if it *is* necessary, then they should take this on board as part of the cost of these wars, but they should *know* about it. And thirdly, the whole point of accreditation for newspaper correspondents is that the army should feel comfortable with the standard and seniority of the journalists who accompany a force in the field.' Alice smiled again, although her eyes were cold. 'Sir Frederick, I am the daughter of a former brigadier in the 64th Foot and have been brought up in an army family. I have covered all of the recent campaign in South Africa and I understand that my reports from there have received commendations from several members of the Government. I *am* accredited and, General, I *can* be trusted to report the facts – even though you and I might disagree from time to time upon certain interpretations of them.'

Covington coughed politely. 'Sir, on this last fact, at least,

I can give some support to Miss Griffith. I knew her father and was with her in Zululand, and—'

Without taking his eyes off Alice, Roberts said, 'That will do, Covington.' Alice shot a swift glance of thanks to the tall man in the corner.

'It won't do to argue like this, Miss Griffith,' said the General. 'Whatever the rights and wrongs of censorship, it is not your place to contravene rules which have been set up by a commander in the field.' There were murmurs of 'Hear, hear' from the two brigadiers flanking him. Roberts straightened his back. 'I must ask you, madam. Did you insert an extra page in your copy and then forge my initials to that page so that it was included in your dispatch telegraphed to London?'

'Of course not, General.' Alice gave him her sweetest smile. 'You must have forgotten that part of the story – or, perhaps, given the fact that you have so many demands on your time, in addition to reading ever single word we scribblers record, maybe you skipped a page?'

It seemed to Alice that every one of the men facing her drew in his breath sharply. 'I am afraid,' said Roberts, 'that I cannot accept that. But I have one further point to make.' He leaned forward again. 'If those references in your dispatches which I have been forced in the past to delete and your report of these recent . . . um . . . judicial executions were balanced and reasonable, why is it that no one else has written them.'

'Ah, but they have, General.' Alice reached inside her cloak and drew out two newspapers. 'I have received only today these copies of two highly respected newspapers in India, *The Bombay Review* and *The Friend of India*. Apropos your executions, the first says, and I quote, "Is it according to the usages of war to treat as felons men who resist invasion?" And the *Friend* writes, "We fear that General

Roberts has done us a serious national injury by lowering our reputation for justice in the eyes of Europe." Now, gentlemen, I repeat that these are respected organs of opinion in India who are not in principle opposed to the British Raj. But here,' she slapped the newssheets with her hand before passing them across the desk, 'they felt that they must speak out.'

The room was silent for a moment. Then Roberts cleared his throat. If he was impressed with Alice's arguments, he gave no sign. 'These opinions are irrelevant, Miss Griffith. I am afraid that you have lost the trust of the command in Afghanistan and I must ask you to leave the country as soon as possible. This will be the day after tomorrow, when you will join a column returning to India.'

Alice sighed. She tried one more ploy – at least audacity seemed to faze the men opposite, if only for a moment.

'I am sorry, General, but I am afraid I cannot do that.'

'What!' For the first time Roberts seemed to lose his temper. He was unaccustomed to being defied.

'I understand that the British Army has sustained a heavy defeat at Maiwand and that you will shortly be taking a flying column out across the hills to march to Kandahar to fight Ayub Khan. I must accompany the press correspondents who are going with you. It is my duty. The readers of the *Morning Post* have a right to know what is happening in western Afghanistan.'

'That is not possible, madam. By your actions – by your deliberate defiance of very necessary rules established by the commanding officer of a British army in the field – you have negated whatever rights you have in this respect. Your editor will be told so. Now, I must ask you to leave and prepare yourself for the journey back to India.'

'I cannot do that, General, for the reasons I have explained.

I have work to do here. You cannot expel me from a country which, in any case, is not yours to govern.'

From the corner of her eye, Alice noticed Covington flinch and shake his head at her.

Roberts stood. 'Ah, but I can, young lady. And I will. If you deliberately disobey me I shall have you arrested and placed in the guardhouse until your departure, when you will be transported under guard back to India. In fetters, if necessary. Do you hear and understand me?' The little man's tone was quietly furious.

Alice sighed. 'Oh, very well, Sir Frederick. I do not wish to add to your considerable burden at this time, when you have so much that is important to do. I am sorry if I have upset you.' She stood. 'But I must give you a warning also.' She saw Covington in the background shake his head again imploringly. 'I shall find some means of reporting this campaign, because, you see, I have my duty.'

'I do not accept that. If you defy me further, I shall have you arrested. Now please leave. We have much to do. Good morning, madam.'

Alice inclined her head to them all. 'Good morning, gentlemen.'

She strode out of the room, her cheeks burning. Damn them! Damn them for their smug authority and hypocrisy. Damn them for interfering with her work, just when she was establishing a reputation. Damn them, in fact, for setting back her career. For that, she realised with sinking heart, was what her inability to accompany the flying column would mean. Cornford and the directors of the *Morning Post* would be furious that their correspondent with the army was being sent out of the country in disgrace, just when one of the most romantic and dangerous expeditions of the whole war was being mounted. She knew that Roberts would have to march through the mountains to get to Kandahar, through a country roused against him. This time there would be no elephants and heavy artillery; all that had been sent back to India. His would truly be a flying column, travelling light and quick – just the sort of march, whether a success or failure, which would set alight the jingoistic public back home. And she would not be here to record it!

Alice held her head high as she walked back through the pale sunshine, but her thoughts were in her boots. Cornford, she knew, had protected her before from criticism from the high Tories on the board. As editor, he had occasionally shaved away some of the more iconoclastic passages in her copy, but he had always allowed the main thrust of her articles to remain. Now he would have few grounds for defending her, even if he wished to. Defying the Commander-in-Chief and forging his initials would, she knew, leave her completely vulnerable to her critics. She was in disgrace.

As she walked through the pale winter sunshine, however – and her stride lengthened as her mind raced – her resolution grew. She would *not* be dictated to by officers of the British Army, however high their rank. She was a civilian working in a neutral country and she would stay in Afghanistan to complete the task assigned to her. But how? She would have to keep up with Roberts's column if she was to get her story, but, clearly, the army would not allow her within its fold and she knew, from travelling with Gough's force up through the passes, that any straggler hobbling along behind the rearguard would be pounced upon and cut to pieces by the tribesmen who lurked on the fringes of the advance. She remembered with a shudder seeing the mutilated bodies of two cooks who had been brought in one morning after straying beyond the pickets. There was no way that a woman could travel independently behind Roberts's column.

Alice entered the Bala Hissar, disregarding the salute of the sentry at the gate, and her mind turned back to Covington's intervention during her interrogation. She smiled at the thought. He had tried to be brave – as one would expect of him – but his gallantry could not go very far. Yet perhaps he could help her travel with the column: in disguise, maybe . . .?

Her reverie was interrupted by Campbell, who put a concerned arm through hers and escorted her to her room. 'Are you going to be shot at dawn?'

'No. Worse than that. I've been sacked. I am to leave Afghanistan with a force which is going back to India in two days' time. The bloody man won't let me go with the Kandahar column.'

Alice sprawled on her bed and Campbell drew up a chair and sat. He leaned forward, his elbow on his knee, his fist supporting his chin. 'Look, I'll do all I can to help. Perhaps I can send my copy back to you at the Frontier and you can rewrite and telegraph on—'

'Good Lord, no.' Alice shook her head in disgust. 'I can't rewrite someone else's copy. I must be with the column and write my own story. You must see that.'

Campbell lifted his eyebrows. 'Well, I can see that all right, Alice. What I can't see, my dear, is how you are going to do it. Trying to smuggle yourself into a fast-moving show, as this is bound to be, will be impossible. You must realise that. Not to mention the danger.'

'I know. I just have to find a way. Perhaps Covington will help me.'

'I don't see how. He will have a war to fight.'

As if on cue, a firm hand rapped on the door and a voice called, 'Alice, I must see you.'

Alice rose and opened the door to reveal a stern-visaged

Covington. His scowl deepened further when he saw Campbell.

'Don't worry,' said the Scotsman. 'I'm just going.' He stood and smiled at Alice and nodded to Covington. At the door, as he brushed past the tall soldier, he whispered, 'Don't be too hard on her.'

Alice gestured to the empty chair and raised a hand in defence. 'I know, I know,' she said. 'I've been foolish. Well, it's not for the first time and I expect it won't be the last.'

Covington sat and, without a word, adjusted the impeccable crease in his trousers. They sat in silence for a moment or two, then, gradually, the Colonel's face relaxed into a smile and he shook his head.

'My darling Alice. Foolish is not the word. Stupid is more like it, but, by God, I like your spirit.' He pushed the chair back until, familiarly, it was balanced on its two back legs. His blue eyes beamed at her above his magnificent moustache. 'You certainly gave those little pricks what for, I'll say. I would give a thousand guineas to hear you call Roberts's hand again with those bloody newspaper articles from India. Never heard him speechless before. Then you told him it wasn't his country to throw you out of . . . Bloody marvellous. Wish you were a soldier and I had you in my regiment. We'd knock these Pathans over on our own. What!'

Alice smiled, despite her gloom. Covington, traditional, conventional, dyed-in-the-wool Victorian Covington, could be magnificently unpredictable. He had a mind of his own – and guts, too. Not for the first time, she realised that this was a man she could love: strong, loyal and attractive. But now he must help her again. He *would* help, she knew.

Suddenly, as though he had read her mind, Covington brought his chair down again with a thud. He reached across and took her hand, raised it to his lips for a moment and then retained it in his own. All trace of laughter had disappeared. 'Now, my dear,' he said, 'there has to be no nonsense about this. I have been put in charge of making sure that you do leave in two days' time.' A half-smile returned for a brief moment. 'Shrewd old bugger, Roberts. I think he suspects that I'm soft on you. So he's given me orders to be hard on you. And so I will. You *will* leave in that India party. I will see to that.'

'But Ralph, I can't go. You must see that. My career depends upon it.'

Covington increased his grip on her hand but his voice softened somewhat. 'My dear, I have a terrible feeling that your career is probably over. You were very stupid to break the rules set up by an army commander in the field. I am afraid you behaved arrogantly, and there is no one in the army, either here or back home, who would say differently. You will never get accreditation again. But, my love,' he cupped her hand in both of his and leaned forward, 'it is of no matter. You have had your fling. Marry me now. You will be mistress of a fine estate back home. There will be good hunting, and children, and even . . .' he waved his hand expansively, 'opportunities very occasionally to accompany me in the field – though not on dangerous postings, of course. I promise you there will be wonderful compensations for this nonsense. I will make it up to you. You'll see.'

Alice smiled into the earnest face so close to hers. She put up a hand and brought his head down so that she could kiss the great moustache. Instinctively, he held her close, but she pushed him away.

'Ralph, you know I do not wish to marry anyone, at least not at present.' She raised his hand and put it to her cheek. 'You also know how fond I am of you. But, just as your career is everything to you, so is mine to me. I know that you think

that unusual and wild-headed, but that is the way I am made.'
She smiled but there was more than a hint of sadness in her
face. 'I do not accept that my career is over and I intend to
fight to see that it is not. Please, please, can you help me with
that?'

Covington withdrew his hand sharply. 'Help you. How?'

'I will not go back to India. Will you help me travel with
the column to Kandahar?'

'Good God. What? How?'

Alice leaned forward and spoke quickly and with emphasis.
'I have not the faintest idea. But you will know. Disguise me
as an Indian woman to travel with the cooks, or something.
You know I am hardy and strong. I will work and keep up.
But I must be in Kandahar to file my story when the battle
comes. I must. I must.'

Covington rose to his feet slowly and stood looking down
at her. Then he broke the silence. 'You know I would do
almost anything for you, Alice. But not this. There are several
reasons why not. Firstly, it is far too dangerous. Do you know
where the main casualties occur when a column goes on active
service on the frontier?'

Alice shook her head.

'It's always with the Indian cooks and baggage train.
However we try and protect them with a rearguard, they are
always vulnerable. They're so easy to pick off, particularly
at night. But there's another reason. I too have my duty to
do. And at the moment, it includes making sure that you are
in that column returning to India. My dear, I shall carry out
that duty, even if it means losing you. I suggest that you
begin packing.'

Covington held her gaze for a moment, then, with a half-
bow, he turned and left, leaving Alice staring at the door with
tears brimming in her eyes. She stayed that way for a while,

cursing her weakness, before lying back on the bed and staring at the ceiling through half-closed eyes. Then, her mind made up, she jumped to her feet, grabbed her cloak and set off for Sherpur.

Simon, Jenkins and W.G. were in their room, beginning their preparations for joining the India column in two days' time, when Alice knocked on the door. She smiled at them all. 'Good afternoon, gentlemen. May I come in?'

Three answering smiles welcomed her and Jenkins and W.G. competed to push forward the solitary chair. She sat and nodded her thanks. 'Mr Jenkins and Mr Grace, would you think me impertinent if I asked if you would be so kind as to leave us so that I can talk privately with the Captain for a moment?'

'Of course not, miss,' said Jenkins, giving Simon as meaningful a look as he dared, and even W.G.'s customary dignity departed him for a moment as his head bobbed up and down in earnest agreement.

As the door closed behind them, Simon regarded Alice rather as a rabbit might a fox – so much so that Alice burst out laughing.

'It's all right, Simon,' she said. 'I am not here to attack you again.'

Simon gave a rueful smile in return. 'Well, I'm not sure whether I am sorry or glad. No. I *do* know. I am sorry.'

'Oh, good. I will take that as a compliment. Now, tell me. How have you been?'

'Oh, fit as a fiddle – thanks to you. I am much better now. In fact, I believe that I am completely recovered; in mind as well as body. Jenkins and I are getting out of the army and W.G. is going back to his regiment. We are all returning to India the day after tomorrow.'

'Oh.' Alice's heart sank immediately and her face showed

her disappointment. Her last chance had disappeared. 'Oh dear. I am glad for you, if that is what you want. I really am.' She paused and looked aimlessly around her: at the rifles leaning in a corner, the clothing strewn on the beds, the remnants of the light lunch still on the table.

Simon followed her gaze and, for a moment, his spirits leaped. She was sorry to be losing him. Her face showed it, there could be no doubting it. She must, *she must*, care a little! Then came disillusion.

'I came to see if you could help me, but I fear you cannot now.' Alice did not record the disappointment that flashed briefly across Simon's face at her words, for she felt herself giving way to despair. All of the humiliation of the interview with Roberts, the disappointment of Covington's rejection and the realisation that her career was ruined pressed in on her, and as she looked into the brown eyes set in the battered young face opposite her, her own eyes filled with tears. She looked down but it was too late. Her shoulders began to heave and she collapsed into great sobs.

Immediately, Simon sprang from the bed, knelt at her side and enfolded her in his arms. She wept on his shoulder like a baby and he, like a father with a child, rocked her to and fro, stroking her hair and murmuring, 'Shush, shush. It will be all right. You'll see. Whatever it is, I will help you. You'll see. Don't cry, Alice. Don't cry.'

But cry she did, uncharacteristically openly, happy to be comforted, all traces of the sophisticated woman-of-the-world completely departed, until, eventually, she pushed him away and groped for her handkerchief.

'Sorry,' she said. 'Isn't it bloody that whenever a person cries, her nose runs too. Please forgive me. I must look a complete wreck.' She dabbed at her nose and swollen eyes with her handkerchief.

Simon returned to the edge of his bed. 'You look fine to me. Now, tell me what has happened. I shall help you, whatever the cost. I owe you everything.'

Alice smiled through her tears. 'No you don't. I didn't come here debt-collecting, and anyway, now that you are out of the army, I don't see how you *can* help me.'

'Tell me anyway.'

'Oh, very well.' Alice blew her nose and regained her composure. Then she related the events of the day. Simon said not a word, although he could not resist a smile when Alice spoke of her evasion of the censoring procedure. At the end she said, 'So you see, I presumed that you would be going with the column to Kandahar and that, somehow, you could take me with you in your scouting party, or whatever it is you do.'

Simon pursed his lips and shook his head. 'Sorry. We are out of the army now, and frankly, I don't see that Roberts would take us back even if we asked him. He will have made other arrangements for scouting and intelligence-gathering now and, frankly, I don't think he's the sort of man who takes kindly to being turned down and then told that we have changed our minds.'

Alice nodded ruefully. 'I can see that.'

For a moment the two regarded each other. To Simon, Alice looked heart-wrenchingly vulnerable. That firm chin was now wobbling slightly as she tried to restrain tears, and the air of cool self-confidence, which, even if it was assumed, had so daunted him when she came to his bed, had been replaced by one of complete and supplicatory dependence. She looked young and quite, quite innocent. It took an effort of will to recall the woman who had, well, seduced him. The memory reminded him of his debt.

'Alice, is this really terribly important to you – I mean, even to the point of risking your life?'

She nodded, her eyes widening as she glimpsed a ray of hope. 'Oh, Simon, yes. You see, my work has meant everything to me. Before I became a journalist I was a complete misfit – a girl with a good mind but with nothing to apply it to. I did not wish to marry and join the breeding circuit and I certainly could not spend the rest of my life helping Mama with good works and arranging fêtes. Writing for the *Morning Post*, I have been good at what I have done. For the first time in my life I have been completely fulfilled. But if I do not have the chance of redeeming myself for this . . . foolishness, I will be finished. Can you, will you, help me?'

'Alice, I don't know, but perhaps I can. Certainly, *I* will try to help you. However, the point is that it would be so much easier if Jenkins and W.G. were involved too, which means that their lives would also be put at risk. I cannot order them in this situation.'

Alice hung her head for a moment. 'I realise I am asking so much.' Then she looked up and held his gaze with that directness he remembered so well. 'Do you think that I am a spoiled brat, Simon, a selfish bitch? Do you?'

Slowly he smiled and shook his head. 'No. A spoiled brat wouldn't have done what you did for me, both here and in South Africa. Stubborn, maybe, but neither selfish nor spoiled. Now, we don't have much time, and even if the others agree, there are practicalities to consider. Can you come back here, say, in two hours?'

'Of course. Oh, Simon. Thank you so much.'

'Wait and see if there is reason to thank us. Give me two hours.'

Alice was back at Sherpur early, of course, so she forced herself to walk around the compound for a while to pass the time, before returning to Simon's room exactly two hours later. She found the three men waiting for her, and to her joy, it was clear from their faces that they all intended to help.

'Now.' Simon put Alice firmly in the chair while the others squatted on their mattresses. 'We have a plan, of sorts, but there is no guarantee that it will work. Alice, I seem to remember that you are a good horsewoman. Is that so?'

'Yes. I used to hunt back home and I have ridden everywhere in South Africa, India and here. I am at home on a horse.'

'There's splendid, then,' murmured Jenkins. 'That makes three of us.'

Simon ignored the interruption. 'Good. We will need to ride hard and fast over very difficult terrain. Look at this.' He pulled forward a hand-sketched map of southern Afghanistan. 'Here we are at Kabul. Here,' he pointed to the south-west, near the border with India, 'is Kandahar, about three hundred miles or more from Kabul. My bet is that Roberts will march directly there. There is a reasonable enough road for the first fifty miles to Ghazni, here, but after that it will be rough tracks and tough mountain country. He will have to cross the Zamburak Kotal, about here, which is more than eight thousand feet high. All the while, he will be vulnerable to attack. But he will go for it as the shortest route. However, my guess, and,' he nodded to the Sikh, 'that of W.G. here, who knows the country, is that he will be harassed by snipers and so on but it is unlikely that he will be confronted by Ayub Khan in a full-pitched battle until the two armies meet at Kandahar. There's a sort of plain in front of the walled city.'

'Yes,' breathed Alice, her eyes wide, 'I must be there, then.' She looked up. 'Can we follow behind the army, keeping in touch with it, so to speak?'

Simon shook his head. 'No. We all think that would be

impossible. Local tribesmen will be trailing the column all the way, reporting on its progress and seeking to cut off stragglers. They would descend on us in a flash.'

Alice nodded slowly. 'Then can we shadow it, from up in the hills?'

'Sorry, no again. It would be awfully difficult for us to ride from peak to peak, and even if we could, we would be picked up again by the Afghans.'

'But I *must* be with the army, to report on its march.'

'Can't be done, Alice. You must reconcile yourself to that. But if we are right, you will not be missing much by not riding with or near the army. There will be no question of Roberts allowing his precious telegraph facility to be used by journalists while on the march – even if it remained unbroken – so it would not be possible for you to send stories back until you reached Kandahar anyway. And we believe there will be no battles on the way, only hard slog.'

Alice saw the point and slowly nodded her head. 'What do you propose, then?'

Simon took a deep breath and looked at the others. 'Well, it is a hell of a risk, but we propose that the four of us ride to Kandahar as fast as we can by a different route to Roberts. Look.' He pulled the map round so that she could see better. 'W.G. believes that we can take a more northerly loop, here,' he traced with his finger, 'through the Hazarajat region and down round the back of Ghazni, and come down to Kandahar, via Baba Wali, here from the north. It will be very tough going indeed, and we may have to lead the horses for much of the way, but it will be safer than trying to shadow the army.'

'But won't we arrive too late? As we have to go so far north, won't Roberts get to Kandahar before us?'

Simon shrugged his shoulders. 'That is quite possible. It is a risk we will have to take. But I hear that the force, although stripped down to the essentials, will still consist of about ten thousand fighting men, some eight thousand followers – baggage carriers, animal handlers and so on – and eighteen guns. Now, Alice, that is a small enough army with which to fight Ayub Khan, but it is a hell of a force to take three hundred miles over mountains. We are riding further but we can travel faster. It all depends when Roberts sets off – and if *we* can stay out of trouble on the way.'

Alice looked at Jenkins and W.G., who had been listening with silent attention. 'Gentlemen,' she said, 'I am very much aware that I am taking you into great danger and I shall quite understand if you feel that this is all too much. After all, you owe me nothing.'

W.G. inclined his head. 'Don't mention it, memsahib. Let us consider it a great adventure, don't you think?'

Jenkins's teeth showed white beneath his moustache. 'Any friend of the Captain's is a friend of ours, miss. Don't worry your head about it. We will get you there . . . or, at least, W.G. will. I'm not too sure of the way, see.'

'Now, Alice,' resumed Simon. 'We three are already natives in appearance, as you see, although,' he rubbed his cheek ruefully, 'I have a feeling that this dye is beginning to lighten by the day. But you will have to black up, I'm afraid. We must join the homeward party the day after tomorrow. As soon as darkness falls on the first day, we will fit you out and colour you up. Then we will slip out of camp and double back. You will ride as a young Pathan boy.' He grinned. 'Though you may have to stay quiet, I'm afraid.'

'But what if we meet tribesmen in the hills on the way?'

'This is where, as ever, we rely on dear old W.G. Don't worry. We've got used to that. When we are near Kabul, we shall be Afghans from the Persian border far to the west, returning to Kandahar from India, where we have been trading, to take part in the attack on the infidels holed up in the city. The lingo is different, you see, in these parts of the country. But W.G. knows most of them and will translate for us. The reverse applies when we near Kandahar. There, we shall be Afridis coming from the North West Frontier. If all else fails, we shoot and ride our way through. Do you . . . er . . . possess a firearm, Alice?'

'Yes, I have a Navy Colt revolver and I have practised with it. I shall have no hesitation in using it, if I must.'

'I don't doubt that, miss,' said Jenkins.

'Good. One more thing, Alice. No one must guess your intentions.'

'Of course not. Except there is one person I must tell, for I shall need *him*, for certain. Johnny Campbell, of the *Standard*, must know, so that he can take notes for me of the march. Please, Simon. I would trust him – as I am trusting you – with my life.'

Simon sighed. 'Well, if you really insist. But he must keep your secret. No more arguments with authority, now. They must presume that you have accepted your lot and will ride obediently back to India.'

'Of course, Simon. Although I will spend much of my last day tomorrow writing and sending my final dispatch back to London about the preparations for the march. Even Roberts can't stop me doing that.'

'Very well. But don't offend him.'

'I promise.'

Alice devoted the next day to gathering whatever facts she could about Roberts's preparations for his epic march. In fact, there were few security precautions evident in the hectic toings and froings which now consumed Sherpur. There was little Roberts could do, in any event, to conceal the detail of his arrangements from the many sharp eyes which followed them from under heavily swathed turbans.

Alice learned that Roberts planned to set out in three days' time, which meant that, in theory at least, she would have one day's march advantage over the army, although this would count for little once she and her escort took their circuitous route north.

The General was making his preparations with typical speed and thoroughness. He was calculating that he could complete his forced march quickly enough to take Ayub Khan if not by surprise, at least before he had been able either to take the city of Kandahar or begin his own march on Kabul. Accordingly, Roberts was ruthlessly engaged in weeding out every man whom he felt would be incapable of standing the strain of a series of forced marches and in stripping down his artillery and reducing it only to lightweight mountain batteries, so that there would be no wheeled guns to delay the march.

More controversially, he reduced the scale of baggage, tents and what he called 'impedimenta' to a minimum. No champagne or other mess luxuries accompanied the officers this time, and each British soldier was allowed only thirty pounds weight for kit and camp equipage, including his greatcoat and waterproof sheet, reduced to twenty pounds for each native soldier. In all, Roberts gathered together a force consisting of just under ten thousand fighting men, divided into three brigades of infantry, one of cavalry and three batteries of mountain guns. He also took eight thousand native camp workers and two thousand, three hundred horses and gun-mules, plus some eight thousand other pack animals and ponies.

Speed was to be the essence of the whole enterprise. Roberts planned to start each day with the 'rouse', sounded at two forty-five a.m., with tents struck and baggage loaded up for a four a.m. start. A halt of ten minutes was to be allowed at the end of each hour which, at eight o'clock, was to be prolonged to twenty minutes to allow for a hasty breakfast. Where the terrain allowed it, the cavalry was to cover the march at a distance of about five miles, with two of the four regiments in the van and the other two on the flanks. The third infantry brigade, with its mountain battery and one or two troops of cavalry, was to form the rearguard.

All of this Alice noted with care before sitting down and writing an article which, she hoped, captured the bustle and urgency of the preparations and the excitement which pervaded Sherpur at what everyone felt would be the last and, whatever the outcome, most decisive encounter with the Afghan army. Somewhat to her surprise, her copy was accepted for censorship without demur and returned shortly afterwards with the initials of the General's ADC on each sheet. Obviously, Roberts was too busy to vet copy at this late stage. Alice took advantage by adding a note to her editor at the end of her story, 'More to follow from Kandahar', before handing it to the telegraph clerk. As she did so, she offered up an inward prayer that the promise would be fulfilled.

The India-bound column was to start before dawn the next day, so, before retiring that evening, Alice sought out John Campbell. The young man was packing the few clothes that he was allowed to take, and Alice's arrival made him embarrassed – a reminder that he was journeying to cover the most important story of his life, while she was being sent out of the country in disgrace.

She quickly told him of what was planned. At first he snorted with derision at the wild ambition of the scheme, then, seeing that she was determined, he pleaded to be allowed to join the party. But Alice remained adamant and extracted a promise that he would keep her secret and, when they met at Kandahar, give her colour details of the march to include in her story. He sighed, kissed her and, with troubled eyes, watched her go.

The promise of the sun was just a glow behind the peaks to the east as Alice joined the Indian contingent the next morning. Covington, erect and stern, although his pillbox hat was set at a jaunty angle, escorted her to the column. He paid no attention to Simon, Jenkins and W.G., who rode up and joined the line towards the rear. Neither did Alice.

Covington cupped his hands to help her mount. 'I am sorry it had to end like this, Alice,' he said. 'Once the General has had his victory, perhaps I can persuade him to be lenient and let you return to Kandahar, by the southern route from India. It might be worth waiting at 'Pindi for that, you know.'

Alice smiled down on him. 'Thank you, Ralph. I appreciate what you have tried to do for me. By all means see if you can wring a concession or two from the old scoundrel. But by then I will probably have been summoned home.'

The tall man's eyes clouded. 'My dear, I shall miss you terribly, you know. Are you ... are you ... sure that you won't reconsider my offer? It still stands, you know.'

'Thank you, Ralph. But no. Perhaps one day – who knows, if we are both then still free – but not now.'

She leaned down and gave him her hand, which he brought to his lips. Then he looked up. 'Ah, forgot to tell you. Some good news for you, at least, to send you on your way. Your man has got in. Gladstone, the old windbag, has won the election and Disraeli has gone. Bad news for the army, I fear, but I know you will be pleased.'

Alice looked down at the Colonel with real affection. 'Ah,

Ralph. Thank you so much for telling me. You knew how much it would mean to me.'

Her heart sang. It was a good omen. Liberal politics at home again at last! She would get to Kandahar. She *would*!

Somewhere far ahead a bugle sounded and, slowly, the column began to move. She dug in her heels, turned and waved to Covington, noticing as she did so that from fifty paces away Simon's eyes were upon her. Then she began the journey she prayed would take her to Kandahar.

Chapter 12

It was summer in Afghanistan, but as soon as the sun touched the edge of the peaks to the west, the temperature dropped by twenty degrees and continued to fall with the dusk, so that by the time the little party of four, high in the mountains, had crawled under their blankets, it was at about zero. The unfortunates who drew the middle and late watches of the night had to be swathed in sheepskins so as not to give away their location by the chattering of their teeth. It was Simon's turn for the latter duty, and he pulled a blanket over his head and tried to wriggle further into the rock crevice that overlooked their camping site as he waited for the dawn. Below him, the inert forms of Alice, Jenkins and W.G. radiated like the spokes of a wheel from the remnants of the fire on which they had cooked a meal of kid and rice. They slept like dogs, worn out by nineteen days of riding and scrambling along a series of goat tracks that climbed and fell relentlessly, shouldering the peaks that loomed over them to the north.

Their escape from the column had been easier than expected. Simon had gambled that, if they chose their moment correctly, they could easily evade the column's flanking cavalry. The problem would be the Pathans who would be watching the troops from the hills. Accordingly, they had decided to go not after dark, when the jackals with their *jezails* would be lurking behind the rocks, but just before dusk, when all was hustle and bustle: the mounted pickets were in and everyone was busy with unlimbering horses, pitching tents and preparing the evening meal. Under cover of the activity, they had slipped, one by one, into a copse of trees that came down low to border the road. It climbed high enough to give them cover for about two hundred feet, after which they could scramble upwards, leading their horses, undetected. Simon knew that Jenkins, W.G. and he would not be missed. They were on no roll-call and were no one's responsibility. But Alice was another matter. She had been invited to dine with the lieutenant colonel commanding the column that evening, and although she had declined, pleading tiredness from the march, her absence would soon be revealed the next morning. The question was: would the column commander send out a search party to look for her? Simon decided that it would be unlikely, but they pressed on in the darkness for four hours anyway before they camped. As important as leaving search parties behind was to get away from the road and the inevitable screen of Afghans who would be shadowing the column. But their luck had held and they seemed to have been undetected. Simon estimated that they had put about ten miles between them and the soldiers by the time they rose at dawn after snatching a brief rest.

Simon and W.G. had decided that their best hope of getting through the hills without running into trouble was to go into the barren heights, away from the settlements that huddled in the valleys. The strategy had been successful in that they had only encountered one goatherd with his flock and ridden through two hamlets of mud and earth huts, from where they had been able to purchase goat's milk and eggs. They excited a sullen curiosity from the old women who seemed the only occupants, but the crones seemed to accept

W.G.'s story that they had become lost on their way from the north to fight for Ayub Khan at Kandahar.

Most days, they rode above the bold birches whose edges signalled, as though with a ruler, the end of the flora and fauna that stretched down to form indistinct purple valleys far below them. Grey eagles sometimes wheeled high above them, and once, they saw a bear, distantly grubbing and rooting at the hillside. Most of the time, however, they could have been the only living things on the planet. Usually they were able to follow a distinct track, sometimes as wide as six feet across, which led roughly in the direction they wished to follow. At other times, however, they had to dismount and lead their horses across rocks and through glissading streams that delayed their progress and induced aching weariness. It was hard, very hard work.

By the light of the moon that half illuminated the flat clearing amidst the rocks where they had made camp, Simon could just make out Alice's fair hair peeping out from beneath her blanket. Despite their protests, she had refused to have it dyed and had promised to keep it coiled at all times within the loose cap she wore. In fact, with her slim form and lithe grace, she made a good-looking Afghan boy – as long as she remembered to keep her glance lowered to hide her grey eyes. She rode like a trooper, even though W.G. had insisted on changing her fine Punjab mount in the bazaar for a sturdy Afghan pony. Cupping his chin on his hand, Simon could trace the sensuous curve of Alice's body beneath the Afghan sheepskin cover. He tingled as he remembered its warmth as she had pressed close to him that night in Kabul and recalled again, as he had a hundred times, the delicious roughness of her tongue and the softness of her lips. Hell and damnation! Why hadn't she left him alone to forget her in India!

She had, of course, been a cheerful, uncomplaining companion to them all on the journey, taking her turn at cooking, strapping Jenkins's ankle when he had turned it in a crevasse and insisting she should stand night guard – although here she had been over-ruled. As she rode, she attempted to make notes of the geography and conditions of the trail, for use, she explained, as background colour when she came to write her articles.

Simon sighed as he looked down at her – though not completely from unrequited love. How the hell were they going to link up with Roberts, if and when he had been able to fight his way through to Kandahar? If the city had resisted attack, it would be surrounded by Ayub Khan's army and Afghan scouts would be out for miles around, attempting to locate Roberts's advancing force. How could they slip through these patrols – and what sort of welcome would they get from Roberts anyway?

His reverie was interrupted by the briefest flicker of light from the tip of the surly, dark peaks to the east. Shivering, he threw away his blanket, climbed down and kicked the smouldering fire into life, so that they could have hot tea, at least, before starting the day's journey. Within the half-hour, they were all mounted and riding to the west, as the newly emerged sun brought some warmth. When they came to a wider part of the trail, Simon dropped back and walked his horse alongside Alice's pony. She had been strangely quiet the previous evening and had uttered no word since resuming the journey. Simon smiled at her but, her eyes downcast, she did not return the smile or look at him.

He cleared his throat. 'I'm afraid that it's been hard pounding, Alice, but we should not have far to go now.'

Alice did not reply for a moment. Then she looked up and gave him a half-smile, and he realised that her eyes were moist. 'Oh, Simon,' she said. 'I have been thinking, and I realise that I have been so foolish and selfish. Making you undertake this journey and . . . and . . . exposing you all to so much danger, just because I want to save what I call *my career*.' She spat out the last two words. 'How could I have been so thoughtless? I realise that once we approach Kandahar we shall be entering the lion's den and I will have been responsible for putting all of your lives at great risk. Is it not too late, even now, to turn back?'

There was no trace left now of the Alice who had so confidently forged a general's signature, who had used her body like a Parisian courtesan, and who had observed executions clinically. That feisty, strong woman seemed to have been blown away, like an autumn leaf, by the hot wind that whistled through these heights. The eyes brimming with tears belonged to a young girl out of her depth for the first time in a harsh world. Simon felt pity and love for her anew, and he reached out and took her hand.

'I don't quite know what to do to comfort you, Alice, except to say that what you did for me showed that you are the most unselfish and caring person in the world. If you can do that for someone you don't love, then you will surely suffocate with unselfishness the man you truly do come to love.'

She smiled at him through her tears.

'I am afraid that we have gone too far to turn back now,' said Simon. 'We have been lucky to have travelled so far undetected and I doubt if we could retrace our steps and keep our luck. Anyway, it would mean returning to the Kabul road, which is unsafe to follow without an army escort. We are not far from our destination now. In less than two days, I judge, we can turn south and go down to look for the valley of the Arghandabad River, which should take us just north of Kandahar.

'And look,' he added, 'it *is* a career worth saving. None of us would be here if we did not believe that.'

Alice sniffed and nodded her thanks, not sure that she could speak. But as the day wore on, her smile returned.

They rode with more caution now, picking their way round the villages they encountered more frequently and shivering without a fire that night. The wood smoke, they felt, would betray their position. W.G. had ridden these hills before, but many years ago, and Simon backed the Sikh's recollections with rough compass bearings. His plan was to find the Arghandabad River, follow it for a few miles north of Kandahar and then loop south to the west of the city. W.G. remembered a flat plain that extended to the south and east of Kandahar, and it was Simon's guess that the Afghan general, whether or not he had taken the city, would draw up his army to receive Roberts there. The Afghans, he knew, were traditionalists when it came to large battles: the British were the invaders, therefore it was they who must attack the fixed positions of the defenders. It was seemly so to do. It was unlikely that Ayub Khan would advance up the Kabul road to confront Roberts in those cramped passes. If this were so – and if Simon and his companions had indeed out-marched the British army – then the four could, perhaps, observe how the Afghans were drawn up, outflank them and ride into Roberts's advance guard and explain the enemy dispositions, so winning the General's grateful forgiveness for Alice's indiscretions. Perhaps, perhaps . . . and perhaps pigs would fly. Simon shrugged his shoulders as he slouched wearily in the saddle. It was the only plan he had, anyway.

Just under three weeks after leaving the column, they turned their horses' heads south at last, down towards the valley far below them, where the real danger lurked. That evening they encountered the shallow, bouncing waters of the Arghandabad and made an uncomfortable camp by its shores, tucked away within a copse of deodar that was feathered and plumed with ferns. They knew that if they followed the river westwards, they would hit the Kabul road on the far side of Kandahar. They also knew, however, that this was the most dangerous part of their journey, for if the Afghans were still laying siege to the city, they would probably have forces to the north as well as to the south, where lay the plain, and to the east, from which direction Roberts was still presumably marching. So, with great caution, they proceeded, W.G. in the lead, Simon ahead of Alice, and Jenkins at the rear, their cocked rifles carried athwart their saddles but with cotton folds across the trigger mechanisms to conceal their British origins.

Inevitably, they encountered a Pathan patrol. They saw them coming from perhaps half a mile away: a group of five horsemen, dressed in the dull khaki of Afghan cavalry, picking their way slowly but purposefully between the boulders fringing the river. The four quickly established that flight would be inadvisable: the stone-strewn track was the last place for a gallop. They decided that they would stick to their original plan, trusting that the men of the patrol would be locals and unfamiliar with the Afridi dialect.

As the two parties closed, W.G. and Simon lifted their hands in greeting and called, *'Allah kerim!'* The leader of the patrol, a hawk-nosed man with black eyes that scanned them all in a second, replied similarly and directed a flow of fluent Pushtu to W.G., who had ridden forward to meet them. The two stayed in conversation for three minutes or so – although it seemed an eternity to Simon, Alice and Jenkins, who leaned wearily on their saddle pommels and gazed about them with what they hoped appeared to be disinterest.

The sun was at its height and the heat made the tension worse. In fact this helped them, for it was clear that the patrol did not wish to linger on such a day interrogating three men and a boy who, it was quickly apparent, were not outriders of the approaching British column nor had information about it. From under lowered brows, Simon saw the patrol leader gesture with his rifle ahead and then to the south, and then wave them on. With a nod of thanks, he urged his horse forward and the four of them walked by, feigning nonchalance and a fatigue which was not altogether assumed.

Once out of sight of the Pathans, Simon called to W.G. and the three of them gathered round the Sikh.

'It was not a problem, lord,' said W.G. 'I explained that you were headman of a village near the Khyber Pass, with your son,' he nodded to Alice, 'and a villager, and that I had been hired to take you to Ayub Khan to join his force. But I said that we had got a bit lost in the outfield, so to speak, in avoiding the British Army.'

Simon nodded. 'Well done, W.G.'

Jenkins snorted. 'Sounds all a bit simple to me. Not proper soldiers, them, not at all.'

The Sikh acknowledged the point with a grave inclination of his head. 'Precisely so, Sergeant bach. But they were tired, like us, and you forget that they are blasted Afghans. Not clever at all, I am saying. Also,' he bowed slightly to Alice, 'the presence of the memsahib helped considerably. We could not be *gora-log* spies, or disguised British patrol, with such a young boy riding with us.' He grinned broadly. 'Very good show, miss, I am thinking.'

'Good.' Simon nodded ahead. 'What were the directions he was giving you?'

'Ah, lord. He said that Kandahar has not fallen and that

Afghan general has withdrawn his forces to the south and the west of the city to wait for the British, who are, perhaps, one day's march only away. He tells me that there is a ford just ahead where we can cross river and then go down to Afghan army. I am thinking, lord, that we do not wish to do this.'

'Blimey,' said Jenkins. 'No fear.'

'I am not so sure,' mused Simon.

'Now come on, bach sir,' said Jenkins, his eyebrows nearly meeting his turban fringe in exaggerated surprise. 'I think we've used up just about all of our nine lives so far in marchin' straight into enemy camps. We've got none left, look you. What would we want to do it for, anyway?'

Simon shook his head. 'No. I don't intend to walk into Ayub Khan's camp, thank you very much. But I would very much like to take a peek at his disposition so that if – no, sorry, *when* – we find Roberts we have something to bring him, so to speak.' He smiled at Alice. 'A sort of peace offering. A present to turn away his wrath.'

Alice smiled back. She had regained something of her composure and had resumed taking notes of the terrain. 'Do whatever you think is right, Simon. But do not do this for me. I do not wish to lead you all into any further danger.'

Jenkins snorted. 'Don't worry about that, miss. We've bin in the fryin' pan so long that I don't think I'd notice if we jumped into the bleedin' fire ... er ... beggin' your pardon, that is, miss.'

They found the ford soon enough, splashed through the shallows and, staying with a narrow trail, immediately began climbing a spur of hills the summit of which, as the day wore on, seemed to recede before them, so that they were forced once again to dismount and lead their horses. The slow progress annoyed Simon, who, with Roberts only a rumoured day's march away, began to fear that they would arrive too late for the battle. Accordingly, they camped late and rose before the dawn the next morning to continue their climb.

Some four hours later, they crested the range and were rewarded with a panoramic vista spread below them, a sight that reminded Simon of the trestle-mounted sand reconstructions of great battle sites that he had studied at Sandhurst. Far to their left, half concealed behind a spur of the hills, they glimpsed the ochre-coloured smudge that, from its size and the heat haze that shimmered above it, was undoubtedly Kandahar. Leading to it, and disappearing into the distance beyond it, was the black, winding road back to Kabul: no traffic on it and certainly no British Army in sight. Directly below them, as W.G. had promised, lay the plain, featuring a large village and gridded, here and there, with low stone walls surrounding cultivated vegetable and fruit patches. Two roads, straight as a die and running roughly east to west, broke the plain and passed out of sight behind a line of rugged peaks to their right.

W.G. indicated with a long forefinger. 'That, lord, is the village of Gundigan, and that line of little mountains there is the Baba Wali Kotal. You see that the Afghan scoundrels are based around the village.'

Indeed they were. Ayub Khan seemed to have drawn up his army on the plain, as Simon had expected, and had used the walls of the village on which to base his right wing and to site artillery. They could see the village teeming with tiny figures, like an anthill. The figures were also to be seen scurrying across the plain, setting up positions behind the walls. It was no country for cavalry, though the two main roads seemed wide and to provide good enough conduits for a two-pronged attack on the Afghan position. Then a flash of light from the Baba Wali Kotal below them and to their right drew Simon's attention. He shaded his eyes.

'Good Lord,' he exclaimed. 'He's put artillery in those hills. The cunning bastard.'

Somehow, the Afghans had manhandled what seemed to be quite heavy pieces of ordnance up the steep sides of the hills and had positioned the guns on ledges and cols so that they commanded the plain below. From their vantage point, Simon and his companions could clearly see the gun emplacements and the white-robed *ghazis* pushing and hauling the pieces into position. From the plain, however, they would be difficult to see. Any force attacking the village and its outlying walled gardens would be vulnerable to this flanking fire from above. It was a perfect trap – another Balaclava.

Simon turned to the others. 'He knows what he's doing, this chap. Our people will be blown away unless those hills are cleared.'

'Yes, well.' Jenkins blew his nose with great ostentation. 'Shall we just nip down and do that before the General arrives, look you? He might be quite glad to see us then, see.'

Alice did not speak, but frowned in consternation as she sketched the scene below in her notebook.

Not for the first time, Simon wished he had a telescope or binoculars. 'W.G., you have the best eyes. Can you see any sign of the British coming down the Kabul road or moving to the city?'

The Sikh turned his head and remained perfectly still for a moment in concentration. He shook his head. 'Nothing I can see, lord.' Then, very slowly, he raised a hand. 'Wait . . . I think there is something. Can you see – beyond the city, where the road disappears into mountains? Can you see?'

They all shielded their eyes and desperately tried to focus on the indistinct end of the black line where it snaked away to the east.

'Either you've got eyes like an eagle, Gracey, or you've got a touch of the sun,' said Jenkins, his nose wrinkled in concentration so that a flash of white teeth appeared behind his moustache. 'As far as I can see, there's bugger-all out there.'

'No, no, there *is* something.' Alice spoke softly, as though she would lose that far-distant something if she raised her voice. 'There is something ... moving out there, just where the road comes down to the plain. Can you see it?'

The others could not at first, but then, after twenty seconds or so of concentration, they spotted it: a tiny brownish block, moving very slowly at that distance. Then a brief flash, another, and yet another as the sun caught something burnished and bright and sent its reflection in an instant some twenty miles across the plain.

'Good.' Simon dug the heel of each hand into his eyes, now watering from the strain of focusing so far. 'That's got to be Roberts. The old devil has done the march in three weeks. Fantastic!'

'But Simon,' said Alice, 'could it not be an Afghan patrol, returning from a scouting mission to look for Roberts?'

'Don't think so. Even at this distance, that looks like the vanguard of an army to me.' He turned to W.G. and Jenkins. 'What do you two think?'

'Wouldn't they be comin' from the other way, then?' asked Jenkins, gesturing to the right. 'Ah, no. Perhaps not.' He squinted upwards. 'If the sun's just there, then, that means the left's the north ... or do I mean the south? Sorry, I'm not much good at this. Can't really tell me arse from me elbow. Oh, sorry, miss.'

The Sikh had never relaxed his gaze on the Kabul road. 'I think, lord,' he said, 'that it is cavalry coming slowly. Perhaps, indeed, it is the advance screen of Punjabis leading the column.' He spoke with proprietorial satisfaction.

'Right.' Simon looked up at the sun. 'If it *is* Roberts, he will go straight to the city and probably camp just outside it for the night. If I know him, he won't waste any time. He will send out patrols to reconnoitre Ayub Khan's position and attack him as soon as possible. They will be running low on supplies at Kandahar now and the General will want to lift the siege right away. W.G., how long do you think it will take for the column to reach the city?'

It was the Sikh's turn to squint up at the sun. 'He will reach it just before nightfall, lord, I believe.'

'Is there a way down from the top here to Kandahar behind us, or will we have to go straight down on to the plain and ride back that way?'

'I am being fairly certain, lord, that we must travel back many miles before we can take a pass down to the city. This is the quickest way.' W.G. gestured forward, where they could see the trail winding downwards until it was lost between the rocks.

'Very well. We will make our way down and find somewhere reasonably hidden to camp before we reach the plain. If we are discovered, we will tell our usual story. Then we must be up just before dawn and ride towards the British position. I suggest that we keep as close to the edge of these hills as possible. Those two roads will be full of Afghan patrols, or even perhaps a sizeable portion of Ayub Khan's army. You see,' Simon turned to Alice, 'he will want Roberts to attack him at these villages below. He may well try to lure him on by making a feint. Then, as Roberts advances along the valley, the guns in these crags below will give him hell.'

Alice nodded gravely. 'I quite understand. You feel we must go and warn him against being drawn into the trap.'

'Absolutely.'

A sigh of great and histrionic weariness came from Jenkins.

'Ah well,' he said, munching his moustache. ' 'Ere we go again. 'Eroes of the Queen an' all that. An' we're not even in the bleedin' army any more. Oh dear, oh dear.' But he pulled his horse's head round and led the descent into the valley.

That night they camped some way off the trail amid rocks and scree about two hundred and fifty feet above the plain. It was uncomfortable, with no fire to provide warmth or hot food, but they were undisturbed and rose well before the sun to begin picking their way down to where the trail broadened out to meet the plain. It was still dark when their descent ended and they turned their horses east, towards Kandahar.

For Simon, blowing on his hands against the pre-dawn cold, it was an anxious time. He looked around at the shadowy figures behind him. They slouched in their saddles and their mounts stepped forward with no enthusiasm. They had all been on the road too long. There was no way they could out-run Afghans on brisk little ponies if it came to a confrontation. Yet they had no story now to explain why they were heading away from the Pathan army and towards the British. It was doubtful if even W.G. could talk his way out of that one. Simon licked his lips and tasted again the dust – the dry, gritty particles that lodged between the teeth and in the corner of the eyes and that would remind him of Afghanistan for ever. In this grim, unforgiving country he was taking his little party into great danger; placing it right between two confronting armies. He must be mad! And yet what else could he do? His gaze took in the slight figure of Alice, riding now with less style, her head bowed and her body arched. What would happen to her if they were captured? He drew in his breath sharply. At all costs he would see that that did not happen.

As though she had sensed his thoughts, Alice lifted up her head, reached into her saddle pack, extracted her Navy Colt revolver and tucked it into her cummerbund.

The light found them making their way over broken ground where the hills to their left rose from the plain. It was difficult going and Simon was forced to veer to the right, on to the plain itself, where the terrain was level. It was a risk, of course, because they became clearly visible once away from the undulations of the foothills. At first, as the sun emerged from a peak ahead and immediately transformed the temperature, they seemed to have the valley to themselves. Ahead of them, Kandahar was tucked out of sight behind a spur, but there was no sign of an encampment, no tell-tale trail of dust from mounted men. Nothing but the flat, seemingly endless plain, pockmarked with stones and, here and there, the low stone walls marking little cultivated squares. Then, far to their right, they could see hundreds of Afghans streaming out from the village of Gundigan going . . . where?

'No, they're not after us,' murmured Simon, in response to the obvious concern of the others. 'I think they are coming out to man those garden walls to bring down the patrols that Roberts is bound to send out early.'

'Yes, bach sir,' muttered Jenkins. 'But what about them lads?' He nodded behind them. At a distance of some three hundred yards, a group of about a dozen mounted Afghans were trotting purposefully towards them, *jezails* and, by the look of it, more modern rifles nestling stocks-down against their thighs, muzzles in the air, like pictures of desert Touregs that Simon had seen in picture books as a boy.

W.G. looked at Simon, his eyebrows raised.

'Tell them,' said Simon, his brain racing, 'tell them, as before, that we are Afridis from the Khyber, on our way to buy horses from Kandahar. Tell them that we lost our way in the hills and that we did not know the city was under siege. Just do what you can, W.G. Play a straight bat for all you're worth.'

'Very good, lord.'

'Let's cock our weapons, but no firing unless we have to. We shall be severely outnumbered. Just keep plodding on. No nervousness, now.'

Within minutes, they were overtaken by the Afghans. Unlike the previous patrol, these were not in uniform. They looked more like brigands in their flowing cotton robes, bandoliers, and arrogantly curled slippers. Some wore skull caps instead of turbans and they all carried long knives or curved swords tucked into their cummerbunds. Two of them had round studded shields, worn on their forearms in medieval fashion. They were not, surmised Simon, regular cavalry, and those who did not carry *jezails*, he noted with relief, were bearing muskets rather than modern breech-loading rifles. Their leader, a small man, his beard flecked with grey, addressed Jenkins, who rode at the rear.

Smoothly, W.G. interjected and began speaking quickly in Pushtu. Simon caught the patrol leader's eye and nodded gravely. While the conversation continued, however, he noticed that one of the Pathans was staring fixedly at Alice. Gradually, the man edged his pony forward until he was by her side. Alice, realising the danger posed by the colour of her eyes, continued to look down, as in a mixture of tiredness and indifference.

Simon was aware that the conversation between W.G. and the leading Afghan was not going well. The man was now raising his voice and gesturing forwards to Kandahar and behind him, presumably to the lines of the Afghan army. W.G. was nodding slowly and shrugging his shoulders, and despite the immediacy of the danger that faced them all, Simon could not help but reflect on the debt they all owed to the Sikh. Without him – his linguistic ability, his knowledge of the country and his cool head in a crisis – they would be like children on a battlefield.

But it was clear that W.G. was losing the argument. The Afghan leader was gesturing back towards Gundigan and the Sikh shot a quick glance of appeal to Simon. Simon weighed the options: could they retreat to the Afghan camp and attempt to talk their way out of there, or should they make a dash for it, across the plain, to what hopefully were the British lines?

The question was answered for him by the man who had edged alongside Alice. In a quick movement, he reached across to tilt her head upwards with his hand under her chin. Instinctively, she knocked his hand upwards but his fingers caught on the edge of her cap, sending it to the ground and releasing her mass of golden hair. For a moment, all action was suspended as everyone looked at Alice, her brown-dyed face incongruously set against her yellow hair. She was no longer a Pathan youth, there was no doubt about that, and a low murmur of, at first, amazement and then anger rose from the Afghans.

For a splendid moment, whatever action was about to be taken by the patrol was diverted by Jenkins. He rose in his stirrups, held up his hand and shouted: 'Now just a minute, boyos, there's good chaps.' He urged his horse forward to that of the leader and addressed him with a huge grin. 'Now, Grandad.' He put a companionable hand on the man's shoulder and pointed back to the village. 'Why don't you and these black gentlemen all fuck off back to that miserable hovel over there and let us get on our way? Yes?' His grin grew even wider. 'Goodness, we don't want to spoil this lovely day with fightin', do we? Not with a lady present, anyway. Eh?'

The look of surprise on the Afghan's face gradually changed to fury, and he reached for the knife at his waist. But Jenkins was quicker. His hand on the man's shoulder slipped to the back of his turban, and in one swift movement he pulled the Afghan's face sharply towards him and head-butted him on the nose. The crack as the nose was shattered echoed clearly on that still morning. Jenkins half lifted, half twisted the leader from the saddle and threw him, with a shrug of his strong shoulders, towards the second Afghan in line, who was fumbling with his musket. The two fell to the ground as a shot rang out – the distinctive, high-pitched crack of a Colt revolver. From the corner of his eye, Simon saw the young Afghan next to Alice crumple as he attempted to pull her from the saddle by her hair. Then a musket ball whistled past Simon's head and he fired instinctively from the waist with his Martini-Henry as his horse bucked. The shot missed his assailant but hit his horse, sending them both to the ground.

To the front, Jenkins and W.G. had had no time to aim and fire their rifles, but both were locked in close combat, using their guns to fend off sword thrusts from three Afghans. It would have been an unequal contest, but the Afghan ponies were rearing, their eyes white with fear at the gunshots, and the thrusts were clumsy and easily parried. Simon had had no time to reload his rifle and he watched impotently as he saw an Afghan pull away from the mêlée, raise his musket and take a sight on Jenkins's back. Then the revolver rang out again and the rifleman clutched at his stomach and slid slowly from the saddle. Alice had pulled away, and although her own pony was excitedly twisting its head, she was coolly reining it in hard with one hand and endeavouring to take aim with the Colt with the other. She put a bullet through the shoulder of one of the men fighting Jenkins and then missed with a fourth shot as her pony reared. She had only two bullets left.

Simon heard a rifle shot as W.G. at last was able to bring his Martini-Henry into play, then, immediately, the double cough as a *jezail* was fired. As in a tableau, he saw the Sikh rise high in the saddle, pause there for a moment, an expression of great surprise on his face and a small black hole in the centre of his forehead, just below his turban, before pitching to the ground.

'No, no!' Simon cried out in a mixture of anger and horror. Then he seized his rifle by the barrel and, swinging it round his head, charged into the knot of Afghans who were attempting to get a bearing for their muskets on their plunging targets. He crashed into them, scattering them by the force of his charge and knocking one from his saddle. At the same time, he felt a thump on his left forearm as a musket shot tore through the flesh. He saw the blood and wondered, for a split second, why no pain came, before a misdirected swing of a sword sent his turban flying. He turned and pushed the sharp muzzle of his rifle hard into the midriff of the Afghan, whose sword swing had left him exposed. The thrust sent a sharp pain surging up from forearm to shoulder and the rifle sagged from his one good hand. But he had unseated the Afghan and given himself a respite for a second so that, breast heaving, he was able to look around at the conflict for the first time.

W.G. lay on the ground, dead, blood oozing from the neat, black-rimmed hole in his forehead. Three Pathans were also dead or badly wounded, while four others, including their leader, from whose shattered nose blood was gushing copiously, were either grovelling on all fours or trying to re-mount their excited ponies. The four remaining members of the band were slightly withdrawn, attempting to calm their mounts so that they could reload and aim their muskets. Alice, revolver in hand, was sitting watching Simon, wide-eyed. To Simon's amazement, Jenkins was gently trotting his pony away from the scene.

The whole confrontation had taken no more than two minutes, yet at least four men had almost certainly lost their lives.

Simon regained his composure. 'Alice,' he shrieked, 'ride like hell to that little compound over there. We may be able to hold them off there. Go now!'

He dug his heels into his horse's flanks and followed Alice, who was riding like a fury. He shouted at Jenkins: 'Follow us, man. Where are you going?' Jenkins, however, raised a languid hand, waved and then turned his horse round so that he faced the little knot of Afghans, who, for a moment, were unsure whether to pursue Alice and Simon or Jenkins himself. They were also detained for a second or two by their leader, who had found his horse and was shouting orders to them, incoherently because he was attempting also to stem the bleeding from his nose with the end of his turban.

'Jenkins. Come on, for God's sake!' Simon shouted as he galloped, his head craned round towards the Welshman. As he watched, he saw Jenkins calmly raise his rifle, fire and bring down the Afghan leader. Suddenly, the little man was galvanised into life. He kicked in his heels, let out a high-pitched screech, put his head down, levelled his rifle as though it was a lance and charged into the Afghans.

There was no time to see more, because Simon's horse had to take the stone wall in a leap which nearly unseated its rider and made him drop the rifle from his injured hand. Alice, already dismounted, seized the reins and held the trembling horse as Simon slid to the ground.

'Did you see that?' gasped Simon. 'Where is he? Where's 352?'

'What? No. I was getting in here. Oh, you've been wounded. Here, let me see.'

'No, it's only a scratch.' He pushed her away and turned his head. 'What's happened to . . . Oh, thank God. Here he is now.'

The Welshman, head down and rifle trailing from one hand, was galloping towards them. He took the stone wall gracefully, wheeled round and dismounted, slipping to the ground with a grin. 'Bloody 'ell,' he said, his cheeks blowing out with exertion, 'that was a bit warm, isn't it? Thought we'd all copped it there for a minute, see. Well done, though, you two.' His grin changed to a frown as he saw the blood dripping from Simon's arm. 'Look you, you've been wounded.'

'No. It's just caught the flesh. What the hell were you doing there?'

The grin came back. 'Thought a bit of a cavalry charge was the only way to give us time to get 'ere. It always works. Takes 'em by surprise, like. An' all that shoutin', it frightens their horses, see. They prance around an' split up an' nobody gets a chance to get a shot in. I was off before they knew whether it was Tuesday or pay day.' He looked round. ' 'Ere, where's old Gracey?'

'I am sorry, 352, but he's dead. He took a slug between the eyes.'

'Ah.' Jenkins pursed his lips and was silent for a moment. 'Now, that is bad, man.' He spoke quietly, as though to himself. 'Bowled middle stump, you might say. Well, 'e might say, anyway. In fact, that's what he *would* say. Lovely bloke.'

'Simon.' Simon turned to Alice, down whose cheeks two distinct tears were running. She gestured with her head. 'I think they're coming again.'

Simon ran to the low wall. What remained of the Afghan patrol – the seven uninjured men – were trotting their ponies towards the compound. As he watched, the little party split into two groups to encircle the enclosure. They now walked their ponies with caution, giving respect to the marksmanship of the defenders. But their determination was evident. They had a score to settle.

They were within range, but Simon resisted the temptation to shoot. Ammunition was limited and he had a feeling that this could be a long haul. He looked around. The walls consisted of roughly piled stones, only about four feet high in most places. They were stout enough, but there would be as much danger from flying stone chips as from bullets. The compound itself was small, about thirty yards square, and contained a little orchard of fruit trees in the centre, which themselves provided a little cover. He caught himself wondering how it was irrigated on this arid plane. With only three of them, it would be difficult to defend four walls. And how long before the shooting attracted more of the Pathans from the village?

He swallowed hard. 'Right. They are going to surround us of course. Jenkins, can you get these horses to lie down. Alice, can you lie with them and keep them down. If they are shot we shall never get out of here.'

Alice shook her head. 'No, Simon. You will need me as one of the walls. I have reloaded my revolver and I have another dozen bullets for it. We must just tie the horses' heads to the trees. I can shoot as well as a man.'

'Better than most, I'd say,' said Jenkins, who was already smoothing the neck of Simon's horse with a practised hand and then persuading it to lie, its head close to the trunk of an orange tree.

'No, Alice.' Simon tried to sound authoritative but it was clear that Alice was not to be ordered. She stood, legs slightly apart, facing him. The tears had traced two rivulets through the dust on her cheeks, but her eyes were bright and she was not crying now. Simon wrinkled his brow. 'Oh my dear. Don't give me trouble.' She shook her head slowly. 'Oh, very well. You take this wall.' He put both hands on her shoulders. 'Keep your head down and keep moving along the wall every time you fire so that they can't get a bearing on you. And Alice . . . don't get yourself killed. Whatever would I say to your father?'

She smiled. 'He would understand, I know he would.'

The cough of a *jezail* made them kneel.

Simon gestured. 'Three five two, you take that eastern wall. I'll dodge between the other two.'

'I'll dodge with you. I'm a better shot than you. You couldn't 'it an elephant if it was sitting on your knee.'

'Don't be impertinent.'

'Very good, sir.'

Alice crawled towards Simon and fumbled with her cotton shirt. She put one end between her teeth and tore off a rough strip. 'Here,' she said, 'let me see your arm.' She inspected it without a grimace. 'Looks only a flesh wound but we should stop the bleeding.' She began winding the cloth tightly around the wound. 'Sorry, we can't clean it now, but we must as soon as we can. Can you use the arm?'

'Yes thank you, nurse.'

The smack of a musket ball into the peach tree above their heads ended the dialogue, and Simon raised his rifle with his good arm and poked it cautiously over the wall. Another slug into the stones was his reward, but a puff of smoke marked where the sniper lay, between two rocks, out on the plain. Simon withdrew and crawled ten paces along behind the wall, then levelled his rifle again and waited, gambling on the inaccuracy of the *jezail*, although he knew that the Afghans were good shots, despite the age and the waywardness of their weapons.

The musket coughed again and the slug whistled over his head, but this time he was able to send a shot straight back into the puff of smoke. He fancied he heard a moan, but could not be sure. Both Jenkins and Alice were firing now, pacing their shots. How long could they all hold out? If only W.G. . . . The pace of events had been so fast that he had had no time to think of the big Sikh. As he scrambled along awkwardly, keeping his head below the edge of the wall, he mourned the man who had devoted his life to the cause of the nation that had defeated his own: a man of morality, resource and complete and utter loyalty. The Sikh had had higher standards than most of the officers who commanded him. If they came out of this mess, Simon resolved, he would make sure that W.G.'s wife and children were well cared for. W.G. W.G. . . . how ridiculous! What the hell was his real name? Lamb would know.

A bullet pinged on to the stone where Simon's rifle barrel showed above the parapet. They were shooting more accurately now. Would they attempt to charge the compound? It was seven against three and the Afghans would know the odds.

He called: 'Have either of you managed to hit any of them?'

Alice shook her head. 'Think I've winged one of 'em,' shouted Jenkins. 'Hey, look out.'

Simon whirled and fired at a white-swathed figure who, sword raised, had jumped a low part of the wall and was running towards Alice. He fell just before her, face down on the stony ground, his sword clattering to a halt at the girl's feet. Blood seeped from under the body and began to form a pool in the dust. Simon scrambled to Alice.

'Are you all right?'

She didn't speak, but her face had blanched under the

dust and cheap dye. She looked at him for a brief moment, her eyes wide, then switched her gaze to the dead man. Slowly she shook her head in some kind of disbelief and the revolver in her hand swung down to her waist, as though it was now too heavy to hold. Simon put his arm around her and gently pushed her to the ground, her back against the wall. He rammed another cartridge into his rifle and shouted to Jenkins: 'Face your front. They may be charging us.'

His arm sent a frisson of pain through to the shoulder again and he realised how useless he would be in a face-to-face encounter, but he levelled his rifle and rose above the parapet to face the new attack. Instead of the expected assault, however, he saw five of the Afghans running back to their horses. Would it be a mounted charge, then? As he watched, they climbed on to the animals, turned away from the orchard and began riding back across the plain towards the outbuildings of Gundigan. Five of them? He ran back to his original position, from where he had fired his first shot. One brown foot, its curled slipper lying by the side, protruded from behind the boulder. He had killed his man.

Elated, he turned away from the wall. 'They're retreating,' he shouted. 'We've seen 'em off. Well done. Oh, bloody well done!'

Jenkins smiled and, his eyes narrowed, gestured behind Simon. 'I don't think it was us, bach sir. More likely that lot, isn't it?'

Simon turned and saw a squadron of Punjab cavalry, pennants fluttering from their lances, galloping across the plain from the direction of Kandahar. They were headed straight for the orchard, and as they neared, Simon saw that they were led by a tall officer, riding awkwardly with his left leg straight and stiff, the boot thrust into a stirrup extended to its full length. Slightly behind him rode a man in the khaki clothes of a civilian, slouch hat on his head.

'Alice, look,' he cried. 'It looks as though we've found the bloody army at last.'

But there was no elation in Alice's gaze. On her knees, she stared at Simon with lacklustre eyes and, with a gesture almost of contempt, let the Colt fall from her hand. Leaning forward, she lifted the head of the Afghan at her feet, looked into his sightless eyes for a second, and then lowered the head back on to the ground. Once again she shook her head slowly.

Simon knelt down beside her and put his arm around her shoulders. 'We are saved, Alice,' he said. 'There is a squadron of cavalry coming. We are going to be all right. There's no need to worry any more.'

'Oh, Simon.' She looked up at him. 'I am so tired of all this . . .' she gestured with her hand, 'all this killing. Poor W.G., such a *good* man. What a waste! This man here was trying to kill me. And I have killed at least two men myself.'

She wiped her cheek with the back of her hand, smudging the dust and so heightening the urchin impression. Big eyes looked up at Simon. 'Do you know what the worst thing was?' Simon shook his head. 'The worst thing was . . .' Alice blew out her cheeks and sighed, 'that I was beginning to enjoy it all for a moment back there. For God's sake – what are we doing here?'

Simon opened his mouth to reply, although he had no idea what answer to give to such a rhetorical question, when an exclamation from Jenkins made him turn. The Welshman had gone to the east side of the compound and was opening a rickety wooden gate to welcome the cavalry when he shielded his eyes and cried: 'Blimey. It's the Colonel!'

The squadron clattered in among the trees, perspiration glistening on the horses' flanks and harnesses all a-jingle.

Colonel Covington looked down at Jenkins and Simon, turned to a stout officer riding immediately behind him and barked, 'Barlow, place these two men under arrest.'

Captain Barlow of the 8th Foot smiled down at the two men he had last seen in a train compartment at Khushalgarh and smiled. 'With pleasure, sir,' he said. He turned and gestured to two troopers. 'You two. Dismount and take their weapons. Bind their hands.'

'What the hell . . .' Simon levelled his rifle at the two Punjabis as they approached. 'Stand back. I'll not be arrested by you, Covington, or anyone else. We're not in the army now.'

Covington lifted an eyebrow and adjusted the chinstrap of his helmet. 'Really? I'd say that's a moot point. But I am not here to argue.' He gestured to the troopers. 'Arrest him and the other man. They will not shoot.'

Slowly, uncertainly, the two troopers advanced until the leading man was able to take Simon's rifle. The second did the same to Jenkins, who had not taken his eyes off Simon. Captain Barlow slid off his horse. 'Give me cord, quickly,' he snapped. Two straps were handed to him and, roughly, he pulled Simon's hands behind his back, sending a shaft of pain up the injured arm, and buckled the strap tightly round his wrists. He did the same for Jenkins. Then he put his face close to Simon's. 'We'll see now whether you can go around kicking people off trains.'

Simon smiled into the face a few inches from his own and lifted his chin. 'Fuck off, you fat prick,' he said.

Alice had remained where she was when the squadron had entered the orchard, kneeling with her back to the wall. Now she rose and walked to Covington. 'What on earth do you think you are doing, Ralph?' she said. 'These men have saved my life several times within the last few weeks. You have no right to arrest them.'

Covington looked down on Alice, as though seeing her for the first time. 'I have every right, Alice,' he said. 'These men were suspected of abducting you, but then it became clear that you had left the India column of your own will and had ridden off with them in wilful disobedience of the General's orders—'

'I can do what I like. I am not a soldier.'

'You cannot do what you like in a country bound by martial law. I—'

He was interrupted by the civilian, who had been dismounting at the rear of the party and who now pushed his way forward and made towards Alice. He took her hand in both his own. 'My dear Alice,' he said, 'thank God you're safe. We have all been so worried.'

'Hello, Johnny,' said Alice, grinning rather shamefacedly. 'What on earth are you doing here?'

Campbell took off his wide-brimmed hat. 'The Colonel here allowed me to ride with him on his scouting party. We are reconnoitring the enemy's position. The General intends to attack at dawn tomorrow.'

'That's enough, Campbell,' interrupted Covington. 'The General's plans are his own concern and should not be bandied about. Now, Barlow, for God's sake help me to dismount, there's a good fellow.'

For the first time, Alice, Simon and Jenkins realised that Covington had been wounded. The once-so-tight trouser on his left leg had been slashed down the side and revealed a glimpse of a now not-so-white bandage that seemed to run from ankle to kneecap. The corpulent Barlow hastened to put his hand under Covington's armpit as the big man gingerly raised his injured leg over his horse's mane, disengaged his other foot from the stirrup and slipped to the ground, grimacing as his wounded leg took the strain.

Alice frowned. 'Ralph, you have been wounded ... how . . .?'

Covington blew out his cheeks. 'It's not much but it's deuced uncomfortable, though I can just about still ride and do my job.' He glowered at her. 'If you must know, my girl, this is your doing.'

'*My* doing?'

'Yes, when the word came that you were missing, I took a small party and followed your trail, as best we could. It took a lot of damned hard talking to get the General's permission, but he allowed me four days. As it turned out, I didn't need that long. On the second day, up in those blasted hills, we were ambushed by a bunch of Pathans and I got a ball in the leg. Had to limp back to Kabul and then catch up with the General as best I could. Damned annoying, I can tell you.'

'Oh, my dear, I am so sorry. But you must rest. You shouldn't be riding.'

'Stuff and nonsense. I wouldn't miss the battle for all the tea in India. In any case, I'm in charge of scouting and intelligence. I've got to be here. Now.' He looked around him. 'Barlow, detail a troop under a subaldar to stay here with Miss Griffith and the two prisoners, while we ride on up the valley and see exactly where Ayub Khan is positioned.'

'You don't need to do that, Covington.' Simon, whose face had become increasingly grim as he had witnessed, first, Campbell's easy informality with Alice, and then her concern at Covington's wound, nodded behind him. 'We've done the job for you. The Afghans' main position is based on the village of Gundigan, back over there. But the major problem is—'

'Fonthill.' Covington took two painful steps towards him. 'If, as is highly unlikely, I should ever want your advice on military or any other matters, I will ask for it. Until then, keep your damned mouth shut. You are under arrest for attacking a brother officer back in Khushalgarh and for deserting in the face of the enemy. This time, I shall make sure that you are convicted at court martial. Now.' He turned and hobbled towards his horse. 'Mount up and . . . oh, damn to hell and blazes . . . Barlow, help me up again, confound it.'

Alice stepped forward and touched the Colonel's arm. She addressed him in a low voice. 'Ralph, you should listen to Simon. If the General attacks directly up the valley, he will be riding into a trap. Simon can tell you exactly—'

Covington grabbed the pommel of his saddle and leaned on Barlow as the latter inserted the boot of his good leg into the stirrup. 'Alice,' he hissed, 'I admire though cannot understand your loyalty to this good-for-nothing. But, I assure you, Fonthill can tell me nothing. Nothing at all. Do you understand? Now wait here in this orchard. I shall be only an hour.' He beckoned to Campbell. 'Come if you're coming. We can't wait around, man.'

Campbell, with a reluctant look at Alice, crushed his hat on to his blond hair and took up the reins of his mount. As he did so, Jenkins, hands bound behind his back, ambled over to Covington.

'With respect, Colonel bach,' he said, 'I don't think you'll be going anywhere.'

'What – what the blazes do you mean? How dare you address me like that.'

Jenkins's turban had never been the most secure headgear seen in Afghanistan and had only achieved a touch of respectability with W.G.'s careful ministrations night and morning. Now, after the exertions of the last few hours, one end hung down to his waist and the rest was coiled precariously on the side of his head. But his face wore that special beam reserved for correcting senior officers.

'Looks to me, see,' he said, 'as though the whole bleedin''

Afghan army is trottin' out to surround us. Look you, Colonel, over there.' And he nodded behind him, through the fruit trees, towards Gundigan.

Without a word, Covington rode forward round the edge of the wall and looked to the south-west with his telescope. The others ran to the wall but they needed no telescope. Riding fast to the east, a group of Afghan cavalry – perhaps three squadrons or more – was already wheeling round to cut off their retreat to Kandahar. Running towards them across the plain from the network of outbuildings to the village were hundreds of white-robed *ghazi* militia, the sun glinting off their spears and shields. As they ran, they fanned out to surround the orchard. Covington's squadron was outnumbered by six or seven to one.

The Colonel twisted in his saddle to gauge their chances of galloping back to Kandahar, but he was already too late. Their escape route was cut off by the Afghan cavalry who now straddled the two roads back to the city. Covington snapped his telescope shut and sauntered his horse back into the compound. Simon realised for the first time why the man had built a reputation for coolness in command in the face of the enemy. He seemed completely unperturbed by their predicament.

'Signaller,' he called.

A trooper pushed his way forward.

'Will your heliograph thing reach Kandahar from here?'

'I am not sure, sahib, but I will try.'

'Well it had better. Signal: "Am surrounded and am in need of urgent assistance." Do it now.'

The trooper dismounted and dismantled an elaborate mirror device from the large haversack behind his saddle. With many a look at the sun's position, he mounted it upon a wall, stood behind it and worked a handle so that the sun was reflected from the mirror's face towards the distant smudge that was Kandahar. He began clicking away.

'Right.' Covington's voice rang out loudly. 'The squadron will dismount and we will defend this compound until reinforcements arrive from Kandahar. Tether the horses to the trees in the middle, and Barlow.'

'Sir.'

'Divide the men so that each wall is equally defended. Position the ammunition reserves in the centre of the orchard and detail a dozen men to stay with me in the middle as a reserve should we need to make a counter-attack.'

'Fonthill.'

'Yes, Covington.'

'Do I have your word that you and your man will make no attempt to escape?'

'You do.'

'Very well. Untie them, Subaldar, and give them back their rifles. Can you shoot, Campbell?'

'Er – yes, if I have to.'

'Then take this.' He removed the Webley revolver from his holster and threw it to the journalist. 'Alice, you will stay in the middle of the orchard with me and you will lie down, out of the line of fire.'

'I will do nothing of the sort. I have a revolver with seven cartridges left and I can take my place on the wall.'

'She's knocked off about seventeen of the black bastards already this morning, Colonel bach,' said Jenkins, 'an' she hasn't really been tryin', see.'

'Don't address me in that fashion,' said Covington coldly, but his face softened as he turned back to Alice. 'No, my dear. You must not help to man the wall. Stay in the middle and protect me. I've got a gammy leg and only a sword. Now, who the hell is going to help me down off this horse?'

As he spoke, a shot rang out and the signaller turned slowly on the wall, leaned over his equipment and, almost in slow motion, brought his heliograph crashing to the ground with himself on top of it, a bullet hole in his back.

'To the walls, quickly,' shouted Covington, and half lowered himself, half fell on to Barlow's stout shoulders.

It was as if the bullet which killed the heliograph operator was a signal in itself, because a fusillade of shots now hit the orchard from all sides. As Simon ran to the west wall with Jenkins at his side, he reflected that if the Afghans had attacked immediately, they must have swept the defenders away, for the walls were poorly manned in those first few moments. Within the orchard all was confusion, as the mounts were tethered among the trees to give them some sort of protection, men ran stooping to their positions and the squadron's few boxes of ammunition reserves were piled into the centre of the compound, where Covington was setting up his command post. Here, the tall man stood on an ammunition box and shouted above the din: 'Keep your heads down. One man only on each wall to watch the enemy – *subaldars* detail him. Then, when they attack, stand and fire volleys in sequence, odd then even numbers. *Subaldars* number the men.'

Jenkins, kneeling next to Simon on the western wall, grinned. 'Seems to know what 'e's doin', all right. That's one good thing, ain't it?'

Simon nodded. 'He's a good soldier, no doubt about that. But if he hadn't been so preoccupied with us, none of us would be in this mess. Good soldiers should watch the enemy at all times.'

Jenkins sucked in his moustache. 'True, true. I'll 'ave a word with 'im about it when we've finished.'

Rifle bullets and balls from the *jezails* were slamming into the stone wall with such ferocity that Simon wondered if they could withstand such hammering. Then, suddenly, everything fell quiet on their side of the square until a high-pitched Punjabi voice called: 'Attack on west wall,' and was followed almost immediately by another: 'Attack on south wall.'

Simon and Jenkins rose and presented their Martini-Henrys. Across the plain, rushing towards them, was what seemed like a solid mass of *ghazi* militiamen, swords held aloft and green banners swinging from high spears. A *subaldar* touched Simon's shoulder. 'Even,' he said. And then to Jenkins: 'Odd. Volley fire when ordered.'

To Simon, it seemed an interminable time before the order to fire came. Holding the heavy Martini-Henry sent throbs of pain through his wounded arm and he was forced to kneel on a stone and rest the barrel on the wall. Whoever was ordering the volleys certainly had nerves of steel, for the attackers were now no more than a hundred and fifty yards from the wall and Simon, squinting down the long barrel, could see the distortion on the face of his target as the man shouted in – what? Exultation, hatred? – as he ran, waving a long curved sword which flashed in the sunlight. As he waited, Simon heard in quick succession, 'Attack on east wall,' 'Attack on north wall.' It was, then, an all-out assault. Could this small group withstand an attack on all fronts? The muzzle of his rifle drooped for a moment, until, with an effort, he re-focused on his target.

Then, Covington's loud voice sounded over the din: 'Volley firing commence on order. Even numbers, FIRE. Even numbers, reload. Odd numbers, FIRE. Odd numbers, reload. Even numbers, FIRE . . . reload . . . FIRE. Reload . . . FIRE . . .'

For three minutes or more, the volleys crashed out, shrouding the wall in a vapour of blue smoke and thrusting the sting of cordite on to the dry lips of the defenders. The concentrated fire from the men behind the walls, rolling out in a series of crashing volleys, could not miss at that short range, and through the blue smoke, Simon could see gaps appearing in the mass in front of him. But the gaps kept being refilled, and although the advance was halted for a moment, it came on again. Would they reach the walls? Simon snatched a glance behind him. Through the trees he could see Covington, still standing on an ammunition box, controlling the volleys, and beyond him a line of khaki figures lining the far wall. There was no sign of Alice. There seemed to have been no breakthrough, thank God. To his right, Jenkins was standing, the butt of his rifle nestling into his massive shoulder, firing and reloading with a half-smile on his face, the perfect fighting machine. Simon coughed at the cordite and forced another cartridge into the breech.

'Cease firing.' Covington's voice rang out again. The smoke cleared and Simon saw that the Afghans were retreating, loping away unhurriedly but leaving behind scores of bodies lying in the dust, shields scattered, spears, *jezails* and swords strewn among the stones. But this was no disorderly rout. The attackers of the west wall were regrouping just out of range of the Punjabis' carbines, although not of Simon and Jenkins's infantry rifles. They were deploying on the flanks and linking with other Afghans, who now began to crawl nearer and direct their own rifle fire on the defendants.

'They ain't pushing off, then,' said Jenkins, wiping his brow with the end of his turban.

'Get your head down,' muttered Simon.

The comment was echoed by Covington from the centre of the grove of trees. 'Heads down,' he shouted. 'One man to look-out on each wall. *Subaldars* to check on casualties and ammunition stocks and report to me within three minutes.'

Simon squinted through the trees to catch a glimpse of

Alice, but there was no sign. Instead, back bent, head down, John Campbell was scrambling towards him.

With a sigh he sat down between Simon and Jenkins. 'Phew,' he said, wiping his face with a bright red handkerchief. 'I wouldn't want to go through that again.'

'Where were you?' asked Simon.

'In the middle with Covington and Alice.' He smiled shyly and Simon noticed that his hand was shaking. He gestured to his Webley. 'To tell you the truth, I'm not much good with this. I've only ever shot at grouse and then I missed most of 'em. I think Covington wanted me to stay in the middle to keep an eye on Alice if . . . if they broke through.' He looked quizzically at Simon. 'Gosh. I wish I could stay as cool as you. To be honest, I think I'm a bit of a coward.'

Simon looked at him sharply. Was he being sarcastic? But the young man's gaze was open, though his eyes looked haunted. 'You're not a coward, Campbell,' he said. 'Nobody enjoys this – except possibly 352 here.'

Jenkins sniffed. 'Oh yes. I'm 'avin' the time of me life, I am, see. I'd much rather be 'ere in among these nice fruit trees than paddlin' in the sea at Rhyl, where it's *really* dangerous with them nasty waves.'

Campbell smiled and, turning to Simon, lowered his voice. 'I ought to get back but I just wanted to ask you something, Fonthill. You see . . .' he wiped the perspiration from his top lip with the back of his hand, 'I'm very fond of Alice, you know.'

Simon stiffened. 'Oh?'

'Yes. And I think you are too. Am I right?'

Simon looked away. Why the hell was this stranger asking him personal questions, questions which went right to the centre of his being and to which he was not sure of the answers himself? His background, his training, the reticence he had developed as a kind of cocoon to protect himself as a child – they united in giving him discomfort at the directness of the question. A bullet clipped the top of the wall and ricocheted away, causing stone splinters to fall on to their hair. Perhaps this was no time for propriety.

'Well, yes. Yes. I suppose I am.'

'Good. I thought so. You see, I think Covington's picked the wrong man to protect Alice. If they break through, I don't think I shall be much good, though I will do what I can.' His voice dropped even lower. 'I would do anything for her, Fonthill, but I am not a fighter. If a wall is breached, will you look after her?'

'Of course.'

'Thanks. Good. I'd better get back.' Bent double to keep below the level of the wall, Campbell scrambled away, back to the centre of the grove, where Simon could now just see Alice, dispensing ammunition to the men.

'What was all that about, then?' asked Jenkins.

Simon frowned. 'I guess he's a bit scared and wanted some moral support.'

Jenkins's teeth flashed beneath the moustache. 'Ah well, then, he's come to the right place. We know all about that, don't we?'

'Look, 352. If they do get over the wall, it could be a bit awkward. These Punjabis don't have bayonets and neither do we. I shall make for Alice to look after her. Will you protect my back?'

'Don't I always?'

'Always.' Simon smiled. He could not imagine Jenkins ever being afraid. It was not that the Welshman lacked imagination; in fact, Simon had several times glimpsed a Celtic sense of wonder and romanticism behind the little man's prosaic exterior. No, Jenkins possessed a strong sense of belief in his powers of survival – a belief based on experience and strengthened in scores of conflicts from childhood onwards. He was a fighter who knew his strengths and always played to them. Simon knew that even now the Welshman would be calculating how they could best fight hand-to-hand with only long-barrelled bayonet-less rifles as weapons.

In fact, Simon was wrong. Jenkins had long since worked out that the best way to use the Martini-Henrys in personal conflict would be to thrust with them, just as if a bayonet was on the end. Such a lunge could wind an opponent long before he could bring his sword down. What was occupying his mind now was how to kill Captain Barlow without being detected. The Welshman could see the stout officer on the end of the south wall, popping his head up and down to observe the enemy. One bullet would do it, but it would have to wait until there was another attack and all the defenders were occupied. Then there would be no question of a court martial for Captain Fonthill, not if the main witness for the prosecution was dead. Yes, one bullet would do it.

'Attack on east wall.'

The volley firing commenced from the other side of the compound and Simon tensed as he waited for the call to defend the west wall. It did not come until the firing from the east had subsided. Then the attack was of a desultory nature, almost like a feint, with a screen of *ghazis* rushing forward only to retreat after the first couple of volleys. The same happened in sequence at the other walls.

'I think they're testing our firepower,' said Simon. 'There's someone out there who knows what he's doing. He's probing the weakest spot.'

'Humph,' said Jenkins. 'There's our weakest spot, look you.' He nodded towards where the west wall met the southern stretch. Along the southern side, the wall had crumbled somewhat and a few pieces of timber had been stretched to bridge the gap. It could be scaled easily and Covington had been forced to leave it unprotected because there was insufficient cover there from rifle fire. 'That cavalry we saw would be over that and in amongst us in a flash, see.'

'You're right,' mused Simon. 'I wonder why they don't send them in? Unless . . . yes, of course.' He slapped his rifle butt in realisation. 'How much ammunition have you got?'

Jenkins fumbled. 'Only about a dozen rounds.'

'That's it. The Afghan commander knows that cavalry patrols carry hardly any reserves of ammunition for their carbines. They are not equipped to get involved in anything but charges, pursuits and skirmishes. He's just drawing our fire to exhaust our ammo. Then he will charge. Clever bastard.'

'Why doesn't old Covey just tell us to mount and make a break for it – charge through 'em?'

'Well, he could have tried it earlier, but then, I suppose, he felt that their cavalry was too much for us. Now he's lost so many of our horses that there wouldn't be enough mounts for us all. And he wouldn't want to leave any of us behind.'

Jenkins snorted. 'Oh no?'

'Stay here. I'll go and have a word with him.'

Simon slung his rifle over his shoulder and, on hands and knees, crawled towards the sparse shelter provided by the punch of low trees in the middle of the compound. He winced as the effort caused the blood to seep through the bandage on his arm again. In the middle, Alice, her back to a tree, was handing out cartridges to the last of the *subaldars*. She looked up and smiled at him – but her eyes had that inanimate expression which he had come to fear. It was as if something inside her had died.

'Don't worry,' he said, slumping down next to her. 'We should be getting help from the city soon.'

Her smile disappeared. 'Well,' she said, 'it had better come soon because I have now handed out all the reserves of ammunition.' She put a hand on his arm and lowered her voice. 'Simon, I cannot help feeling that we are all about to be killed.'

'Nonsense. There are—'

'No. I know the situation. Look.' She pointed to the carcasses of horses killed in the crossfire. 'We have few horses left and I have heard the reports of the wounded – we have lost about a quarter of the men. If they break in, we are finished. Listen, my dear, I want you to know how sorry I am that I have led you to this and how deeply grateful I am for all that you have done.'

The tears were now back, brimming in her eyes. 'If it had not been for me, W.G. would still be alive and you and Jenkins would be safely back in India. I am ashamed of myself, of my selfishness. I am so sorry, my dear.'

'Fonthill. Get back to the wall.' Covington came through the trees, limping heavily and using his sabre as support. 'Back to your post, man.'

'Very well, but I need a word with you first.'

'No time. Get back to the wall.'

Simon rose awkwardly to his feet and pulled Covington away from Alice. 'Look,' he said, 'the Afghans are luring us into using all our ammunition by making these dummy attacks. Then they will come at us and send their cavalry in over that breach in the wall.'

The blue eyes stared at Simon. 'How very kind of you, Fonthill, to tell me my job. You will be staggered to hear that I have given orders for us to hold our fire.' His lips curved into a smile but his eyes remained cold. 'But you are right about the breach. Take your Welshman and fill it immediately. Stand and fire as soon as they charge. Bring down the leading horsemen and make the rest veer away.'

'But there's no cover. It would be suicide.'

'Frightened again, Fonthill?'

Simon clenched his fist for a moment and then sighed. 'You really are an arsehole, Covington,' he said. But he turned away, stooped and scrambled back towards the wall. As he went, he caught Alice's frightened eye. Campbell had come to kneel beside her and was slipping a cartridge into his revolver.

Jenkins watched Simon approach. 'It's gone a bit deathly quiet, like,' he said as Simon dropped to one knee beside him. 'Either they've all gone off for a beer, see, or they're pullin' up their knickers before comin' in on us 'ard, like.'

'Oh, they'll be coming in all right. Come on. We've been ordered to defend the breach.'

The Welshman's big eyebrows rose. 'Oh, how simply splendid,' he lisped in the manner of a young officer. 'Shall I stand in the middle and 'it the 'orses with me rifle as they ride by?'

'Something like that. Come on.'

Together they crawled to the breach, Jenkins jumping across to take one side, Simon crouching at the other. The gap was about eight feet wide, with the remains of the wall rising to an irregular two feet or so and with two poles stretching across some four feet high, like a practice jump in a riders' field for beginners. Simon studied it carefully. It was an easy jump for any competent horseman but it was too narrow for two to take side by side at speed. If snipers didn't get them, he and Jenkins could easily bring down the first two riders, but the second and third would probably be through before they could reload their single-shot rifles. Jumping . . . jumping. Jumping meant landing.

'Look,' he called across to Jenkins. 'Get as many of these rocks as you can find and push and scatter them just where

363

the horses will land. If they don't cause them to shy, at least they might bring them down when they're over. Don't go into the breach to fire until the horses charge. Then jump away at the last minute.'

Jenkins nodded, and they began desperately to scrabble about in the debris, pushing and throwing the sun-bleached stones so that they were strewn haphazardly on the ground beyond the breach. They had had little time to build an effective deterrent, however, when the cry of 'Attack on the north wall' caused them to seize their rifles and huddle behind the wall. The volley firing – less closely synchronised this time – had hardly begun before the defenders of the other three walls were called into action. Simon shot a glance backwards. He could not see Alice, but he caught a glimpse of Campbell, one arm around a tree, the other hanging at his side, revolver in hand, staring wide-eyed at the north wall. Simon raised his heavy rifle with an effort and rose above the wall. He realised that he was frightened but there was absolutely nothing he could do about it.

The wave of Pathans ahead of him seemed somehow thinner, less impenetrable, and he soon realised why. As predicted, they formed only a thin screen for a body of horsemen who were trotting at their rear, lances held high, shields on their left forearms. He had time to reflect for a second that Alexander's spearmen must have been confronted with the same sight when they came through these passes two thousand years before. Then he took aim and fired.

Almost immediately, the white-robed *ghazis* in front of him parted and were replaced by the vanguard of the cavalry. It was a splendid and terrifying sight. With a shout which could be heard above the firing, the horsemen formed into a V, led by a man wearing a black-fringed sheepskin cap and carrying a shield and a lance which he now lowered as he urged his horse into a gallop. The other horsemen slipped into line behind him as they headed for the gap in the wall. As they charged, they kicked up thick dust that rose behind them like smoke from hell. To the defenders on the wall, they seemed to be the very angels of death.

Simon ran a tongue around lips that felt like blotting paper as he slipped another cartridge into the breech. Only five more bullets lay on the wall beside him. 'Aim for the horses, bach,' called Jenkins.

The leader of the charge was soon brought down, in the flurry of dust and rolling eyes from his beast, and so too were the second and third, and then the fourth and fifth as the fire of the defenders of the south wall took effect. But there were no volleys now, only sporadic firing, and the riders did not flinch from the fire nor veer their horses away from the wall. With impeccable discipline and courage they kept on coming, aiming for that narrow, jumpable gap in the wall, their lances levelled, their heads down over their horses' manes.

Simon fired his last bullet at point-blank range and brought down the mount of the first horseman attempting the jump. The rider wrenched his horse's head away at the last minute, so leaving room for the man behind him to take the jump. As this man urged his horse into the leap, Jenkins's bullet caught him on the chest and he slumped away in the saddle so that, in mid-jump, his head caught the side of the wall.

'Fall back into the middle,' shouted Simon. He threw his now useless rifle at the next horse, causing him to shy, and then doubled back towards the trees, turning his head to see Jenkins, his white teeth bared under his moustache, running after him. To the right, he saw that there was hand-to-hand fighting at the wall, although no Afghans had yet been able, it seemed, to climb it. As he approached the trees, twelve Punjabi cavalrymen, in impeccable order, emerged with Covington in the centre, sabre in hand. He raised his sword. 'Present,' he shouted. The Punjabis levelled their carbines.

'Down, Jenkins, for God's sake,' screamed Simon and threw himself to the ground. The volley thundered over his head. Then the two men picked themselves up and scrambled forward to push through the rank of riflemen. 'You could have killed us,' Simon gasped to Covington.

The big man, blood now trickling down his injured leg on to his boot, paid no attention. 'Present,' he thundered. 'Fire!' Another volley crashed out and Simon turned and saw that the breach in the wall was now completely closed by the bodies of horses, some of them with legs still thrashing. The terrible mound rose higher than the wall on either side and could not be jumped. Cavalry could be seen milling around beyond the wall.

'They will come to the gate in the east wall,' shouted Covington to his reserve. 'Move there at the double. AT THE DOUBLE, I SAID.' His men turned and ran through the trees and he limped after them, sabre in hand, without sparing a glance for Simon or Jenkins. The Punjabis on the south and west walls, at least, were still holding fast, firing with care. Simon ran back to the breach and retrieved from the ground one of the Afghan lances, its green pennant still attached. He now had a weapon, of sorts – and lighter than his rifle. Jenkins, he noticed, still had his gun. 'How much ammo do you have left?' he asked.

'Just the one,' said Jenkins. 'Savin' it for a bit, see.'

'We'd best help at the gate, then,' said Simon. 'If Alice is all right, that is.'

Alice was where they had last seen her, but now she was on her knees, kneeling beside the prostrate body of Campbell, cradling his head and wiping his face with a tattered handkerchief.

'What's happened?' asked Simon, lowering himself to her side.

'A bullet took him in the chest as he was trying to fire his revolver. I think he's gone.' She spoke without emotion, in a flat monotone. Her action with the handkerchief seemed quite redundant, for as Simon took the young man's hand to feel for the pulse, it was quite cold. The bullet had entered his chest just by the heart. He was no longer breathing and his eyes were staring at the sky, with that slightly puzzled look of the dead.

'I am afraid you are right,' said Simon, leaning forward and gently closing Campbell's eyes. 'He would have been killed outright. You can do no more, my dear.'

She looked at him expressionlessly. 'Very well,' she said flatly. She drew her Colt revolver from the cummerbund round her waist. 'Then I shall go to the wall and fight.'

Jenkins interrupted. 'Bach, sir. I think they're overwhelmin' us at that gate. We'd better go and 'elp the Colonel.'

'No.' Simon turned to Alice. 'Keep your pistol and stay here among the trees. Here.' He bent down and retrieved the Webley from the ground near Campbell's body and opened the magazine. There were four cartridges left. He threw it to Jenkins. 'Stay with her. There's a bit of cover among the trees. If they break through, I'll run back.'

'Hey,' shouted Jenkins, 'I'm supposed to protect your back.' But Simon was gone.

He ran to the east wall, jumping over the carcasses of the dead horses, to find that the rickety five-barred gate was now the scene of a heaving mass of fighting men, as the *ghazis* attempted to push it open to let the cavalry through and the Punjabis, using their carbines as clubs, desperately defended it. In the centre, balancing awkwardly on his good leg, Covington cut and hacked with his sabre, using a retrieved

Afghan shield to fend off sword thrusts. The Pathans' very advantage in numbers handicapped them, however, for as the host behind them pressed them forward, they could find little room to swing their weapons, whereas the Punjabis were able to stand back from the gate to swing their rifles.

Simon pushed to Covington's side and lunged with his long lance. He heard the scream as it found soft flesh and, dimly remembering the technique of the Zulu warriors, he twisted the lance and pulled back, hearing on the retrieval that sucking noise, *iklwa* – the name the Zulus had given their assegais. A curved sword swung at his head and Covington thrust forward his shield to parry it, allowing Simon to thrust again and then again and again into the mass of figures beyond the gate. Another sword swung, and this time Covington was only able partly to parry it, deflecting the back of the blade on to his own head. He went down immediately, half stunned, at Simon's feet, and two Pathans immediately took the opportunity to climb on to the top of the gate. Simon stood astride the fallen Colonel and speared the first tribesman but was unable to retrieve the lance in time to stop the second from leaping on to him, and the two went down together, falling across Covington. Simon, momentarily winded, stared up into a face that exuded hate. He struggled to find the man's throat, but his wounded arm was now quite useless and the uneven contest would have been over in a second had not a shot rung out and Simon felt the Pathan go inert above him. Covington and Simon crawled from under the Afghan together and were helped to their feet by Jenkins, revolver in hand.

'Thanks, 352,' gasped Simon.

'Not me,' said Jenkins, nodding over his shoulder and then coolly taking aim. 'You try keepin' 'er in the trees. I couldn't.'

Alice was standing a few paces back from the mêlée, thrusting cartridges into her Colt. She twirled the revolving magazine, levelled the gun and fired again into the crowd.

'Back into the trees, Alice,' shouted Covington, sucking air into his lungs.

'Go to hell, Ralph,' she retorted, shooting again.

Suddenly, there was a crack as the top bar of the gate split. Jenkins immediately picked up his rifle and pushed into the middle of the Punjabis. He thrust the Martini-Henry straight into the midriff of a *ghazi* attempting to scale the gate and the man bent at the middle like a mattress and collapsed backwards. Simon, his left arm now virtually useless, short-handled his lance and thrust away with it across the broken wood. A 'Confound you, you black devil' from his side told him that Covington had rejoined the fray.

Yet it was now clearly hopeless. Firing had petered out at the walls of the compound and it was obvious that the defenders' ammunition had been exhausted and that, all around the perimeter, they were now reduced to fighting with their rifles as clubs. It could only be a matter of minutes before the Afghans would make a breach and attack from behind. Then it would all be over.

The series of *crumps* that now came surprised everyone, attackers and defenders alike. Beyond the crowd still thronging the gate, Simon saw a red-cored column of earth and stone erupt vertically; and then another and another. The thud of the gunfire came a second after the shells exploded. The first overshot and landed behind the cavalry who were milling at the rear of the *ghazis* attempting to force the gate. But the second and third fell among the mounted men, causing havoc as horses reared and bodies were hurled to the ground.

'They've brought up their artillery,' Simon cried in despair.

'Don't be a bloody fool,' growled Covington. 'They're our seven-pounders. Screw guns. Knew they'd come. Saw a flicker from their heliograph, before our signaller was shot.' He wiped the back of a blood-stained hand across his moustache. 'Left it a bit late, though. Get Alice under cover. Go on, man. They may drop short.'

Chapter 13

Simon winced as the medical orderly pulled the two ends of the bandage together on his forearm and fastened it just below the wound. He was sitting on a camp stool outside the Commander-in-Chief's tent, under the walls of Kandahar. For a man who had never been on the general staff, he reflected, he had spent an inordinate amount of time on this campaign waiting to see General Roberts. Now, as he watched the sun slipping down behind the peaks of the Baba Wali Kotal, he was dog tired and wanted no awkward interrogation from the Commander-in-Chief – just the chance to crawl under blankets and forget the happenings of an horrific day. The deaths of W.G. and, to a lesser extent, John Campbell had saddened him, but he was also perturbed at the way the conflicts of the day had reduced Alice to a shrunken, uncommunicative figure, huddled and shrouded in a blanket in an ammunition cart as they had been escorted back to Kandahar by the battalion that had rescued them from the orchard.

Roberts, he had been told, had been suffering from fever for the last week of the march to Kandahar. Nevertheless, he had led his force over three hundred miles of mountainous, hostile territory to arrive at the besieged city in twenty-two days. It was a march that was to make him famous throughout the Empire. Now, however, he had arrived to find the defenders of the city huddled behind their thirty-foot-high walls, still cowed by the defeat at Maiwand and too despondent even to hoist the Union Jack until the relieving force was in sight. Weak with fever, furious at the inertia of the garrison, he had immediately thrown out reconnaissance parties to discover the deposition of the Afghan army and prepared, weak as he was, to lead the attack on it as soon as possible.

Simon knew that the little general would have been less than pleased to be forced to dispatch a battalion of his tired troops to rescue his main scouting party, but he was past caring. Covington had exchanged not a word as they had ridden back to Kandahar and the Colonel had been closeted with Roberts for at least half an hour now. After a brief word with a puzzled but less than welcoming Brigadier Lamb, Simon had been told to get his wound dressed and wait until the C-in-C was ready to see him.

Shivering as the cold descended with the twilight, Simon rose from his stool and pondered what he should tell the General. The main objective was to protect Alice and to prevent her from being further censured for following the army. He suspected that, despite her despondent state, she would be determined to report the imminent battle. But Roberts would be more than likely to put her under guard in Kandahar and ship her out to India without giving her the chance to file a word. How to stop that . . .?

His reverie was interrupted by Lamb, who put his head round the tent flap and gestured. 'Come in, Fonthill.'

Sir Frederick Roberts, deep rings under his eyes and his usual pink complexion reduced to a dull grey, was sitting at a camp table, a greatcoat hunched over his shoulders. An ADC was bustling with an orderly at another table, laying out maps. To Roberts's right sat Lamb, and at his left sprawled Brigadier

MacPherson, red face glowing in the fading light. At the end
of the table sat Covington, his wounded leg thrust straight
out.

Wearily, Roberts gestured to Simon to pull up a folding
chair. 'How is the arm?' he enquired.

'Just a scratch, sir.'

'Hmnnn.' Despite the air of fatigue, the General's blue
eyes retained that look of familiar icy penetration. His voice
was equally cold. 'Now, tell me what you were doing five
miles to the west of Kandahar, wearing native dress and
accompanying Miss . . . what's her name . . . Griffith, when
you left Kabul three weeks ago to return to India. I have to
tell you, Fonthill, that I find your behaviour increasingly
irritating – if not disturbing.'

Simon took a deep breath and shot a glance at Lamb. But
the Brigadier's face showed no trace of friendliness. Only
MacPherson wore a half-smile of – what? Sympathy, amusement? – on his lips.

'Well, sir,' began Simon, 'after I resigned my commission
I heard about Maiwand and the fact that you had been
ordered to form a flying column to march across the hills
and relieve the siege of Kandahar. I talked with my two
colleagues – you will remember my Welsh sergeant and our
Sikh guide?'

Roberts nodded.

'We agreed that we ought to be able to help you, knowing
the country as we do . . .'

The General cut in sharply. 'So why didn't you re-enlist or
just offer your services to me?'

Simon sighed inwardly. He had known this would be
the difficult part. 'I am sorry, sir, but I knew that that
would mean serving under the command of Colonel
Covington here, and I did not wish to do that. So we decided

to act independently. We reasoned that Ayub Khan would not attack you in the passes or on the march but would confront you here, on the plain beyond Kandahar. So we resolved to loop north through the hills, come down behind the city, take a look at the Afghan positions and meet you here and tell you what we could. We were on our way this morning when we fell foul of an Afghan patrol and were cornered in an orchard. It was there that Colonel Covington found us.'

It was clear that Roberts was intrigued, despite his initial disapproval. 'I have to say, Fonthill,' he said, 'that I find your story remarkable – if it is true. But what on earth was Miss Griffith of the *Morning Post* doing with you?'

'She heard of our plan just before leaving Kabul and begged to be allowed to come with us. We are old childhood friends, you see – our fathers served together in the 24th Regiment – and I knew how desperately she wished to be present at the forthcoming battle. So we blacked her up and disguised her as a Pathan boy. It worked until this morning when we fell in with this Afghan patrol.'

Lamb now spoke for the first time. 'You came all this way, over a most difficult and dangerous route, to discover the Afghan dispositions? Well, what did you find?'

'Ayub Khan seems to have centred his main force in and around the village of Gundigan on your left, sir. He will have fortified the villages across the plain, but that is not the real danger.'

'What do you mean?'

The tent was now silent, and even the ADC and his orderly were openly listening. The faint air of incredulity with which Simon's story had first been received had now vanished. He cleared his throat. 'The Afghans have dragged guns up into the Baba Wali Kotal range to your right.

They are positioned to fire down on to you as you attack up the valley towards Gundigan. It is, then, a kind of trap. You will need to clear those guns before you launch your main attack.'

'How many guns?'

'Sixteen or seventeen. Enough to cause a lot of damage.'

Roberts turned to Covington. 'Did you see these guns, Covington?'

'No, sir. Don't believe a word of it. Doubt if it is possible to haul artillery up there anyway.'

'It is virtually impossible to see the emplacements from the plain,' said Simon. 'We came down from the north, from the higher hills, and looked down on them. They are positioned to fire virtually south-east, towards the Gundigan approach. It will take time to haul them round, so it should be possible to attack them before they can be turned to fire on a force climbing up towards them. There are good tracks.'

As Simon spoke, Lamb had been making notes. Roberts turned and looked at the Brigadier, who nodded, almost imperceptibly. He then turned to MacPherson, who scratched one red jowl. 'This young feller served me well to the north of Kabul,' MacPherson said. 'I understand that he also did well at Sherpur. Give me a brigade first thing in the morning, Sir Frederick, and I'll spike all those guns.'

Roberts smiled for the first time. 'Very well, Mac.' He turned back to Simon. 'Young man, you will stay in camp tomorrow.' The General held up a hand as Simon began to intervene. 'No. I think you have had enough adventures to last you for a while. We shall not need you to guide us to the Baba Wali Kotal – Brigadier MacPherson can see plainly where it is, and anyway, you should nurse that wound. Go and get some rest now and we will talk further when I have sent the Afghans running. And get out of those rags.'

Simon stood and paused uncertainly. 'Am I still under arrest, sir?'

The General's eyebrows rose. 'Who placed you under arrest?'

'I did, sir,' said Covington. 'Two charges. Firstly I was under the impression that Fonthill had deserted from the India Column in the face of the enemy, though perhaps I was wrong on that count. But the other charge remains, that of attacking a fellow officer on the frontier a little under a year ago.'

'Good Lord,' said Roberts. 'What else is there to learn about this young man? Who was the officer?'

'Captain Barlow, 8th Foot.'

'And where is that officer now?'

'Dead, sir. Died in the orchard this morning. A single shot took him in the head.'

'And were there any witnesses to the assault a year ago?'

'No, sir.'

Roberts waved a dismissive hand. 'Then the charge no longer has substance. Dismiss it. I have a battle to fight, gentlemen. Fonthill, you are no longer under arrest. But don't go wandering off.'

'No, sir. Er . . . General. May I make one request?'

Roberts wiped a weary hand across his forehead. 'If it is quick and relevant, you may do so.'

Simon took a deep breath. 'It concerns Miss Griffith, sir.'

The General's brows descended like thunder. 'What about her?'

'Sir, she felt she was only doing her duty by coming with us. She knew that she did wrong in . . . er . . . evading the censorship rules and now regrets it, but she is desperate to serve her newspaper and her readers and she risked everything – including her life – to get here. Sir, she fought like a soldier back there in the orchard. Will you please allow her to join the other correspondents tomorrow in reporting the battle?'

Roberts's face remained expressionless. 'I will consider it,' he said. 'You are now dismissed, Fonthill.'

'Sir.' Simon turned and bent his head to exit through the tent flap, but Roberts's voice brought him back.

'Speaking of fighting like a soldier,' said the General drily, 'and referring to your obvious dislike of Colonel Covington here, you should know that the Colonel has commended you and your man for the way you fought this morning. You should remember that, Fonthill. Good evening.'

'Thank you, sir. Good evening.' Simon looked quickly at Covington, but the Colonel, his face drained of colour, no doubt by the pain from his wound, was considering the texture of the timber of the tent pole by his head.

Outside the tent, Simon blew out his cheeks and pulled in a draught of cold twilight air. Had they believed him? It seemed like it. But had he helped Alice? He doubted it. He now felt a tide of weariness lap his brain. His wounded arm was throbbing again after the tightness of the bandaging had worn off and he realised that he was very, very hungry. The cold was now almost visible in the half-light. Camp fires glowed and all around him there was bustle and purposefulness and that kind of quiet apprehension that soldiers exude on the eve of a battle. Except that he would not be fighting that battle. He did not feel sorry. But where to now? He remembered that the doctor had said that a tent had been allocated for him and Jenkins, but where? And where was Alice?

A shout made him turn. The unmistakable figure of Jenkins was walking towards him: a Jenkins who had shed his tattered

Pathan cotton and was now attired in a linen suit of uncertain fit but of some respectability, which was let down a little by the Afghan sandals on his feet. Jenkins stopped and waved. 'Come on, this way. The kettle's boiling.'

Slowly Simon walked towards him. 'Three five two,' he said, stopping and laying a weary hand on the little man's broad shoulder, 'you look like a Calcutta stage door masher – if there are such people. Where did you get those clothes?'

Jenkins's eyes twinkled. 'In the bazaar, in the town.'

'But you don't have any money.'

'Gave 'em me rifle. 'Ad good reason to lose it, but the bloody thing's jammed anyway. Over'eated again. They're always doin' it, them Martini-Horaces.'

'You'll get shot for selling an army rifle.'

'No I won't. We're out of the army now – until you put us back in again, that is, of course – and if asked, I shall say I lost it in the bloody battle. Anyway, it was a good trade. I also got a suit for you, a kettle, a cookin' pot, some rice and a chicken, see. Oh, and some tea, look you.'

Simon shook his head and, with his good hand on the shoulder of his friend, walked with him down the tent lines. 'You're what's known in a good officers' mess as a bloody marvel, Jenkins,' he said. 'Do we have somewhere to sleep?'

'Nice little bell tent. It's by the 'orse lines, so it's a bit pongy, but I didn't think you'd complain. Got two bed rolls 'an all.'

'Where's Alice?'

'Ah.' The Welshman's ragged moustache drooped as he frowned. 'The doctor took 'er off somewhere, look you. She didn't look too good, see, but I felt she would be in better 'ands with 'im than with us, if you get my meanin'.'

Simon sighed. 'I'm sure you're right.'

'I forgot to ask you about the General. Are we goin' to be court-martialled again? 'Ung like them poor bastards in Kyball?'

'All in a minute.'

They were now on the edge of the lines, where horses were tethered and munching oats. In front of a small bell tent, a fire was blazing under a cooking pot and a kettle. Simon pulled out a bed roll from the tent, laid it in front of the welcoming blaze and lowered himself on to it with a sigh. As Jenkins busied himself making tea, he told him of the interview with Roberts. By the end, he had finished his tea and was almost asleep.

He was woken the next morning before dawn by a hand shaking his shoulder. He looked into the face of Alice, a few inches from his own. She was wearing no perfume but he remembered with a little lurch of the heart her warm, feminine smell. 'I am sorry to wake you, Simon,' she whispered. 'But I had to tell you that I am being allowed to report the battle and I am on my way now with the army.'

He struggled to sit but she restrained him. 'No. Don't get up.' She smiled, her face still close to his. 'I understand that you are to stay here. Covington has told me that it was your intervention with the General that made him change his mind and allow me to go. I came to thank you and to tell you where I was,' she lowered her gaze for a second, 'in case you were worried.' She kissed him quickly. 'Thank you, my dear. Stay and rest, and if all goes well, I shall see you tonight.'

'But Alice, Alice . . . Are you . . . are you all right now?'

Her voice was quite even. 'Yes, perfectly all right, thank you.' Then she was gone.

A black moustache rose for a moment from the bed roll on

the other side of the tent. 'Well,' said Jenkins, 'she sounded better'n yesterday, I'll say that. Let's 'ope she doesn't go and get 'erself killed, eh?'

'Shut up. I've had enough of battles. We've got the day off, so go back to sleep.'

In fact, neither of them could do so. Simon lay watching the tent canvas turn gradually white as the sun came up, and shortly afterwards he heard the sound of firing from the west. He cupped his ear the better to listen. But there was no deep booming from heavy ordnance, only the distant sharp cracks of light artillery: the screw guns that Roberts had brought with him across the mountains and the manoeuvrable cannon that the Afghans had put in place behind the village walls. He was relieved. It sounded as though the bigger Afghan guns up in the hills had not been brought into play.

Simon sat up. 'We can't just lie here,' he said. 'Let's go and see what's happening.'

Jenkins threw back his blanket and pushed his fingers through his spiky black hair. 'Not until we've 'ad some breakfast, bach,' he said, 'and not until I've dressed that arm of yours. We'll not be 'avin' another fever, now, will we?'

The camp had a deserted air. Cooks and a few band boys were preparing strange concoctions in huge cooking pots, ready for the return of hungry troops. A medical post had been set up near the site of Roberts's HQ tent and everywhere, doolie bearers and other native non-combatants were going about their leisurely business. In the distance, towards the west, Simon could make out mounted piquets moving on the plain. Detachments of men from regiments that he did not recognise – presumably from the Kandahar garrison – were formed up behind primitive defences facing west. Obviously Roberts did not contemplate defeat and he had made no elaborate plans to defend his baggage. The general tenor was that of a base camp on Salisbury Plain whose regiment was away on a day's exercise.

It was not until well after noon, in fact, before Simon could find anyone with sufficient seniority to allow him to borrow two rather elderly horses to ride out towards the fighting. In their civilian clothing they were not challenged by any of the piquets that were patrolling the plain near the city and they headed towards the distant firing, the intensity of which had now decreased markedly. As they rode, the noise of battle seemed to recede before them until, after they had been riding for less than an hour, it disappeared altogether. They passed several ambulance wagons, carrying wounded back to Kandahar, but no steady stream of such vehicles denoting fierce fighting. A small figure in the distance soon revealed itself to be a horseman, galloping towards them and leaving a cloud of dust in his wake. As he approached, Simon recognised the blond-moustached young ADC who had served him tea in Roberts's anteroom, and he waved him down.

'What's the news?'

The young man looked quizzically at the two men in their dusty linen suits and then his eyes lit up. 'Ah, Captain Fonthill. Didn't recognise you in your mufti for a minute.' A broad smile extended his moustache. 'Great news, sir. Bobs has won the day. I am just dashing back to the city to tell the old ladies of the garrison there that they can stop shakin' and come out of their boudoirs. Oh.' His smile disappeared for a second. 'Sorry. Speakin' out of turn there for a minute. But,' the smile returned, 'I'm sure you know what I mean. What?'

Simon smiled back. 'Yes. Don't worry. Look. I mustn't detain you. Just tell me the main details. Did he manage to clear the guns from the hills up ahead?'

'Oh yes. Old Mac had no problem. Then the 1st and 2nd Brigades went straight down the plain, and after a bit of a shindig at Pir Paimal and then the back of the Baba Wali Kotal, they advanced on old Ayub's camp and found that the bird had flown. Buggered off back to Herat with what's left of his army. The cavalry are out after them still. We took thirty-two pieces of artillery at his camp. A damned good day's work, I'd say.' The young man gathered in his reins. 'Must get on, sir.'

'Yes, of course. Where's the General now?'

'Straight ahead. About two miles. Must go.'

He dug in his heels and was off in a cloud of dust. Jenkins wiped his moustache with the back of his hand. 'Well now. And they did all that without us. Amazin', isn't it?'

Simon nodded slowly. 'That surely must be the end of it in this country. The Afghans have had three substantial defeats in different parts of this godforsaken place. They won't be able to put another army in the field. They'll probably make old Bobs a field marshal now.'

'Do we ride on now and see 'im to pick up our medals?'

'No. I don't want to be roasted for leaving camp. Anyway, we have something more important to do. Come on.' He turned his horse's head to the north, to where the slopes of the Baba Wali Kotal rose from the plain. Soon they passed the orchard where they had so nearly met their deaths the day before, and shortly afterwards they found what they were looking for.

W.G.'s body lay where it had fallen, one arm crumpled beneath him and flies crawling round the neat blue hole in his forehead. Rigor mortis had set in and he was difficult to lift, but between them they were able to wrap the big Sikh in a horse blanket and then lay him across the saddle of Simon's horse. Simon climbed up behind Jenkins and slowly they made their way back to Kandahar, provoking a few curious glances from piquets and returning ambulances but nothing more. No one queried their mission and they arrived back in the late afternoon to find the camp already buzzing with the news of the great victory.

They rode through the camp until they came to the lines of one of the Punjabi regiments. Here they found an elderly *rissaldar*, his beard grey and his blue turban faded, but his back straight and his manner courteous. Because of his age, he explained, he had been detailed to remain behind to prepare the reception of the seriously wounded, but so far none had come back from the battlefield. He nodded to the blanket-swathed figure on Simon's horse. 'Is this, sahib, the first?' he enquired with grave dignity. Simon explained a little of W.G.'s background and how he had met his death.

The old man inclined his head. 'Is this, then, one Inderjit Singh, who used to ride to the north with Captain Cavendish of the Guides?'

'Ah.' Simon was surprised but relieved. 'I believe that was his name, although I called him by another. You knew him, then?'

For a moment the black eyes of the *rissaldar* lit up. 'He was the best batsman in his regiment,' he said. 'I knew his father and I know his wife. There will be great sadness.'

'Where can I find his wife?'

'She is at Amritsar. Anyone at the great barracks there will tell you how to find her. Does the sahib wish to visit her?'

'Yes. We both wish to pay our respects to her and to tell her how much we admired her husband.'

The Sikh nodded again. 'It is fitting. You may leave his body with me. I will attend to it. It must be bathed and properly swathed.'

'Excuse me,' said Jenkins. 'We would both like to attend the . . . er . . . burial or whatever. When will that be, then?'

'We do not bury, sahib. We shall cremate his body tomorrow shortly after dawn, together with the other shells, if we are unfortunate enough to have any after this battle.'

'Shells?' Jenkins looked puzzled.

The *rissaldar* inclined his head again. 'The body is not important,' he said. 'It is merely a shell for the soul. Death is a natural process – even sudden death in war – and it is God's will. We do not approve of a public display of mourning nor of erecting gravestones. We shall scatter his ashes in the river and begin the reading of the Sri Guru Granth Sahib.'

'Ah, yes,' said Simon, a little uncertainly. 'Well, thank you, *Rissaldar*. It is good for us to know that W.G. . . . er . . . Inderjit Singh – or his shell, that is – is in good hands. We shall join you, if we may, in the morning. In the background, that is, of course.'

The Sikh bowed again and Simon and Jenkins carefully lifted W.G.'s body from the horse and took it to a little cleared area behind the tents. Then, wearily, they made their way back to their own tent. Simon thought of attempting to find the correspondents' quarters and of seeing Alice, but rejected it. The task of finding W.G. and bringing his body back had induced a feeling of sadness and of rejection of the whole process of warfare – even the reporting of it. He wanted no further part in it, and the sounds of celebration from the lines as the victorious army returned drove him into his bed roll long before dusk fell.

This feeling of lassitude returned in the morning as, just before dawn, Simon and Jenkins made their way to the Punjabi lines. Sixteen other bodies had been brought back from the plain after the battle, and the funeral pyres crackled and lit up the early day as the warriors were committed to the flames. A sepulchral hymn began to be half chanted, half sung, and, feeling out of place, the two crept away, their heads bowed.

At their tent, a small note was handed to Simon. It was written in pencil and had obviously been hurriedly scribbled:

> I have returned safely from the battlefield and have been up all night writing my story – or rather my stories. I felt that I had to cover for Johnny Campbell too, so I have also filed a story to the London *Standard*. It was the least I could do. I am now attempting to get some sleep and hope perhaps to see you later, if you wish. A.

Simon had hardly tucked the note into his pocket when an orderly arrived, asking him to report to Brigadier Lamb. With a sigh, Simon attempted to brush some of the all-pervasive Afghan dust from his new but now-crumpled suit and followed the man through the British lines. Despite the early hour and the fact that he had obviously been in the thick of the battle yesterday – a bandaged hand testified to that – Lamb had clearly been at work for some time. Papers were strewn across his camp table in a fashion Simon remembered well.

'Right,' said the little man. 'Take a pew.'

Simon sat down and looked into the familiar bright blue eyes. The gaze which met his was not smiling but nor was it unfriendly.

'Bobs has asked me to see you, Fonthill, and to express his thanks for the information you gave us. Saved us a lot of time and trouble yesterday, and, in all probability, lives too.'

Simon nodded in acknowledgement. 'Glad to hear it, sir.'

The Brigadier pursed his lips and nodded back. 'Yes. Good

old Mac had no trouble in clearing the hills, mind you, but it was good to be forewarned.'

Good to be forewarned! Simon frowned. In gaining that information, that *forewarning*, W.G. had lost his life. Once again the arrogance of this army struck home. The loftiness, the other-worldliness of the officer caste in its dealings with the native troops; its sanguine acceptance of the need to lose life to gain an objective; its extension of the ethics of the playing field to the field of battle ('good old Mac') – he hated it all, with the passion of the convert. God, was he becoming a pacifist? No, some fighting was necessary. But was this? He swallowed and looked at the roof of the tent.

Lamb followed his gaze, partly puzzled and partly exasperated at Simon's lack of enthusiasm at the victory. He picked up a pencil and tapped it on the table, as a schoolmaster would to regain the attention of an erring pupil. 'Now, Fonthill,' he said, 'the General believes that you and your Welshman, 362—'

'Nearly got it this time, sir.'

'Don't be so bloody impertinent, young man.'

'Sir.'

'The General believes that you have earned some reward for your efforts, even though you have left the army.' The Brigadier coughed. 'He has therefore awarded you both an extra month's back pay. In addition, your Sikh has been promoted with effect from the time that he began working with you, so that his widow will receive a considerable sum – by Indian standards, that is.'

'Now *that* will be appreciated.'

The irony in Simon's tone was not lost on Lamb. His nutmeg face crinkled into a hatch of lines as he frowned in annoyance. 'I have to tell you, Fonthill, that the General does not know what to make of you. In fact, he does not like you and has always been rather suspicious of your motives and your methods. He wants you out of Afghanistan as soon as possible.'

Anger began to mount within Simon. 'Well, that's fine by me, Brigadier,' he said. 'I shall be glad to leave this sad country. But it is damned unfair of Sir Frederick to doubt my motives and my methods. I am here because you blackmailed me to do a job which I did not want – *that* was my motive. And as for my methods, it is impossible to play by the Horse Guards' rules of etiquette when your balls are being burned off or when pompous line officers try to throw the best soldier in the world off a train just because he doesn't wear stars on his shoulder. Anyway, those methods brought the results that the General wanted. He should be satisfied.'

Simon's anger had prompted him to half rise from the chair, but a twinge of pain as he thrust his hand on to the table forced him to sit again and bestowed a sullen note to his closing sentence, which he immediately regretted. But he held Lamb's gaze defiantly until, characteristically, the face opposite broke into a smile.

'Damn me, Fonthill,' chuckled the Brigadier. 'I think it's just as well you've left this army, otherwise we would have been forced to shoot you.' Lamb stood. 'Look. I've told you the General's view. Now, mine is that you've done a damned fine job under difficult conditions, and I would like to thank you and your Welshman, whatever his damned number is.' He extended his hand. 'Good luck to you in whatever you are going to do.'

Simon rose and took the hand. 'Thank you, sir. When do we have to get out, and how do we go?'

'There is a column leaving tomorrow with wounded who are able to travel but need treatment in India.'

'Tomorrow?' Simon's face betrayed his surprise. Would he be able to see Alice before he left?

'Yes. Sorry about the short notice, but Bobs wants you out before you shoot Covington.' His smile was steely. 'Start shortly after dawn. See the quartermaster about gear and clothing – he may be able to better that suit. You won't have to slog back the way we came. The column will march through the Bolan Pass and you can pick up the railway which takes you through to Rohri on the Indus. What are you going to do, anyway?'

'I don't really know. Haven't had much time to think about it. Jenkins and I want to visit W.G.'s widow. Then we will decide.'

'Very well. Thank you again. Good luck, Fonthill.'

'Goodbye, sir.'

Outside the tent, Simon stood for a moment in indecision. His mind was a mixture of emotions. He wanted to get out of Afghanistan and shake off the confines of the army as quickly as possible, but this abrupt departure was redolent of expulsion. He disliked the implication of wrongdoing which that prompted. Also, he wanted to see Alice. In fact, he wanted to see her very much – but what to say to her? He frowned, as his brain tried to be logical and handle the questions that came flooding in. Which Alice would he meet: the warm, worldly and slightly cynical woman, or the frightened, disturbed girl? How should he pose his question? Was this the time? Was it the place? Well, damn it, it had to be. He kicked the soil angrily and strode off back to the tent.

There, Jenkins heard the news of their departure stoically. 'Time to go is time to go, see,' he said, with that air of native wisdom he wore on occasions and which always infuriated Simon. Seeing the warning signs, the Welshman sniffed and nodded towards the city. 'I'll wander off to see the QM, then, and pick up our 'Avana cigars for the journey. Oh, by the way,' he turned at the tent flap, 'the newspaper people 'ave been moved into the city. Their quarters are just off the main gate. Thought you might like to know, see.' Then he was gone.

Simon waited for two hours, lying on his bed roll, then he threw his few personal possessions into a bag, before washing, brushing his hair and walking towards the massive gate that gave entrance to Kandahar. A sentry showed him the low house that had become the working centre for the correspondents covering the campaign and he sent a note through to ask if Alice was available to see him. He hoped she had recovered from her night's labours. From the deserted look of the press centre, her colleagues had been similarly employed.

But she came to the door quickly enough and it was clear that she had been up and about for some time. The makeshift dye had been scrubbed away from her face and only traces now showed in thin brown lines under her eyes. She was wearing her hair in a tight bun at the nape of her neck, wound round with that familiar lime-green scarf, and for once, she had forsaken riding breeches and had somehow acquired a simple shift-like dress of khaki cotton which gave her a girlish air of unsophistication. The haunted look had left her face, though the grey eyes looked strained and sad and there was a slight hint of melancholy in the smile with which she greeted Simon.

'I am so glad to see you,' she said. 'I have just been moving into the little hovel they have given me. Much cooler than a tent and at least it's my own. Do come and see it.'

Simon followed her through the house into a courtyard, off which several doors led. She ushered him through one and he sat on the only chair, while she sprawled on the narrow camp bed.

'Did you manage to sleep well, after all your work?' Simon enquired.

'I rested a little, thank you. But I have been up for a couple of hours now, sorting myself out and . . . er . . . seeing a few people. It seems I am now forgiven and they are letting me stay on for a short while, to cover the installation of the new amir and so on.' She smiled that sad smile again. 'My editor liked my story of the battle and I have also received a cable of thanks from the *Standard*, so, for once, it seems I am in everyone's good books, though I don't suppose that will last long. Now, how about you? Has the arm recovered, and how are you feeling, my dear?'

'I am quite well now, thank you, Alice.' Simon felt a slight sense of annoyance at the formal way the conversation was developing, as though Alice was erecting a barrier of convention between them. This was not the way he wished to introduce the matter he had come to put to the lovely woman sitting opposite him, her chin now resting schoolgirlishly on her knees.

'Alice,' he began hesitantly, 'I have something I wish to—'

Alice held up her hand to interrupt. This was the moment she had been dreading. Telling Simon.

The filing of her stories had perforce taken her back again into the minutiae of the battle. She had had to discover and then break down the numbers of the killed and wounded and then to report the detail dispassionately. On previous occasions this task, while never pleasant, had not fazed her, for she had been able to retain a professional distance when writing about carnage. Now, however, she could not help recalling Campbell's dead face, and the cries of the Afghans as her own bullets had hit their targets. The memories pressed heavier when, after sending her dispatches, she lay down for a precious moment or two of rest. Sleep evaded her and she began to feel a deep and personal responsibility for those she had seen killed in the compound. They would not have perished, brown and white, if she had not insisted on evading Roberts's edict and persuading Simon and his friends to take her to Kandahar.

Alice was never short of confidence and by nature she was not introspective. But the events of that day had been cathartic. They had forced her to examine her motives and attitude to life. Was she not completely selfish and, indeed, self-centred? The answer, of course, was yes. Yet, as she lay looking at the white fabric of her tent and tasted the dust of the army camp on her tongue, she realised that she could not change her personality simply by the exercise of self-analysis, like Mesmer clicking his fingers to bring someone out of a hypnotic state. Nevertheless, it was necessary – it was *vital* – to alter the direction of her life.

Alice had allowed herself a half-smile: the change of course need not lead to a nunnery exactly but certainly towards something which would contain an element of sacrifice and yet still be creative and, perhaps, of some use to others. Slowly an idea began to form in her mind, one that would take her away from all that now revolted her but which would be not at all unpleasant . . . In fact, it would relieve the pressure on her. But – and here she had frowned – it would not please Simon. Simon, her dear friend for whom she felt so much gratitude and affection. Nevertheless, that could not be helped. It offered the best solution.

In consequence, now she flushed slightly as she stopped Simon. 'May I interrupt you?' she asked. 'For I have something to tell you and wish you to be the first to know.'

'Of course.'

'Well.' Alice's eyes left his and roamed over the ceiling, as though looking for something to help her begin. Eventually, they returned to his face and Simon realised that whatever she had to tell him would not please him. She seemed almost ashamed of what she was about to say. 'You know how much gratitude I have to you and to Jenkins and poor W.G. for enabling me to reach this place and to report the battle?'

He nodded.

'And I know that it was you who pleaded with Roberts so that I was allowed to go out yesterday. So I am doubly grateful.'

He remained silent, his eyes fixed on hers, willing her to get on with whatever it was she found so difficult to impart.

'Yes, well. I think you also know that I have found the violence of the last few days to be very . . . disturbing. Oh, Simon.' Now she reached across impulsively and took his hand, and her eyes regained that expression of intensity that he remembered so well. 'I killed W.G. and Johnny Campbell as surely as if I had pulled the trigger. I killed others, too – more directly. I never thought that I would ever do that.'

She shook her head as though to dispel the memories. 'I have been thinking of that and I realise that I must never put myself again into that position of kill or be killed. That is a soldier's world. A man's world. I was wrong to have strayed into it.'

'But Alice.' Simon found himself searching for words. 'You knew all this when you set out – even, perhaps, when you decided to become a journalist, a war correspondent. To get your story you had to take that risk. It's what a man would have done.'

Alice looked away again for a moment and her voice was

low. 'Yes, well, perhaps I should never have done that. And I have decided not to run that risk again.'

Simon waited, and then was forced to break the silence. 'So . . . what are you going to do?'

She turned and looked him full in the face. 'I am going to resign my position and marry Ralph Covington.'

The silence in the little room hung over them both. Slowly, unbelievingly, Simon repeated: 'You are going to marry Ralph Covington? To marry that man? For God's sake, why?'

Alice relinquished his hand and sat back on the bed, as though in retreat. 'Because . . . because I think I love him. And he offers me the chance of doing something else. Of running a large estate, of doing something worthwhile with his land and the estate employees. Of having money, and children, and bringing them up as I believe they ought to be raised. Of . . . of . . . oh, I don't know.' She gestured wildly. 'Of getting away from all this.'

Simon ran his fingers through his hair. 'You – staying at home and bringing up children! That's not you. Anyway, the man's a bully and a monster. He would have had me court-martialled on a trumped-up charge.'

'I don't believe he would have gone on with that. And anyway, he is also a gallant soldier and a brave man. And he loves me.' She stared almost defiantly at Simon.

A feeling akin to nausea ran through Simon. A large estate, money – he had none of those things. Whatever he had to offer could not match what she had accepted. The nausea turned to anger – to marry Covington, of all people! Never, for one moment, had he imagined that competition would come from that quarter, nor that Covington's feelings would be reciprocated. Was Alice out of her mind? He opened his mouth to remonstrate further. She was watching him closely, defensively, expecting an argument and bracing herself for it. There was that familiar look of determination now in her face. A stubbornness he knew he could not shift. He realised, with deep, deep sadness, that there was nothing he could do.

He rose and put out his hand. 'Congratulations, Alice. I hope you will be very happy. Whatever I think of Covington – and I would be a hypocrite if I said I liked the man – he is indeed a gallant soldier and a brave one.' His words, he knew, sounded stilted even to himself and he made an effort to appear more gracious. He pulled her up from the bed when she took his hand, and embraced her gently. 'You deserve only the very best, my dear. Let me know where I should send the rubies and diamonds as your wedding present.'

She laughed for the first time and kissed him on the cheek. 'You are the first person I have told. Both you and Jenkins will be invited to the wedding.' She pulled back with an expression of remorse. 'But I forgot. You came to tell me something and I have been prattling on about myself as usual. What was it?'

'Oh.' Simon paused for a second and cleared his throat. 'Only to say that Jenkins and I are being thrown out of Afghanistan by Roberts. He has given us a derisory extra month's pay for our efforts and told us that we must be with the column of wounded who are leaving for India at dawn tomorrow. I believe he thinks we are troublemakers. I came to say goodbye.'

A look of righteous indignation flooded Alice's face. 'The old bastard! After all the lives you saved at Kabul and here. I will not let him get away with that.' She took his arm. 'Please let me write about it. I will see that questions are asked about it at home.'

Simon shook his head. 'No thank you. Jenkins and I don't give a damn really. And I would not want you to get back into hot water again. No, my dear, we shall slip away quietly tomorrow. But thank you all the same.'

The hurtful sadness deepened into a real sense of loss as he looked into the concerned face a few inches from his own. The beautiful grey eyes were full of feeling for him, he could tell, but what sort of feeling? Certainly not love. She knew, of course, what he had been about to ask her when she interrupted him, and she knew he had been wounded. But – what the hell! He had to get out of there. He kissed her quickly, chastely, on the lips, then turned and left.

Shortly after Simon arrived back at the tent, Jenkins came staggering in, loaded down with two bulging kit bags. 'Well,' he puffed, 'we've done well. I've been to the bazaar and traded in the army boots and the shirts they gave us and I've got some fine cotton stuff . . .' His voice trailed away as he looked at the mournful face opposite him. 'Ah. We're not gettin' married, then?'

'How did you know?'

'Your face is as long as the Severn.'

'How did you know I was going to ask her?'

'Call it an old soldier's institution . . . intwit . . .'

'Intuition.'

'That's what I was goin' to say. Anyway, you've been moonin' about since we stopped fightin' the fierce Pataan. I guessed you was screwin' up your courage, look you. 'Ard luck, bach.'

'She's going to marry Covington.'

'Blimey!' The look of, first, surprise and then disgust on the Welshman's face almost made Simon's disappointment worthwhile.

'Well,' said Simon, 'he's rich and has land and much to offer.'

Jenkins sat down slowly and sucked in his moustache. For a moment or two he considered the proposition. 'She's a fine lass, that's for sure,' he said eventually. 'But she's old enough and, by golly, brave enough to make her own bed. Now she must lie on it.' He shot a quick glance at Simon. 'So what are we going to do now?'

Simon looked across at the familiar face opposite, now wearing an apprehensive, even wistful expression. Somehow, he felt better. 'I've been wondering about that. I think we should go to my home – just for a short while. What do you think?'

'What – to Wales?'

'Yes. I would like to see my people again.'

Jenkins screwed up his face. 'Aw, they wouldn't want somethin' rough like me about the place.'

'Rubbish. They will love you. Particularly my father. Don't forget he was a soldier. He respects good soldiers.'

Jenkins's habitual beam returned. 'Are you sure? Back to Brecon?'

'Yes, but only for a while. While we decide what to do next.'

'And what *will* we do next?'

Simon linked his hands behind his head and lay back on the narrow bed. 'I haven't had much time to consider it, but I can't help thinking that people ought to do what they're good at. I will never make a farmer or a businessman, and I have a few pennies of my own, so we don't need a big income. What *we* are good at is soldiering. No, no.' He held up his hand to stop an incredulous Jenkins interrupting. 'I don't like the army and we could never be line soldiers again. But I realise that the army needs people like us . . . sort of freelances who operate on the edges as we have been doing. Scouts and that sort of thing.' He lifted his head. 'Do you know what I mean?'

'Suppose so. I must say, I should miss a bit of excitement. But I don't want no more salutin' and that sort of stuff, see.'

'Of course not. But I can see things boiling over rather in South Africa sooner or later, and perhaps in Egypt. We could be of use in places like that – as long as there were no strings attached to the brass. We would have to keep a degree of independence. But first, a spell at home. What do you think?'

Jenkins blinked and turned to one of the kit bags. He pulled out a shirt and began smoothing it with his big, broad hand. 'I'll go anywhere you go,' he said. 'Somebody's got to look after you, after all.'

Author's Note

The Road to Kandahar is a work of fiction, of course, but the flesh of the story has been hung upon a skeleton of fact. The events leading up to the second Anglo–Afghanistan War, related in the novel by Colonel Lamb, are as accurate as I can make them, relying upon the work of respected historians, as, too, are the details of the battles described in the book. The leading characters – Fonthill, Jenkins, Alice, Covington, W.G., Colonel Lamb, et al. – are all fictional. But the mullah very much existed, as did the other named Afghan leaders, and also Sir Louis Cavagnari, Brigadiers Massey and MacPherson, and John Dunn. Sir Frederick Roberts, of course, remains one of Britain's best-loved Victorian generals, dying a field marshal in 1914 and revered for his long but rapid march on Kandahar. Many of the opinions expressed by Roberts in the novel and by Cavagnari to Simon have been taken from the field marshal's memoirs, *Forty One Years in India* (first published by Richard Bentley and Son in London in 1897). I am also indebted to these recollections for much of the military and logistical detail contained in my account of the war. The spelling of Afghan place names has changed bewilderingly over the years. For the sake of consistency, I have stayed in the narrative with the version used in the map of the time, included at the front of this novel.

Alice's evasion of Roberts's censorship and her

subsequent banishment from Afghanistan are based on fact. They happened to the London *Standard*'s reporter accredited to Roberts's army. The indictment of Roberts's vengeful hangings, contained in *The Bombay Review* and *The Friend of India* and cited by Alice in her defence, *were* printed in those respected journals and were quoted by the London *Times* at the time.

A punctilious student of historical chronology might cock an eyebrow at Alice reporting the first stage of Gladstone's Midlothian campaign in late November 1879 and still being able to arrive at Kabul shortly after the Battle of Sherpur in late December of the same year. I can only hope he might allow me a few weeks of poetic licence.

If the idea of a woman war correspondent in 1879 jars, then I must cite – as does Alice to John Campbell over dinner in Edinburgh – Frances, Viscountess de Peyronnet (born in Suffolk plain Frances Whitfield), who reported the siege of Paris for the *Times* of London in 1871, seven years before Alice began filing her stories from the Cape. Then, in 1881 – the year after Alice reported from Kandahar – the grand *Morning Post*, Alice's own newspaper, sent Florence Dixie to the Transvaal to cover the first Anglo–Boer War. Even in Victorian Britain, you couldn't keep a good gel down!

J.W.
Chilmark

The Horns of the Buffalo

John Wilcox

In 1879 the redcoats of the British army are universally regarded as the finest fighting force in the world. Among them is Lieutenant Simon Fonthill, dispatched to South Africa with much to prove: for Colonel Covington, his former Commanding Officer, has slanderously branded him a coward.

In the Cape, tension is high. The Zulus, an independent nation of magnificently militant tribesmen, threaten the colonial government's vision of a united South Africa. And Simon has been chosen for a particularly dangerous mission: to travel deep into Zululand to discover the intentions of the king.

Simon encounters violence and imprisonment before he is faced with his greatest challenge. Escaping from the massacre at the Battle of Islandlwana, he must warn the tiny garrison at Rorke's Drift of the threat posed by advancing Zulu impis. He has a chance to prove Covington a liar, but he may pay the ultimate price.

Both a gripping adventure and a powerful exploration of courage and comradeship, THE HORNS OF THE BUFFALO introduces a young hero fit to stand shoulder to shoulder with Hornblower and Sharpe on any battlefield of the nineteenth century.

0 7553 0983 9

headline

The Eagle and the Wolves

Simon Scarrow

As the Roman armies invading Britain face bitter resistance from unyielding natives, Macro and Cato find themselves standing between the destiny of Rome and bloody defeat.

In the summer of AD 44, tense undercurrents amongst the tribe of nominally friendly Atrebatans are ready to explode into open revolt. It falls to centurions Macro and Cato to provide aged ruler Verica with an army, training his tribal levies to protect their king and enforce his rule. With a scratch force of raw recruits, unversed in the techniques of war, they must find and destroy a resourceful and cunning opponent. But can they do this whilst surviving the deadly cross-currents of plotters threatening to destroy not only Macro and Cato, but all their comrades serving with the Eagles?

Praise for Simon Scarrow's previous tales of military adventure:

'A thoroughly enjoyable read . . . The engrossing storyline is full of teeth-clenching battles, political machinations, treachery, honour, love and death' Elizabeth Chadwick

'A good, uncomplicated, rip-roaring read' *Mail on Sunday*

'Scarrow . . . sweeps the reader into the past as if the fighting were happening today' *Oxford Times*

'When it comes to the battle scenes few can surely touch Scarrow in his vivid descriptions' *Eastern Daily Press*

0 7553 0114 5

headline

Now you can buy any of these other bestselling
Headline books from your bookshop or
direct from the publisher.

FREE P&P AND UK DELIVERY
(Overseas and Ireland £3.50 per book)

The Horns of the Buffalo	John Wilcox	£6.99
The Eagle and the Wolves	Simon Scarrow	£6.99
Killigrew's Run	Jonathan Lunn	£6.99
The Templar's Penance	Michael Jecks	£6.99
The Ghosts of Glevum	Rosemary Rowe	£6.99
The Occupation	Guy Walters	£6.99
None But the Brave	Joy Chambers	£7.99
The King's Touch	Jude Morgan	£7.99
The Magician's Death	Paul Doherty	£6.99
The Leger's Bell	Peter Tremayne	£6.99
Shoulder the Sky	Anne Perry	£6.99

TO ORDER SIMPLY CALL THIS NUMBER

01235 400 414

or visit our website: www.madaboutbooks.com

Prices and availability subject to change without notice.